Torn in Two

by

Vincent Morrone

The Torn Series, Book 2

Torn in Two

COPYRIGHT © 2019 by Vincent Morrone

Cover Art by *Kristian Norris*

The Wild Rose Press, Inc.
PO Box 708
Adams Basin, NY 14410-0708
Visit us at www.thewildrosepress.com

Publishing History
First Mainstream Thriller Edition, 2019
Print ISBN 978-1-5092-2387-9
Digital ISBN 978-1-5092-2388-6

The Torn Series, Book 2
Published in the United States of America

She closed her eyes as she continued. "I can still smell the cheap beer on his breath, the smell of cigarettes on his clothes. He held me by the throat, and I couldn't breathe as his bloodshot eyes looked me up and down. I swear to God, I thought he was going to rape me. He probably would have if Drew hadn't come home. Drew kicked at him, and Dad broke his arm."

"Oh no," Ollie said. "Oh baby. I'm sorry. I never knew."

Ashley nodded in his chest. "Now you do. That wasn't the only horrible thing he did. He was always vulgar. Always saying things like that, but that was the one time I really thought he'd do *that*." She let him pull her into his arms. "I'm sorry, but this is what you're getting with me. I'm broken."

"No, you're not," Ollie insisted.

"You need to see me for what I am."

"I do," Ollie said. "I know you're not perfect. I know you have a past. I love you. That's never going to change. And if you're broken, then I'll break myself to fit."

Kudos for Vincent Morrone

The follow-up to the First Place Winner
of the SRWA Great Beginnings Contest.

Dedication

Sometime after the final draft of book one of the Torn series was finished, and before the polishing of book two, something amazing happened. Our family grew. I never expected it to happen, but it did and I couldn't be more thrilled.

Hannah, your animated personality and your drive are an inspiration. Yotham, watching you become an amazing young man is an honor, and your humor always makes me smile. Eliana, you're wise beyond your years, but it fills me with joy when I see you laugh. (Even if it is often at me.)

A few years ago, I never would have guessed you guys would become a part of our lives. Now, I can't imagine my life without you in it.

I'd like to dedicate this book to you and your siblings. You've made me a happier and better man, and our family wouldn't be complete without you.

Chapter 1
Leave 'em with a Smile

For the first time since her arrest, Diana Lakeland thought she might actually survive. Making good on her word, the Chief of Ember Falls PD actually arranged for a decent lawyer to come from out of town, one that she was sure had no connection with anyone who wanted her dead.

Well, that wasn't *quite* true. Attorney Stephanie Howard very much knew someone who would like her dead. She was friends with Drew Duncan. Close friends in fact. How close, Diana wasn't sure, but while Ms. Howard was able to remain professional, the lawyer had also made her disdain for Diana very clear from the start.

"The only reason I'm doing this is because Drew asked me to," Stephanie said within seconds of meeting Diana.

"You'll be paid." Diana extended her hand. Seeing Stephanie curl her lip in disgust, she put it down.

"I don't want to shake your hand." Stephanie tossed her briefcase on the table. "And I don't want your money. What I want is for you to tell the chief what it is you know. You were Kelli Duncan's counselor and you worked with the two cops who murdered her. Helped kidnap her son. I want to know why. Who had Kelli Duncan killed?"

Diana folded her arms and smiled. The open hostility made her feel better. She knew when people were faking, and this bitch wasn't. There was something in the pretty lawyer's eyes that told Diana that Stephanie wanted to punch her new client in the nose. It wasn't someone who wanted Diana dead that was the problem. It was those people who were actively plotting her demise that Diana worried about. They'd act nice and sweet to Diana's face, and first chance they had, stab her in the back.

"I'll talk," Diana said. "Once there's a deal and I know you'll be able to keep me alive."

Stephanie leaned on the table between them, putting herself right in Diana's face. "You're not getting any deal without telling me what you know."

Diana grinned and took a seat, studying the woman in front of her. Stephanie was easily described as stunningly beautiful, and everything about her; her perfect figure contained in a smart black pants suit, her red hair that was flawlessly styled, her immaculate pedicured nails, screamed class and elegance.

"Tell me something." Diana leaned back in her chair and let her gaze slowly run up Stephanie's body. "How close are you and Drew Duncan?"

Stephanie stiffened. "What?" She shook her head. "Why?"

With raised eyebrows, Diana leaned in closer. "Are. You. Fucking. Him? Or for that matter, have you ever?"

Stephanie looked positively scandalized, which gave Diana her first true laugh since her life hit the shitter. Being a trained therapist, Diana considered herself a pretty decent read of people, and the outrage displayed on her new lawyer's face wasn't because Stephanie was a prude, but because she'd touched a nerve somewhere under that flawless skin.

"My relationship with Drew is none of your business," Stephanie said.

"I'm afraid we have a difference of opinion there." Diana studied Stephanie, measuring every facial tic, trying to read what was going on behind those pretty eyes of hers. "Let me make my meaning clear. I know Duncan wouldn't shed a single tear if I suddenly found myself on the wrong end of a shiv while in jail, and sooner or later, that's what's going to happen to me, but I also know that he wants something. He wants to know what I know. So, I need to know if you're loyal to him."

Stephanie scowled as she pulled out the chair and sat down. "Let me lay my cards on the table. I am here for one reason and one reason alone. Because Drew asked me to be here. I'm not going to talk about my relationship with him, but know this. If it could help Drew, I'd sell you down the river. Lawyer/client privilege be damned."

Diana arched an eyebrow as she considered Stephanie. "You love him, don't you?"

Stephanie folded her hands, crossed her legs and stayed quiet, and her silence spoke volumes to Diana.

"Fine." Diana shrugged. "I know the real reason why Kelli Duncan was killed. If it makes you feel better, I tried to keep it from happening. I actually did feel sorry for her." Diana recalled the first time she'd seen Kelli Duncan, a pathetic shadow of a real woman. "She was weak. I tried to make her strong enough so she wouldn't need her damn brother back in her life, but she just had to go there." Diana began to examine her nails which she'd bitten down to the stubs since being arrested. The worst part was that she had nothing left to chew.

Stephanie opened her briefcase and pulled out papers. "Needing family is not weak."

Diana rolled her eyes. "Sister, let me tell you something I've learned over the years. Family will fuck you over more than anyone else." Her hands fidgeted, and not for the last time she wished she had a cigarette. "I don't suppose you smoke."

Stephanie looked up briefly. "No. And if I did, the answer would still be no. Let's go over today. It should be very simple. You go in and say nothing. I speak for you. If you're asked a question, you whisper in my ear and I answer for you. With the charges you're facing, you won't be granted bail and quite frankly, if you're as worried about your life as you say you are, it's better for you to remain in custody."

Diana laughed. "You sure about that?"

Stephanie put down the paper she was reading and met Diana's gaze. "Yes. The General has called in over a dozen favors. Right after you're arraigned, you're going to be transported to a federal prison."

"The General?" Diana asked. "Is that the old man that Wilson kept bitching about?" Seeing the insult show on Stephanie's face, she realized she was not only correct, but that she'd also hit another nerve. "Man, Wilson hated him. If he had gotten the chance, he said he was going to find him and beat the crap out of him."

"Really?" Stephanie surprised Diana with the almost amused tone. "That would have been fun to see. The General would have kicked his teeth down his throat and handed him his own ass."

Stephanie placed the papers on the table. "Nobody who has any connection here in Ember Falls, past or present, has any connection there. The warden is a personal friend of the General. You'll be in extreme high protective custody. You'll be as safe as possible, which is safer than you deserve. Once there, you'll meet with a special prosecutor at the federal level. Another favor the General called in for Drew from some well-connected associates who have owed him. He's not going to be pleased if this all turns out not to be worth the chips he's cashed in, so you better not disappoint. You get one shot and only one. You tell us everything you know and we'll do right by you. That doesn't mean you walk."

Stephanie leaned in close. "Be very clear on that. You will see the inside of a very small cage for a very long time and I will personally toast when they turn the key. But you get to live and maybe even breathe free air one day, although it'll be at an age where your long, dark hair has gone grey." Stephanie allowed herself a small smile. "You screw us over, I will make sure you're put into general population with a very big target on your back."

Diana had thought she might be able to cut a sweeter deal, maybe when she gave more details on who she could hand them, but the cold stare she was getting from her lawyer told her she was shit out of luck. Maybe she could get a country club of a prison when she met this special prosecutor, but somehow she felt that unlikely.

It was, however, probably the best she could hope for.

"Fine." Diana blew out a breath in frustration. "You get me to the special prosecutor, I'll sing like a fucking bird."

Stephanie pushed paperwork forward. "You better. Or I may just kill you myself."

****

Two hours later, Stephanie accompanied Diana as she was escorted to the court building. They were driven there in a police van, but the good Chief of Ember Falls had allowed a single man from McAlister Security to ride with them. His name was Brent Stevens, a dark-skinned man who Stephanie had gotten to know on the way over here. He had a lovely wife, three young children and was just a bit of a Star Wars nerd. All the other court officers were dressed in body armor with helmets and faceguards. Diana was now wearing a pants suit that Stephanie had picked up for her in her place, accessorized by a thick, bullet proof vest.

They made it to the court without incident. Once there, they waited in a private room. Everyone remained stoic, except for Diana who was becoming more and more fidgety. She'd tap her foot, pull at her clothing, bite at the corner of her mouth and grind her teeth. "God, doesn't anyone have a cigarette?"

Stephanie shook her head, happy to see the woman so worried. Normally with clients, she was very good at trying to soothe them. In her briefcase, Stephanie always carried cigarettes and a lighter even though she hadn't smoked in nearly a decade. Stephanie also carried a pack of gum with her for the nonsmokers, but she had no desire to do anything remotely nice for a woman who had hurt Drew so badly. "No, and there's no smoking in a court building."

"What about gum?" Diana asked.

Stephanie resisted the urge to pull out a stick for herself while insisting she had none. Instead, she ignored Diana as several officers came into the room and tried to walk past them. Brent quickly put himself in front of Stephanie and insisted the officers find an alternative route. They shot several dirty looks, but didn't argue for more than a few seconds. Just as they cleared out, another officer came into the room. This one signaled that it was time to head in.

They all rose and headed into the courtroom. As they entered, Stephanie saw Drew Duncan standing with his family. He was dressed in a jacket and tie, which he filled out like it was a suit of armor. He still sported a few small scratches from his deadly struggle with his sister's killer last week, but otherwise he looked healthy. To his right was the very pretty officer that Stephanie had met briefly on her last trip to Ember Falls. Even while on duty, she was extraordinarily beautiful. She wore her long, dark hair back in a tightly pulled ponytail and very little makeup, but her big brown eyes and olive toned skin made her striking.

Stephanie couldn't recall her name, but despite being in uniform, the officer reached down and took Drew's hand the moment they were in sight.

To Drew's left was Ashley Duncan. She was tall, thin with auburn hair that was wavy and a little wild. Stephanie heard that Ashley had been the one to deck Diana, and it looked like she'd like to do it again. Her eyes were narrow slits and her hands were balled into fists.

There was another face that Stephanie recognized,

although it took her a moment to place him. It was the son of Ember Fall's Chief's, although the last time Stephanie had seen him, he was in uniform like the female officer who was now whispering something comforting into Drew's ear. Looked like Ember Falls had a new detective.

"Bitch," Diana muttered just loud enough for Ashley to hear her.

Ashley started to come forward, but both Drew and the man on her other side stopped her.

"Shut your damn mouth," Stephanie ordered. "Or I swear to God, I'll slap your face right here and—" Stephanie spotted movement in Diana's mouth. "Where the hell did you get a piece of gum?"

Diana grinned. "One of those uniformed guards. Some men can't help but take pity on a defenseless damsel in distress." She looked over to the door where the armed guards had disappeared behind. "I'd say he was the cute one, but I couldn't see any of their faces. Who cares?"

Stephanie nearly did hit her. "I do. You can't chew gum in a court room." Stephanie reached into her pocket and pulled out a small tissue. "Get rid of it."

With a roll of her eyes, Diana took the tissue, spit the gum out into it, and shoved it into Stephanie's hand. Revolted, Stephanie put it in her jacket pocket for lack of a garbage pail. "You're disgusting."

Diana shot another dirty look back at the Duncans, and Stephanie followed her gaze.

Ashley Duncan was visibly shaking with a desire to choke the life out of Diana, refusing to blink. Drew's face was a mask of fury.

Grinning, Diana was the first to look away.

"They're going to kill me."

Stephanie shook her head. "We'd have an easier time protecting you from them if you told us who *they* were."

Diana started to shake. "No, I mean the Duncans. They want me dead."

Refusing to look at her client, Stephanie reviewed the paperwork in front of her. "You bet your ass they do, but they *need* you alive."

Diana searched the rest of the courtroom, rubbing her arms.

"Would you calm down," Stephanie hissed. "You're shaking like a leaf and I don't have the patience *or* compassion to try and talk gentle to you. And why are you smiling?"

Diana pulled at her collar. Her skin was clammy and she was beginning to sweat.

Diana undid her top button, rubbed her arms and continued to tremble. Resigned to having to try to calm the woman, Stephanie mustered what little compassion she could and spoke in a soft voice. "Diana."

Diana nearly jumped out of her seat. She rubbed her neck and continued to search for the threat she seemed certain was coming.

"Here, drink some water." Stephanie picked up the pitcher that was provided at the defense table, poured some into a glass and handed it to Diana who accepted with hands that were shaking so badly that she could barely sip the liquid without spilling it all over herself. Drops of water splashed Stephanie's hands.

Diana swallowed the water in one gulp and her grin widened.

Stephanie recognized the panic in Diana's

widening eyes and realized this was more than just jitters.

Diana began to spasm uncontrollably. Her legs kicked out, knocking the table away, and Diana tried to grab onto to Stephanie. Amid the screams from the courtroom, Diana fell out of her chair, her skull hitting the hardwood floor with a crack.

Diana tried to say something, but nothing came out except a gurgle. Her back arched painfully and her legs continued to kick and seize. Her chest contracted as if her lungs were on fire.

Ashley Duncan was yelling, "Don't let that fucking bitch die."

It was Stephanie's green eyes that Diana locked onto. Somehow, she'd managed to grab Stephanie's hand. For the first time since they met, Stephanie felt a hint of compassion for Diana.

"Diana, we're going to get you to the hospital," Stephanie said. "Tell me who did this."

Diana gasped desperately for breath as if she were drowning. She cried for help, cursed, and called out for her father as she continued to spasm violently, grinning the entire time, her eyes wide with fear and agony. She bucked hard, arching her back so much that she lifted off the ground.

With one last strangled gasp, the spasms stopped and Diana collapsed. Her spine bent backwards and her eyes opened wide. She gave one last twitch and died with an unnatural and haunted grin permanently cemented on her lifeless face.

Chapter 2
Jericho

"What the hell happened?" Chief Ann Miller asked the moment she burst through the door of the conference room at the police station. Ollie sat at the table wearing his brand-new suit. His grey tie was loosened, but still around his neck. He started to stand, but Ann quickly waved him back into his seat. "We'd been so careful. How the hell did someone get close enough to kill her?"

"I don't know." Ollie rubbed his hand over his face. He sank back into the chair and sighed. "I've been trying to get in touch with the entire crew that escorted Diana to the court building, but one of them is missing."

Ann's eyes narrowed. "Who?"

"Vic Miranda." Ollie shook his head. "I can't believe Vic would do anything. He's a good guy."

Ann took a seat opposite her son. "I tend to agree, but Vic has a new baby at home. Any chance someone threatened him?"

Ollie wanted to say no. Vic Miranda had been one of his first friends since coming into the Ember Falls PD. Most officers had kept him at a distance, afraid to get too close to the son of the chief, but Vic was a nice guy and it just wasn't in his nature to be anything but friendly.

Loyalty couldn't be used to explain away Vic's disappearance from the courthouse. Or the fact that he was late today, something very out of character for Vic. According to the others in the detail, Vic had shown up just as they were getting ready to load Diana onto the transport van.

"Where's Duncan," Ann asked.

Ollie couldn't help but notice how tired his mother looked. "He's looking for Vic."

Ann nodded. "How are you and he getting along? Still okay with the thought of him being brought on as your partner?"

Without hesitation, Ollie nodded. "Yes. We've put our issues behind us and he's good at what he does. He was pissed today."

"I don't blame him," Ann said. "Is he so pissed that he can't do his job?"

Once again, Ollie didn't hesitate. "He'll do it." Of that, Ollie was sure. When Cole was missing, Drew had been scared to death, but he kept his head on straight and did what needed to be done. Somewhere during his temporary exile from Ember Falls, Drew had managed to learn self-control.

As if on cue, Ollie's phone beeped. Pulling it out, he read the Caller ID. "Drew, you're on speaker. I'm with my mom. What's going on?"

"I found Vic Miranda," Drew said.

Relief flooded through Ollie. If he was trying to hide, he wouldn't have been found that quickly. "Where is he?"

The momentary pause from Drew had something twisting in Ollie's stomach. "I found him in his own garage. He's dead. I'd say he was killed a few hours ago."

Ann and Ollie both got up at the same time. "What? But he was there today. I saw—" Ollie stopped himself in midsentence as his mother cursed. "I guess I didn't."

"Yeah," Drew said from the other side of Ollie's cell. "He never took off his helmet. None of them did. He got there late. Still, it was a fucking ballsy move. If anyone had recognized him, it would all have gone bad fast."

"Mr. Duncan," Ann said. "Where's his wife?"

There was a momentary pause, followed by a weary sigh. "She's still in the house. I told her that it was probably nothing, but I could tell she's worried. I should probably go and tell her, but she's going to flip out. She's alone with their baby girl."

Ann closed her eyes. "I'm on my way with Ollie and additional personal. I'd prefer it if you can wait until I get there, but don't let her into that garage. It's now an active crime scene."

"Got it," Drew answered.

Since earning his shield, this would be the first Line of Duty death Ollie would ever deal with. All he could think as he followed his mother out was, *let it be his last.*

****

You will not be a jealous bitch. You will not be a jealous bitch.

Sam repeated the mantra over and over again in her mind. She had no reason to be jealous. Drew was with her, wasn't he? She was wearing the ring he'd given her.

After knowing him for about three weeks. He'd

known Stephanie Howard a lot longer, and probably a lot better.

How *much* better, was the question?

The first time she'd met the attorney was when Drew had been arrested by two detectives in connection with his own sister's murder. She had arrived with the General to confront both Wilson and Harrington, the detectives in charge of the investigation. The moment she'd walked into the police station, with her stunning good looks and kind and friendly face, it was clear that she was concerned for Drew on a personal level.

Deeply concerned.

Sam hadn't liked that one bit.

During the interrogation, Drew had done a good job of turning things around on the detectives, making them look guilty as hell. Of course, they *were* guilty, not only of once again trying to railroad Drew, but of the murder of Kelli Duncan.

As Drew hammered away at them, Wilson lost control for a moment, and Sam watched as Drew had protected Stephanie, as if it were the most natural thing in the world to him.

Sam had liked that even less.

She'd tried to convince herself that it was nothing. Drew had probably worked with the woman for years. He'd naturally gotten close to the people he'd spent so much time with. And besides, Stephanie wore a ring that indicated she was married.

But even now, as Sam wore the engagement ring that Drew had placed on her finger, she knew that rings didn't mean much to some people.

Once released, Sam saw Drew with Stephanie. The affection they shared, the concern Stephanie had shown about Drew, was bad enough, but seeing her radiant smile when she thanked Drew for the flowers that Drew had just recently sent her had been enough to cause Sam to give Drew the cold shoulder that day.

Drew had come to Sam's home later that night, told her that he and Stephanie were just friends. He hadn't gone into details. No explanation for the flowers had been offered and Sam hadn't asked, not once Drew dropped the bombshell that he was falling in love with her.

In that moment, the sincerity in his eyes had washed away all of her insecurities, and she'd found herself taking Drew to bed for the first time. Lying in his arms, tracing the pattern of his tattoo that covered his scars, Sam knew she was done for. It wasn't just the incredibly hot sex, although that certainly factored in. It was the connection. Suddenly, her past life of discovering that her ex-fiancé had been boning some slut no longer cast a shadow over her new relationship.

When Drew had put down a deposit on a new home, literally right behind the one where his sister lived with Cole, Sam had thought she had left all of those doubts behind. After all, she was the one who got to get him naked in her bed. (Or his bed, the shower, and in one crazy moment while her grandmother was out, on the kitchen floor.)

Then Stephanie Howard had come back into town, at Drew's request.

Sam was determined to keep that little-green-monster at bay, but it wasn't easy when she didn't know what his relationship with Stephanie had been before he'd come back to Ember Falls. Maybe they had just been friends. Or maybe they once had a casual tryst that sizzled out. (Although, it was hard to believe sex with Drew could sizzle out.) Maybe they had never been lovers at all, yet there was something about the way she looked at him, turned to him in that moment of fear, that just seemed somehow intimate.

Knocking at the door to the exam room, Sam waited for Stephanie to invite her in. Sam had escorted her to the hospital as a personal favor to Drew. She'd done her best to remain both supportive and, failing that, professional. It's not like she didn't feel sorry for Stephanie. Diana's death was particularly gruesome to watch. What little color had been in the lawyer's fair skinned face had quickly drained away to leave her a ghostly white.

Diana's last, desperate breath had happened while she'd held tightly onto Stephanie's hand, and once dead, her body seemed frozen.

It would be enough to give anyone nightmares.

Sam looked down at her left hand. Normally, she'd never wear her engagement ring while on duty, but she'd known Stephanie would be at the courtroom and so she'd made a decision to wear it today. Drew was taken, move on.

Did that make her insecure about her relationship with Drew, or did it mean she was just a bitch? She didn't like the former, but the strangely enough, she was fine with the latter.

"Come on in," Stephanie called.

Sam pushed the door open and found the lawyer sitting on the edge of the hospital bed, her sharp, elegant suit jacket was lying over the arm of a nearby chair and her shoes were on the floor. The make up around her eyes was smeared, but she still looked as if she could grace the cover of a magazine.

You will not be a jealous bitch. You will not be a jealous bitch.

"How are you doing?" Sam tried her best to sound friendly.

Stephanie offered a weak smile. "I'll live, which is more than I can say for Diana. I'm supposed to wait for test results, but I'm sure I'm fine."

Sam nodded in agreement. It had been Drew's idea and Sam was trying not to resent the concern that had been so evident in her fiancé's eyes when he had been pleading with Stephanie to go get checked out. "You're probably right, but let's play it safe. You want anything? Coffee? Tea? Water?"

Shaking her head, Stephanie ran her fingers through her hair. "What I want is to get out of here. I hate hospitals."

"Doesn't everyone?"

"Not the way I do," Stephanie countered, as she wrapped her arms around herself as if she were cold, although as far as Sam was concerned the temperature was fine.

Stephanie was definitely on edge. Every sound from the hallway made her jump. Her eyes watched every shadow pass by the door. "I appreciate you coming with me."

Sam forced a smile. "Not a problem."

Stephanie rubbed her hand over her face as she slid off the bed. "I've never seen anyone die before. That was… horrible." Stephanie closed her eyes. "I was pretty cold to her. And I keep thinking, I should feel bad. She was a human being and I was the last person to talk to her. I should feel bad that she died like that, calling out for her father." She looked up at Sam. "But I really don't. Does that make me a bad person?"

Since Sam felt the same way, she was able to understand exactly what Stephanie meant. It was like watching a horrible death on TV. It was gruesome, and not easy to witness, but in the end, you weren't heartbroken. "I wouldn't lose sleep over it. I just wish we knew what she was going to tell us."

Stephanie exhaled sharply and began to pace. "So do I, but she was keeping that to herself until we got to the special prosecutor. She was convinced someone was going to try and kill her, which I guess they were." Someone paused in front of the door and Stephanie seemed to hold her breath until they moved on. "Y'know, before I worked for the General, I'd defended other killers. I once defended someone who'd killed his twin brother over their collection of Star Wars action figures."

Sam's eyebrows shot up and she put her hand in front of her mouth to hide her gasp. "Oh, that's horrible. Child deaths are the worst. How old were they?"

Stephanie didn't answer right away, she was too busy staring at the door as if she was afraid the doctor might come in with horrible news. "They had just celebrated their fiftieth birthday." She shrugged and shook her head. "Boys and their toys."

Sam nearly chuckled. It was still horrible that one brother had killed another, but to be that angry over a stupid doll. Of course, now that she thought about it, Ollie had some of those things and he got upset when she called them dolls. Ollie made a big deal out of the fact that they were still in box, mint condition, never opened Star Wars *action figures* and referring to them as anything else was blasphemy.

"It's a little difficult for me to care about her either." Sam checked her phone again, looking for a text from someone to let her know what was going on. "That was my grandmother she kidnapped along with Cole."

Stephanie nodded as she sat down in the chair in the corner. "Are you and your grandmother close?"

Sam almost talked about how she lived with her grandmother, but decided that wasn't something she wanted to tell the ginger haired beauty. She imagined Stephanie living in a fancy, Manhattan apartment with a doorman where she could have visitors spend the night without worrying about a grandmother who would walk in on your lovemaking, something that still mortified her.

Instead, she nodded. "Very."

Drawing her arms up to her chest, Stephanie smiled. "I was close with my grandmother when I was little, but things changed by the time I was in high school. She didn't approve of my," she made little quotation mark gestures in the air with her fingers, "life choices."

Sam wondered what those life choices were, but decided against asking. Accepting that there was nothing between Drew and Stephanie didn't mean she had to become BFF's with her. The entire situation was very frustrating. Sam didn't like feeling insecure or jealous. Normally she wasn't, but after her last fiancé had cheated on her, it was a tender spot.

"She wasn't the first client I've had that I couldn't stand. I know every person deserves representation, but there were times I got stuck with some pretty scuzzy characters. Domestic violence and sexual assault cases were the worst, but I wasn't given a choice."

Stephanie winced for a moment, as if feeling a sharp, sudden pain.

It was enough to have Sam concerned.

Stephanie shook her head, shaking away whatever dark thoughts had her rubbing her arms. "I was actually thinking about giving up the law and looking for something else when Drew introduced me to the General." The hint of a smile tugged at the corner of her mouth and her face softened.

Sam shifted uncomfortably as she realized that even when he was nowhere to be found, the mere thought of Drew was managing to rescue Stephanie from whatever painful memory was trying to haunt her.

Dammit, you will not be a jealous bitch! "I always thought you met Drew while working *for* the General."

Stephanie got up, looked out the window. "No, Drew was the one who introduced us. The General was looking to expand the legal arm of McAlister Security and Drew thought I'd be a good fit."

Sam waited for her to continue, but Stephanie seemed to decide that she'd said enough.

"So... how *did* you two meet?" Sam asked.

Stephanie took a deep breath, exhaled sharply and looked away. "I think Drew should tell you that."

Sam felt her back stiffen. Okay, maybe it *was* okay to be a jealous bitch after all. "Why?"

Stephanie stayed quiet for a long moment, and Sam wondered if the lawyer was just going to ignore her, until finally Stephanie glanced her way. "Because it's private and not my place."

Sam opened her mouth to say something, but couldn't think of anything that didn't involve name calling, so she stayed silent. This woman was important to Drew and she had no right to demand she tell her intimate details of their lives, but dammit, she didn't want any secrets between her and the man she was going to marry. Was that too much to ask?

Absently, she looked down at the ring on her finger. Suddenly, it felt very heavy on her hand.

"May I see?" Stephanie took her hand to examine the diamond.

Sam was about to snatch her hand away, but she caught the look in Stephanie's eye as she grinned down at the engagement ring. The stunning red head looked truly happy.

Stephanie smiled. "He's over the moon over you. For the first time since I've known Drew, I feel like he might really be happy. And if there's anyone who deserves happiness in his life, it's Drew. I don't want to lose Drew in my life."

Sam frowned, and now she did pull her hand away. She crossed her arms and leaned against the wall behind her. "I don't plan on being one of those girls who dictates who their husband can or can't be friends with. I refuse to be. Just as I refuse to be the one with a husband with secrets."

Stephanie gently placed a hand on Sam's shoulder. "You may never tell Drew that he can't see me, but that doesn't mean you can't put up walls. I really want us to be friends Samantha. When Drew and I met, we were both in pretty dark places. You have, I'm sure, a pretty good idea of what he's been through, but I doubt he's filled in all the blanks. He never does." Stephanie shook her head. "For what it's worth, I agree, there should be no secrets between you, but be patient. Some things are hard to share, *especially* with someone you're in love with."

Someone came to the door, and Sam could feel Stephanie's hand that was still on her shoulder begin to tremble. The shadow on the other side of the door seemed to hesitate, and Sam imagined they were reading something, probably test results. It seemed normal enough, but Stephanie was holding her breath.

"I'm sure your test results are fine," Sam offered.

Absently, Stephanie nodded. "I'm not worried about the results. I just want to get out of here."

Instinctively, Sam put her hand on Stephanie's. She hated seeing anyone this scared over nothing.

The shadow on the other side of the door knocked and without waiting for an invitation, the door opened. A man with stubble on his face and wearing doctor scrubs came in, his eyes on a clipboard. He appeared like he hadn't slept in two days and didn't bother to look up. He never came all way in. "Ms. Howard, there's nothing here. Whatever the victim was exposed to, you're fine. If you feel any symptoms, please come back in, but you're free to go."

Stephanie rapidly started to gather up her things. She signed a few forms from a nurse, none of which she bothered to read. The two women hurried for the door and once outside, Stephanie took several deep breaths, as if she had been under water. When Sam put a sympathetic hand on her arm, Stephanie smiled. "Thank you for staying with me."

The sincerity in Stephanie's words had sympathy stirring in her, and Sam didn't want to be hateful. Her instinct told her that Stephanie was a good person and genuinely wanted Drew to be happy.

Sam decided to try a different approach. "Look, I'm not naïve. We both have a past and it's not like I think Drew hasn't been with anyone before me, and while I'm not friends with anyone from my past, I can understand that you and Drew—"

Stephanie eyes widened in amusement and her hand shot to her mouth to hide a laugh. "Wait, hold on."

Sam fought the urge to smack the smirk off her face.

"Is that what you think? That Drew and I were an item?"

Sam rolled her shoulders. "Well… I assumed…"

Stephanie threw her head back and laughed. Not just a small chuckle, but a full-throated belly laugh. Sam felt her face burn and had to resist the urge to slug the attorney. What was worse is that the laughter made Stephanie even more beautiful.

"Oh Samantha, you don't have anything to be worried about. Drew's a sweetheart and I love him like a brother, but he's not exactly my type."

Frowning, Sam put her hands on her hips. "Why not? What exactly *is* your type?"

Stephanie smiled radiantly and even managed a wink. "If I was available, you would be."

Sam found herself going into blink overdrive. "I'm sorry, but… huh? But I overhead you thank Drew for sending you flowers."

Stephanie dug inside her purse and pulled out her cell phone. She held it up for Sam to see. "He bought flowers for *us*."

Sam took the cell and studied the image of

Stephanie, beaming as she leaned next to a mocha skinned woman in a hospital bed. The woman was very pretty, if exhausted. In her arms, she held a newborn baby.

"Drew sent us the flowers right after Tanya gave birth to Isabella." Stephanie smiled broadly. "She was born two days after Drew came back to Ember Falls. It was very sweet that he'd think of us while he was going through all of that."

Sam forced herself to look Stephanie in the eye as she handed her phone back. "I'm sorry. You must be thinking that I'm some insecure bitch, but…"

Stephanie shook her head as she took her phone back. "No, I can understand how it must have looked." She took one more look at the picture before closing the screen and putting it away.

Sam's cell beeped. Pulling it out, she read a text from Drew, and felt a tear roll down her cheek.

"What is it?" Stephanie asked.

Putting away her cell, Sam looked up and wiped the tear away. "It was from Drew. They just notified Vic Miranda's widow."

The two women exchanged a look of heartbreak.

"Is there anything else that you can remember," Sam asked as they made their way through the parking lot. "Any detail, no matter how small?"

Stephanie stopped walking for a moment and closed her eyes. She had her business jacket folded up, draped over her arms which were crossed in front of her, her purse slung over her shoulder.

Sam came to a stop as well, turning to face her. Realizing that Stephanie was beginning to shake her head, Sam stepped closer. "Just walk me through it again, from the moment you first met her."

Stephanie took a deep breath. "I was brought to the interview room. She was under three guards at all times, and camera surveillance. They had to step outside for us to talk. I handed her the clothes I'd brought her and—"

"Wait." Sam held up a hand. "Where did you get the clothing? Did someone from the department hand it to you?"

Stephanie shook her head. "No, I got an outfit from her apartment. I was told that there were two business suits that looked like they had just been picked up from the dry cleaners. Still in plastic. There was a teal one and a grey one. I took the teal." She smiled. "I thought it was uglier."

Sam shared the smile. "Where did you take the outfit?"

Stephanie considered for a moment. "I got it first thing this morning when I flew in. Brent from McAlister drove me. I grabbed a pair of shoes, underwear, stuff like that. I almost didn't grab makeup, but I could see how she could spin that into my not doing my best, so I took the basics."

They started to walk again as Stephanie outlined everything that happened from when she walked in the interview room to the moment it was time to leave for court.

"And nobody came in while you were speaking with her?"

Stephanie shook her head just as they reached the patrol car Sam had driven to the hospital. She went to the passenger side as Sam opened the door.

They both got in, and Sam buckled in. "So, it was

all the cops on the detail that came in with you, right?"

Stephanie nodded. "Yes. Chief Miller was there too. She drove in a separate car to the court house."

Sam pictured it in her mind. Ollie would have driven her, leading the way to the courthouse. She would have had another patrol car behind them.

"You guys went into a hallway to wait, right?" Sam asked as she started the car.

Buckling her seatbelt, Stephanie went through the details. "Nobody spoke except myself and Diana. Well." She propped her elbow on the side door panel and rested her head on her fingers. "Mostly Diana. She was really nervous, which I was happy about. I wanted her to suffer. And then—"

Sam saw Stephanie close her eyes, watched her frown deepen. "What?"

Blowing out a breath, Stephanie opened her eyes and glanced over at Sam. "She was complaining, bitching really. Wanted a cigarette or at least a stick of gum. You see it all the time. Back when I was a defense attorney, I used to carry a pack for clients. Of course, I smoked then myself, but I carried a pack just for them. I know when you're nervous, it can really help."

Sam shrugged. Something in Stephanie's eyes spoke of guilt, but she didn't understand why. Still, this was something new. "If you don't carry cigarettes anymore, then you couldn't have done anything, right?"

Stephanie sighed and reached into her bag. "Right." She dug around for a few moments, before she pulled out a small package of gum and held it up. "I did have these. When nobody would give her a smoke, she asked for gum. I didn't want to give her any. I wanted her to suffer." Shrugging, Stephanie pulled out a stick and offered it to Sam, who accepted it. Taking one herself, she tossed the package in her bag, along with the gum wrapper. "I even made her spit out the one someone else gave her."

Sam unwrapped her own stick of gum, tossed the wrapper in her pocket and froze, the stick of gum half way to her mouth. "Wait? Did you say that someone gave her gum?"

Stephanie rolled her eyes. "Yeah. I didn't see it until we were in the court room. We were waiting for the judge to come in when I noticed. I made her spit it into a tissue and give it to me, just to be a bitch."

Sam spun in her seat. "What did you do with it?" Sam's mind was flooded with images of getting every uniform in Ember Falls PD to start dumpster diving through the court house trash. Wasn't she going to be popular at the annual picnic? She imagined this was going to go over worse than killing Harrington.

Stephanie frowned. "I shoved it in my coat pocket. Probably still there."

Stephanie started to reach for the small side pocket on her jacket when Sam grabbed her hand. "Stop. Don't touch it."

She waited until she saw the acknowledgement if not the understanding in Stephanie's eyes before she got out and ran to the back of the patrol car. Popping the hood, Sam grabbed a black container the size of a large tool box. Flipping the latches open, Sam dug out a small plastic bag and a pair of plastic gloves. She rushed back to the driver's seat and climbed in to find Stephanie holding the jacket up, ready. "Here's what I'm thinking." Sam snapped on a plastic glove and reached into the right-hand pocket.

"I figured it out." Stephanie watched Sam pull out a tissue with a wadded-up piece of gum balled up inside of it. "I've been walking around with the murder weapon in my pocket."

****

Ashley had taken the long way back to the house as she tried to figure out what, if anything, to tell Cole. She had floated the idea of lying, but both Ollie and Drew had shot her down, insisting he'd find out and it was better if it came from one of them. She also thought about waiting until Drew was able to be there. As much as it irritated her, Cole seemed to feel safer with his uncle around.

She tried not to resent that. Drew was a former marine. He looked deadly, with his massive build of muscles, and his right arm covered in that cool, black, phoenix tattoo he'd gotten after he'd left Ember Falls, while Ashley was tall, thin with barely much meat on her bones. She was scrappy, but there was no way for the kid to know that.

Whatever thought Ashley had entertained of hiding or delaying the truth disappeared the moment she saw his grim, little eyes.

He stood waiting for her in the living room. He was wearing jeans that were getting too short for him and a Batman shirt. He held a dust rag in one hand, and a can of Pledge in the other. "What happened?"

Ashley sighed. "Did Lilly say something?"

Cole shook his head, but held up the cleaning supplies as an answer.

Ashley rolled her eyes as she tossed her purse on a nearby desk. She'd texted Lilly the basics, instructing her not to say anything. And while Lilly hadn't, she'd gone into cleaning overdrive, something she was prone to do, and the kid was too smart to not to pick up on the clues.

"Where's Lilly? I don't want to have to tell this story more than once."

Cole pointed to the kitchen with the can of furniture polish. "She's mopping the kitchen floor for the second time."

Shaking her head, Ashley went into the kitchen to find Lilly pushing a mop back and forth across the kitchen floor which shined. Lilly was a red headed girl who was short, especially when standing next to Ashley.

Ashley did a quick survey. When she was younger, Lilly had sometimes gone into panic attacks that resulted in her cleaning until someone stopped her. The last time was right after she'd broken up with her high school boyfriend and Ashley had found Lilly on her hands and knees scrubbing the floor, her skin scraped raw.

Satisfied that Lilly wasn't in such a state, Ashley beckoned Lilly to follow with one finger. With a sigh, Lilly put the mop into the nearby bucket.

When they came back to the living room, they found Cole had put down the Pledge and dust rag and had taken a seat on the couch. Lilly sat next to him, careful not to touch him. Cole still didn't like being touched.

Pacing back and forth, Ashley described what had happened, leaving out the details of Diana thrashing about. Cole didn't need to hear it and she had no desire to relive it.

"So now what?" Cole asked.

Ashley thought about it. She was probably supposed to say something about how the police would keep looking and they'd figure it all out, but the fact was she had very little faith in the cops' ability to do their jobs. They'd completely screwed Drew when Molly Winters had disappeared, making the entire town believe her brother had been responsible.

"This isn't the same police force," Lilly said, reading the look in Ashley's eyes. "Chief Miller isn't corrupt, and Ollie won't give up. Neither will your Uncle Drew."

Ashley didn't trust cops, but she trusted Ollie. He'd promised he'd find the truth. Ollie wouldn't break his word to her.

"So, what do *we* do now?" Cole asked.

Lilly smiled at the small boy. "We just live our lives. Your aunt and I go back to work. You go back to school."

Cole scowled, but he held his tongue. He'd gotten a short reprieve from school after being kidnapped and nearly killed a week ago, but he was expected back at school the next day. The only reason he hadn't gone back today was because his aunt, uncle and Lilly were all going in to have a meeting with the school principal in the morning and none of them were available today because of the hearing.

"I know you don't want to go," Lilly said. "But it'll be okay, I promise. And remember what Ollie told you. You give it your best shot, he'll take you to that… what is it again?"

"Dragon-Con," Cole supplied. "JD Vincent is going to be there. He's like the best writer like… ever, but something will probably come up."

Ashley read Cole's face. Meeting that author was so important to him, and he was assuming he would be disappointed. "Ollie promised you, right?"

Cole nodded glumly. "Yeah, but…"

Ashley held up her hand like a crossing guard. "Stop. Ollie doesn't break his word. He hasn't once since I've known him. He knows how much this means to you. You're going to that Dragon thing."

Cole sat back and sighed. "Dragon-con."

Lilly put on a cheerful face. "Why don't you decide what you want for dinner tonight? You can have anything you want."

"Good idea," Ashley said. "A final meal. I'll go to the market."

Cole narrowed his eyes.

Ashley scowled and pointed a finger at her nephew. "Don't give me that look. I'm not going to ruin dinner just by being the one to go get the ingredients at the store, but if you're worried you can always come with me."

Cole sneered. He hated trips to the grocery store.

"Or," Ashley said as she went to retrieve her purse and keys. "You can stay here and help Lilly finish cleaning. Knowing her, she'll want to make another pass at everything."

Cole glanced at Lilly who smiled brightly. He groaned and slid off the couch. "I'll go put my sneakers on."

As Cole left the room, Lilly walked over to Ashley. "Since you're going, I'll make a list of things we need."

Ashley rolled her eyes. "Are you okay? You're not… Over-cleaning, are you?"

Lilly shook her head as she scribbled items on a

small piece of paper. "No. I was upset, but... I was just trying to keep him busy and away from the TV. I promise, I'm okay."

Ashley decided to believe Lilly as Cole came running down the stairs. She took the list Lilly handed to her, scanned it and sighed. "Let's go, before she adds more crap to this."

She and Cole headed out to her car and pulled out of the driveway to head into town. She barely noticed the dented, green car that was parked across the street.

****

Police officers swarmed around the home of the late Vic Miranda. Mostly, they concentrated on the garage where his body had been found, but others went in and out of the house.

Across the street, a house sat with a For Sale sign in the front yard. In the end, it was that sign that had been the deciding factor in Vic Miranda's death. Its sole occupant knew it would only be a matter of time until Vic's body had been found and he wanted to have a front row seat for the show.

He had many names. So many, it was hard to sometimes remember his real one. He hadn't used it in a long time. It was such a simple name. Boring and routine. He much preferred his chosen professional name.

Jericho.

It had a nice ring to it and it used the same initial as the name his whore of a mother had called him for years, so he felt like he hadn't completely lost his boyhood identity. It was important to remember where you came from, even if at times you'd much rather forget.

Of course, nobody who he ever met face to face with knew that name. He never used it in person, not unless he knew the person he used it with was going to die at his own hand. It just wasn't very professional for a hired killer.

Jericho was a professional, hired to do a job, but that didn't mean he didn't take pride in his work. It was true that the officer's death had been less that satisfying. It had been child's play to snap his neck from behind. The man was dead before he even realized he wasn't alone in his own garage.

Still, it was worth it to be able to witness how his true target had died. The confusion turning to terror. The elegant spasms of pain, the sweet ballet of having each of her muscles contracting. He loved it when that particular poison resulted in a grin of agony for his victims. It had been a challenge, but Jericho loved challenges.

Jericho sat quietly, listening to Bach as he watched the activity. He kept the house dark, so as to not attract attention, and used binoculars to focus in on points of interest.

It would have been interesting to be able to see what was happening inside the house, but that just wasn't meant to be. He'd have to try and get to the funeral at least and pay his respects. Maybe they would even wake him in the home? The chance to touch the widow was exciting. Perhaps he'd be given the chance to hold the baby?

He loved children.

It was too bad the child was too young to fully appreciate the loss of her father. Jericho wondered if he'd sentenced the young girl to a life of grief, or spared her one. He had no idea what sort of father Vic Miranda would have been.

The killer pushed these thoughts to the side as he saw the front door open. A few minutes ago, the wife's sister had arrived. She'd been met by one off the officers and escorted into the home.

Now, the Chief of Ember Fall's PD exited the house. Small towns like this weren't used to losing officers in the line of duty. The only time it had happened since this Chief had taken control was when one of her officers suffered a fatal heart attack in the middle of shift. Jericho liked to think of him being fat and overweight, dying while sitting in his patrol car, with a doughnut in his mouth, and powdered sugar on the cheesy cop moustache that covered his upper lip.

During his research, Jericho had purposely avoided seeing a picture of Officer Jim Valance. Why ruin that image?

Vic Miranda had no moustache, but he was an attractive male and Jericho liked to imagine he'd married a hot piece of ass. Hopefully, his wife hadn't let herself get too fat from being pregnant. He liked to think that Vic had enjoyed a little morning nookie before heading to his garage to have his neck snapped.

Across the street, someone else came out of the house. Most of the cops in this town held little to no interest, but this one did. Oliver Miller. Jericho believed him to be a sad excuse for a man and an officer. Most likely his position as the newest detective in Ember Falls was because he'd been squirted out from the body of the town Chief.

Still, he'd seen the man interact with the other officers earlier and Jericho couldn't detect any resentment on their part.

He was close with one of the Duncans and was rumored to be working with the other one, so he bore scrutiny.

Jericho watched as Detective Miller walked his mother to her car. They had arrived together, but apparently, they wouldn't leave in the same vehicle. Had he arranged to leave with one of the other officers? Or perhaps he was to stay behind, try and give comfort to the poor grieving widow, in the hopes that in a moment of vulnerability, she'd spread her legs for him?

Jericho focused in on Detective Miller. He spoke to some of the officers who were coming out of the garage. He imagined him to be a Mamma's boy, but he conducted himself with authority.

Someone else came out of the garage.

Andrew Duncan.

According to his file, everyone called him Drew. From what Jericho had learned, he and the young detective weren't the best of friends in high school. In fact, from what he'd heard, Drew had bullied young Oliver. He imagined it must burn Miller's ass to have to work with Duncan. Yet when the two made eye contact, he saw no hint of resentment.

Interesting.

Even more interesting, the pair headed to the car that Duncan had arrived in. Duncan made his way to the driver's side and got in. A moment later, the engine roared to life.

Detective Miller didn't get in right away. Was he steeling himself to have to appear friendly with his former tormentor? Or perhaps he was thinking about going inside one last time to see if there was anything else he could do to curry favor with the late Vic Miranda's wife?

With both hands on the roof of the car, Ollie gazed around in the early dusk. The shadows of night were just beginning to fall and a nearby streetlamp had come on, basking the young detective in a silhouette as he narrowed his eyes. Looking for something. Searching.

Jericho could imagine the hairs on the back of Miller's neck prickling as somehow, he sensed the presence of a nearby predator.

Jericho smiled. He had been warned to be wary of Drew Duncan, and he would be, but tonight it had been Oliver Miller who had impressed him.

Perhaps the chance would come to introduce himself to the young detective. The question would be, what name would he chose to give?

Chapter 3
Back to School

By the time Ollie pulled into the parking spot across the street from his third-floor apartment, it was well nearly ten PM. The moon was bright in the sky, and the stars twinkled in the blackness of the night. Ollie sniffed the air as he got out. Somebody had a wood fire burning, which reminded him of when he'd gone camping with his Dad as a kid. Dad's birthday was just around the corner. If it hadn't been for that heart attack, he would have turned fifty-four.

He'd been eleven when his father had passed, and the loss had devastated him. Peter Miller had been a huge fan of science fiction movies, graphic novels, and fantasy books. His mother had always teased Ollie when he got geeked up that he was channeling his father.

He wondered how little Francesca Miranda might take after her father. What personality traits she'd share with the Dad who never got to raise her. Would she have his laugh? His smile? Would little Frannie share her father's ability to make friends with almost anyone?

She'd never remember her father. As Ollie crossed the street to his apartment, he wondered which was worse. Losing a parent that you loved, or losing them so early, you never knew them.

Ollie unlocked his front door and flipped on the

lights. The walls were plastered with movie posters. Everything from Alien to Zorro and every letter in-between. He had a fifty-six-inch flat screen TV with four different gaming systems plugged in. There were knickknacks displayed in places of honor. The best part was the extensive movie collection he owned.

No, I wouldn't give up that time I had with Dad for anything in the world.

As he hadn't eaten yet, it would make sense to order dinner, but Ollie felt the need to wash the day off of him. Going into the bedroom, he stripped down, putting his wallet, shield and gun on his bedroom dresser, then headed into the shower in his bedroom bath.

With the water on hot, he lathered up and tried to rinse away the grief and disgust that he'd accumulated throughout the day. He tried not to think about Diana in her last moments. She didn't deserve his pity, not after everything she'd done, but Ollie just wasn't able to turn that part of him off that easily.

In those last few moments of her life, she must have known she was done for. Why couldn't she have managed to get out some piece of vital information, some hint as to who had done this?

Instead, she called for her father.

Ollie wondered what would go through his mind if he were about to die. Would he think of his dad? Knowing himself, Ollie figured he'd probably call out for his mom. He was, at heart, a mamma's boy. He'd long ago made peace with that. He had a wonderful mother, so what was wrong with being close with her.

While Diana didn't exactly strike him as a 'Daddy's Little Princess' type, that moment when she called for her father would stay with him a long time.

As Ollie scrubbed his blonde hair, he tried not to let her death bother him so much. She was an evil woman. She may not have physically done it, but she was as responsible for Kelli's death as Wilson was. She would have stood by and watched Wilson murder both Cole and Sam's grandmother.

So why was it that he felt like he needed to get her justice as well?

Ollie's thoughts were disturbed by a noise. He shut the water off to listen, but didn't hear anything further besides the drip from the shower head.

It was probably nothing. Mrs. Rosenthal, who lived below him, was probably just putting out one of her cats. She often slammed the door at all hours of the night.

Ollie was on edge. Someone had taken a big risk in killing Diana.

Then there had been that feeling outside Vic's house tonight. It had only lasted a moment, but he was positive someone was watching them. Probably just more evidence that he was being paranoid, which is why he hadn't said anything to Drew.

Ollie put the water back on, and rinsed off the last of the suds.

Maybe he should have said something. Drew clearly believed in instincts. Drew had sat in the small, stone alcove near where his sister's body was found, looked out on that area of dirt and just knew something was off. He'd been right.

Of course, maybe Drew simply had better instincts then Ollie did.

Getting out of the shower, Ollie grabbed the large,

white terry cloth towel and started to dry off. The bathroom was small, so he stepped out into the bedroom and towards the dresser. Wrapping the towel around his waist, he opened the top drawer.

The sound of glass shattering had Ollie's heart racing. He grabbed the gun on the dresser and rushed through his bedroom door, and down the hallway. He burst into the living area, instantly training his gun on the source of the disturbance.

"Police, don't move!" Ollie commanded.

Hands went up. It was a woman, thin and tall, with auburn hair. The familiarity of her curves was just setting in when she turned her head and grinned. "Don't shoot officer. I surrender."

Ollie lowered his gun. "Ashley?"

She turned the rest of the way around, lowered her hands and folded her arms. "No wonder you made detective. Planning on shooting me with that, stud?"

Ollie scowled. "Of course not. The safety is back on already."

Ashley's smirk turned into a grin. "I wasn't talking about your gun." She glanced down.

Ollie followed her gaze and saw the towel had fallen down around his ankles. "Fuck!"

He grabbed at the towel with one hand, trying to cover himself with the other. As he was still holding his gun, he was afraid he was going to shoot his dick off, but that couldn't be much more embarrassing.

Ashley snorted as he wrapped the towel around his waist again. "Easy there, stud. It's not like you have anything to be embarrassed about. Go get dressed and don't shoot anything important off."

He slinked away to the bedroom, cringing as he

heard her laugh.

Minutes later, still feeling the heat in his face, Ollie came out to find Ashley standing by the microwave as something heated up. She smiled. "You didn't need to get dressed on my account."

Ollie rubbed his hand over his face. "Stop. Just… stop."

She chuckled. "I broke a wine glass. Sorry about that. Thankfully, you had more."

On the table was a single place setting, but two glasses. There was a bottle of red, uncorked, between them, and a plastic bag from a local store that wasn't opened.

"Sit," Ashley said. "You've had a hell of a day. I figured you probably didn't eat."

Still unable to look at her, he sat at the table. "I wasn't that hungry. You didn't have to go to any trouble."

The microwave beeped and she sneered. "Relax. I'm just serving. Lilly cooked." She opened the door and pulled out a Tupperware bowl filled with a spicy smelling meat. "Homemade Sloppy Joes. I know you're a fan. There are buns in the bag, along with potato chips."

The scent of the meat made Ollie's mouth drool. "Well, since you brought it all the way over here."

Ashley brought over the meat as he poured two glasses of wine. Taking hers, she watched as he built himself a sandwich. "It was Cole's idea. A last meal before he goes back to school tomorrow."

Ollie nodded as he took a bite. Bits of meat fell out of the sandwich and onto his nice, clean shirt.

That didn't take long.

He reached for a napkin. "How's he holding up? I know he's not thrilled about going back."

Ashley exhaled. "He's miserable, but he's keeping it to himself. He doesn't want to miss out on going to that crazy wizard's ball."

Ollie tucked a napkin into his shirt, wishing he'd done that to begin with. "Dragon-Con and I'm looking forward to it to. It'll be fun going with him." He took another bite, washed it down with some wine. "Does he know what happened?"

The smile quickly faded from Ashley's face. "He knows Diana was killed. I didn't go into descriptive detail. I didn't tell him about Vic Miranda. You know, I kissed Vic once."

Ollie stopped mid-bite, scowling at the Sloppy Joe. "When?"

Ashley shrugged. "It was at a party, back in junior high. We were playing Spin the Bottle. You weren't there. It was innocent enough." Ashley smiled. "Although that was the night when Chad Bollington slipped me the tongue for the first time."

Ollie dropped his sandwich on his plate. He remembered the party. He was one of the few kids in school that hadn't been invited. He sat home, playing video games, wondering if the kids at the party might play some game like Spin the Bottle. If he had been there, it might have given him a chance to kiss Ashley.

With a sigh, Ollie forced the thought from his mind. It wasn't Ashley's fault that he'd been too much of a nerd to have been invited. Or that he'd been too afraid to make a move.

He studied her face as she helped herself to potato chips. He always loved the way her hair framed her long face. She had a small nose, but generous lips that were amazing when she smiled. Her hazel eyes twinkled in amusement at him as she sipped wine.

"Whatcha lookin' at, stud." She helped herself to another chip.

Ollie groaned, feeling his face grow hot again. "Is that going to be your new nickname for me now?" If so, he took it at a sign that the entire town of Ember Falls was going to hear the story how his towel got the drop on her.

"Oh relax. It was a sight to behold. I hadn't realized how much of a sight," she grinned, "but you don't have anything to be embarrassed about."

Ollie smiled, feeling somewhat cheered. At least she wasn't going all 'ew, I saw your thingie.' Maybe she even liked what she saw?

Ashley pointed down at his half eaten Sloppy Joe. "Aren't you hungry? I slaved over a hot microwave oven to reheat that for you."

Allowing himself a small laugh, he picked up the sandwich and took another bite. He wished she'd eat more than just chips. He liked having dinner with her. There was something so homey about it.

"You sure you don't want?" Ollie offered. "It's really good."

Ashley leaned back in the chair and closed her eyes. "I still haven't gotten my appetite back after today." Her fingers started to press over her right temple. "You want to know what pisses me off? I felt bad for her. Seeing her die like that, so much pain. If you had asked me this morning, I would say she deserved it, but watching it?" She shook her head. "It was different with Wilson. Watching Drew kill him didn't bother me. Maybe because I was holding Cole and knew if Drew hadn't done it, the bastard would come after him again. Besides, it was self-defense. Drew didn't have a choice."

Ashley pushed back from the table, took her wine glass and walked over to a nearby window. The moonlight bathed her face in a glow that made her look both beautiful and haunted. She brought the wine to her lips, but didn't drink. "I hate feeling sorry for that bitch. She had a hand in killing Kelli. I shouldn't feel bad for her." She finally took that sip, a big one. Gulped it down and winced.

Leaving his sandwich alone, Ollie joined her at the window. "It was a horrible thing to see. It was one thing when Sam shot Harrington. He was an active threat. I don't think there's anything wrong with feeling pity for Diana in that moment. It bothers you because it feels like a betrayal of Kelli, but you're raising her son now, and I don't think Kelli would want Cole raised by a woman so cold that she could witness the death of a defenseless person and just shrug it off."

Ashley studied Ollie's face, looking for some sign that he was deceiving her.

"What did she say? Right before she died. I couldn't hear."

Ollie sighed. "Nothing of importance. She begged for help, and called for her father."

Ashley rolled her eyes. "Stupid bitch. Couldn't do the right thing at the last moment. Who the hell calls for their father when they die? I thought people called out for their mothers. I know you would." She took another sip. "I don't think I would. Not that I didn't love mom, but I never could count on her."

She finished of her wine and scowled. "Fuck it. You can't count on anyone. Why bother?"

Something twisted in Ollie's gut as she walked away from him. "That's not true."

Ashley glared at him. "Jesus. I know you and Drew put your issues to rest and you're working with him now, but don't go getting all defensive over him. He's just like every other male on the planet. Some are worse than others, but all are assholes."

Drew hadn't told Ashley the real reason why he'd left Ember Falls, and Ollie had given his word that he'd keep Drew's secret, but that didn't stop Ollie from thinking he ought to. That betrayal was still a wall between them, keeping Ashley and Drew from fully reconnecting. Ashley continued to castigate him for it, and Drew took it, feeling he deserved the punishment. He'd probably never forgive himself for leaving his sisters.

However, defending Drew Duncan wasn't something that was first on Ollie's mind. "I wasn't talking about Drew." He wanted to touch her, but was afraid she'd pull away. "I've always been here for you Ashley."

Ashley's glare softened. Exhaling, she managed a small smile. "Of course you have been." Putting her glass down, she walked over to Ollie, wrapped her arms around him, and rested her head on his chest. "But I imagine someday some smart woman will snap you up and you'll leave me. Whoever that is, she'll be the luckiest woman on the face of the planet."

Kissing the top of her head, Ollie embraced her back. He felt his blood burn as he smelled her cherry blossom perfume, felt the warmth of her skin. Why couldn't she see that he was hers if she wanted him? Why couldn't he tell her?

"I'll never leave you alone." Ollie wished he could find the courage to finally tell her that all he wanted in life was her. The words were right there, ready for him to say.

Instead, he just held her. The thought of losing her as a friend because she didn't want anything more from him was too frightening. He promised that he'd never leave her, because it was true. The question was would she ever leave him.

****

The next morning, Cole sat on a small bench outside of the Ember Falls elementary school administrative office, trying to concentrate on the words to his favorite book which he was re-reading in preparation to meet the author. He was still convinced something would come up, some excuse would be made, and he'd never get the chance to meet J.D. Vincent. He knew nobody understood why it was so important to him.

Someday, he wanted to be the person who put words down on paper, creating a story that allowed the reader to escape into a magical realm where real monsters of the world couldn't follow them.

So, Cole had kept his word. He hadn't given anyone a hard time about coming back to school today, even though he knew it was going to be horrible. Everyone told him they'd deal with things at school. Uncle Drew, Aunt Ashley, and Lilly had assured him things wouldn't be as bad as he thought. They didn't get it.

None of them understood. Mrs. Collins hated him

from the moment he'd stepped foot in her classroom. Nothing he ever did was good enough for her. She got mad at him for not knowing things that the class had done before he'd moved to Ember Falls and she ignored it when the other kids picked on him.

Cole sighed as he turned the page. He'd dealt with far worse than Mrs. Collins. He could ignore her for the rest of the school year if he had to.

"Good book?"

Cole looked up. Standing a few feet away was a boy he'd seen coming in and out of school. He was a good couple of inches taller than Cole, with crazy, black hair. His skin was the color of chocolate milk and his eyes had a hint of Asian ancestry in them. He wore a T-shirt with a picture of a cowboy riding a dinosaur.

Cole squirmed in his seat. The kid was twice his size and he doubted he'd be able to fight him off if he tried to take his things. Instinct had Cole holding the book closer.

The boy didn't seem put off by Cole's silence. He tilted his head as he studied the cover. "Dragons are pretty cool, as long as they don't talk. That's just stupid." He rolled his eyes. "My cousin likes the cute ones that sing and dance, but to me, dragons should roar and breathe fire. I've always loved drawing them." He shifted his weight, letting his backpack fall off his shoulder. Grabbing it, he unzipped the top and reached inside. A moment later, he pulled out a sketch pad. "I'm not so crazy about the Chinese ones, but my grandmother likes those." He started to flip pages, his eyebrows going up as he did. "Personally, I like the big ones."

He offered the pad to Cole who glanced at the

picture. A golden dragon stared back at him. The drawing was completely awesome in all of its amazing details, from the scales that covered its body, to the enormous golden wings, and the sharp talons that looked ready to slice into someone. It's had jagged ridges on its back and a head crowned in horns.

Cole couldn't help but be impressed. The illustration had been done in colored pencils. He'd seen comic books that weren't that detailed or well done. It looked almost exactly like the dragon from the book he was reading. Strong and mighty. Fierce and majestic.

"I'm not happy with the eyes." The artist kid shrugged. "They're too big and make him look like a toy that squeaks when you squeeze it."

Cole snorted. They were white, with a simple black dot. "You should make them blue," Cole said. "Not like the middle, like my uncle's eyes. I mean the whole eye should be blue. Then make the black part—"

"The pupil?"

Cole nodded. "Yeah. Make that black, but not round. Like this." Cole handed back the notebook and opened his novel. At the beginning of each chapter was a small, black and white illustration. It showed a dragon's eye. The pupil was a black sliver of a moon. Mysterious and deadly.

The artist kid studied it intently. "Yeah, yeah… That'll work. I knew I was doing it wrong. I was trying to make it like Godzilla, but this would work. Blue?" He stood up straight, scratched his chin as he considered the idea. "That might work. It's regal, right? It would stand out. I like it."

There was more yelling from the office, which made Cole wince. He saw the other boy look curiously at the door. He could hear Aunt Ash's voice the clearest, using language that wasn't suitable for a school.

Quickly, Cole looked down and started to flip through the pages of the sketch book. He was surprised to see that it wasn't just filled with dragons, but with vampires, zombies, superheroes, soldiers and girls.

"These are cool." Cole found a picture of a costumed hero dressed in a yellow outfit with red trimming. The outfit looked almost like a military uniform, with a star-like emblem over the heart, not over the middle of the chest like you see in most superheroes. Cole thought it was an interesting detail. "What's his name?"

Looking down, the artist kid shrugged. "I don't know. I see these pictures in my head and draw them, but I can't come up with names or back stories."

Cole studied the picture some more. The character had a yellow burst of energy in the palm of his right hand. His left hand was pointing outward. "How about something like Star Man. Or wait…" Cole shook his head. That was lame. "Captain Nova."

The artist's eyes widened as he slowly smiled. "Hey, that's pretty cool."

Continuing to examine the picture, Cole tried to bring the character to life. He heard him speak with a raspy, deep voice, barking out orders as he commanded others. "His outfit isn't like a regular hero. Maybe he's part of a group. An inter-galactic group that fights an enemy from another galaxy, but he's human so when he's not… what's the word?"

Taking a seat next to Cole, the other boy tossed his bag down on the floor. "Deployed."

"Yeah, that's it," Cole said, enjoying himself.

Sticking out his hand, the artist smiled broadly. "By the way, my name's Jay Lancaster. What are you in for?"

Cole sighed as he glanced at the door. It was a long story, and he wasn't sure how much he wanted to share.

"Ah." Jay gave a knowing smile. "Parent's in with the principal? What'd you do?"

Cole handed the sketch pad back and averted his eyes. "I *didn't* do anything."

Jay nodded as he took back the pad. "Good. Never admit anything. Plead the fifth. They ain't got nothing on ya."

Crossing his arms, Cole looked at the door as he heard raised voices again. "I *didn't.*"

Jay held up his hands. "Hey, I believe you, but someone in there isn't very happy. You think you're gonna get grounded?"

Cole shook his head. He wasn't really in trouble, although he was certain that they were probably making things worse for him. "I don't think so. Why?"

Jay shrugged. "I was thinking that maybe we could hang out. I've always wanted to do a comic book. Maybe you could help. You have good ideas. You think you could come up with more characters?"

Excited, Cole saw an army of costumed heroes in his mind. Visions of giant, mutant lizards terrorizing a city while the newly baptized Captain Nova and his crew of colorful cohorts rode to the rescue, saving lives. He turned to give his enthusiastic support of the idea when the door to the office opened. Cole's teacher Mrs. Collins came out. She glanced at Cole, sending him a venomous glare. Her mouth opened with a barbed comment on the tip of her tongue, when someone came up behind her.

"Thank you, Barbara," Mrs. Harris, the school principal said. "You should probably go greet your class. We'll speak again *after* dismissal."

With a huff, Mrs. Collins stormed off. As she did, Mrs. Harris glanced to the small bench where Cole sat. She blinked a few moments as her eyes settled on Jay. "Oh. Mr. Lancaster. I'd forgotten about you. If you have that paperwork, just give it to Ms. Pulaski. She'll be out in a moment."

Jay grinned and sent her a thumbs up. As he went into his bookbag, Mrs. Harris looked to Cole. "Mr. Duncan, why don't you come in so we can talk a bit."

Cole sent Jay one last, desperate look before he got up.

"See ya later buddy," Jay called, never looking up from his backpack.

Buddy? Had he just made his first friend? Suddenly, Mrs. Harris didn't seem quite as scary as he let her steer him inside her office.

Chapter 4
A Bet's a Bet

Cole trailed behind Mrs. Harris, unsure if he fully understood what had just transpired. She was taking her time, talking about how much she loved the school and the students in it, telling him how important they were to her.

Cole had assumed when he'd gone in that he was bound to be reprimanded. He'd been stunned when Mrs. Harris told him that she felt he might do better in a different fourth grade class. So much so, he stood with his mouth wide open, looking around the room, going person to person. Aunt Ashley had a small, satisfied look on her face. Lilly was nearly giddy. Uncle Drew looked pissed, but Cole was mostly sure it wasn't at him.

His time in the principal's officer was quick and painless, and before he'd fully processed that he was getting a new teacher, he was saying goodbye to everyone so Mrs. Harris could escort him to class.

"Your new classroom is just around the corner," Mrs. Harris said as they approached the intersection. Mrs. Collin's class was all the way down in the opposite direction, making Cole wonder if his classroom had been chosen for the simple fact that it was far away from his old one. If so, it was fine with him.

The walls didn't have just artwork on it, but handwritten pages as well. Cole could see many of the words were highlighted in yellow. He examined one a little closer and quickly realized the emphasized words were all verbs. Each page had an accompanying picture of a bird's head. Red birds, blue ones, yellow ones. Displayed above the work were big red letters that read 'Angry Verbs.'

Mrs. Harris paused a few feet short of the classroom door, signaled for Cole to wait, as she knocked on the door.

A shadow appeared on the other side of the frosted window. When the door opened, a woman smiled out at Mrs. Harris. Slightly heavy set, with long, fizzy hair that was a dull shade of red, she had a smiling face that displayed a splattering of freckles.

"This is Ms. Hanley." Mrs. Harris gestured towards the teacher. "Ms. Hanley, meet Cole Duncan. Why don't I go in and say hello to your class?"

Mrs. Harris stepped inside as Ms. Hanley came over. "Hi Cole. Mrs. Harris and I spoke about you. I read the homework assignment you did where you had to write a story of what it would be like to live on another planet. You did a really amazing job."

Suspicious of compliments, Cole narrowed his eyes. She stood a good few feet away from Cole, which was much better than Mrs. Collins, who always seemed to like to be hover. Mrs. Collins was always putting her hand on his shoulder, or the back of his neck, no matter how uncomfortable it made him.

Mrs. Hanley stood with her hands folded in front of her, patiently waiting for Cole to say something. She was probably going to have to wait a while, as Cole didn't know what to say.

"I'm big into writing," Mrs. Hanley said. "That's why I was so excited to hear you'd be coming to my class. You were very descriptive in that story you did. You did a wonderful job painting the picture of how your character Drake saw himself and the world he was on. Most of the time, you'd just get a basic sense of what it was like on the planet, but you managed to tell a full story. How Drake had been part of a space mission and had issues with his ship. He'd managed to crash land on a planet that he could live on, but there was no food for him to eat at first. And that creature that was living nearby, watching him at all times. He knew it was there, but wasn't sure what to do about it."

She frowned. "You didn't wrap it up. I wanted to know what happened. Did that creature ever come out? Did they become friends? I kept waiting for it to try and eat Drake?"

Cole felt the back of his neck grow warm as he felt his teacher's eyes on him. It was just a stupid assignment, what did it matter? He was told to write one page and he did. Mrs. Collins chose some to display. Not his, but that hadn't bothered him.

"I got the feeling like you wanted to finish the story," Mrs. Hanley said.

Cole shrugged again. She was right, but that didn't mean anything. He hated not being able to finish stories.

"The creature wouldn't eat Drake," Cole said, surprising himself. "He doesn't like the way he would taste."

Mrs. Hanley nodded. "So, they become friends?"

Cole shook his head. "No, Drake and the creature

can never be friends. It can kill Drake if it wants to, but right now it's just waiting. Watching. Drake knows that. He's trying to get ready, but he knows the only way to survive is if someone comes to get him."

Mrs. Hanley's eyebrows went up. "Does anyone ever come for Drake?"

Cole was careful to avoid eye contact. "After about a year, just as he thinks nobody will. Another ship comes. Some friends from Earth were out looking for him."

Mrs. Hanley straightened out a poem about Mindy and her eventual Presidential aspirations. "So, it's got a happy ending. Drake goes home."

Everyone loved a happy ending, but not all stories had one. "The creature kills everyone except Drake. Drake turns off the equipment that sends the distress signal, so nobody else will come. The creature doesn't hurt Drake, but he wants him to stay where he can watch. He thinks of him like a pet."

Mrs. Hanley blinked in surprise and bit the bottom of her lip. "You've got a very good imagination. And you write wonderfully. I know you and Mrs. Collins didn't get along very well, but I'm really hoping you'll be willing to give me a chance. I really want you in my class Cole. I want to read all the amazing things you're going to write."

Cole didn't respond. He didn't like the ending to his own story, but the story had a life of its own and the creature was just too powerful to stop.

Careful not to touch Cole, she indicated the door. "Let's go meet the rest of your class."

Cole followed Mrs. Hanley inside the classroom. He felt his face burn as about twenty sets of eyes looked at him, sizing up the new kid. Nobody sneered, which was at least something. Mrs. Hanley was introducing Cole and saying something about finding him a place to sit.

A hand shot up in the back of the class, waving furiously, and Cole's heart did a little leap.

"He can sit next to me!" Jay indicated a small desk next to him which was empty.

Cole looked to Mrs. Hanley who considered for a moment. "I think that's the perfect spot. Cole, go sit next to Jay and make yourself at home."

Grabbing his bookbag, Cole made his way to his new desk and took his spot next to Jay who was grinning ear to ear.

Jay leaned into Cole. "Cool. Mrs. Hanley is the best. She loves my drawings, even the gross ones. We can work on our comic during lunch."

Their comic.

It was really going to be a thing. He was really doing this. He really had a friend.

Mrs. Harris said goodbye to the entire class and Mrs. Hanley instructed everyone to take out their history books. "Cole, we'll get you your own books by tomorrow. Can you look on with Jay for now?"

Grinning, Cole scooted over so he could read on with his new buddy. He pulled out his own notebook, which was crammed full of story ideas. Looking over, he saw every page of Jay's notebook had a doodle on it of one sort or another.

It was a match made in heaven.

****

Drew pulled up in front of the police station, unsure of what to expect when he walked in. He'd been connected to the deaths of both Wilson and Harington, the two cops who'd gone rogue, conspired with Diana to murder his sister, but they had been so far beyond the line that nobody had held their deaths against him.

Vic Miranda was a different story. He was a nice guy who was a new father. Everyone liked Vic. He was always quick with a grin and a joke, and even faster to pull out pictures of his baby girl. Vic was all about being a dad. It was the most important thing to ever happen to him and he loved every part of it.

Drew knew he didn't kill Vic, but he died because of his attempt to get justice for his sister.

Drew flashed the ID card that he'd been presented by Chief Miller, and made his way down the hall of the police station. Everyone wore black bands over their police shields today. He received nods of acknowledgement as he made his way to the briefing room.

He paused at the door to the room, his hand hovering over the doorknob. Would they all blame him?

Only one way to find out.

He opened the door and found a room full of cops. Most were in uniform, but there were a few plain clothes people around. There were half empty cups of coffee scattered around and two murder boards set up. One had pictures related to Diana, the other one dedicated to Vic.

Most everyone avoided looking at the one for their fallen comrade, but Drew couldn't help but stare. Vic's body on the ground, his neck bent at an unnatural angle. This had happened less than twenty feet from where his infant daughter slept.

Drew felt someone come stand by his side. He glanced over to see the tired eyes of Bryan O'Malley. He had been Vic's best friend and partner. Bryan was in his late twenties, with very short blonde hair and a face that made him look like he could still be in college. "I was supposed to work yesterday, but my kid had to have surgery. Tonsillitis. Nothing major, but he's my kid. I had to go, right?"

Drew exhaled sharply. "Of course, you did."

Bryan folded his arms and shook his head. "If I'd have been there…"

"Stop." Drew moved over so the officer could look at him without seeing Vic's picture. "You can't think like that. Vic was killed early in the morning, right as he was leaving."

Bryan refused to look up. "I would have seen it wasn't him. I know Vic. I…" He sighed, looked up. "Crap. I *knew* Vic." He rubbed his hands over his face. "We need to get this son of a bitch."

Drew put his hand on Bryan's shoulder. "We will."

Chief Miller came into the room, followed by her son Ollie and his former partner, Sam.

On duty, Samantha Rossi was still quite stunningly beautiful. She was all business, with her long, luxurious hair pulled back into a ponytail, and her body wrapped in the Ember Falls PD uniform. Her eyes, the color of milk chocolate, found his.

Something twitched in his stomach when she looked at him. He hadn't realized he could fall in love so hard or so fast.

Once, when he was young, he thought he'd fallen in love, but the girl who stole his heart had laughed at him and slapped his face. Shortly afterwards, she'd disappeared and Drew was assumed guilty. He'd nearly gone to prison for the rest of his life.

It took Drew years to come to terms with the fact that he wanted somebody to love him so desperately that he mistook sex for affection.

Now, Molly Winter's body was lying on a slab in the coroner's office, and Drew wasn't quite sure how he felt about it.

This time was different. He wasn't a boy, feeling trapped under the thumb of his abusive, alcoholic father. He was a man, who knew what he wanted, and he wanted Sam Rossi. And she wanted him.

So why did he see uncertainty when he looked into those big, beautiful eyes?

Chief Ann Miller signaled everyone that she was ready to start, and took her spot at the head of the table. She let everyone settle into their seat, bringing their Styrofoam coffee cups and bagels on small paper plates with them. Ollie took the seat to her right, across from Drew.

Sam sat next to Drew, put her hand gently on his for a moment, before folding them in front of herself, back to all business mode.

Drew noticed that she wasn't wearing her engagement ring like she had the day before, but assured himself that it was nothing. She normally didn't wear it while in uniform.

Everyone looked to Chief Miller, waiting for her to start. Ann's face was grim and she appeared as if she'd aged overnight. Lack of sleep was evident from the bags under her eyes, but those eyes were stern and resolute.

"Vic Miranda was one of us." Ann's voice was

steady, firm and had the men and women around her nodding. "He was a good man, a good father, and a damn good cop. I still remember when he came on the force as a rookie about six years ago. Vic was proud to wear the uniform. He was a friend to each and every one of us in this room. Vic was more than a coworker. He was family."

She stood up, glanced at the cop sitting nearest Ollie. He was one of the last old timers, his dark hair showing hints of gray. "Sanders, if I recall, whenever you have that fund raiser walk for your granddaughter with cancer, Vic was the first to sign up."

Sanders nodded grimly. "Each and every year. He was thrilled when Amy went into remission. My girl has a bit of a crush on Vic. She—" Sanders closed his eyes for a moment as he caught his mistake in using the present tense. "I haven't told her yet. My wife and I were going to do it tomorrow."

Ann nodded, before her eyes shifted to the other end of the table. "Fredricks, wasn't Vic the one who took your mom to the hospital? Stayed with her, when she had that heart attack, and you and your family were out of town on vacation?"

Fredricks, one of the other detectives in the department rubbed his hand over his balding head. "Yeah. Stayed with her all night until we could get back. We drove all night from Cape Cod. Found them laughing it up while he helped her eat breakfast."

"I'd bet we could all tell at least one story about Vic." Ann's eyes moved around the table until they settled on Bryan O'Malley. "Bryan, you and he weren't just partners. You're godfather to his little girl, aren't you?"

Bryan didn't look up. His eyes remained locked to the picture of Vic on the murder board. "Yeah. We haven't told anyone, but Sally's pregnant." Murmurs of congratulations filled the room, but Bryan didn't acknowledge it. "We were keeping it quiet, until we hit that three-month mark. Only close family knows. That included Vic and Mindy. They were supposed to be Godparents for us."

Ann folded her hands in front of her. "Vic was family to us all and we're going to do right by him and his family. His shield number will be retired from this point going forward. We'll set up a college fund for his daughter. And we will bring his killer to justice." She leaned forward. "Let me be very clear. When I say justice, I mean *justice*. Not revenge. We will not sully the memory of Vic Miranda by breaking the law he swore to uphold. We're going to do this the right way. Through solid police work. Teamwork. This is a good department. The business with Wilson and Harrington is a stain that won't be forgotten, but that's what started this. We won't add to that by seeking vigilante justice. We will find his killer and we will nail his ass to the wall. Is that understood?"

There were reluctant nods from all around the table and Ann made sure to make eye contact with everyone until she was satisfied that they were all on the same page. "Let's get started."

She turned to Ollie, who cleared his throat. "We have the murder weapon. Officer Rossi recovered a chewed piece of gum from Ms. Howard, one that Diana had been given by the killer posing as Vic. We're still waiting on tests." Ollie leaned back in his chair, making small motions with his hands as he spoke. "The lab wants to pull DNA, just for verifications sake, but we're sure it was Diana's gum. The big tests are what it was laced with. They're still pending, but prelim reports is that it's a very concentrated form of strychnine."

Ollie outlined Stephanie's statement, explaining how the unsub must have passed a piece of gum to Diana as she was waiting.

Fredricks frowned as he scribbled notes. "Poisoned gum? Can you really get enough into a stick of gum?"

Drew nodded. "I spoke to an expert from McAlister last night. It's possible, but it's not cheap or easy. You can't just dip a piece into strychnine. It would have to be tailor made gum."

Sanders, who was about to take a sip of coffee, scowled and put his Styrofoam cup down. "Tailor made gum? Where the hell would you get that from?"

Drew exchanged an uneasy glance with Chief Miller. He'd spent a long-time last night in her office with her, on the phone with different experts. They spoke with about half a dozen McAlister personnel, including the General who was footing the bill for Drew's involvement in the case. By hiring his own firm to investigate Kelli's death, it allowed Drew to stay employed by McAlister Security, and bypass any police regulation on investigating a homicide where he had a personal involvement.

From the resigned nod from Chief Miller, Drew understood it was time to put all their cards on the table.

"Most likely," Drew said, "we're dealing with a hired killer, one that was sent to Ember Falls to keep us from hearing what Diana had to tell us about my sister's murder."

Fredricks put voice to what everyone else was

thinking. "A hired killer? In Ember Falls? Who the hell would have deep enough pockets for that? And why?"

With a sigh of resignation, Ann continued. "There's an aspect of this investigation that I've kept private and away from most of you in this room. The exceptions have been my son, Detective Sanders, Officer Rossi and Mr. Duncan. This was my decision, and any issues with it can be addressed directly to me on a one on one."

There was a stirring of uncomfortable glances and nobody appeared as surprised as Drew had expected. Many eyes shot down towards the end of the table, where a uniformed officer sat.

Sergeant Bart Polansky was the only officer with nearly two decades worth of experience under his belt, a belt that was a little bigger than all of the other cops in the room. His bulldog face almost never smiled, except when he was playing poker and he had just won a big pot. He had a thin moustache on his lip and a thinner hair line on top of his head. Jutting a chin or two towards the chief, Polansky folded his arms. "Is this about the body dumpsite you've kept on the down low?"

Chief Miller reacted with a small arch of her eyebrow. "You already know?"

Polansky scowled, grinding his jaw. "I know what happens in my house." He said this with enough disdain in his voice to make it clear he found it insulting that she was surprised. "Look Chief, everyone in the room has known that there was something going on, something bigger than Kelli Duncan getting on the wrong side of two bad cops." His beetle eyes slid towards Drew. "I never liked Harrington or Wilson, and

I've got the rips to prove it."

"I didn't care for him myself," Ann said. "But that didn't give you the right to punch Wilson that time, although you never did tell me why you did that."

Polansky took a sip of coffee and sneered. "Bastard took the last jelly doughnut. He knew those were mine." To punctuate the point, he took a bite out of his powdered jelly doughnut, washed it down with more coffee.

Ann shook her head. "If you knew, why didn't you come to me?"

Unaware of the small powder smear on his lip, Polansky shrugged. "I figured you had your reasons. You're the chief." With that, he looked away.

Ann sighed as she sat back down, glancing at Ollie as she did. Polansky was the hard ass of the station, the one all the uniforms went to for advice on how to do the job. He was old school cop, cynical to the bone and unafraid to butt heads with anyone, including the Chief of the Ember Falls PD.

"That's right," Ann said. "*I'm* the chief. I was brought into this town to clean it up. I grew up in Ember Falls. Same as many of you. This town deserves a good, clean department, and all of us in this room have worked hard to make the changes that were needed." She clenched her fist as she spoke. "I thought we had done enough. I didn't like Wilson, but he closed cases. I knew Harrington was a lazy cop, but I thought he was clean. I was wrong. *They* were wrong. I needed to be sure, not only that nobody else was corrupt, but also that you weren't connected to someone who was, even if you didn't know it. So, I waited and looked. I'm not about to apologize for it, but if I had been wrong about the people in this room, I would be turning in my shield today, not running this meeting."

Polansky shrugged as he turned back to Chief Miller, his scowl still firmly in place. "Let's not get dramatic." He rolled his eyes and managed to spot Sam who signaled him to wipe his lip.

"Mr. Duncan," Chief Miller said. "Why don't you fill in the rest of what we know? Start from the beginning."

Drew sighed as he looked out to the varied cop faces, all waiting. This was the part he had been dreading. Explaining to all of these people what had happened and what he'd done, seeing the judgement in their eyes.

He glanced over to Sam, and this time, her eyes spoke volumes. She was in his corner, solidly.

That was enough.

"Let me start with Molly Winters." Drew pictured her face in his mind, pictured her body under his for the first time. He could still smell her perfume, and remember that feeling of losing himself in her. All the secrets he'd told her, and how she always listened. He believed then it was because she truly cared. "We got into a fight that night at the dance and I stormed off. I honestly can't tell you where I went. I think I might have been going to see a friend, but I don't think I ever got there. Pretty much everything after the slap is a blur, but when I woke up, I was under arrest for her murder. Cuffed to a hospital bed and being told they had tons of evidence against me. Witnesses, blood splatter, DNA, the fucking works. I was told right then and there by the DA that I was fried and if I didn't cop a plea deal, I'd get a needle in my arm."

"Bullshit." Polansky pointed at Drew. "I was a beat cop back then, and we didn't have squat. I did the canvasing. I was the one who found the damn blood. It looked bad, but it wasn't enough to verify death." He shook his head as he squinted as if he were trying to read something without his glasses. "I'll admit, I wondered for a while if it you did something, but no way we had that."

"I never said they *had* that evidence," Drew said over the din. He waited a moment until everyone quieted down. He met Polansky's eyes dead on. Let the man read his face. "What I'm saying is that McGrath insisted they did. More than once. So did his shit for brains partner, Harington. I can barely remember the first time they had a go at me, I was still half way out of it." Drew couldn't recall the entire interrogation, but whenever he tried to, he could still smell the disinfectant of the hospital. Still remember the face of a nurse that came to his rescue. "Someone stepped in, told them to get out. I can't say for sure, but I don't think they read me my rights."

Polansky got up, taking his cup with him. He went over to the coffee pot in the corner. "Any lawyer would have been able to get that thrown out, even a first-year public defender with his head up his ass."

Drew crossed his arms and settled back, understanding the dance he was in with Polansky. The uniforms looked to him for their lead. If Polansky was on board, they were on board.

"I didn't have a lawyer." Drew scowled at the memory. "Not for a week of being in the hospital. I met Robert Gillman at the court house about five minutes before I had to enter my plea. I was advised"—Drew paused for a beat—"strenuously advised, to plead guilty, right up to when the judge asked. Gillman even started to tell the judge that I was most likely pleading guilty, and asking for a few moments longer. I spoke up and told the judge I was never taking a plea."

Polansky sat back down, his eyes never leaving Drew. "What judge was it?"

"Roberts." Drew never forgot a single name of who was involved. Once his head cleared in that hospital bed, he memorized every face and every name. He could recall the conversations in amazing detail. "He seemed to nudge me that way too, but I didn't give him any wiggle room."

Polansky nodded. "Roberts was a dirty bird himself. If I recall, he was pulled down by that same prostitute ring where our old Chief was involved. Chief Barber got off easy."

That earned a rare snort from Ann. "If you want to call a married man, pillar of the community, and a man who loved to quote the bible, suffering a fatal heart attack while he was in bed with a pair of handcuffed, underage male prostitutes getting off easy, then I hate to see your definition of not getting off easy."

Polansky smiled, a rare and stunning sight. "Getting caught like that and surviving, but maybe that's just me."

Snickers circulated through the room, and Drew allowed himself to join in for a moment before continuing. "While I was held, Gillman kept telling me to take a plea. I won't bore you with the details, but he rode me on it nearly as much as the DA did."

Polansky held his cup up. "You're talking about District Attorney Reynolds. He was a moron and lapdog of our old mayor, Brooks."

Drew nodded. "One and the same. I got better advice from some of the inmates. I had pressure put on me from everyone, including those who were supposed to be on my side." Drew took a long sip of coffee, swallowed hard, hurting his throat.

Polansky's eyes sharpened as he seemed to ponder the meaning of what Drew meant. "And you didn't take it with that much pressure?"

Drew shook his head. "No. I'm a stubborn bastard. I refused to admit I did something like that when I knew I didn't. I was determined to die first, and the more pressure they put on me, the more I dug in my heels. I started to educate myself in prison on my rights, and requested a different public defender. I was pretty sure I'd end up dead, but that's when everything blew up with Chief Barbar and the judge. I remember there were rumors that someone thought the DA was involved as well, but he was appointed by the Governor to the State DA's office, and nothing ever came of it." Drew shrugged. "New Ember Falls DA. New Chief." He looked to Chief Miller, who nodded in his direction. It occurred to Drew just then he'd never really thanked her for her role in stopping the never-ending cycle of awaiting trial. That was something he was going to have to remedy soon.

"So, it was you against all of them," Polansky said, considering. "What about your family? Your old man."

Drew stared into his now cold coffee. "I wasn't in contact with my sisters. I was under the impression that they had bought into the idea that I was guilty."

"They hadn't." Ollie waited for Drew to make eye contact. "Ashley tried to write, email. She tried to go up to see you, but was always turned away. Kelli told me she snuck into the hospital to see you, but you weren't allowed visitors because you were under arrest. Neither of them ever believed you hurt Molly, even after you were out and left Ember Falls. Ashley was devastated, but she never believed you were guilty. Just…" Ollie flushed, quickly picked up his coffee to hide his face.

"Just thought I was a bastard for leaving?" Drew finished for him. "Yeah, Ash has made that clear."

Polansky was starting to make notes, but wasn't looking up. "And your father?"

Drew grimaced. "You know my dad is retired EFPD. I don't know if any of you knew him."

Polansky leaned back in his chair and snorted. "I did. He was a son of a bitch, no offense. I slugged him once too."

Drew grinned, picturing his father getting punched in the face by the rotund Polansky, and the image helped his nerves.

"None taken," Drew replied. "Trust me, nobody here has a lower opinion of my father than I do."

Polansky arched an eyebrow. "You got a twenty you want to put on that? I've got a damn low opinion of your old man."

Drew couldn't help but think it would be the easiest twenty he'd ever make.

"My father did come to see me," Drew said. "Six times. Amazingly, he never had a problem getting in. I had no desire to talk to him, but I was told I didn't have a choice. He was one of the loudest ones telling me to take the deal."

Polansky frowned as he started to pick up the pencil again. "Your dad thought you were guilty?"

Drew shook his head. "Not as far as I know. He made it clear he didn't give a shit. On his second visit, he tried to pull off the concerned father act. Said if I took the plea, I could tell everyone I was high and didn't remember it. Say I was having flashbacks and feeling guilty, I could convince them to not give me life. Be out by the time I was fifty maybe. Still have a life. It's what my mother would have wanted." Drew had to resist the urge to pound the table. "By the time he walked out, he was making threats, telling me I'd be sorry."

Polansky's eyebrows went up and he whistled. "He was always an ass."

Drew heaved out a breath, desperately trying to maintain control. "You have no idea, but you're about to get one. His last visit came a week before the chief died. It was the day before Easter. He didn't even try with the pretense. Just threats. He said there would be a new lawyer coming up to see me in a week. He wanted me to take the," Drew made quotation marks in the air with his fingers, "*sweetheart deal* that he managed to work out for me. Twenty years, for involuntary manslaughter. He threatened me. Even assaulted me, which was nothing new. I told him to shove it up his ass."

A few of the cops nodded, as if to say they agreed with the sentiment. Others shook their heads, unable to believe his father's level of cruelty. They still had no idea.

Drew rubbed his hands on his jeans fighting the nausea. "When he left, he told me to be careful. Prison was a scary place. I thought it was just another lame attempt to scare me, but I found out the next night that there was more to it than that."

Drew swallowed hard, forced himself to look up. He concentrated on Polansky. Kept his eyes off of Sam as he chose his words very carefully. "I was jumped the next night. I spent a week in the prison infirmary." Drew glanced around, attempting to gauge everyone's face. Most seemed to believe what he was saying. Ollie frowned in sympathy. Drew still couldn't look at Sam, but she took his hand again, giving it a gentle squeeze.

He was sure she could feel him tremble.

Drew felt the sweat on the back of his neck as Polansky studied him with intense, calculating eyes. It was like Polansky was hearing every word Drew said, and was reading Drew's mind to know the truth he refused to say.

The sergeant took a swig of coffee, scowled at the cup before putting it down. When he looked up at Drew, it was clear he was still weighing his next question in his head.

"And what happened when you got out?" Polansky asked.

Drew, unaware that he had been holding his breath, inhaled slowly. His throat felt dry and raw, and he desperately wanted to drink something, but didn't dare pick up his cup.

"I had no idea I was getting out until about fifteen minutes before I was brought to the door," Drew said. "Dad had let it slip months ago that both Ashley and Kelli had moved out and I wasn't sure how to get in touch with them. I wasn't given the chance to call anyone. I figured I'd hike down the road, find a phone somewhere. Figured to try my friend Brooke first, then if I couldn't get him, Lilly."

He'd later learned that Brooke had left Ember Falls by that point, and upon the death of Lilly's grandmother, both Ashley and Lilly were living in her house, the same one they lived in now.

"However, when I got outside the prison, I found my father waiting for me. He was driving a brand new, black Ford Truck, with all the extras. My father hasn't owned a brand-new vehicle his entire life up until then."

The implication of Drew's words registered on everyone's face, including Polansky. "Your old man was forced to retire. Many were pissed, but they took the money and ran." His eyes went to Chief Miller, and Drew understood that had been part of her cleanup of the department. "Lots of people get to that point, they splurge on something. I've got my eye on getting a boat whenever I turn in my papers."

Drew already knew his father had stopped working for the EFPD during the time he was awaiting trial. "He didn't seem pissed when he picked me up. He was happy. Nearly giddy."

O'Malley shrugged, held his hands out and furrowed his brow. "So? He was happy to see you. His son was out of jail and coming home instead of facing the rest of his life behind bars for a murder he didn't do."

Huffing out a humorless laugh, Drew shook his head. "He never wanted me out and he never cared that I was innocent. And he never brought me home. He drove me a few miles, then turned off a back road and pulled his gun on me."

A sea of raised eyebrows, widened eyes and several open mouths displayed in front of Drew.

Drew pulled his hand away from Sam and crossed his arms. He wanted to curse Polansky. Drew was supposed to be working with these cops, but Polansky was turning it into an interrogation. Intellectually, Drew understood why. He knew if their positions were reversed, he'd do the same thing, but that doesn't mean he had to like it. "He wanted me to leave town." Drew forced himself to look up. "And I did."

Polansky rose from his chair. "You want us to believe that your own father pulled a gun on you? I'm not about to win any father of the year awards from my son. I spent most of his childhood on the wrong side of a bottle, but I'd never hurt my kid. I checked, there were never any reports of any abuse in your home."

Drew shot out of his chair, his hands clenched in fists. "There were reports. Ask the man who used to live behind me. He called in twice and got his ass kicked by my father for his trouble in front of his kid. Ask Sam's Nana who called it in when she suspected it and how my father paid her a visit."

Sam rose beside Drew, gently putting her hand on his arm. "It's true. You can talk to her if you like, but Nana told me she called it in, and it when she pushed to get something done, Frank Duncan showed up in her home."

Polansky frowned, folded his arms. "He threatened her?"

Sam shook her head. "No. He threatened me. Threatened to have someone pay me a visit. As a cop, he knew people who liked little girls."

The reaction from the room was immediate and visceral. O'Malley's curled lip, Sander's flinched and crinkled his nose, and raised voices called Drew's father a son of a bitch and a bastard and a variety of other names.

Polansky however, stayed passive. His dark eyes watched Drew, studied him, while Chief Miller tried to quiet down the room and deal with the calls from some to find Frank Duncan and kick his ass.

"Stop it," Ann said. "We will deal with retired officer Duncan in due time and we'll do so professionally. There will be no tuning him up, slapping him around or any other of the more colorful suggestions. Am I understood?"

Now it was O'Malley who got up and stormed forward. He jabbed a finger at Ollie. "You're telling me you're okay with not feeding this punk his own teeth."

Ann slowly rose. "Detective Miller understands that's not the way we do things.

Ollie, who was staring straight ahead with his arms crossed, scowling in contempt, slowly looked at his mother. "Maybe we should."

The room exploded again as mother and son stared at each other, neither blinking.

It was Drew who finally brought the tension in the room down. "There's nothing more I'd like than pound my father into the ground, but he's not the one behind Kelli's murder."

Polansky jutted his chin up. "How can you be so sure? If we're to believe what you're saying, how are we supposed to believe that he'd never hurt his own kid."

Drew's eyes narrowed and he turned slightly away from Sam.

Ollie rose to stand next to Polansky, but kept his eyes on his new partner. "Tell him," Ollie ordered. "All of it."

With a glare of disgust that was as much for himself as it was for his father, Drew nodded.

But not all of it. Never all of it.

"When I learned that Kelli had been murdered and her punk of an ex was locked up at the time, my next thought was my father." Drew took a deep breath, held it for a moment, before exhaling. "When my father forced me from the car by gunpoint, he told me that there was nobody left in Ember Falls who thought I hadn't killed Molly Winters. That's why my sisters or my friends hadn't come to see me. He told me that nobody would believe me if I tried to convince anyone I hadn't done it. And it was better if I didn't."

Polansky's eyebrows shot up. "Better? For who?"

"For my sisters," Drew snapped. "You need me to spell it out for you? He told me if I ever came back into this town, both of my sisters would be raped, tortured and killed. He'd make sure they suffered as long as possible and that they knew it was my fault."

Feeling as if the air had been sucked out of the room, Drew stalked away from the cluster of cops, rubbing his hand over his head. Sam moved to his side, but he pulled away from her, ignored the hurt look in her eyes and turned back to the room full of cop's eyes. "I confronted my father about Kelli when I came back to town. I was with General McAlister. Dad made it clear that if he had done it, he would have kept his word."

As everyone tried to absorb what he had said, Drew moved back to the table, closer to Sam, who made no attempt to touch him. Everyone watched him, waiting.

Polansky was leaning on the table with his hip, his arms folded, and his eyes on the chief who seemed to be avoiding eye contact.

Drew sighed and decided to say what he knew everyone was thinking.

"Kelli was murdered because she wanted me back in town. She started to poke around in the Molly Winter's case. I wouldn't be surprised if she even told Diana during one of her counseling sessions about the email she sent me." He rubbed his face with his hand and felt bone weary tired. "If she hadn't, Kelli would still be alive. If I hadn't come back, Vic's wife wouldn't be a widow. His daughter wouldn't have lost her father before she's able to speak."

Polansky's eye narrowed. "Bullshit." He moved off the table, and started to circle it like a shark, pointing a finger at Drew as he stalked over. "That's bullshit. You didn't kill Vic, any more than you killed your damn sister. Some asshole is pulling strings, that's the person who we need to hold responsible. You put this on yourself, you're taking some of the blame off where it needs to be."

The sergeant reached to his back pocket, pulled out his wallet. "And as for your fucking old man, I've been on this job for a long time. I've seen fathers who've beat their own kids to death in a drunken rage, but cold threats like that? Just when you think you've fucking seen it all, you realize you haven't." Shaking his head, he pulled out a twenty and shoved it into Drew's hand. "Now, let's figure out what our next step is."

Slowly, Drew made his way back to Sam, but he was unable to make eye contact. Instead, the pair of them stared down at the twenty. "I hate talking about that."

Tentatively, Sam reached out and put a hand on his arm. "Nobody in this room blames you for what happened to Kelli or Vic, except you. Have you told Ashley yet why you left?"

Drew shook his head. "I don't want to make excuses. Bottom line is, I walked away from her and Kelli."

Sam sighed and pulled him into a hug. He was a massive man, over six feet tall and solid as steel. He had the body of a pro-wrestler, with a mess of dark hair on his head and a black, dangerous looking phoenix tattoo that ran up his right arm right to his chest. Yet right now, he felt like an eight-year-old boy left in a heap on the floor, and a fresh cigarette burn seared into his skin.

The pair of them made their way back to the table, where Drew tossed the twenty down on a clean empty plate. "Let that be the start of a college fund for little Frannie, and let's nail the son of a bitch who killed her father."

Chapter 5
That's the Way the Cookie Crumbles

Ashley pulled her car in front of the school and glanced at the dashboard clock that told her she still had fifteen minutes left before the hordes of maniacs known as children were released to wreak havoc on the populace of Ember Falls. Killing the engine, she got out and walked over to the school entrance, intending to wait there for the bell to ring. She wanted to get a look at Cole the moment he walked out and if he was still miserable, she'd know, and by God there would be hell to pay.

Ashley was done with not being able to protect the kid. Unlike most other hellions, Cole was sweet and quiet and she just couldn't take the sadness in his eyes. There had been a time when Ashley had thought about becoming a mom, but the idea scared the crap out of her. What kind of mother would she be? She couldn't bake cookies or any of that other mom crap. Her own mother was usually so depressed that she wasn't much of a cookie baker herself. And whenever Mom attempted to, she burnt them to a crisp. Just like Ashley would do now if she tried.

But if she needed to take a class to learn to bake a damn cookie, she would.

Ashley once held a fantasy of being a wife and a mom, back when she was a little girl. She'd meet a sweet guy who loved her more than the world itself. Someone who'd dote on her, and wanted nothing more than to start a family. Even back then, she knew how babies were made, thanks to the crudeness of her father. Somehow, she thought girls weren't supposed to like sex, but she'd find a guy who was more interested in getting into her heart than her pants and they'd run off and get married and have a whole bunch of babies.

And that man would be gentle, and kind, and he'd never hurt her. The sound of him coming home wouldn't make her go pale and tremble like it had with her father.

Ashley thought back to the first time she'd imagined getting married. She'd have her brother give her away, never her father. No, her father wouldn't even be there, wherever *there* was. Kelli would be her Maid of Honor. And the guy would watch her walk down the aisle with a look of wonder on his face as if he were watching her walk on water. She must have been just a little girl, because she could still remember asking her mom when she'd be old enough to get married.

Those were silly little dreams, which died a sad and painful death.

Men looked at her, wanted her, but not as a wife. Nobody was interested in a forever with her and she'd long since stopped looking for Mr. Right and had been quite happy with the string of Mr. Right Nows. Dad had been correct, guys just wanted in her pants. However, the first time she let someone do that with her, she found she liked it just as much as they did.

Unbidden, a memory surfaced of her father walking in when Ashley had been curled up in her mother's bed. It was near the end, when Mom could barely stay awake for more than an hour at a time, and everyone was telling her that it would be a matter of days. Ashley had still refused to believe it, no matter how hard it was for Mom to breathe.

Dad had come in and hadn't yet gotten drunk for the night. He really was just passing by from getting out of uniform and had overheard Ashley's dream of getting married to the sweetest, kindest boy and having a lot of babies with him.

Dad had announced his presence by laughing at her. "You think some asshole who isn't a desperate loser would think about marrying you?" He shook his head as he lit a cigarette. Blowing out smoke, he jabbed his finger at her. "Get real. Plenty of guys will want a ride, but they won't want you. Your sister might find a man. She'd got that quiet, knows her place thing, but you've got a mouth on you." He took another drag, and laughed again, the smoke escaping from his mouth as he did. "You'll probably be a good lay, but don't expect more than that."

Mom sighed, squeezing Ashley's hand. "Don't say that Frank. She'll find a nice man and—"

"Blow him until he shoots a ring out?" Dad said. "Please. Some girls are the ones you marry. Some are the ones you fuck while you're married. Guess which one you are?"

Never one to just allow herself to be insulted, Ashley started to scream at her father. Sometimes it actually amused him. This hadn't been one of those times. He'd closed the distance between them and grabbed her by the hair, yanking her out of the bed. Cigarette still in his mouth, he smacked her face. The memory had Ashley place her own hand over her cheek, remembering the loud smack and sharp pain. The mortification and utter terror as her father's hand formed a fist.

That's when Drew had come running in. One quick punch to Dad's balls, he'd let go of Ashley and went after her brother. Drew fought and managed to get outside.

"Fucking old man can't even catch me anymore," Drew said as he backed up to the stairs.

Dad took off after her brother. She'd found out later that night their father had indeed caught Drew. Most of her brother's bruises were hidden from plain sight, but he was limping and his lip was split. He'd gotten Kelli and the three of them spend the night in their mother's room, with the door locked. Their father had gone out to drink and hadn't returned until the next day.

That was the night Mom had died.

"Hey Ashley."

Spinning around with a gasp, Ashley saw Drew's new fiancé trotting up to her. Her beautiful smile was replaced with a frown of concern.

"You okay?" Sam was still in uniform and Ashley could see her patrol car only a few feet away. "I didn't mean to startle you."

After a moment, Ashley started to breathe again. "Yeah, sorry. I was just…" Ashley scowled, hating the fact that she'd taken such a bad trip down memory lane. She settled back into place to wait for Cole. "Lost in thought. What are you doing here?"

Sam took a spot next to her, propping her butt next to Ashley, so they were both facing the same direction.

"Chief wants a police presence outside the school for now at dismissal. She sent me since I know Cole." Sam glanced over at Ashley. "It's just a precaution," she added. "It was really Drew's idea, but he couldn't be here. He and Ollie are driving out to the neighboring communities to get any missing person reports for the last ten years."

Ashley frowned. "In today's day and age? Can't someone email them?"

Sam shook her head. "They want everything low key. Only people the chief knows personally are involved. We had a big meeting today. The sergeant went at Drew pretty hard. It was a little difficult to watch."

Ashley's eyes narrowed as she turned to Sam with her jaw set. "What sergeant and why the hell is he going after my brother?"

Sam grinned a little, but managed to wipe it away quickly enough. "Polansky. All the uniforms look to him for guidance. He pushed at Drew to get the details. Chief Miller was trying to connect the dots and Polansky wanted to make sure we got the whole story, but the cops in that room followed Polansky's lead. He put to rest any doubts about Drew."

"Good." She turned back to the school, determined not to miss Cole when he came out, but she stole a quick glance back to Sam. Ashley felt like she was still missing something, but put it out of her mind. She'd seen the smirk from Sam at the display of concern and anger over someone giving Drew a hard time, and she wasn't going to give Sam any additional ammo. Drew wasn't off the hook. She still hadn't forgiven him for leaving and she never would. She may be glad that he's back, although she'd never say that out loud to anyone, but she wasn't going to forgive him.

"Has Drew talked to you at all about what he did while he was away?" Sam asked.

Ashley shook her head and squared her shoulders, but didn't take her eyes off the school doors. "No. I don't want to hear about his adventures with McAlister."

"I mean beyond that," Sam asked. "Anything about what he did for fun. Or anyone he hung out with or dated or anything?"

Arching an eyebrow, Ashley glanced at Sam. "If you've got any questions about Drew's past, then you should speak to your fiancé, not me."

Sam sighed. "You're right. And we have. It's just that…" She shook her head. "Never mind. I should and I will, but maybe you should also talk to your brother about everything. You two have a lot of catching up to do."

Ashley turned back to the school. "No, we don't. He made his choice when he got out of prison. Now maybe some of that can be overlooked because he'd been through hell. I guess for some reason, he never got the letters we sent him, but he still should have come back."

"He's back now."

Ashley let out a dry, humorless laugh, and crossed her arms. "So, he changed his mind and came back, a decade later. I'm over it. If he leaves now, he'll crush that little boy."

"Drew's not going anywhere," Sam insisted. "He's never leaving Cole *or* you."

Ashley responded with a derisive snort.

Both women remained quiet for the next two minutes, their eyes on the school, not on each other. More and more parents arrived, mostly mothers, but a few fathers as well. Ashley checked her cell for the time. She still had six minutes.

"I'm sorry," Sam said, breaking the silence.

Ashley glanced over. "For what?"

Sam sighed. "For poking my nose in where I shouldn't. I don't want you to hate me. I want you and your brother to mend your fences, and I want us to be close. I've never had any sisters, or brothers for that matter. I was an only child. So were my parents, so no cousins. I know that you and Lilly are like besties, but I was kind of looking forward to having a sister-in-law."

Ashley liked Sam, and Lord knows, she'd been there when Cole was in trouble, and Ollie swore by her. "What are you doing Saturday night?"

Furrowing her brow. "I've got that self-defense class. Drew volunteered to help and I signed you up, remember?"

"Yeah, yeah." Ashley made a waving motion with her hands. "That's over at eight? I mean after that. We're not your Nana's age, you know, we can stay out past dark."

Sam laughed. "Nana goes out more than I do. And before I met your brother, had more sex than I do." Her hand shot to her mouth and her face turned red. "Oh, I'm sorry."

Ashley just snorted. "Glad he's good for something. I say we have him stay with the kid afterwards. Your Nana said she'd watch him while we were at the class, but we can send Drew home and you, me and Lilly can go out and get drinks." Ashley smiled, leaned back on the car and crossed her arms. "Lots of drinks."

"Sound great. Consider it a date." Sam grinned, mimicked Ashley's pose. "To be honest, I haven't gone out much since moving back to Ember Falls. Except with either Nana or Ollie."

Ashley turned quickly to look at Sam, her arms dropping to her sides. "You and Ollie used to date?"

Sam's head slowly turned, and her eyebrows drew together. "No. He's my partner. Or at least he was. We hung out sometimes. He wanted to drag me to a Comic-Con once down in the city, but I refused to wear the costume." Sam gave a shiver. "But no, we never dated. Ollie would never have hit on me when we were partners, and now I'm with Drew."

Ashley settled back on the car, nodded slowly and turned back to watch the school doors. "All right." She refolded her arms again. "Okay."

Sam watched her carefully. "Why? Would that have been an issue?"

With a deep frown, Ashley shook her head, ignoring the flush she felt in her cheeks. "No. Just curious since he never mentioned it. Which if you never went out with him, would be why, but it's none of my business who Ollie dates, if anyone."

"Uh huh." Sam scooted a little closer. "You know, he's not seeing anyone right now. In fact, I don't think he's dated once since I first met him."

Feeling guilty for the fact that she was relieved, Ashley tried to keep her face passive. "That's too bad."

"It is," Sam agreed, grinning like an idiot. "I think someone ought to snatch him up."

Ashley concentrated on the front doors of the

school. "Whoever does, will be the luckiest girl in the world."

The school bell rang, none too soon for Ashley's taste, and within moments, the doors opened and a flood of children came pouring out. Some ran, as if they'd just escaped through the gates of hell, while others did what you'd call a mosey, deep in conversation with their friends.

Ashley became worried when the doors opened again and Cole came out. He was walking shoulder to shoulder with a boy much bigger than he was, but the two of them seemed to both be staring at the same notebook. The larger boy was pointing to the pictures and talking, while Cole nodded, made comments and smiled.

Cole was *smiling*.

Cole being happy was a rare and beautiful thing. He'd giggle here or grin there when something happened that was amusing, but seeing Cole truly joyful was something that happened far too infrequently.

The pair stopped dead, Cole grabbing the notebook and saying something that had the other boy's eyes going wide in astonishment. A slow grin appeared on the larger boy's face.

"Looks like someone made a friend," Sam said.

Ashley nodded slowly, wiping away the tears that she just realized she had cried upon seeing Cole with his new bestie.

"What in the world are they reading?" Sam asked as she stood on her toes for a moment, trying to get a better look. "What's Cole's favorite subject?"

Ashley shrugged. "I don't think he has one. I guess

reading, knowing him." She gave Sam a quick, annoyed glance. "Get off your toes and act normal. Don't make a big deal out of this." Cole and the other boy had started forward again. Now it was Cole doing the talking and the other boy nodding along. "I mean, it *is* a big deal, but don't make it out to be one."

Sam nodded, settled back onto the car and tried to stop grinning.

Cole and the boy stopped again, flipping pages in the note book furiously, when Cole looked up. He said something to the other boy and the pair launched themselves forward.

"Aunt Ash!" Cole came skidding to a stop, his eyes filled with excitement. "Sam! This is Jay." He indicated the boy next to him who was smiling up at Ashley. "He's in my new class. We're going to do a comic book together. *Look.*"

He shoved the notebook in her hands, which she accepted, but didn't open right away. "Hi Jay, it's nice to meet you."

Jay continued to smile shyly, giving a little wave.

"Look Aunt Ash," Cole insisted, pointing to the notebook again. "Look inside."

Exchanging a quick grin with Sam, Ashley flipped open the notebook. She knew that whatever doodles were in there, she needed to act completely enthralled and mesmerized, but she wasn't expecting to really be impressed. "Wow, these are good. You both drew these?" She continued to flip the pages, moving the notebook so Sam could look on.

"No, Jay's the artist." Cole jabbed a thumb at his new friend. "I'm in charge of the stories. I've got tons of ideas. We want to get together and work on them."

Ashley studied the pictures, many of which of superheroes. They were detailed, thought out and really well done. She was pleased that the women superheroes weren't wearing costumes that looked like they were strippers with capes.

Man, Ollie would love this.

Some of the characters had names and even origin stories. Ashley found one that reminded her of Ollie, dressed in a superhero-military like costume. "Captain Nova is the first human recruit to the Nova Force, an interstellar military organization dedicated to keeping the Galaxy safe from interdimensional creatures, hostile aliens and galactic domination. Captain Nova's mother was part of a crew of NASA that was thought killed in the first manned mission to Mars when their vessel exploded in space, but after he joins the Nova Force, he learns she's been held captive by the evil overlord Galactor and will stop at nothing to save her."

Ashley exchanged an impressed nod with Sam before going back to studying the illustration. "Wow. You came up with all of this Jay?"

When Jay didn't answer, Ashley looked to see if he'd wandered off, but he was still there, grinning. His eyes fixated on Ashley. "Jay?"

Blinking rapidly, Jay blushed and shook his head. "No ma'am. I mean, I drew the picture. I showed it to Cole this morning and he came up with all of that. The name, the story. Everything. And he did it just like that." Jay snapped his fingers. "Just wham."

"It was nothing." Cole couldn't stop grinning, clearly pleased with the fact that his new friend thought so highly of him. "You came up with the picture on your own."

Ashley flipped through the pages again, looking for names and character descriptions again, now that she knew Cole was responsible for those. There were only a few, but the ones she found all had catchy monikers and often tragic backstories. It was really impressive. "You've got to show Ollie these." Ashley closed the notebook and handed it back to Jay who took it with a shy smile. "He'll love them."

Once again, Cole beamed with pride. "Can Jay come over? We don't have much homework and we can get started on the comic after we're done. *Please*!"

It wasn't often Cole asked for anything. When he first arrived, he never did. He took what was given, did what he was told, and tried to stay under the radar as much as possible. Ashley loved the fact that he felt comfortable enough to ask for this. More so, the fact that he wanted to have his friend over. When she was young, she never let her friends come over, not even Lilly. The thought of it had terrified her.

"It's fine by me." Ashley held up her hand to stop Cole from doing a celebratory jump. "But Jay needs to ask his mom or dad first."

Cole turned to Jay, pleading in his eyes.

Jay just shrugged. "I texted my aunt during lunch, she said it was fine and she'd pick me up, just let her know when."

"You live with your aunt?" Ashley asked.

Jay nodded, pulling out his phone to show her the text. "Dad is overseas on deployment. He's a marine."

"My uncle was a marine," Cole volunteered.

Noticing there was no mention of a mother, Ashley read the text, figured it was legit, but decided to do her due diligence. "I'm going to call your aunt, just to go over some things." She pulled out her own cell, got the number from Jay and called.

Less than five minutes later, she had both Cole and Jay in the car, the two boys chattering on about powers and backstories and plots. Which heroes would get their powers from green goo or were genetic mutations or came from another planet, universe or dimension. It was very in depth and quite intense and Ashley, who had no idea what they were talking about, was thrilled.

Sam was still behind her in the squad car, driving with a fresh-faced cop, right out of the academy. She wondered if this was going to be routine now, to have Sam or another uniform at the school and escorting them home. It was a little annoying, but considering the fact that both Drew and Lilly had to talk Ashley out of sitting in her car in the parking lot the entire day, she decided not to complain.

She went to make a turn and, just for a moment, she thought she spotted her father in a distant car. She blinked and he was gone.

What color was the vehicle? Dad would never drive a green car. Black, maybe red. And a truck. Something that looked like it could run you over. Something that if it were in an animated movie, would be the bully car character.

Ashley shook her head as she pulled into the driveway. She was being paranoid. That's what happened when you had a cop following you home. And having your nephew kidnapped. And everything else that happened. It wasn't her father's car, that much she was sure.

Drew's car was in the driveway, and two seconds after they pulled up, he came out of the house. Ashley barely had the car in park before Cole was out, racing up to him with the notebook to tell him all about his day, his comic plans, and his new friend.

Jay, however, was still in the car, taking his time getting his seatbelt off. "You need any help with anything Ms. Duncan?" His face looked so hopeful.

Ashley smiled. "No sweetie. I'm good. Your aunt said it was fine to keep you for dinner. Is there anything you'd like?"

Taking his time grabbing his bag, Jay shrugged. "I eat anything. Make whatever you were gonna anyway."

"I'll put you in the hospital if I cook," Ashley said. "Go hang out with Cole and meet his uncle."

Reluctantly, Jay got out and ran to the porch where Drew was standing, listening patiently as he flipped through the notebook. Ashley could tell Jay was impressed by Drew. Drew kept his attention on the boys, looking up only momentarily when Sam came over, her partner staying in the car. Ashley went over to join them as Drew continued to study the drawings.

"This stuff looks real impressive," Drew said. "And I like the back story. I had a friend, long time ago. He could draw too. He was good, but nothing this good." Drew flipped through a few more pages, then handed the book back to Cole. "Very cool. Look, I don't have much time. I wanted to see how your first day of your new class went. I've got to work late and I just came home for a bit, but I want to read everything you guys come up with. I really do."

Ashley caught the flash of concern Drew sent as Cole and Jay were concentrating on their notebook.

"Hey guys," Ashley said, clapping her hands. Cole barely looked up, but Jay smiled. "You've both got some homework to do, right?" Both boys moaned in unison. "Go. I'll be in soon. The quicker it's done, the faster you two can get to work on Captain Nova."

Exchanging glances of defeat, the boys headed in through the screen door, shed their jackets and started for the stairs.

"You have the coolest looking family," Jay said, apparently unaware that sound traveled. "I'm definitely modeling new heroes on them. Especially your aunt."

The pair stomped up the stairs to Cole's room.

Drew grinned and turned to Ashley, wiggled his eyebrows.

Sam snorted. "I think someone has a crush."

Ashley's face grew hot. "What are you...?" She glanced towards the stairs inside. "Oh, Jay. Yeah, he's a cutie." She turned to Drew. "What's up?"

Drew moved closer. "Not much to tell right now, but Ollie's mom wants to talk to dad."

Ashley scowled. "Why? That asshole doesn't know anything."

Drew and Sam glanced at each other, and Ashley could see the unspoken communication between them.

"Someone warned Diana we were coming," Drew said. "She got a message from a burner phone. We all know that the EFPD had a corrupt streak a mile wide before Ollie's Mom came in. She's cleaned house, but someone was missed. Dad was a cop and if there was dirt to be getting into while he was on the force, he was in it up to his neck. He may be able to point us in the right direction. Until we know who warned Diana, we're keeping that part of the investigation off the books. That's why Ollie and I have to go one town over to Glenford tonight. Look at their files, without putting in a formal request. We just got back from Tuscarora."

Ashley folded her arms and pursed her lips. Everything Drew said made sense, but she wondered if there was more. "What aren't you telling me?"

He glanced at his watch. "Nothing."

Ashley was positive there was more, but it was clear that was all she was getting. She supposed she should tell Drew that for a moment, she thought she'd seen their father on the way home, but decided against it. The more she thought about it, the more convinced she was that it hadn't been him. And she couldn't describe the car to save her life.

Besides, if Drew was going to hold out on her, she could do the same.

Dad will always be an asshole, but he couldn't hurt her anymore. No man could. Ashley wouldn't allow it.

"I should go in," Ashley said. "Just in case those two burn down the house or something."

Drew nodded. "I'll see you tonight." He turned to Sam. "Can you spare a few minutes?"

Sam looked a little surprised by the request, but she nodded and followed Drew to the back, using her cell to tell her partner she'd be back soon. He waved from the passenger seat, then went back to whatever he was doing on his cell phone.

Knowing that Lilly would be at least another hour before she got home, Ashley decided it was on her to make the boys a snack. She decided to make cookies. How hard could it be? She headed inside, pulling out her phone and googled how to become Betty Crocker.

****

Sam followed Drew to the garage apartment where he'd been staying. He had just purchased the home behind Lilly's house, one where the back door was nearly as close as the entrance to the tiny upper level studio. She knew Drew had wanted to move in as soon as possible. Personally, she couldn't wait. The garage apartment was nice, but it was tiny. There was no place to cook, the shower was so small it made her claustrophobic, and the bed was lumpy and uncomfortable.

As they climbed the steps, Sam considered asking Drew about Stephanie. She was satisfied that there was nothing romantic between her and Drew, but the fact that Stephanie wouldn't explain how they met bothered her.

He shouldn't have secrets, not from me.

Drew unlocked the door, swung it open and stepped aside, allowing Sam to enter. The door closed and he was on her, spinning her around and crushing his mouth to hers. She staggered until her back was against the wall and his body pressed against her. Drew had a way of expressing more want and need in a kiss then a poet could in a long, drawn out sonnet.

When the kiss ended, she was panting for air. He rested his forehead against hers. "I'm sorry."

Sam gently placed her hands against his chest, the massiveness of it never ceasing to amaze her, and looked up into his blue eyes. "What for?"

"This morning." Drew closed his eyes. "You were trying to comfort me as Polansky went at me and…" He forced a breath. "Talking about that. Remembering how I fucked up by when I left Ember Falls, it twists me up inside. It really does."

Drew had been put in an impossible position when he was still just a kid himself, and he had made the best choice he could at the time. *Would he ever stop punishing himself over it?*

"Stop." Sam kissed him gently. "I understand. I'll admit it was jarring, but it's fine. And Polansky wanted to see what you were made of. There's been some resistance to working with you, but Polansky is on your side now, and everyone in uniform looks up to him. He's the Sarg."

"Yeah, I figured that out, but it still burned. I wonder what the General would make of the Sarg."

Both of them laughed, and that was almost as good as the kiss. He kissed her again. She felt the need in his body. "I want you Sam. I need you. Under me. Over me. I need to touch you."

"I'll come over after shift, wait for you to come home. I like waking up with you."

Drew nibbled at her neck. "I've got twenty minutes before I have to pick up Ollie. And he'll have to wait if I'm late."

She gave him a playful smack. "I'm still on duty and I've got a very young new partner waiting for me in the car. And trust me, you're going to need way more than twenty minutes to even recover when we're done." With an amazing amount of reluctance, she pushed Drew away. "Now let me go and stop it. I've got to get back out there. And no hickeys on duty. It doesn't go with the uniform."

Drew grinned. "I want what's under that uniform."

Flushed with pleasure, she headed for the door, knowing if she didn't get out soon she was going to handcuff him to the bed herself.

****

"You're dead. You have no chance of surviving.

Unless you run. You've got to run away." Cole's wide eyes took in the devastation, his hands over his ears to block out the noise and screams of desperation.

"Shut up already!" Ashley stood by the open back door, waving a kitchen towel, trying to get the black smoke that permeated the kitchen out into the back yard. The faucet was on full while tiny pieces of black charcoal of what were supposed to be cookies dissolved in the sink. "Just please shut up."

A red light blinked from a white smoke detector while it emitted an ear-splitting squeal. "I don't think it's gonna listen."

Ashley narrowed her eyes. "Why don't you do something useful?"

Cole and Jay, who had come downstairs a few moments earlier to the smell of smoke and the sound of Ashley's cursing, glanced at each other, shrugged and then grabbed kitchen towels themselves. Soon all three were flapping them in the air. Cole stood on a chair right under the alarm, while Jay slowly meandered towards Ashley.

Five minutes of towel waving, the smoke started to dissipate, and the alarm finally went silent. Throwing his towel on the counter, Cole took a closer look at the kitchen carnage. Egg shells littered the space near the sink, the package of sugar was overturned and there were chocolate chips on the floor. Everything, including Ashley, was covered in flour.

"What happened?" Cole asked.

Ashley slumped against the counter. "I figured I'd make you guys a snack. Cookies." Ashley looked towards the black, soggy things in the sink. "I looked it up online. I thought, cookies. I can do cookies."

Cole walked over to the sink, turned off the faucet, and tried to pick up one of the blobs that were supposed to be his snack. It didn't as much crumble as it did dissolve through his fingers. "I don't think you *can* do cookies."

Ashley scowled and was about to reply when the sound of a car pulling into the driveway cut off her retort. "Shit, it's Lilly."

Cole glanced towards the door. "You are *so* dead."

"Shit, shit, shit." Ashley pushed her fingers through her long, auburn hair. She had hoped to try and clean the place before Lilly got home, but that was clearly out of the question. There was no way her best friend was not going to freak. Best thing was to avoid collateral damage. "Go." She jabbed a thumb towards back stairs. "Both of you. Save yourself."

Not needing to be told twice, Cole and Jay scampered up the stairs. The moment they closed the door, they heard Lilly scream.

Jay grinned. "Man, I love your house."

****

The officer was no longer in uniform, which was unfortunate. If Jericho had his way, he'd fuck her while she was on duty. Use her handcuffs on her too. It'd be fun.

She looked like she was going to head to the house, but before she could, Drew Duncan pulled into the driveway. The two of them ended up going straight to the small apartment over the garage, pausing just long enough for a very long, passionate kiss.

The lights in the apartment never went on. Jericho grinned. The Duncan boy was getting himself some right now. Good for him.

He'd studied Duncan. Plenty of citations and awards for bravery from his time as a marine. An excellent record since joining McAlister Security, although that was more difficult to dig up. Duncan never appeared in any news articles whenever the company did. He was not an attention hog.

Glancing towards the house, he saw the lights downstairs were out. It was late, and the kid was in bed. He'd had a friend over tonight. Jericho would have to look into Jay as well, although most likely he wouldn't factor in. Besides, he was more curious about Cole himself. Jericho understood what Cole had been through better than any of the adults in the child's life.

He frowned and shrugged off an uncomfortable sensation in his gut.

Right now, his job was to simply observe. See how close they were getting to the truth. And find the father.

Still, there was so much that he'd *like* to do.

The front door opened, and the sister came out. Ashley Duncan.

In Jericho's opinion, she was the most fuckable. The one he'd really like to have his way with. The things he could do with her would be magnificent. It was unlikely he'd be sanctioned to go after her, but it was nice to dream.

Still, he was a professional. He took his work, his art, very seriously. Diana had been a masterpiece.

When Ashley got into her car, he decided to follow. From what he'd seen and heard about her, she had a few guys who were regular hook ups, but he had a feeling that wasn't where she was heading.

Jericho kept enough of a distance that she wouldn't have noticed him following her through the streets of

Ember Falls. He realized where they were going within a few blocks.

Ashley parked the car across the street from Oliver Miller's place. The new detective lived in a third-floor apartment. It was a corner house, where the landlord lived on the first floor, and some old biddy on the second, along with her clowder of cats.

Ashley went up, dug into her purse, but then stopped as if she were thinking about something. She closed her purse, and knocked on the door.

A few moments later, Oliver Miller answered. Jericho watched them closely. Was Duncan screwing the detective? He'd seen them together in public. Never touching, never holding hands, but he'd seen how Miller watched the Duncan girl, mostly whenever she was looking away. Had something changed?

Jericho studied them through binoculars, saw that the woman still wasn't touching him romantically, but she stood close.

Was she laughing?

Ashley buried her head in Ollie's chest. He awkwardly put his arms around her. Slowly, they went inside.

She was crying!

Something had happened that had upset the Duncan girl and she went running to him for a shoulder to cry on.

Jericho laughed. He could see the detective wanted the Duncan girl, but he hadn't realized at this point that he was practically her girlfriend.

Jericho killed the engine and settled down to wait. He wanted to see how late Miller could get her to stay. He had a feeling it wouldn't be long. What he wouldn't do to be able to hear what was being said. Miller's pathetic attempts to be super sweet, hoping to get the Duncan girl to spread her legs. And Ashley Duncan, prattling on and on, not able to see what was right before her eyes.

Jericho used his phone to check his emails, to make sure nothing had changed. So far, he was still in a hold pattern. Observe only, interact just enough to study. Boring, but understandable.

Still, he wanted to plan. To plot. To imagine.

Chapter 6
You didn't know that?

"I think somebody has a crush on somebody."

The morning sky was just starting to turn a lighter shade of blue, although the clouds in the sky looked to keep the sun hidden for most of the day. The sound of rain gently tapping on the roof of the garage apartment sounded strange, amplified compared to what it would sound like in an actual home. A solitary bird chirped outside, almost as if it were singing, 'rain, rain, go away.' Sam was pretty sure the rain wouldn't listen.

The alarm had yet to go off, but the same couldn't be said for Drew. Somehow, he'd sensed the moment she was awake. His hand had reached out, cupping her breast, while his mouth tasted her. That had been an hour ago, and they were now lying in each other's arms, basking in the afterglow.

A few times last night, despite her internal promise to let it drop, Sam had almost asked where he'd met Stephanie. She kept telling herself it didn't matter. She knew there had never been anything romantic between the lawyer and Drew. Even if there had been, it wouldn't have been any of her business.

Yet it bugged her.

It bugged her because she felt it was a part of Drew that he intentionally kept hidden. She didn't want secrets between them.

So just ask him, she thought. Maybe it was no big deal. Maybe it was a night of drinking. Maybe Drew had tried to pick Stephanie up, not realizing she was into girls, and the two of them had become good friends. That was reasonable. Heck, it was kind of sweet. So just ask him. *Casually.*

'Stephanie said you got her the job at McAlister's. How'd you two meet, anyway?' He might just tell her, because there was nothing to hide. Nothing to be worried about.

Yet she never did. Because something in her gut told her that it just wouldn't be that easy.

Drew pulled her close, nuzzled into her neck. "What was that? I was still in aftershock."

Sam giggled and gently elbowed him in the ribs. "I said, someone we know has a crush on someone else we know."

Drew sighed in her ear. "That's not exactly news. I've known Ollie has had a thing for Ash since we were kids. I was just too much of an ass to see it was a good thing."

Sam rolled on her back so she could look at Drew. He had that sexy stubble on his face, and his hair was tousled on his head. "I wasn't talking about Ollie liking your sister."

Drew grinned. "Oh, you mean Cole's new friend, Jay? Yeah, I saw the way the kid looked at her."

Sam touched his arm, tracing the pattern of his phoenix tattoo, feeling the textures of his skin. Smooth, with patches of roughness from years of abuse. "No, not that. Although that was awfully cute. You were closer the first time."

"Huh?" Drew narrowed his eyes. "Ollie has a crush

on someone else now?" Drew frowned.

"No, he's still hung up on Ashley." Sam scooted up in bed so she was sitting, glanced at the clock, and saw the alarm would go off in a few minutes. "I'm starting to think that Ashley likes Ollie too."

"Really?" Drew considered that a moment. "After all this time? How do you know?"

Sam shrugged, but grinned. "I just have a feeling. In fact, I'd lay money on it. You may want to clue Ollie in. If he's going to ever make a move, now would be the time."

Now Drew sat up, so he was side by side with Sam. "You're not serious."

She bumped him with her shoulder. "I know you'd like her to be with him. Ollie might need a little nudge."

Drew rolled his eyes. "Sure. He's a great guy. He stuck when I didn't, but I can't talk to him about this. We're guys. We don't talk about having crushes and deep feelings. We burp. Make dirty jokes. Talk football."

"I was Ollie's partner, and he doesn't talk about football." Sam arched an eyebrow at Drew. "Quidditch maybe. And I wish you wouldn't say that."

Drew frowned. "What? That we tell dirty jokes? Ollie doesn't know any. And he blushes when he hears one."

Sam gave am 'hmph' as she slid out of the bed. She walked to the nearby chair and grabbed her shirt, pulling it on. She wasn't having this conversation naked. "That's not what I mean. You didn't leave your sisters."

Drew scowled as he got up. He grabbed a pair of pants. "You know that's not true. I was gone for nearly ten years. Kelli got pregnant, had Cole's fuck up of a father run out and steal everything she had. If I had been here, I could have helped. She never would have gotten together with Edward Hunter. Imagine how different Cole's life would have been if I hadn't fucked up and ran."

He stood facing the window. Despite having the blinds closed, the oncoming storm was visible.

Sam stalked over and pulled his arm so he turned to face her. "You didn't run. You weren't given a choice. Not really. Damn it Drew, you were put in an impossible position. You didn't *choose* to leave them."

With arms folded, he shook his head. "I wanted to get the hell out of this town."

"Who could blame you?" Sam held her hands out. "As far as you knew, everyone in town, including Kelli and Ashley, thought you were guilty of killing Molly Winters. You had a nightmare of a childhood." She grasped his arm, ran her fingers against his skin. "Every time I touch you, I feel these burns your father gave you. I picture you as a kid, fighting him. Kicking and bucking and screaming as he pressed his cigarette against your skin. All to have you call your sisters." She placed her hand over his heart. "And you never did."

He took her hand, pulled it away gently. "It doesn't matter. I did what I did."

She sighed and step closer. "And you're just determined to punish yourself, for the rest of your life? Or to let Ashley do it? You need to talk with Ashley. Tell her the rest."

He stalked across the room, shaking his head. "No. She doesn't need to know. Let her hate me. It's her way of dealing with it."

"Is she dealing with it?" Sam followed him. "Have you ever wondered why Ashley and Ollie have never gotten together?"

Drew laughed. "He's a chicken. At least when it comes to her." He ran his hand over his head. "I don't know. Maybe he's still afraid because I fucking bullied him for following her around when we were kids."

"But what about her? Ashley is a lot of things. Shy isn't one of them. Why don't you ask her?"

"None of my business."

She rolled her eyes. "She's your sister. You keep too much from her. You have too many secrets." She moved over to the bed, sat down on the edge and sighed. *So much for keeping it casual.* "I've been trying to talk myself out of asking you something, but I'm just going to do it, because I should be able to ask you anything, right?"

Drew managed a nod.

Taking a deep breath, Sam exhaled. "How did you and Stephanie meet?"

Sam hoped he would just shrug, say she was a friend of a friend. Or that the lawyer had rear ended him. Or anything except staying silent. The nothingness of his words crashed down on her like a tidal wave of cold water.

Sam continued to get dressed.

"Wait, don't go." Drew came over, reached out as if he were about to pull her shirt away from her, but pulled his hand back. "Please."

Sam looked around for her socks. "I know there was nothing between the two of you. She told me about Tanya, but that's not the point." She found one sock, but the other seemed to have disappeared. "She happened to say that you got her the job with McAlister. I always thought you met there. And when I asked how you met, she wouldn't tell me. Said you should." Giving up on the missing sock, she got up, grabbed her sneakers and put them on.

Just as she grabbed her purse, Drew moved to block her. "Please. Don't go."

Sam folded her arms. "Why won't you tell me? Drew, I love you, but I don't deal with secrets well."

He closed his eyes and for a moment, she thought he was going to finally tell her. Her hopes faded the moment he shook his head. "I can't. It's not something I talk about." He looked at her. "To anyone."

Sam swallowed hard. "I'm not supposed to be just anyone. I'm your fiancé." She held up her hand with the ring. "I've got to go home, get ready for work."

She brushed by him, but he touched her arm. "Please Sam, I love you."

His words felt like a fist tightening around her heart. "I know. And I love you too, but I really need to go." She pulled away, and left without looking back.

****

Drew resisted the urge to go stand by the curb and wait for Ollie in the rain. Instead he went inside to see Cole. He felt bad for getting home so late the night before that he missed being able to spend any time with him.

He found Cole sitting at the table, barely eating the french toast that Lilly had lovingly prepared. His sole concentration was on a notebook that he was scribbling in. Cole didn't stiffen the way he used to whenever Drew walked into the room, but he didn't light up at the sight of him. If anything, he ignored him.

Drew poured himself a cup of coffee. "Didn't finish your homework last night?"

Cole glanced up, frowned, but avoided eye contact. "Yeah I did. I'm not doing anything wrong."

Drew sighed. *I guess we still have a ways to go.* "I didn't mean to imply you did. What are you working on?"

Cole glanced down suspiciously at his notebook. "It's the comic book. I'm putting together some ideas. Jay is coming over again and I want to be ready."

Drew did his best to look impressed. "Sounds like fun. I might get in late again, but I hope to see what you guys are working on."

Drew carried his mug to the table, sat down next to Cole who gave him a sideways glance, before returning to his notebook.

Drew leaned closer. "So, tell me what you guys are planning."

Cole paused, but didn't move. "You don't really want to hear."

"Sure, I do." Drew put his mug down. "I've got a few minutes before Ollie picks me up. Talk to me."

"Yeah?" Cole looked up, excitement in his eyes. "It's really cool. We're making it so this guy, he was someone who wanted to be in the army, but couldn't. He was weak, but he was brave and smart. And then he's recruited by the Nova Corps. Look."

Cole pushed his notebook in front of Drew, which had four pages of a backstory. It was pretty detailed and intense. As Cole continued to talk, Drew skimmed. Chris Sampson was a weak, small man. Always picked on through his entire life by everyone except his mother Kelly, who worked for NASA. Drew couldn't help but notice that Cole had used the more traditional spelling of his mother's name, as if that would hide where it came from. He didn't point out the fact that he spelled the word Corps as core. He'd make sure it was correct before he put anything in the comic, but didn't want to interrupt Cole as he continued to talk.

Just as Cole was getting to the part about Galactor, ruler of a dark dimension who kidnapped women and used their life-force to power his weapons, Ollie came in holding a plastic bag.

"Hey guys." Ollie smiled at Cole, and pointed to Ashley who had just come downstairs. "I need to speak to your aunt for a minute, then your uncle and I have to go. I heard about your new friend and the graphic novel you two are going to work on. Sounds cool. I should show you my collection someday."

Cole nodded. "That'd be cool." He went back to Drew. "So then, just as he's all alone, he gets recruited by the Nova Corps and they change him. So now he's big and strong and can fly and bullets bounce off of him." And once again, he was off, talking so fast that Drew had a hard time keeping up.

****

Ollie held up a small bag to Ashley, who frowned at him. "Here, this is for later," he whispered.

Ashley put down her own coffee mug. "What?"

From the bag, Ollie pulled out a tub that was yellow and white, with pictures of cookies on it.

She nearly hit him, but didn't want to draw attention to herself. She'd sworn everyone *in the know* to secrecy.

"In case you want to make them cookies." Ollie held up the container. "It's easy. Look." He pointed to the back where there were instructions. "Just preheat the oven all the way first. Then you ball up the cookie dough, it's already made. Press it down into a cookie shape. Bake. It's really simple. See." He handed her the tub.

Ashley examined the tub, reading the instructions. It certainly seemed simple enough.

"Oh, one other thing." Ollie pulled out a folded piece of paper from his shirt pocket. "This place? It's a great comic shop in town. I thought they might have kits for Jay and Cole." Ollie shrugged. "I just thought you might like to—"

Ashley cut Ollie off by pulling him into a hug, pressing her body into his. The warmth of his touch filled her with a sense of completeness.

Ollie got it. He understood how much her relationship with Cole meant to her. How desperate she was to really connect.

"Ollie, this is amazing," she whispered in his ear. "I'm going to be a friggin' hero when I get this stuff. *And* when I bake him cookies without risking burning the house down with him in it. Thank you."

He blushed, as Ollie was prone to do.

She loved the kindness in his eyes. Ollie had one of those faces that was just open and trustworthy. He'd come a long way from the chubby, awkward kid. Of course, Ashley got a full view of how far he'd come a couple of nights ago when he'd dropped his towel. For those few moments when he hadn't quite realized he was standing there naked in front of her, he had really been a sight to behold. She hadn't been able to get the image of him out of her mind. He looked like a man she'd want under her.

But she couldn't risk thinking of Ollie that way. A wave of queasiness had filled her as she remembered the time she nearly thrown her friendship with him away in a moment of drunken desperation.

Besides, if Ollie wanted her, he'd had plenty of chances. It was clear that he didn't think of her that way. Why would he? He was everything that was good in the world, wrapped up in one beautiful package.

Ashley hugged him again. "Thank you. Really."

"Hey Ollie," Drew said as he got up from the table, watching them in a way that made Ashley uneasy. "We'd better go."

Ollie stepped back and nodded. "Right."

Ashley wondered how her brother was treating Ollie. Because even when Ollie followed Drew, he looked like he didn't want to go.

****

"We got one."

Polansky held up a small vanilla folder as he entered Chief Miller's office. His round, bulldog face was already sweating and he had a dab of powdered sugar on his uniform tie, but his eyes were all business.

Ann stood up behind her desk, holding her hand out to accept the folder. "We identified one of the bodies?"

Polansky nodded, handing the folder to her. "Yeah. Some girl who went missing about a dozen years ago. Caitlyn Maynard." He sat as Ann started to flip through the file. "She was seventeen at the time. Ran away more than a few times. Her father wasn't in the picture, mother had remarried and had more kids. Caitlyn was a teen when the others were little, got into trouble, ran away. The last time she disappeared, it took a week for the mom to file a report." Polansky shook his head in disgust. "She wasn't looked for real hard."

Ann lowered herself into her chair and opened the file. "Her friends all said she was talking about heading to the city. Had enough money to make it until her eighteenth birthday, and then she'd be able to make money on her own." She skimmed the file and scowled. "Well, it's good we identified one. Ollie and Drew can interview the mother and stepfather. See if anything useful turns up."

Polansky arched an eyebrow. "You seem almost disappointed there, Chief."

Ann sighed. "I was hoping it was one of the other bodies. One of the more recent ones."

Nodding his understanding, Polansky wiped his brow with his handkerchief. "One that disappeared while Duncan was behind bars. You don't think he's connected to this Caitlyn? Duncan would have been just fifteen when she was disappeared. He wouldn't even have his license by then. This girl was snatched from two towns over, if not more."

"More?" Ann asked.

Polansky pointed to the folder. "If she was grabbed up while running away from home, she would have been heading downstate, towards the city." Polansky said. "That's where she was picked up the other times." He folded his arms. "Duncan doesn't fit. You need a car for this. It doesn't jibe."

Ann skimmed the file again, before closing it. "It doesn't, but when you take a good look at the Molly Winter's case, he didn't fit there either. Nobody saw Duncan anywhere near the school after he stormed off. Everyone said the Winter's girl laughed at him and smacked his face. He never threatened her. He just walked away, but that didn't stop the former Chief from trying to pin it on him. The DA from going along with it."

Polansky rubbed his face. "We look at the old chief? I can tell you, he was an ass through and through. Gave me a hard time if I didn't write enough tickets. Made it clear to jam someone up and give them the summons even if they didn't deserve it."

That had been one of the practices that Ann had ended when she took over. She had no problem with her cops writing someone up when they did wrong, but not bullshit tickets. She'd rather they give warnings than one ticket after another. Improve relations. Tickets would always be given, but the town wasn't going to use its population as its personal ATM.

"We looked at him," Ann answered. "I even talked to Ollie about it the other night. He made a good point. Chief Lewis is dead. Who would kill Kelli Duncan or hire a hitman to take out Diana to keep his name clear."

"There is that." Polansky shoved his hanky away, leaned forward. "You ever ask Drew Duncan what exactly was said between him and Winters that she slapped him?"

Ann shook her head. "It didn't seem germane to investigation and I wasn't about to ask him something so personal when there was no official reason to ask." She smiled. "You feel free."

Polansky gave Ann a scowl that nearly made her laugh, before he retreated from her office.

****

Drew and Ollie approached a small, run down house. The yellow siding was faded and dusty, and the lawn was unkempt. There were bikes on the lawn, a basketball net that was well used and tons of hop scotch chalk marks in the driveway. This was where Caitlyn's mother and stepfather lived. The file gave their names as Susan and Rob Crosswell.

"You ever do a notification like this?" Drew asked.

"A few. Ember Falls doesn't have much by way of murder, but we have accidents." Ollie sighed. "Plus, there was Dad."

Drew stopped dead, grabbed Ollie's arm. "*Your* dad?"

Ollie frowned. "Yeah, I was home with him when he had the heart attack. I had to be the one to call my mom. She was at work and it all happened so fast."

Drew felt as if he'd just swallowed a bowling ball. How did he not know this? And why couldn't he had been a pal back when they were kids, instead of such an ass. "Jesus Ollie. I'm sorry."

Ollie managed a shrug. "It was a long time ago." He turned back to the door. "Let's do this." Before Drew could say anything else, he stepped up onto the front porch and rang the bell.

A chorus of dog barks followed, and a TV was shut off from inside. A man's voice started to yell. "Get back. It's okay. Good boy." The door swung open and revealed a tall man who was badly in need of a shave. He was plump, wearing ripped sweatpants and a stained Tee. He held a large, black dog by the collar who was still barking his head off, but looked like it wanted to play. "Yeah?"

Ollie held out his badge. "Sir, my name is Detective Miller. My partner, Drew Duncan. We're looking for the parents of Caitlyn Maynard."

The man frowned, huffed out a breath. "Give me a minute, will you. I need to put the dogs in the back." He pulled the black dog back, headed into the kitchen. A second dog, a much bigger white one, sniffed at the screen, wagged its tail at Ollie, then scampered off when called. "Susan!" The man called the moment he had the back door closed.

He took his time coming back to the door. When he arrived, a thin woman with greying hair and lines on her face had joined him. He whispered something in her ear. Her hand shot to her heart, and her eyes went glassy. "Oh no. Oh my baby."

The man opened the door and invited them in. As they entered, Drew saw a house in complete disarray. Kids toys were everywhere, the kitchen sink was filled with so many dirty dishes that they could be seen from here, and the carpet looked like it wouldn't recognize what a vacuum cleaner was.

A door opened from upstairs. Footsteps thundered down. A teen boy appeared, coughing the entire way. His face was pale white, with neat black hair on top. He looked to his parents. "Mom? Dad? What's up?"

"Nothing Matt." The father never looked at his son, too busy pulling a beer from the fridge. "You need to get better so you ain't sick no more. Leave us be."

The kid sneered, but ran up the stairs, disappearing with a cough.

Ollie ignored all of this and sat near the mother. "I'm sorry. Your daughter was killed."

Silent tears ran down her face as she reached for a pack of cigarettes. "I should quit these. My youngest can't be around them, but…" She lit it, took a long drag and exhaled. "I've known it would happen. I figured sooner or later, but I always hoped I'd hear from her again. At least once. She called me a bitch the last time she was here. Thought I favored Rob over her." She took another drag. "But he's my husband and has to come first, right?"

Drew clenched his jaw, and glanced at Rob who was coming in with a beer. Studied his knuckles for bruises. They were clean.

"So, what happened?" Susan kept the cigarette close to her mouth, ready for her next drag. "Caitlyn was always a pretty girl. She knew it. She took after her father's side of the family."

Rob sat down holding his beer, snatched the pack of cigarettes with his free hand, and pulled one out with his lips. "She sure didn't get those tits from you."

Drew had to stop himself from punching the man.

Ollie didn't flinch, but Drew could see something in his eyes. They were on the same page, but Ollie was in full sympathy mode. "Do you remember the last time you saw her?"

Susan nodded as she smoked. "Oh, I'll never forget. She wanted to go out. She had a job, but Rob said…" She shifted her eyes to her husband. "Well, we both felt at her age, she'd just turned seventeen, she needed to contribute here. It's not cheap raising children. I've had two." She took a puff. "Well, three if you count Caitlyn."

Rob put his beer down just long enough to light his cigarette. "The thing was, she wasn't my kid, but I let her stay on the agreement that she put her money back into my home. Not all of her check. She kept half. Just enough to cover what we had to pay for her food and board."

Susan was nodding along. "She didn't want to share her money with us. She was willing to give some for her brother and sister, but that's what our money is for, right?"

Ollie patted her hand, but Drew noticed, never agreed. "What happened that last day?"

The tears were gone now as the shock had subsided. She shrugged as she exhaled more smoke. "No, she was pissed. Called me a bitch because I didn't yell at Rob for... Well she knew she was supposed to share the paycheck. And so, she didn't have any money to go out, but what did that matter? She could flirt her way into any man's car. I always assumed that's what she did."

Rob snorted as he took a swig of beer. "Yeah, she knew how to get men to do what she wanted. She was no stranger to the backseat of their cars."

Drew stood up quickly. "Excuse me." He pulled out his phone. "I need to take this. I'll step outside."

Before anyone could say anything, Drew went out through the front door. Ollie was handling this like a seasoned pro, and it was all Drew could do from slugging the father.

He checked his cell, hoping that there was a message from Sam, but there wasn't.

What the hell was he going to do? He knew things had moved quickly with Sam, but he also knew he was in love with her. She got him. Maybe too well. She knew he was hiding something. Why couldn't she just leave it alone?

He opened the text he'd gotten from Stephanie earlier.

I'm sorry I put you in this position, but you should

tell her. I'm fine with it. You can tell her all about me, because if she's with you, she's family. I like her too. Stop being a stubborn ass and talk to her. She loves you, you idiot.

Drew put the cell away. He knew she did. That's why he couldn't tell her.

"Psst."

Drew spun around. The Crosswell's son was standing in the neighbor's yard, behind a row of tall bushes that ran across the property line. Drew casually stepped over, glancing at the house to make sure nobody was watching.

"Matt, right?" Drew asked.

The teen nodded as he coughed into his sleeve.

"Should you even be out here?"

Shaking his head and coughing, Matt moved further away from his own home. "I've got pneumonia, so probably not, but I've got to go out now and then. I'm going to have to go out tonight. I've got work."

Drew frowned. "Where?"

Matt jabbed his thumb over his shoulder. "Over in the Food Lot."

"Call in sick, kid." Drew watched as the kid coughed again. "Nobody wants you coughing over their groceries."

Matt shook his head. "I need the money. I've called in twice already, but the fever's gone. I just can't get rid of this fucking cough." He narrowed his eyes, as if waiting for Drew to yell at him for language. "I need to get to the pharmacy, but I wanted to talk to you about Caitlyn. I don't remember her much, but she was nice. I remember she gave me a stuffed dog." Matt shrugged, embarrassed with himself. "I always wondered about her. I thought, maybe someday when I was on my own, I'd look for her. I guess that's out. Did she suffer?"

Drew wasn't sure what to say to the kid. They hadn't had full details, the remains were very old and degraded, but all things pointed to someone who enjoyed hurting their victims. "I don't know. The coroner isn't sure what happened to her."

Matt's eyes narrowed. "I've seen TV. They can tell if she's been hurt."

Drew sighed. "She was just found, but she was killed a while ago. We don't think she ever made it down to the city. Probably never made it out of town."

Matt didn't say anything, he just kept coughing. Drew watched him, thought about taking the kid to a doctor himself.

"I can hear my parents from my room. You left so you wouldn't punch Dad, right?"

Drew didn't answer, just thought about how Cole overheard everything as well.

Matt laughed, which turned into a cough. "I don't blame you. He's an ass. Both he and my mom smoke. She tried to quit and he keeps offering her cigarettes, even though my little sister sneezes when she's around it. Cassie has asthma. That's what I have to pick up. Her inhaler was nearly empty last night. I'll be lucky to get her to last until tomorrow."

"I'm sorry for your loss." Drew should have said it earlier.

Matt shrugged. "I didn't know her much. She's more of a memory." He went into a fit that had him bending at the knees. Drew put his hand on the kids back.

Drew waited until the kid stopped coughing. "You

been to a doctor?"

Matt nodded. "Yeah. I told you, its pneumonia. I've had it before. I'll be fine."

Choosing to believe him for now, Drew decided to see if the kid knew anything. "Tell me anything about Caitlyn that you remember."

"Not much. She was pretty. I can remember that. More I heard whenever her name comes up, which isn't often. I know she used to ditch school. Hook up with different guys. My Dad didn't like her, but he's an ass. Still, I got the impression Caitlyn liked to piss Dad off. Maybe that's why I remember liking her."

Drew thought about Molly Winters and how she liked to drive her father nuts.

"What will happen to my sister?"

Drew frowned at the question. "After they're done with her, we'll release her body to your parents for the burial."

Matt exhaled sharply. "If they can get out of it, they will. Dad'll be like, it wasn't his kid and Mom will cave like she always does. How much is a burial? I can try and save up some. Once I'm better, I can pull extra shifts, get one or two hundred."

"Don't worry about it." Drew pulled out his wallet. He had some cards with his info and the McAlister Security logo on them. He handed one to Matt. "Here. That's my cell. If you hear anything, call. Matt, I want to ask you a question. Don't lie. I'll know. Did your father ever put hands on her? Or on you? Has he ever—"

"No." Matt shook his head. "I know what you're asking. Dad's mostly just a lump. He drinks beer, smokes cigarettes and not much else. He works. He'd tell you he was a good dad because he puts food on the table, and I guess he does, but he doesn't have the energy to raise his fist. Besides, if he ever hurt my sister, I'd kill him and he knows it. He just says stupid things."

Satisfied that Matt was telling the truth, he opened the bill section of his wallet. He had nearly two hundred in there. He handed it all to Matt. "Here."

Matt didn't take it. "What? Why?"

"The pharmacy delivers, right? Call in the prescription for your sister. Have them throw in some cough syrup for you. You have a cell?"

Matt nodded. "It's shit, but it works."

"Text me your contact info. I'll let you know about the arraignments for Caitlyn. If your parents won't pay, we'll put her to rest ourselves. I'll make sure you're there." He shoved the money into Matt's hand. "Stay in bed and rest kid. And call if you need something."

Matt stared at Drew, opening his mouth to try and say thank you, but unable to find the words. He started to slowly back away.

"Take care of your sister." Drew said as Matt ran to slip back in his house. "Better than I did."

Ollie emerged from the house and Drew met him at the car. "Sorry."

Ollie smiled as they got in. "I get it. I wanted to clock him myself. The stepfather doesn't think he should have to pay to bury a kid that isn't his." Ollie shook his head as he started the engine.

Drew strapped his seat belt on. "Matt called that right."

Ollie's eyebrows went up. "You talked to the son?"

Drew nodded. "He snuck out when he heard me

leaving. Let's get the fuck out of here. I'll tell you what he said and you'll fill me in on your side, but I think our girl Caitlyn probably got into this dude's car. I can see Molly doing that too."

It only took a few minutes to realize that Matt covered most of what Ollie had learned inside. Neither was sure how much help it was, but it added to what they knew.

"Maybe we'll get more as we ID the others." Ollie turned onto the main highway, started to head back to Ember Falls. "You know what stands out to me about the bodies?"

Drew nodded. "The outliner. The one guy. Why him? All the others were girls." Of the bodies found, the coroner was able to determine that the male body was the last one killed. "That one is going to be key. We need to ID him."

Ollie merged lanes. "We'd be able to get them faster if we weren't keeping everything hush-hush."

Drew checked his cell, again hoping he'd see a message from Sam. There was none. "You know one of the reasons why your mom is keeping everything so quiet is me, right?"

Ollie frowned as he watched a black sports car go speeding by on his left. "What are you talking about?"

Drew felt fidgety. Driving in a car was one of those times he'd light up. The urges were coming less and less after quitting cold turkey the moment he'd come back to Ember Falls and realized Cole was allergic, but when they did come, they hit him hard. "She's hoping one of those bodies can be traced back to someone who died while I was in prison. Once people know that Molly Winters body is among them, they're going to point the finger at me."

Ollie shook his head. "You didn't kill Molly."

"I didn't kill her a decade ago. I still spent months in prison awaiting trial." Drew played with his phone again, just for something to do with his hands. He hated being in the passenger seat when he felt this restless. He wanted coffee, but coffee just reminded him of Sam. "If she can tie just *one* body to when I was behind bars, one that was seen after I was placed under arrest, nobody will be able to still insist that I killed Molly." Drew shrugged. "It'll make things neater. For her and for me."

"This isn't then," Ollie said as he slowed down. "Mom won't put the investigation on you."

"She may be pressured. Pushed from the State to look at me."

Ollie shook his head as he sped back up to the speed limit. "She'll push back."

"I could see someone from Albany trying to force her out over this," Drew said. "And if they do, they can put someone in who will cave to political pressure."

"Knock it off," Ollie insisted. "You're in a pisser of a mood today. Did you and Ashley have a go at it this morning?"

Drew shook his head. "Sam."

"You'll work it out. Just apologize and get it over with."

Drew checked his phone again. "Why do you assume I was in the wrong?"

Ollie shrugged. "I'm not. Apologize and get it over with either way."

Drew sighed. "It's not that simple."

When Drew didn't say anything else, Ollie glanced

his way. "You want to talk about it or something."

That was the last thing Drew wanted to do, so he remained mute.

Thankfully, Ollie didn't push. "If you do, I'll buy the beer."

And that was Ollie. Always eager to help. Never too busy to lend an ear or offer his input or just listen. Steady, solid and loyal. He would have been Drew's friend back in school if Drew hadn't had his head up his ass. Ollie was the poster child for 'good guy.'

Drew thought about how even when they were young, he picked up on Ollie liking Ashley. He wanted to pound anyone who looked at his sisters. He'd been such a moron and maybe it was time to make up for it. "What's going on between you and Ashley?"

Ollie's eye widened. "Huh?"

Drew felt like an idiot. Guys didn't do this. "You and Ashley. What's going on?"

Ollie stared at Drew so hard that Drew was surprised Ollie didn't accidently run them off the road. "Are you kidding me? We're doing *this*? Here and now?"

Drew pointed to the road so they wouldn't die. He realized that both of them were so mortified that dying might be preferable to continuing, but Drew decided to finish what he started. "Not what you think. I know I gave you a hard time back when we were young. I was an idiot. Ashley would be lucky to be with a guy like you. I hope you're not hesitating because of me. I won't stand in your way."

Ollie's eyes crossed, and his head tilted as if he'd just come off one of those whirly rides that spin you so fast it makes you feel as if you're still spinning. "Good to know. Stop talking." He finally stared back at the road. "*Please.*"

Drew couldn't look at him, so he stared out the window. "Okay. Sorry."

Suddenly the car noises seemed much louder and the distance between here and Ember Falls so much further. Drew considered putting on the radio, but that would require turning towards Ollie and he'd just as soon open the door and throw himself onto the highway.

"Look," Ollie said. "You were gone a long time. I had my chance to make my move. I need to accept that Ashley doesn't see me that way. I can't help how I feel, but…" Ollie shook his head, blushed a deeper shade of red than Drew thought possible. "Whatever. Point is, it's not on you."

Drew closed his eyes. Should he take that next step?

Oh hell, Ollie hadn't shot him yet.

"Sam thinks Ashley likes you." Even with his eyes focused on the side view mirror, he could see Ollie's head turn towards him. The car swerved and Drew was forced to yell at Ollie not to get them killed.

With one hand on the wheel, Ollie used the other to rub his face. "Why is Sam telling you this?"

"I don't know." Drew focused on the mirror again. "Maybe Ashley passed her a note in class. She thought I should say something to Ashley, but I can't. And quite honestly, I think that would hurt any chance you have, but I gritted my teeth and said something to you. I'm sorry."

Ollie nodded. "You should be. Let us never speak of this again."

"Agreed."

"Good." Ollie gripped the wheel with both hands, concentrated on the road. "So, what *should* I do?"

Drew moaned. Before he could answer, he felt his phone vibrate. He pulled it out so quickly, he nearly dropped it, praying it was from Sam. It wasn't. He quickly scanned the message before turning to Ollie. "It's from your mom. They've identified two more."

****

Polansky returned to the front desk, carrying his fifth cup of coffee for the day. His doctor wanted him to cut out the caffeine, but Polansky had told the doc he would have to pry his mug out of his cold, dead hands. He'd already changed his life considerably over the last few years. He'd kicked the bottle and chucked the cigarettes. Somehow, he'd managed to lose about thirty pounds and had lowered his cholesterol. He even had started to have an actual relationship with his son, who had quite rightly told him to go fuck himself back when he had been in a drunken stupor.

But giving up coffee? Might as well give up breathing.

Sighing, Polansky logged into the computer and started to read through the reports on the bodies found where Duncan's sister was found.

All showed matching signs of being restrained and tortured. Burn marks from a small torch, razor cuts that weren't deep enough to be dangerous, but would have hurt like hell, broken bones, and other various injuries. These women didn't die easily.

The pattern of the chains, crossed over their heart was identical in each one. There could be no question the same bastard did all of them.

The man was a different story. It was a knife to the back of the skull. The rest of the mutilation had been done post mortem, not for jollies but with the intention of making the job of identifying the poor SOB difficult. The man's face had been bashed in, and his fingers had been snipped off, but he had been killed quickly.

Who was this guy?

He'd been stripped naked and dumped into a grave several feet away from the women, closer in fact to where they'd found Kelli Duncan's body, although that was still farther away.

As Polansky placed his mug back on his desk, he saw the front door to the station open. A man in a crumpled trench coat and a cheesy moustache came in. He ran his fingers through his unkempt hair and made his way over to Polansky.

Something about Trench Coat made Polansky sneer, but he wasn't sure what. Despite the stubble on his face, he reeked of aftershave that smelled like dead flowers.

Chief Miller had said on a few occasions that whoever was working the front desk should try and look pleasant whenever someone came in. "Appear friendly and approachable," she'd told him.

Well, Polansky didn't do friendly and approachable, but even if he could fake it, he wouldn't put forth the effort with this jackass.

"I'm here to see the chief."

"Yeah?" Polanski shrugged and deliberately tapped at his computer, deleting a few random emails just to make the schmuck wait. "You got an appointment?"

Trench Coat started to answer, paused, and smiled. "Sure."

Polanski knew the man was lying, but he checked in the system where the chief would put her schedule of meetings. As expected, it was blank for the day, as Chief Miller had far more important things to do. "Funny, she doesn't have anyone penciled in. What's your name?"

Trench Coat narrowed his eyes and clenched his jaw. "Caesar. Jack Caesar."

Scowling, Polansky rolled the name around in his head. "Don't you write for that rag, the Tablet?"

Jack grinned. "You bet. Award winning online news site."

Polansky's lips thinned and his eyebrow went up. "What half-assed award did you win?"

The smile quickly faded from Jack's face. "We placed fifth in the Wonderful-World-Webbing for alt news of a small town."

Scowling, Polansky tilted his head like a dog did when exposed to a strange, high pitched sound. Instead of barking, he just jabbed his thumb towards the door. "Get out of here."

With a scowl, Polansky went back to work, hoping that Jack Caesar would shuffle out without another word.

Jack didn't budge. He cleared his throat and waited.

"You still here?" Polansky didn't bother to look up now.

Jack pulled out a small recording device and clicked it on. He held it up for a moment, allowing the sergeant to recognize what it was. "I'm here to ask the chief about the bodies that were found."

Using his best poker face, Polansky narrowed his

eyes. "What the hell are you talking about?"

Jack grinned. "I think you know."

The pair kept eyeing each other as Polansky weighed his options. An out and out lie would come back to haunt them when the truth finally came out, but he'd be damned if he was going to break the news to some hack with a laptop and a blog.

Sighing, Polansky pulled out a pen and scribbled onto a piece of paper. "Here." He shoved it forward with as much disinterest as he could muster.

Jack took the slip of paper and read it quickly, frowning. "What's this?"

With an impatient air, Polansky went back to his computer. "The EFPD Media Liaison. If there's something going on that I don't know, they're the ones to ask. I don't deal with press." Unable to help himself, he glanced up with disdain. "Award winning or not."

Keeping his eyes on the computer screen, Polansky carefully watched Jack Caesar peripherally. The blogger seemed both annoyed and overly impressed with himself. He'd clearly been hoping for more of a scoop, but was secretly thrilled to be given the telephone number for the media liaison like a real reporter, never mind the fact that it was easily accessible on the Ember Falls PD website.

Finally, Jack nodded and held up the paper. "Um... all right then. I guess this story is a little big for a peon like you."

Polansky stopped typing. "A what? What am I?"

Jack stammered. "A peon? You know. A subordinate. An unimportant person? I didn't mean anything by it."

Polansky pointed to the stripes on his sleeve. "See

these? I'm a sergeant. Just because I don't handle media inquiries or get briefed on whatever bullshit rumors are going around, doesn't mean I'm a fucking nobody."

Jack held up his hands. "All right." He backed up.

Polansky gave his fiercest bulldog scowl. "Aren't you the guy who wrote that piece on 'Best ways to scoop the poop,' or some shit like that?" He was sure that was the name of the article he'd just seen online as he'd searched for Jack Caesar, Ember Falls Tablet. It was on the third page of google searches.

Jack nodded, clearly pleased that the sergeant had finally recognized him.

"And you're calling me a fucking peon?"

The smile faded, and Jack backed towards the door. "Have a good day."

Polansky waited a good twenty seconds, drank down the last of his coffee, and then went to find the chief. They had a new problem.

****

Drew and Ollie made it back to the Ember Falls in record time. As soon as they walked in the police station, Polansky signaled for them to follow him to a secluded area. They quickly gave their report about what little they'd learned about Caitlyn Maynard, and Polansky brought them up to speed on the other two names.

Holly Anderson was also a runaway. She had several busts for solicitation. She'd often disappear weeks at a time, and had last been seen in September of the year Molly had been killed.

"My money is that she was taken a month before the dance. Then there's Fiona Richards."

Drew read the file he had been handed. His heart

did a little leap when he saw the date that she'd been reported missing. It was two weeks after he'd taken Molly to the dance.

As if reading his mind, Polansky shook his head. "Best we can tell, she left home two days before the dance. Told her mother she was going to stay with the father. The father thought she was with the mom. They both hated each other. Still do. Her friends told us she was tired of both of them. Neither of them bothered to check on her at the other's house." He shrugged. "She might have been grabbed up before or after. Hard to know."

Sighing, Drew nodded. They had found six bodies. With Molly, that was four who they identified. There was one more girl, and then the man. One of them had to be taken after Molly.

"I think we'll find the same timeline for the remaining girl." Ollie said.

Drew closed the file. "Why? Why can't our last Jane Doe have been taken after Molly?"

"Besides the fact that it would be too easy?" Ollie gave a shrug. "Because as far as we can tell from what we know, the killer took the others from local areas, but not from Ember Falls. Molly comes from here."

Drew pursed his lips. "You think he's from Ember Falls?"

Ollie nodded. "Yeah. He takes from other counties and neighboring towns. Brings them here to bury. Someplace he can visit them to relive what he did, but he grabbed them from outside Ember Falls. I'll bet that there was something about Molly that was just too tempting to pass up."

Drew exchanged glances with Polansky who was

standing with his arms folded. "I don't like it, but it makes sense. Pretty girls who weren't afraid to flirt and take risks. Molly was a flirt." Drew felt his face flush as he remembered how she liked to tease him back in school. "You think that after he took Molly, he realized it was too close to home."

Ollie nodded. "Yeah. He got lucky that the focus was on you. Or maybe it wasn't luck." Ollie gestured with his finger. "Maybe he wanted suspicion on you, but realized it was a one and done."

Polansky scowled. "Makes sense. I'd finger the old Chief, but if it were him, we'd have a bunch of boys on that table, not girls."

Drew paced the small room they were in. "No. The Chief's dead. Nobody is going to kill to protect him, but the DA. His name was Reynolds. Where's he at?"

"He's the Deputy State Attorney General," Polansky said. "He's got his eye on running for the Governor's office, last I heard. I dealt with him and he's a putz. I was surprised he didn't get caught up in that whole scandal himself. He was sleazy. He hid it well, but I saw the way he looked at young women. He's married. Has a son who is a punk. He pulled every string you can imagine to get his son out of trouble."

"I remember the son." Ollie pointed at Drew. "Sam Reynolds. He was a couple of years older than us, remember. He was on the football team. Went through half the cheerleaders. He was an ass."

Drew nodded. "Sam was dealing too."

Polansky's eyebrows shot up. "How you know that?"

Drew laughed, seeing the curious look on Ollie's face as well. "I ran with a rougher crowd. I'm not just talking pot. He was the connection for anything upwards of that. Molly smoked weed. She told me she got it from Sam and didn't have to pay for it. That was just as we were getting together." He shrugged. "I tried it once. Didn't care for it. Made me too… passive."

Polansky's lip curled. "Damn drugs. Rot your brain."

"Aren't you in AA?" Ollie asked.

Polansky jutted his chin up. "That's different. Even Jesus drank wine."

Ollie grinned. "Not to the point where he passed out under the table during the last supper."

Someone knocked on the door. Polansky scowled at Ollie before opening it.

As the door opened, raised voices echoed from down the hallway. An officer leaned in and pointed in the direction of the ruckus. "Chief has company, and they're getting loud."

Polansky led the way towards the chief's closed door. Two shadows were visible behind the frosted glass, neither looked like Chief Miller. One jabbed a finger to punctuate the points he was loudly making. The other figure stood still and silent.

"I'm sorry for your loss sir." Ann's voice was polite, yet firm. "I couldn't begin to imagine your pain. This department is doing everything in its power to bring your family justice."

The angry shadow raised a fist. "Your department is working with her killer."

Polansky narrowed his eyes and glanced at Drew and Ollie. All of them knew they should let the chief handle this herself, but none of them moved.

The other shadow inched closer to the angry one.

"Why don't we calm down? We're not going to solve anything by insulting Chief Miller."

"I don't give a fuck if she's insulted. I want Duncan arrested and charged. I want him thrown in jail and to rot there for the rest of his miserable life."

For a moment, Drew could hear the slamming of the cage door.

"Enough," Ann said. "Mr. Duncan is no longer under suspicion. The evidence against him was flimsy to begin with and new evidence proves that he's not a killer. This office will aggressively pursue any and all avenues of investigation until the correct perpetrator is identified and brought to justice. We will not cave in to pressure, political or otherwise. This isn't the same corrupt department that existed under Chief Barbar and we won't be making the same mistakes. This time, when we arrest someone, it'll be the right man and the charges *will* stick."

The two shadows merged into one large figure as if someone was stopping the angry man from surging forward. "You're a corrupt bitch who is protecting a man that killed his own sister and I'll make sure you lose your fucking badge over this."

Both Ollie and Drew tensed, glanced at each other, ready to hold the other back. Neither of them were prepared to stop Polansky from slamming the door open and stepping inside uninvited.

"All right, that's enough." Polansky grabbed the shoulder of a man who was pointing at Chief Miller, turned him around. "You're not coming in this house and threatening anyone asshole."

The man who spun around was taller than Polansky, with gray hair and a reddening face. He wore a finely tailored suit and looked perfectly groomed, despite the fact that he appeared ready to leap over the desk and attack the chief. He narrowed his eyes at Polansky, opening his mouth to say something, until he spotted Drew.

"You!" He stepped towards the door, and pulled his fist back.

Drew knew the punch was coming. He resisted the natural instinct to dodge or block the blow, and instead stepped into it. His head snapped back as Ollie and Polansky grabbed the man and pulled him away. Polansky reached for his cuffs.

"No," Drew said. "There's no need for that."

Scowling, Polansky moved his hand away from his restraints.

Drew wiped a small drop of blood from his lip. "Mr. Winters, I never had the chance to tell you how sorry I was for Molly's death. I know you don't believe that I'm innocent, but I will make sure the person who hurt Molly pays."

Darren Winters stiffened, glared at Drew. "Don't you talk to me, you son of a bitch. You murdered my little girl. You took away my baby. You…" His breath hitched. "If it weren't for you, she'd be here today."

Everyone waited for Drew to respond, but he didn't say a word.

Polansky pointed down the hallway. "All right, time to go home. Now." He started to guide Mr. Winters down the hall, but the man yanked his arm free.

"Do you have any idea who I am," Mr. Winters snapped. "I have friends in the Senate and the State DA's office."

Polansky rolled his eyes. "Yeah, yeah. And I've

got friends in the 'I don't give a shit' club. Now you move your ass out the door and if you come back here again, you'll see the inside of a cage."

The other man, who had remained quiet until this point, stepped up to Molly Winters' father and put a comforting hand on his shoulder. "Darren, let me deal with things here. Please."

The man was tall, clean shaven and dressed in a dark blue suit that concealed both his build and a sidearm. He had neatly trimmed brown hair and his face was filled with sympathy as he tried to calm Mr. Winters down.

Mr. Winters sneered at the unnamed man, before pointing an accusatory finger at Drew. "I'll see you in hell." He glared at everyone else present. "All of you." He yanked free of Polansky, and with one last, snarling glare at Drew and stormed away. Polansky trailed behind to make sure he left.

"Detective Miller, please close the door." Ann waited until Ollie had done so before fixing her gaze on Drew. "Are you all right, Mr. Duncan?"

Drew touched his lower lip. The bleeding had already stopped. "Yeah, I'm fine."

The stranger stepped forward and offered Drew a smile. "Darren Winters doesn't strike me as someone who packs a huge punch. I imagine that hurt his hand more than your jaw, but I'm a little surprised he got the drop on you. A decorated, former marine; I'd have thought you'd have seen that punch a mile away."

Drew scowled. "What was I supposed to do? Break the nose of a man who lost his daughter and knock him on his ass? No thank you."

The stranger extended a hand to Drew. "I'm sorry.

Let me introduce myself. My name is Detective Ian Corvidae. I work for the State DA."

Ollie glanced at his mother. "I wasn't aware that we called in the State yet."

Ann settled back in her chair. "We haven't. Someone called Darren Winters and told him that we found a body which may belong to Molly Winters." She fixed her eyes on Corvidae. "I'm still waiting to hear exactly who told him this, since we don't have an official ID on the body we found."

Drew exchanged a quick glance with Ollie, one that Corvidae didn't seem to notice.

"We don't know," Corvidae said. "He told the State D.A. that he received an anonymous call." He shrugged. "Whether he was telling the truth, I don't know, but he went to D.A. Reynolds. They've been friends since childhood. I was called in this morning, asked to come with Darren to see you."

Corvidae casually lowered himself into a chair in front of the desk as if he were a frequent guest in the chief's office. "I do want to apologize for the way he spoke to you Chief. He's been through an awful ordeal. Over the last decade, he and his wife split up. She took their son, moved near her parents in Saratoga. It's really hard to get past the death of a child. I don't have children myself, but I couldn't imagine it."

Ann nodded. "Neither can I, and I'm very sympathetic to Mr. Winters. We'll do everything we can to get justice for his daughter."

Corvidae smiled. "I'm confident you will. What can you tell me about the case so far?"

Chief Miller settled back in her chair and returned the smile. "That our detectives are doggedly pursuing any and all leads and I firmly believe that we will find the person responsible for her murder." She folded her hands and placed them on her desk.

Corvidae leaned forward. "Chief, I don't want to step on any toes, but the DA wants to know what's happening. Plus, I can help. I'm an experienced investigator. I can be of service."

Ann stood up, offered her hand. "I'll keep that in mind."

Recognizing that he was being dismissed, Corvidae rose and shook hands with Ann. "I'll be staying close. You'll contact me if there's any break in the case?"

"Count on it. We have a lovely town. In fact, we have a concert in the park scheduled for this weekend. And in a few weeks, we'll have Chowder Fest." She glanced to Ollie. "Detective Miller, please make sure that we have contact information for Detective Corvidae."

Ollie nodded as he opened the door for Corvidae, making it clear that it was time for him to depart.

Corvidae smiled as he nodded to Drew, then glanced at Ollie as he passed. "I don't suppose you could suggest a decent place to stay in town?"

Ever the affable one, Ollie started to name hotels in town as he closed the door behind them.

Drew exhaled sharply as he moved to stand directly in front of Ann. "At least he seemed to only know about Molly. How'd he find that out even?"

Ann shrugged, pointed to a chair, indicating for Drew to sit. "Not sure. We've been keeping a tight lid on things here. You're sure there's no possible leak through McAlister?"

With a scowl that made it clear Drew felt there was

no chance that the leak had come from the General's company, but he'd entertain the notion out of respect. "I can certainly have them do a check, but we kept our people isolated when they came. Nobody except myself has any connection to Ember Falls, past or present. And the General runs a tight ship. Nothing happens there that he doesn't know about it."

Drew winced as he realized how that might sound. "Not that you don't, but things happen in small towns. Your medical examiner seems solid, but if he mentioned it to his wife, and one of their kids overheard?" Drew shrugged. "Same with any number of cops, civilian aids. Again, one slip to a family member. Someone says to them, 'I hear you're working with that Duncan kid. They ever find out what happened to that girlfriend of his who disappeared'." He shrugged. "It doesn't have to be that someone intentionally leaked it or sold us out, just a small slip of the tongue would explain Detective Corvidae coming down on our asses."

Ann nodded. "What did you think of Corvidae?"

Drew looked over his shoulder, as if to make sure the shadow of the detective was truly gone. "He doesn't strike me as an ass. Not sure if that's a good or not."

Chief Miller grinned. "You'd rather he *did* came across as an ass?"

Drew nodded. "How would you approach the group you wanted to fit in with?"

With a sigh, Ann sat forward. "I'll see what I can find out about him. It's possible Corvidae is just a nice guy who was sent here to poke around. He's being upfront about it, so I can't fault him. Maybe you could reach out to McAlister and see what they can find out?"

Drew nodded, started to rise only to settle back again when the chief signaled that she wasn't done.

"Corvidae was right about one thing." Ann's eyes narrowed on his. "Your nephew could have seen that punch coming. I know you feel responsible for what happened to Molly, but you're not, just like you're not responsible for what happened to Kelli."

Drew shook his head, but couldn't look the chief in the eye. "I appreciate what you're telling me, but—"

"No." Ann held up a hand. "Consider this an order, Mr. Duncan. Stop letting yourself be a punching bag. If you let people like Daren Winters treat you as if you're guilty, you're just making it easier for others to believe that you are, and that doesn't just reflect poorly on you anymore. It reflects poorly on your family, including your nephew. *And* on this department, which I will not allow. Are we understood?"

This time, Drew did look in her eyes. "Yes ma'am."

She nodded, and Drew took his leave, rolling her words around in his head as he went to find Ollie.

If necessary, he'd tell each and every person he wasn't guilty for the deaths of Molly and his sister. He'd buy a bullhorn and shout if from the streets if it would help Cole.

It didn't mean he had to believe it himself.

****

Ashley stepped into nerd nirvana. That wasn't the actual name of the store, although as she passed by a pair of teen boys having a heated argument over which Green Lantern was the best (*There was more than one of them?*) she realized it might as well be. Instead, she wandered the aisles of The Comic Crate, Ember Falls biggest store for all comic related crap, looking for supplies to make homemade comics.

She needed to get the things Cole and Jay would need to make their comic book together, and then get to the school in time to pick them up. Jay's aunt was thrilled that Jay could come over as she usually worked past five, and otherwise he'd have to stay in an afterschool program that Jay found boring.

Ashley was just beyond ecstatic that Cole had made a friend. There was also something about Jay that made Ashley believe that the pair would be friends for the rest of their lives, like her and Lilly.

Ashley was determined to make that a reality. And right now, that meant finding the stuff for the pair to make their comic book.

Mostly, the Comic Crate stocked actual comics. Not only the current issues of everything from classics like Superman, Spiderman and Jughead, but also things like The Walking Dead, Priest, and an area that held mature comics titled Sex Criminals and Bitch Planet. She'd found books with everything from auto biographies of famous comic book writers and artists to in- depth looks into how a comic became a famous movie.

Since Ashley still wasn't finding what she needed, she decided to ask. The first guy she spoke to was at least two hundred pounds overweight, had a severe case of acne and mumbled. It took nearly ten minutes for Ashley to understand that he was new and wasn't sure. He finally told her to ask the manager who was one or two aisles over.

One row down, Ashley found a trio of gangly teenagers practicing their flirting techniques on life size cardboard cutouts of female superheroes. Two of them were vying for the attention of Supergirl, while the oldest and dorkiest was putting the moves on Wonder Woman. Neither the Kryptonian nor the Amazon looked impressed. Ashley quickly moved down one more aisle and spotted a man in a dark blue suit, holding a few comic books and staring at the display in front of him.

Finally, someone who's done with puberty.

"Excuse me," Ashley said as she turned down the aisle. "Can you help me? I need to find something."

The man blinked and smiled.

"I'd be happy to try." He shuffled the stack of comics in his hands, so that were in a neat pile and put them on a nearby box. "What do you need?"

Relief flooded through Ashley. "A friend told me that you sell stuff here to make comic books. The books with panels. Pencils and stuff?"

The man frowned and Ashley couldn't help but think that was even cuter. "I guess that might be true. I mean…" He shrugged. "It'd make sense, right?"

Ashley cocked an eyebrow. "You seem unsure? Don't you work here?"

Shaking his head, the man smiled again. "Sorry, no. I'm trying to get some comics for my nephew. He's really into them, although he'd get mad at me for calling them comics. They're graphic novels."

Ashley picked up one of the thick comics on the nearby crate. "What's the difference?"

The man sighed, picked up another one of the comics, and shrugged. "As far as I can tell, they're bigger."

Ashley snorted. "Okay then. Sorry to bother you.

Let me find one of the managers."

The man motioned towards the previous aisle. "I'm pretty sure I saw him trying to dry hump the Invisible Woman an aisle down."

With a wince, Ashley rolled her eyes. "I guess I'll go ask them, but if they look at me like they do those cardboard cut outs, I'm going to slap them so hard they'll think they're on the planet Klingon."

"The planet what?"

"Klingon," Ashley said. "Where Superman comes from?"

A slow grin spread across the man's face. "I think you mean Krypton. Klingon is Star Trek. The actual Klingon planet is…" He shook his head. "Never mind. You know, I think there's a store next door that has what you need. Let me take you. I was in there earlier looking for something for my niece."

Ashley grinned as they headed for the door. "You must be their favorite uncle."

"I give world class pony rides." He returned the smile and held his hand out. "My name's Ian Corvidae."

With a practiced flip of her hair, Ashley accepted the hand shake. "Ashley Duncan."

Corvidae held the door to the comic shop open for Ashley. "Duncan? Any relationship to Drew Duncan?"

A steel fist squeezed her heart as she prepared to defend her brother's name. "Yes, why?"

Corvidae's smile stayed in place as he led her to the arts and crafts store one door over. "I just met him at the station. I work for the State DA's office, and I'm in town to assist on an investigation. I don't think your brother's having a good day."

She stopped short. "Why? What happened?"

Corvidae sighed. "He came face to face with Darren Winters who just can't accept that your brother wasn't responsible for his daughter's death."

Relief turned to gratitude. She didn't have to defend Drew. "I feel terrible for what the Winters went through. I know how horrible that must have been."

Corvidae pointed to a display where all the supplies one might need for a comic book were stacked neatly. "Yeah, I guess you do. I'm very sorry about your sister."

Ashley pretended to study the display. "Thank you." She was very aware of Corvidae watching her.

"Hey, after you get what you need, could I buy you a cup of coffee? I'd really like to hear your take on what happened. I'll understand if you don't want to talk about it." He gave her a lopsided grin. "Even if you don't, I'd still like to buy you a cup of coffee."

Ashley glanced at her watch as she loaded up on colored pencils and drawing pads. She still had nearly two hours before she had to get to the school. "Sure."

****

Two hours later, Ashley raced out of the coffee shop and to her car. She had spent far more time with Ian Corvidae than she'd planned. He was just easy to talk to, but she needed to get to the school. Like yesterday, she intended to be early.

She'd hidden the bags in the trunk of her red Toyota Camry where Cole wouldn't see them until they got home. She wanted to see his face. It was true, it would be Jay who would use most of the supplies, but there were some things in there for Cole himself. She'd spent part of the morning getting an old laptop ready for him. She'd removed the internet ability, and made sure he had a program to write.

This morning, for the first time since he'd come into her life, Cole was actually excited to go to school. Although most of the enthusiasm was because of his friend Jay, some of it was also his new teacher. Apparently, Mrs. Hanley was very nice and liked the beginning of a story he had written that the mean Mrs. Collins hadn't.

Ashley asked if she could read the story, but Cole told her he wanted to finish it first. "Besides, it's not that good. You'd probably hate it."

Ashley assured Cole that she wouldn't, but he didn't seem convinced. Somehow, she had to find a way to help Cole scale over that wall of self-doubt and insecurity.

Ashley pulled in front of the school and found Sam was already there, waiting near the entrance while her new partner patiently sat in the squad car like yesterday.

Ashley started to wave to Sam, but realized her soon to be sister-in-law didn't see her. She was deep in thought, and she didn't look happy.

"Hey Sam," Ashley said as she took a spot next to the pretty cop who had captured her brother's heart. She leaned her butt up against the brick half wall that was near the entrance. "What's up?"

Sam didn't answer right away, and something about her eyes made Ashley think she'd been crying. "Nothing."

"You sure?" Ashley inched closer. Yeah, she'd definitely been crying and that meant one thing. "What did my idiot brother do?"

Sam's head went down. "You don't want to hear

about it."

"Sure, I do. And I can help you beat him up." Ashley grinned. "What did he do?"

Sam crossed her arms and blew out a breath in frustration. "It's not so much what he did as much as what he didn't do."

"Oh wait." Ashley squirmed, crinkled her nose. "This isn't where you tell me that Drew didn't get your eyes to roll back to the back of your skull? Or where you had to tell him that it's not a big deal and it happens to everyone?"

Sam's mouth dropped open. "Oh my God, no. Trust me, that's not the issue. It's more to do with your brother not being honest."

Ashley's eyebrows shot up. "Drew lied to you?"

"Not *exactly*." Sam avoided eye contact. "I asked him a question about something that happened from before we met. He won't tell me. He's not *lying*, he just won't talk to me about it. And I can't decide if I have the right to be angry at him."

Ashley frowned. "So, you asked him about women from his past? Like…" Ashley looked around. "Molly Winters?"

Sam shook her head. "Not like her. I'm probably being stupid. He has a right to his privacy. It's just that I have issues with secrets." Sam sighed. "I never told you I was engaged once before."

Ashley started to blink rapidly. "What? When?"

"A few years ago, before I moved here. Long story short, he cheated on me. When I found out and confronted him, he shrugged it off, as if were no big deal. I tossed the ring in his face and he slapped mine."

Ashley gasped. "He hit you? What did you do?"

Sam grinned. "I broke his nose."

Slowly, Ashley nodded. "Good." She glanced towards the door, but her mind pictured Sam slugging some douche in the face, drawing blood. "Very good."

Sam sighed. "Point is, honesty is a sore subject with me. And Drew knows it." She shrugged. "But he *didn't* lie. He could have. He could have made up some story that fit easily enough and I wouldn't have known. I just can't stand that he won't tell me." She moved away from the half wall, paced a few feet and turned away. "I love your brother, but I don't want secrets between us."

Ashley mulled it over, choosing her words carefully. "You have a right not to, and if my brother wasn't such a moron, he'd tell you whatever you want to know. He's an asshole."

Sam frowned. "He's anything but. Ashley, you're really too hard on him. I understand how hurt you were when he left, but you have to know how sorry he is for that."

Ashley's lips formed a small line as she rolled her shoulders, as if it wasn't important. "Whatever."

Sam moved closer. "Have you talked to your brother about why he left?"

Ashley scowled. "I can't imagine he's got anything to say that I want to hear. He's just more proof that the entire male species are liars and bastards."

Sam grabbed Ashley's hand, giving it a squeeze. "No, he's not. Drew is one of the best men I've ever known, and I know what a good man is. My father. Ollie."

Ashley snorted, but still avoided eye contact. "Ollie is nothing like Drew. Ollie's solid and stuck with me.

He's stayed with me through it all, and hopefully he always will, even when he meets a woman who might actually deserve him." She stared intently at the doors.

Sam moved so she was in Ashley's line of sight. At first, Ashley seemed to pretend not to see notice, but when it was clear Sam wasn't moving, their eyes finally met. "Ashley, you do know how Ollie feels about you, right? That he loves you."

Ashley narrowed her eyes. "Of course. He's been the best friend that I could ever ask—"

Sam took a step closer. "No. That's not what I mean. He doesn't love you the way that Lilly loves you or even how Drew loves you. He's *in* love with you."

With her mouth forming the perfect 'O', Ashley tried to formulate a response, but before any coherent thought could form, the bell rang and the doors began to open. Ashley was still blinking as the children started to race out to capture the rest of the day.

"Why would you say something like that?" Ashley asked. "Did Ollie tell you?"

Sam shook her head. "No. But it's pretty clear. I think everyone knows." She shrugged. "Except maybe you."

Ashley started to point a finger at Sam, ready to argue the point, but nothing came out. She tried to remember a decade's worth of memories, all of the sweet things Ollie would do. All of the times she'd cried on his shoulder. The one night she'd been drunk and heartbroken and she'd nearly thrown their friendship away. This morning.

"He brought me cookie dough. I tried to bake cookies for Cole and Jay yesterday, nearly burnt the house down. He came to pick Drew up and brought me a tub of cookie dough. It was supposed to be easy to do. I made a small batch as practice." Ashley looked back at Sam who was grinning. "Shut up. He's a sweet guy. That doesn't mean anything. Why are you even saying this?"

Sam stepped closer. "Because I think you want him that way too. I want you both to be happy. You're both wonderful people."

Before Ashley could comprehend what she was being told, Cole and Jay came running out together.

"I'll follow you home," Sam said. "Just to be safe, but think about it. And do me a favor. Tell Drew I need a day or two, but I'll see him Friday when we do that class. Tell him I love him. I just need to think."

Ashley did her best to push everything out of her mind once Cole was there. She wanted to hear about Cole's day, to bring him home, bake him cookies and give him and Jay the things for their comic. Then she'd deal with this.

Sam had to be wrong. She was just loopy from being in love herself and it was making her nuts. Because Ollie didn't love her that way. The very idea that he might terrified her beyond words.

Chapter 7
Drew's first houseguest

"So, your mom is dead? I'm sorry, I didn't know."

Jay was sitting on the floor of Cole's room, sampling the cool new drawing supplies that Ashley had purchased for them. "Yeah, she died when I was in second grade. She was sick for a long time." He shrugged, picked up a peach pencil, and touched the tip with his finger. "I can't really remember when she wasn't sick, but it got real bad. Lost her hair. Couldn't even get out of bed." Tossing aside the peach, he found one that was basic black. "I thought I'd have another year or two, but she died while I was at school."

Cole picked up the plate of cookies, carried them over to Jay and knelt down beside him. "I'm sorry." The words sounded awkward coming out of his mouth. People had been saying it to him for weeks now, and it didn't ever make him feel better, so why was he saying it to Jay? Because he didn't know what else to say, he supposed.

Jay took a cookie, but didn't eat it.

Cole sat back down, taking one for himself. "My mom died too, but you probably knew that."

Jay nodded. "I did. I thought you were the kid they were talking about. My dad, he told me that I should say something, like maybe you'd feel better if you knew about my mom. I know it's not the same…" Jay

149

shrugged and bit into the cookie, sprinkling crumbs onto his shirt which he wiped onto the floor.

Cole stared at the paper as Jay started to sketch, bringing the latest version of Captain Nova to life. They had made some adjustments to his uniform, making it even less superhero like, and more military. They had thought about making it green, like a soldier, but decided that since his field of battle was space, they'd make it black, with a star pattern. Seeing a character that he was helping to create come to life on paper was easily one of the most awesome feelings in the world.

"I've got an idea," Cole said. "When we're ready to put out our first issue, why don't we…" Cole frowned as he looked up, trying to remember the right word. "What do they call it?"

Jay sampled another cookie. "I don't know dude, what?"

Cole tapped his finger on his chin for a moment before rising. Going to his bookcase, he sifted through one book after another until he found the first book of the Dragon's Pride series. Bringing it over to Jay, he opened it and sat back down, offering the book to Jay. "Look. The author's mom died just before he finished this. He wrote to her in it."

Jay accepted the book, read the part Cole was pointing to.

This book is dedicated to you Mom, for always believing in me, even when I didn't. I know you're soaring around in heaven on the back of a golden dragon, reading everything I write as you always did. I love you, and I'll miss you always.

Jay grinned, liking the idea of that. His father had often told him that he got his artistic abilities from his mother, and he'd like to think she'd be reading his comics in heaven. "Yeah." He handed the book back to Cole. "You write it, though. You're better with that. We'll make it clear it's from both of us. My mom's name was Janet. What about your mom?"

"Kelli. With an I at the end." Cole placed the book back on the shelf.

"So how goes the story?" Jay asked as he grabbed a fresh piece of paper. "You said that Captain Nova's mother was being held captive. Where?"

Cole grabbed some papers that he had scribbled on. "Someplace dark and very cold." He took a seat on the floor near Jay.

Jay nodded. "Why is he doing this? Most bad guys have a reason."

Cole glanced down at his notes. "I'm thinking he like…" Cole shrugged, unsure how to say what he had in mind. "He wants them afraid, and in pain. Maybe that's how he gets his powers. He eats their fear."

Jay curled his lip as he pondered the idea of someone eating fear. "How does he keep them afraid? He can't just keep them locked up."

Cole kept studying the notes on different characters he held in front of him. "He hurts them. Makes them think he's gonna murder them. Maybe even does… you know…" He shrugged again. "Kill them."

Jay didn't react, he just went back to what he was working on. "We can do something like that, I guess." He reached for a different pencil. "Why don't you write out the story, and then I'll sketch out the panels. You think you could get together this weekend?"

Cole started to nod, but caught himself. "Wait, I've got plans this weekend. There's a Dragon-Con going on. The author of my favorite book is going to be there. Ollie is going to take me."

"Oh yeah," Jay continued to work. "I wanted to go, but my dad is overseas and my aunt hates those things."

Cole smiled. "Maybe you could come with us? I'd have to ask Ollie and see if he can get an extra ticket, but if Aunt Ashley asks him to take us both, he will."

"Cool." Jay grinned. "I'll be skyping with Dad tonight, so I'll ask him if it's okay, but I'm sure it'll be fine. He'd take me himself if he weren't deployed."

Cole carefully selected another cookie. "Are you ever scared about your dad?"

Jay absently reached for the cookie plate himself. "Yeah, I worry, but dad's tough. He'll be okay. He'll be back soon."

Pausing with the cookie halfway to his mouth, Cole frowned. "You won't have to move, will you?"

Jay shook his head as he chewed. "No. Dad said this is his last tour, and Aunt Jeanette moved in, so I could stay in school here. I'm staying."

Cole grinned as he finished his cookie. Wiping stray crumbs away, he reached for another, but saw there was only one more and Jay was about to take it.

Jay laughed. "Split it?"

Cole grinned, grabbed it and carefully divided it into two pieces, trying to make them as even as possible. One was definitely a little bigger, but he gave that half to Jay. "What are you working on now?"

Jay held up a finger, continued to work for a few moments as Cole munched his half a cookie. When he was done, he held the paper up for display.

To Kelli and Janet, the two best moms in the world. We miss you

Jay had used fancy letters, and decorated it with hearts. It was perfect. "It's just an idea of what it'll look like. I'll make it nicer when we do the actual comic."

Cole took it, studied it a moment before smiling. "Cool." He handed the picture back to Jay.

Jay took it, added it to the pile of approved sketches and took out another piece of paper. "Let's talk about Galactor's lair and how he's got the mom locked up. We thinking a jail cell? Or you got something else in mind?"

Picking up the empty plate, Cole carried it over to his desk where he wouldn't worry about stepping on it. "I was thinking chains."

****

Ashley walked into Deja Brew, the local coffee shop, and took the same seat where she'd first talked to Ian Corvidae. He'd sent a text earlier, asking if she'd be willing to meet him for a late-night cup of Joe.

She had planned on going to see Ollie, but last she heard, he was still working late with Drew and Ashley was bursting with the excitement over how Cole nearly hugged her when she'd given him and Jay the comic book stuff. There was a moment, just one moment, where it almost looked like Cole might shed tears of happiness. Someone believed in him, and that someone had been Ashley. Drew might be the big, bad ass uncle, and Lilly the one who made him his favorite meals, but Ashley would be his biggest fan. She would forever be the one who bought him his first comic book kit.

He'd also shown her the draft of the dedication he and Jay had come up with. Ashley hadn't known that Jay had lost his mother to cancer, but somehow, she wasn't surprised. Kindred spirits found each other.

She ordered a chai tea for Corvidae, as that was what he'd gotten the last time, a coffee for herself, and pulled her phone out to see if she'd gotten any messages. She was still hoping to see Ollie tonight. She wanted to tell him everything about her afternoon with Cole. It was probably silly. She managed to bake cookies and not nearly burn the house down. People did that all the time.

Lilly would probably roll her eyes. The woman could make cookies from scratch, while putting together an elaborate four course meal without blinking an eye. Drew would have grinned and said something snarky, like 'You never know Ash, maybe those cookies are a slow acting poison.'

Ollie would just share in her excitement.

The things Sam had said echoed in her mind. Could Ollie really have those feelings for her? If she was being honest, she had realized back when they were young that Ollie had a tiny crush on her, but she knew then it wouldn't last. Ollie had quickly become an important friend. Someone who was a small beacon of hope. Something solid to hold onto when her daily life was hidden nightmares and secret terrors.

She hadn't wanted to risk that when she first caught him blushing at her in sixth grade. By the time they were in high school and she was making her way from one guy to another, she knew he'd be better off without her. And besides, he'd grown up. That silly, innocent crush would have died by then.

There was nothing innocent about Ashley.

A shadow fell over the table, and Ashley smiled as she looked up. She'd expected to see Ian Corvidae standing there, with that cute, lopsided grin of his.

Instead, Ashley saw a crumpled trench coat, covering an even more crumpled man, who reeked of whisky. His upper lip was covered in a disgusting moustache that looked like it had grime under it, and his white shirt was misbuttoned and stained. He held a coffee in one hand and a cruller in the other.

Her smile melted into a scowl. "Can I help you?"

The moustache grinned down at her as he helped himself to the chair opposite of Ashley. "You bet you can sweetheart. I'm Jack Caesar. Let me buy you a cup of coffee."

Ashley held up her cup. "I just bought my own cup Jack, and I'm expecting a friend." She indicated the chai tea.

"You want a bite of my cruller?"

Ashley curled her lip, but said nothing.

Jack laughed, sat back and tore off a bite of his cruller with his teeth. Powdered sugar fell onto his coat. "So how does it feel to have your little brother home with you? Happy? Or worried he might kill again?"

Ashley narrowed her eyes. Slowly, she placed her coffee on the table to resist the urge to throw the hot liquid in his face. "My brother is no killer."

Jack wiped his mouth with his sleeve. "Sure, he is sweetheart. He was a marine in Iraq. I did my homework. Do you have any idea how many insurgents your brother killed? He got a medal for killing over a dozen single handedly and defending a fellow marine who was injured and unconscious."

Ashley's heart tightened. Drew was awarded a medal? Why didn't she know that? Wasn't that a big deal?

Because you've told him you have no interest in

anything that happened to him since he'd left Ember Falls.

"That was war," Ashley said.

Jack sipped coffee. "Sure, but it wasn't war when he killed a man in front of his son. I heard the kid is still in therapy."

Ashley shot up from her chair and grabbed Jack by his trench coat, knocking her purse onto the floor and causing him to spill his coffee. "You want to watch your fucking mouth about my brother." She shoved him away from her.

Jack seemed amused at her reaction. "Hey, he got off, didn't he? Just like with Molly Winters."

Seeing red, Ashley came at Jack with a clenched fist, ready to pound his skull, when the manager from Deja Brew stepped in-between them. Ashley gave the young, high school senior a lesson in offensive language as she cursed at Jack who watched her, grinning shrewdly.

"What the hell is going on here?" Corvidae said as he walked in. He was dressed down, in simple jeans and a t-shirt, but his long, lanky frame and serious face still managed to exude a quiet authority.

Caesar had bent down to pick up Ashley's purse, but Corvidae grabbed it.

Jack offered his hand. "Jack Caesar. I'm a reporter for the Tablet. I was just trying to get a quote from Ms. Duncan about her brother."

Ashley jabbed a finger in Jack's face. "This fucker was calling Drew a murderer. Talking shit about him, trying to get me to turn against him."

Jack smiled. "From my sources, you already have."

Corvidae tossed Ashley's purse on the table and

quickly stepped in front of Jack, to prevent Ashley from ripping his throat out. He pulled out his identification, and showed it to Jack and the manager. "I'm with the Governor's office. I think you want to remember you're talking about a dedicated marine. A man who has served this country with honor and distinction."

Jack shrugged. "I just wanted a quote."

Corvidae studied Jack for a moment before shoving him against the wall and frisking him. He pulled out a small recording device. "Did you let her know you were recording your conversation?"

"It's New York. One party consent is all that's required."

Corvidae turned to Ashley. "Did he ask you about your brother committing crimes?"

Ashley nodded. "Fucker said Drew killed Molly Winters and some guy in front of his family."

Corvidae held up the device and Jack tried to grab it. "Those are pretty serious allegations."

"It's all true," Jack insisted.

"Well then." Corvidae grinned. "I better investigate. I'll just confiscate this as evidence. The Winters case is still open."

Jack's face turned red. "You can't do that. I'm a reporter."

Pocketing the recorder, Corvidae held his other hand out. "Let's see your press credentials."

Jack just scowled.

"Didn't bring them with you?" Corvidae grabbed Jack's arm and began to steer him towards the door. "That's okay. We'll hold this until such time as you can produce them. Now, stop harassing Ms. Duncan, or you'll find yourself locked up." He opened the door, shoved Jack outside and watched as he stomped off down the street.

Ashley was slowly calming down. "Thank you."

Corvidae smiled. "No problem, but I think someone should inform Chief Miller about Mr. Caesar."

"I'll tell Ollie. That's Detective Miller, the chief's son." Ashley sat down again, sipped her coffee, and scowled. "Your tea is probably as cold as my coffee."

Corvidae smiled. "You want a fresh one?"

Ashley shook her head, so Corvidae sat down opposite of her, sampled his tea, and winced while he swallowed. "It's still warm."

Lifting her own cup to hide her grin, Ashley shook her head. "You're a horrible liar. You'd probably be best keeping away from me. I'm in a bad place these days."

He reached across the table and gently placed his hand over hers. "I can only imagine what you're going through right now. You're adjusting to being a mother to Cole, still grieving over your sister, and here comes your brother. And with him, all the accusations that chased him out of town."

Corvidae shook his head and leaned in closer. "I know it's not the same thing, but I had this friend when I was a kid. Bobby Nevins. Nicest guy you could ever meet. One day, this old guy across the street from him came stomping over to Bobby's house. Old Man Canktell was already a few cards short of a full deck, and he started to scream at Bobby about letting his dog out of the yard, saying the dog ran away. His mother and father came running out to stop him. Bobby was crying. He was always a sensitive kid. I think the old guy probably let the dog out himself and forgot."

Corvidae shrugged. "Who knows what happened, but it wasn't Bobby. I know he liked to pet the thing. Bobby loved all animals, and he'd never have done that even by accident and not told someone. We were seven and poor Bobby was scared to go outside for the next year. He'd run away if he saw the old codger. Or wait on the corner when we got off of the school bus and hide until Old Man Canktell went inside. I stayed with him, watching until the coast was clear. It didn't matter if it was raining or snowing, he wouldn't walk down the block if Canktell was outside."

"You stayed with him?" Ashley asked. "That was sweet of you."

Corvidae gave an uncomfortable shrug. "What was I going to do? Leave him there, standing in the rain behind a tree? If I'd been smart, I would have told his parents, but I pinky swore I wouldn't. It upset me that he didn't want to go outside and play anymore."

Memories of how Drew often acted annoyed when he was protecting Ashley or her sister floated to her mind, yet he never failed to try, until he left.

"You said it lasted a year?" Ashley asked.

Corvidae nodded. "Yeah, Canktell died in a fire. We were told he fell asleep in his bed while smoking. Happened in the middle of the night. It was pretty sad, but at least Bobby could walk down his own street if he wanted to again."

Ashley's phone buzzed. She quickly checked to see if it was Ollie, but it was just a message from Lilly about the bookstore.

"You need to go? It's okay. I've got work to catch up on at the hotel."

She did want to go if Ollie texted, and yet she was terrified of seeing him since Sam's pronouncement.

"Problem?" Corvidae asked.

Ashley bit her lower lip. She really wanted to talk to someone, and normally that would be either Lilly or Ollie. Lilly was picking up the slack at the bookstore so Ashley could spend more time with Cole, and she certainly couldn't talk to Ollie about this.

The idea of talking to Drew had passed through her mind, but she'd dismissed that just as quickly. He'd lost the right to be there for her when he'd left Ember Falls without a word.

"It's Ollie." She sighed as she settled back in her seat. "We've been friends since we were kids. Someone I know thinks he would like to be more than friends. I don't know if he sees me that way. We've been friends for ages. I'm sure he just thinks of me as a sister. His crazy, obnoxious sister."

Corvidae thought silently for a moment. "I met him today. He seems like a nice guy. Have you thought about asking him?"

Ashley shook her head. "What am I supposed to do? Hey Ollie, have you ever had the hots for me? No, besides, I can't imagine—" She felt her cheeks flush at a memory. "So I got really drunk once. I was very upset over something, and I sort of threw myself at him." She looked away. "God, I can't believe I'm telling you this."

Corvidae offered her a friendly smile. "I've got that kind of face. And I'm a good listener. Go ahead. No judgements."

Ashley closed her eyes for a brief moment before deciding to go for it. "It was one of the worst nights of my life. I'd just learned that Drew had been let out of prison. The charges were dropped and he was a free man. Instead of coming home, he left. He didn't call, he didn't write. He just left. Up until his arrest, Drew and I were really close. The three of us, me, him and Kelli went through so much. I'd spent nearly a year worrying, and praying he was going to be all right. And then he left without even so much as a goodbye."

She grabbed her cup, swallowed bitter, cold coffee. "I got drunker than I'd ever been before. I called Ollie crying and he came running." *Like he always does.* "And after crying in his arms for an hour or so, I threw myself at him." She looked away, unable to watch Corvidae study her. "Drew was the one person who always made me believe I was loveable. When my father told me I'd be nothing to anyone except a good lay, Drew managed to make me believe that I'd meet a guy who would live or die for me. And in that moment, I thought Ollie was that guy. He's the kindest, gentlest person I've ever known, and I just needed him."

Corvidae reached out once again for hand. "Do you think he took advantage of you?"

Ashley's eyes widened and she looked him right in the eye. "God no, Ollie would never…" She shook her head. "I wasn't so drunk that I was out of control, just drunk enough to be vulnerable. Vulnerable enough to risk throwing away a friendship that meant the world to me in the hopes that he would return it. But he didn't.

"Ollie carried me to bed, tucked me in and when I begged him not to leave me. Ollie promised me he never would. He laid down beside me, and held me all night. I just remember feeling safe and…" She tried to think of the right word. "Complete. The next day when

I woke up, he stayed to tend to me. I expected him to joke about it, but he pretended like it never happened. I realized that he just didn't see me that way."

Ashley stared at her coffee cup, then the window. Anywhere but at Corvidae's eyes, which were watching her with just too much understanding.

"And now your friend told you that Ollie might have romantic feelings for you?" he asked. "Are you worried she's right? Or that she's wrong?"

Ashley sat tapping her foot and looking at her phone, wishing that she'd get a call about an emergency. Anything so she didn't have to answer that question.

"Look," Corvidae said. "Forget about how he feels about you. You need to ask yourself how you feel about him."

Ashley nodded absently. How *did* she really feel about Ollie? Was there a chance there was something there?

Sighing, she glanced up to see Corvidae studying her. "You seemed to know a lot about my brother."

Corvidae shrugged. "I was sent here by the State DA's office to assist and monitor the case. I knew coming in that your brother was not only front and center, but had been accused. I made myself familiar with him as much as I could. I'm sure I don't need to tell you how impressive a record he's had since he first left Ember Falls."

Ashley stiffened.

"Uh oh," Corvidae said. "I just said something I shouldn't have."

Ashley forced a smile. "I hadn't seen or heard from Drew since he left. Not until after my sister was killed and he came back. I don't know all much about his life between his arrest and now."

Corvidae nodded. "And that bothers you?"

Unable to make eye contact, Ashley shook her head. "No. I don't care. I mean, I don't like hearing lies from that ass wipe Caesar that my brother killed some man in front of his kid."

She glanced up, expecting… even hoping to see confusion on Corvidae's face. Instead, he was watching her. "What happened?"

Corvidae forced a sip of his cold tea. "I shouldn't say anything."

"My brother is no killer." Ashley's blood boiled as she jabbed a finger in Corvidae's face. "Drew spent his life protecting me and my sister from an abusive father. He'd never kill an innocent man and terrify their kid…"

Corvidae held up his hands. "Whoa there. I never said he did anything wrong. You really have no idea, do you?"

Ashley frowned. Slowly, she lowered herself back into the chair that she hadn't realized she'd risen from. "Idea about what?"

Corvidae hesitated. "You should probably ask your brother."

He was right. She should. But while she didn't want to hear anyone else talk bad about Drew, she also didn't want hear Drew defend himself. "I'm asking you."

Corvidae sighed. "Okay, but don't shoot the messenger. As I understand it, Drew had just signed on to be point man with McAlister Security. A woman hired the firm to locate her son, daughter-in-law and grandson. They'd disappeared and the grandmother was worried. The son was too much like her late husband. Fond of the drink and quick with the fist. She'd suspected abuse for some time. Tried to get the wife to leave, offered to help even if it meant her own son hating her. She also tried to get her son to admit he had a problem. Offered to pay for counseling. It didn't seem to be working. But the old woman had a few tricks up her sleeve. She was in charge of her late husband's estate. She managed to buy up shares in the company and told the son if he didn't get help and stay away from his family, she'd not only force him out of the family business, she'd cut him out of the will. She'd really managed to get his balls in a vice grip."

Ashley nodded. "Good. Bastard deserved it. What happened next?"

Corvidae's face grew dark. "What you'd expect when you have an animal trapped. It lashes out. In this case, he left his mother on the floor with a broken leg. He'd never hit her before, but had certainly seen his own father do it enough times. He dragged his ex-wife and kid out by their hair in front of her. Told her if she called the police, he'd mail pieces of her grandson to her, one chunk at a time."

Ashley's mouth fell open as she pictured the depravity. She saw her father's face in place of the abusive husband, her sister for the wife and Cole as the son. She closed her eyes as if that would block out the images. "What happened?"

Corvidae waited until Ashley opened her eyes again. "He contacted Mom, wanted money and the company jet to leave the US. Said he'd make a fresh start in another country with his son. She knew she couldn't call the cops. He had buddies who would tell him. So she called General McAlister. And he sent Drew."

Her brother. Always the protector. "Did he find them? Save them?"

Corvidae heaved a sigh. "It was too late for the mother. The husband smashed her face into a million pieces right in front of his son. Drew tried to get the kid out. He was the priority, but the husband wasn't having any of it. He pointed a gun at the son and fired."

Ashley leaned forward. "He killed the son?"

Corvidae shook his head. "Drew managed to get in the way. Luckily, the bullet just grazed him. Drew managed to tackle the father, they struggled for the gun. Bastard found out your brother isn't as easy to beat up as a six year old."

Corvidae picked up his tea and considered it. "From the kid's statement, your brother begged for him to surrender. He didn't want to kill him in front of his son, but the bastard gave him no choice."

He sighed. "Kid's being raised by his grandmother. Might be for the best. She had balls, trying to take on her son like that."

Ashley felt herself shaking with rage. Was it because she saw her own family in the story? Or was it because it was clear Drew had never lost any of his protective instincts.

He just learned to not care about her.

"I need to go," she said as she rose. She couldn't stay here, in public, around people. She felt the need to scream. "I'm sorry."

Corvidae rose. "No, I'm sorry. I've upset you."

Ashley waved her hand. "It's not you. I just... I need to go."

She didn't wait for another goodbye as she left the coffee shop. Just as she got in her car, her cell buzzed. It was Ollie. He was going to be late, because he was still out with Drew.

The one person who might make her feel better was with the brother she wanted to scream about.

****

Drew pulled into the driveway of his new home. The house needed a lot of work. The siding was old and disgusting, the lawn was overgrown and full of weeds, except in a few areas where it was nothing but dirt. The shutters were missing, and the so was the screen from the front door.

And it was all his.

Stepping onto the front porch, Drew pulled out the keys and went inside. The door swung open with a squeak. Something else to add to the list.

He had the closing coming up, so technically it wasn't his yet. He might be able to get out of it if he wanted, but the fact was he needed his own place, and this was perfect. It was close to Cole, without being too close to Ashley. Repairing his relationship with his sister was one of his top priorities, but he wasn't going to do that if the pair of them kept butting heads. Ashley was getting more abrasive, which he hadn't thought was possible. Something was annoying her.

Sam seemed to think that she needed someone to nudge her in Ollie's direction. What the hell was he supposed to do about it?

If Drew tried to stick his nose into Ashley's relationship with Ollie, she'd probably break it.

What in the world was Sam thinking anyway? What did he know about relationships? Apparently, he couldn't even handle his own.

Drew didn't want to think about it. He climbed the stairs and started at the top of the house, making a list of things that needed to be done. The attic needed new insulation, and there were trunks of old clothing and antiquated Christmas decorations that needed to go. Once it was cleared up, there'd be decent storage space up here.

Drew made his way down to the second floor, going room by room. The master bedroom was in the rear of the home, with a private bath and walk- in closet. The bathroom was out of date, with peeling wallpaper and an old pedestal sink that appeared ready to fall off the wall. There wasn't much by way of lighting, but that was something easily fixed. The nicely sized shower needed to be re-tiled, and the bathtub was so rusty he wouldn't wash his socks in it, but he had the idea to rip it all out and start over from scratch. He wanted Sam to have a hand in designing it, but now he was afraid she might never even live here.

Drew made a few notes, then went to inspect the other bathroom and three bedrooms. All could use a little modernization. He'd let Cole pick out the color of paint for his own bedroom, but imagined he'd keep the other's neutral toned, at least for now.

It was a good house. Lots of potential to become a home for a family. He never realized how much he wanted that until Kelli had been killed, but he did. He wanted to have children that were never afraid of their father, never screamed for a mother who was too terrified to save them. He wanted to do what his own father had no interest in doing.

He wanted to be a husband and a dad, build a

family that he could cherish, and he wanted to build that family with Sam.

Drew pictured Sam walking through the house, all furnished and picture perfect. He'd never lied to her, never pretended to be something he wasn't. Yes, he had a secret. He had something he wanted to keep private. Wasn't he entitled? Did he have to expose every nook and cranny of his life?

Even now, thinking about it made him want to scream.

He dealt with that part of his past, put it behind him, and moved on. He didn't want to go back.

Yet there was a part of him that wanted to find Sam right now and tell her anything she wanted to know.

A noise from down the first floor caught his attention. The sound of floorboards creaking. Pulling out his sidearm, Drew quickly and quietly descended the stairs.

He saw the shadow first. Thin. Female.

His heart leapt as he let the tip of his gun lower.

Sam?

"Jesus fucking Christ, what is it with men pulling guns on me?"

Drew scowled at his sister, shoving his gun away. "Who the hell pulled a gun on you?"

Ashley went back to examining the kitchen, turning her back on Drew. "I surprised Ollie the other night. Brought him some of the Sloppy Joes that Lilly made. I guess I caught him with his pants down…" She snickered. "More or less."

Drew started to ask what exactly she meant by that, then changed his mind. He was better off not knowing. "What's up?"

Ashley opened up cabinet doors as if she were searching for a snack. "Just wanted a look at the place. I see you haven't done much. Thinking of getting out of it?"

Drew folded his arms across his chest and leaned against the kitchen door frame. "No. I need a place of my own. That apartment over the garage is just too small. Why would I get out of it?"

Ashley shrugged as she tested the faucet. "Maybe you were getting itchy feet. When's the closing?"

Drew's patience was wearing thin. How long would it be before Ashley accepted that he was back to stay? "Next week. And even once that's all over, you'll probably expect me to put it up for sale every other weekend. You're going to have to trust me sooner or later Ash."

Ashley sneered as she went to the stove, which was rusted over and covered in grease. She opened the oven door to look inside. "Why the hell would I do that? Besides, it doesn't matter to me if you stay or go. I told you, I've moved on from needing you, but Cole would be crushed."

Drew strode over to her. "Listen to me. I'm not going anywhere. I'm not making the same mistake again."

The pair stared at each other for several long seconds, neither blinking. Ashley remained calm, but underneath it, Drew could tell she was looking for a reason to scream at him. Something was under her skin.

Finally, she walked around him to begin examining the counter top, which was stained. "From what I hear, you're making new fuck ups."

Drew's stomach turned and he narrowed his eyes.

"What's that supposed to mean?"

Ashley shrugged as she opened the pantry. "I hear you're keeping secrets from Sam, and she called you out on your lies."

Drew closed the distance, slammed the pantry door shut. "I never lied to Sam. I've been upfront and honest about everything, including how much of an ass I was to you. I just want to keep some things private."

"Really? You've told her how you broke your promises before? How many times did you swear you'd always be there?" She shoved him, pointing a finger in his face. "Do you have any idea what that did to me? I was fucking alone! You were never just a brother to me, and suddenly I was nothing to you!"

Drew winced. "You were never nothing to me. You can't believe that. Ashley, I've said it a thousand times and I'll say it a thousand more. I'm sorry."

"You can say it a million times," Ashley retorted. "You fucking broke me." Her voice cracked and the first hint of tears appeared in her eyes.

Drew's eyes snapped open. "Don't say that. Hate me all you want, but you're not broken. Don't ever think that."

This time, it was Ashley who looked away. "You don't get to tell me that anymore." She swatted at him as he tried to reach out to her.

"Ashley."

"Don't. Just..." Her breath hitched. "You don't know how you fucked me up. You can't know. Kelli was *always* like a ghost, scared of her own shadow. Mom just cried and pretended everything was okay as we were getting our asses kicked. You were the only one I thought would always be there, and then just like that, you were done with me. You were fucking done. I would have understood if you just didn't want to live in Ember Falls, but you didn't want me anywhere near you. I was just another bad memory for you to forget."

Drew didn't look at his sister. He couldn't stand to see her this way. If someone else had Ashley in tears, he'd have found them and kicked their ass. Right now, he wished someone would kick his.

He opened his mouth to apologize again, to beg her forgiveness, and to confess his secrets, but no words came out. He felt the crushing weight of the consequences of his choices.

When he took step towards her, she waved him off. "Just don't. I don't want to hear that you're sorry. Don't you think I want to forgive you? I can't. *"*

The anger was gone from her voice. The heat had cooled and left a cold, dark sadness, which clawed at his heart even more.

"You made me realize that there was just something…" She shook her head and turned away, disgusted with herself. "Unlovable about me."

"No." Drew's voice cracked as he spoke, but he knew he couldn't be silent anymore. "There's nothing wrong with you."

Ashley snorted as she wiped away a tear. "Face it Drew, we're both losers. So was Kelli. She latched on to a bastard who was just like Dad. You're fucking up your relationship with Sam. And me…" She shook her head.

"You're wrong Ash," Drew said. "You've always been loved."

She sneered. "Yeah you loved me so much you couldn't stand to be around."

Drew's eyes closed from the verbal backhand. "I never stopped loving you, but that's not what I meant. There's Ollie."

Ashley's back stiffened. "What the hell are you talking about?"

Drew moved in closer. "You've got to see it. Ash, he's been in love with you since we were kids. I knew he had a thing for you back then, but I was too much of a fucking moron to realize he was the type of guy I should *want* for you."

Ashley backed away, groping for the door. "Shut up. Shut the fuck up. You don't have any fucking idea what you're talking about."

Just as she found the handle, Drew put his hand on the door, keeping it closed. "I *do* know what I'm talking about. Ash, I was the one who fucked up, and I can never make it up to you, but Ollie never left. And he'll tell you what I'm telling you. I fucked up. I was messed up, and I convinced myself that you were better off without me. There's not a God damned thing wrong with you."

Ashley slapped Drew's face. "I need to get away from you." She looked up, tears in her eyes. "Please."

With a sigh, Drew let go of the door. Ashley didn't look back as she ripped the door open and ran out of his house.

Chapter 8
Slippery When Wet

Tires squealed as Ashley's car tore out of the driveway. She drove without any thought to her destination, wiping away the tears she refused to acknowledge were there. She just needed to get some space between her and Drew. She hadn't meant to be so damn vicious. She'd just wanted to give him a hard time and deliver Sam's message, which she had forgotten. Instead, she ripped into him with a vengeance.

But he fucking deserved to know how broken he'd left her. Why shouldn't she say those things? Just because he'd come back, was she supposed to just forgive and forget?

She'd hurt him. And he deserved it and so much more.

So why did she feel like such a bitch for saying it? And the satisfaction that surged through her when she slapped Drew was drowned out by a tidal wave of guilt and shame. She had to get away, or she would have begged him to forgive *her*.

Ashley pulled into the space next to Ollie's car, but didn't get out. She hadn't realized that she was driving here until she'd arrived. Not that it should make a difference. This was Ollie. She could always go to him.

So why wasn't she getting out of the car?

Drew was wrong. Ollie didn't see her that way. That was just Drew making a mess out of things again. What the hell did Drew know?

Ollie would probably laugh at the idea.

But Sam had said the same thing.

Ashley froze as she watched his window from below. The light was on and she could see his silhouette pass by. She could go up. Heck, Ollie wouldn't care if she came up while he was asleep.

Ashley reached for the door handle, but didn't pull it open.

This was stupid. She should go and tell Ollie everything that Drew had said. They'd have a few beers, a few good laughs and everything would be okay again. That's why she came here. Ollie would make everything all right. He always did.

So why couldn't she get out of the car. With far more effort than it should have taken, Ashley pushed her door open and undid her seatbelt. Getting out, she leaned on the car while standing behind the open door.

It was dark already, and the night seemed especially quiet, as if the entire neighborhood was anxiously awaiting to see if she'd cross the street and go in. There was a bite in the air from the cold breeze, and the sky was nearly pitch black. The stars were all hiding.

Ashley cursed herself for being such a baby and closed her car door. She started across the street, then retreated back. Leaning down to see her reflection in the mirror, she inspected her face to make sure she didn't look like a wreck.

Not that Ollie would care what she looked like. A small smile spread across her face as she recalled a time when Lilly was out of town at a bookseller's convention, and she'd come down with the flu. Ollie had come over to care for her, bringing chicken soup from Marie's Deli. Her hair had been a rat's nest and she'd just thrown up five minutes before he'd arrived. She had told him to look away because she was hideous, but he'd just smiled and insisted that she wasn't capable of being anything but beautiful.

He'd stayed with her throughout the next two days, taking her temperature, bringing her cold compresses, and cooking for her. He actually seemed to enjoy caring for her, and didn't go running every time she'd ended up on her knees, heaving into the toilet.

Well, she certainly looked better now than she did then. Her eyes weren't too puffy from crying, not that she would admit that she had cried. Still, Ollie would notice. He'd never say anything about her eyes, but he'd notice right away that she was upset. He always did.

With long, purposeful strides, Ashley started to head across the street. She only got halfway when she stopped again, the picture of Ollie wiping puke off of her face. Who the hell does that? The way he took care of her, the way he always takes care of her…

Could Drew and Sam be right?

She shook her head and took another step. No, they were wrong. Sam was in love and wanted the world to be in love and Drew was just an idiot. Ollie didn't love her.

Well, he did. That much was clear, but he wasn't *in* love with her.

He'd never tried anything. Never made any indication that he wanted to get in her pants, or her bed.

Just into her heart.

Ashley scowled as she looked up to his window, spotting his shadow moving once more.

In the distance, a cat hissed and Ashley turned on her heel. She gazed down the street. The night was still and dark, like a predator ready to strike. All the houses had lights coming from their windows, making them look like peeping toms, able to see into her soul as she battled her internal struggle.

The field across from Ollie's apartment was a sea of black shadows, untouched by the yellowish streetlights that bathed the road in an eerie illumination.

About five houses down, one of the street lamps was dark, allowing for a sliver of shadow to be cast on the car across the street.

The cold breeze carried the subtle scent of rotted meat from the field as she studied the car. It was probably empty, but she felt like she was being watched.

She imagined what her sister's final moments on Earth were like. Her hand went to her throat as she envisioned Wilson's blade cutting into Kelli's neck, and she wondered if the instant before the attack Kelli had felt the same chill in her bones.

She glanced back to Ollie's window, needing to go to him even more now that the feeling of dread had overwhelmed her. Somehow, that sensation was the last push she needed to head back to her car. She fumbled with the key fob, nearly dropping the remote as she glanced over her shoulder towards the dark car down the street. Once inside, she locked the doors, started the engine and pulled away.

She wasn't doing this. She had nearly ruined her

friendship with Ollie by trying to sleep with him while drunk once, she wasn't going to ask him now if he'd been secretly in love with her for years. There was too much at stake for her to risk her friendship with Ollie. Cole was so looking forward to his trip to that stupid convention and she'd just screw that up. Kid needed to have a man in his life he could count on, and who knew if or when her idiot brother would decide to vanish again.

Besides, she had no business thinking of Ollie Miller that way. The truth was, he was sweet, honest and the best man she'd ever known.

Which meant he was way too good for her.

****

Not wanting to go home, Ashley headed down Route 50 which ran into Broadway. Downtown Ember Falls featured several trendy restaurants and shops, including a cupcake store, a clothing retailer, and the art shop where Ashley had bought the supplies for Cole's comic book.

Ashley passed them all by and took a right, pulling into a small lot near the epicenter of what passed for nightlife here in Ember Falls. She ran across the street, dodging slowly moving cars and ignoring honking horns as she passed the crowded venues of bars and night clubs. She held her breathe as she moved through the small crowd out on the street breathing out cigarette smoke and vapor, and entered the front doors of Clancy's.

Clancy's was a small hole in the wall bar, stuck between a dance club and a café. It was the place she went to when she just wanted to be alone and drink herself stupid, something she hadn't done in too long.

Lilly was home with Cole, and God help her, Drew was right there too. The kid would be fine.

Ashley surveyed the room, taking in the old, mahogany wood bar and the high back stools. The walls were decorated with old posters, patches from local unions, and pictures of the children of the bartenders and waitresses. Glasses were suspended upside-down above, while rows of liquor bottles lined the shelves. There was a TV screen with a college football game displayed with the volume turned down.

The crowd was sparse and muted, with a few old timers sitting in a corner, eating peanuts and sipping beers as they told each other the same old stories and jokes they'd told a thousand times. A pair of middle-aged men played darts, debating the wisdom of going home versus staying for one more game. A short waitress in her mid-forties with dark, curly hair served drinks to a group of business men with their ties loosened, while Steve the bartender wiped the counter between pouring drinks.

Ashley made a beeline for the far end of the bar where she could drink, stew and be left alone. She didn't want to talk to anybody except the bartender, and to him, she just wanted to tell him what to pour and to keep it coming.

Ashley barely made eye contact as she ordered a Guinness. She pulled over a small bowl of nuts, pretended to watch the game and prayed everyone would leave her alone.

Ashley sensed more than saw someone sit down next to her. She kept her eyes on the screen, barely acknowledging Steve the barkeep when he placed her Guinness down in front of her.

Shit, I so don't want to get hit on.

"I know who you are."

Slowly, Ashley turned. The man was familiar, but Ashley couldn't quite place the face. He was older, with greying hair and an expensive suit. He reeked of alcohol. He was as drunk as she wanted to be, and he appeared just as angry. The glare of hatred he wore made it clear she wasn't about to get hit on.

"I'm sorry, have we met?"

The man emptied the contents of the glass he had carried over. "I know your bastard of a brother. He killed my little girl."

It clicked into place. "Mr. Winters. I'm sorry for what happened to Molly."

Darren Winters scoffed as he held his glass up for another whiskey which Steve gave him as if he'd been expecting it. "Is that all you have to say?"

Ashley picked up her Guinness. "Yes. Have a good night."

She began to rise to look for someplace else to sit, but Mr. Winter's grabbed her arm, causing her to spill the Guinness down her front. The dark, amber liquid soaked into her clothes, making her smell like a brewery. She yanked her arm away. "Son of a bitch!"

Everyone in the bar went quiet and watched in stunned silence as Ashley dripped Guinness all over the floor. She pushed Winters away and his drink toppled out of his hand and splashed over the one dry spot on her red blouse.

"That's exactly what your brother is." Mr. Winters leaned in right into Ashley's face, and her nostrils flared from the sour scent of alcohol that permeated from him. It wasn't just his breath that reeked, his entire body had a strong, putrid smell when you got close to him, as if he were already dead and decomposing, but nobody had told him to stop walking around. "He's a son of a worthless bitch, from a whore who couldn't keep her legs together, doing whatever and whoever your bastard of a father told her to. Drew Duncan is a coward that preys on innocent little girls and murders them and hasn't got a decent bone in his worthless body."

She jutted her chin out and stepped closer to Winters, making sure he knew he wasn't intimidating her. "You better watch your fucking mouth about my family. My brother is a better man than you could ever hope to be, and your daughter was hardly an innocent little lamb."

More red-faced by the moment, Winters grabbed Ashley by the shoulders. "Don't you fucking talk about my little girl like that you fucking bitch."

Ashley brought her hands up sharply and knocked Winters back. He stumbled into the arms of a pair of hipsters with their oversized glasses and flannel shirts. "You're fucking nuts. No wonder Molly was sleeping with half the guys in school."

Winters face went from red to deep purple as he let out a scream like a tortured cat. He elbowed one of the men holding him and shoved the other before launching himself at Ashley, grabbing her by the throat.

Ashley fell back into a waitress who was balancing a tray full of beers in her hand. Glass shattered as the brew showered down Ashley's already soaked clothing. She grabbed his fingers and began to pry them loose while her knee came up and found Winters' groin.

Winters staggered back, heaving for breath. Steve

was coming out from behind the bar as most of the patrons stood and watched, their mouths open in shock.

Just as Winters looked like he was going to charge again, someone came up from behind him. "Woah there Darren, you need to stop now." Corvidae pulled Winters towards the door.

"Let go of me!" Winters struggled widely.

Corvidae seemed to have no intention of doing so. "Darren, you're drunk. You need to go home and sleep it off, not do something *else* you'll regret."

Winters's face went from red to white, as if he'd gone from madman to cadaver in a second. His eyes hardened as he stopped struggled. "What are you talking about?"

Corvidae narrowed his eyes. "You need to concentrate on your son. It's not too late to repair your relationship with him. You can't throw your life away over your daughter. She's gone. And I promise to make sure the chief gets the person responsible, no matter *who* it is."

Winters sent a venomous glare towards Ashley. "Everyone from her family is disgusting. They're a cancer in this town. Her father was a sick, twisted, bastard. You have no idea the things he and the others did. Even I couldn't…" He shook his head and for a moment, Ashley thought he might puke.

Ashley curled a lip. "You'll get no argument from me about my father. You want to go kill him, be my guest, but you stay away from me and my family."

She stalked into the small and disgusting ladies' room. There were two stalls, one of which was occupied by someone smoking and the other Ashley knew had a door that wouldn't stay closed. Ashley headed to the sink to try and clean up, but her blouse and jeans were soaked in Guinness, tap beer and cheap whiskey. It was useless. She'd just won the world's most depressing wet t-shirt contest.

The idea of going home didn't appeal to her, but she wasn't going to sit in a bar smelling like she'd taken a dip in a beer distillery.

Hearing the sounds of the woman's ass exploding on the toilet, Ashley retreated from the bathroom. Steve had cleaned up the bar, and there was a yellow 'Wet Surface' sign displayed where he had mopped. Ashley felt like the stick figure who was in a perpetual state of slipping.

The door to the bar opened, and Corvidae came in from outside. He scanned the room, spotted Ashley, and made his way over. "Are you all right?" He studied Ashley's neck.

Ashley ignored the question. "What are you doing here Ian?"

Corvidae sighed and gestured towards the door. "I came looking for Darren. I know he has a drinking problem. Molly's death has destroyed him."

Ashley scowled. "I never liked Molly. She had Drew wrapped around her little finger. Idiot thought he loved her, but Molly was always a cold, heartless bitch. Still, she didn't deserve what happened to her."

Corvidae rubbed his hand over his head. "I never met her, but I know that Molly was very difficult. Still, it's hard to get past the loss of a child, even one who you were never close to. It pretty much destroyed their entire family."

Despite herself, Ashley couldn't help but pity Winters. She remembered that moment when Ollie had come to her doorstep to tell her Kelli had been killed. She'd gotten so angry, she was ready to throw things at him, but she knew Ollie would never be so cruel. She'd ended up crying in his arms the entire night.

"He needs help. He didn't seem well."

Corvidae sighed, glancing around. "He's not. I'm not supposed to say anything, but he has cancer." He frowned and shook his head. "I don't think he has long, and he'd like to get justice for his daughter before he goes."

Ashley folded her arms and narrowed her eyes. "Well, he's not going to get it by going after my brother." She glanced around the bar. "Where is he?"

"I poured him in a cab, sent him back to the hotel. Normally, I would have taken him myself, but he refused to let me. Besides, I wanted to come back and make sure you were okay."

Ashley cocked an eyebrow. "Aw, aren't you sweet. You hoping to ride to the rescue? Save the damsel in distress?"

Laughing, Corvidae shook his head. "You don't strike me as anyone's damsel."

Ashley smirked. "Damn right."

Corvidae pulled out a chair for her, which she accepted. "I'm sorry if I upset you earlier with what I told you about your brother."

She shrugged.

"Did you talk to him?"

Ashley nodded while studying her shoes.

Corvidae sighed. "I'm guessing things didn't go well."

Finally, Ashley made eye contact. "I'm here in this dump looking to dive head first into a Guinness." She sniffed her shirt. "By the smell of me, you'd think that's exactly what I did. I tried to talk. It didn't end well."

Corvidae gave her a sympathetic smile. "He doesn't want to talk about it?"

It would be easy for Ashley to blame Drew. That seemed to be her favorite pastime, but it wouldn't be true. "I didn't give him the chance. He keeps begging me to forgive him. And dammit I want to, but every time I think about it, I feel like I'm getting kicked in the gut again, and I rip into him."

Corvidae folded his arms. "Can I make an observation?"

Ashley considered for a moment, then nodded.

Corvidae took his time, choosing his words carefully. "You have issues to work out with him. I think you're scared of him hurting you again. I get that. With how the three of you grew up, he was the only male family member that ever loved you. I can understand why it messed you up."

Ashley rolled his words around in her head. Of course, it messed her up. It destroyed her in ways she could never explain.

"There's something else I notice," Corvidae said. "You may rip into him, but you never hesitate in defending him when someone else says anything bad about him. Clearly you still love him."

Ashley turned away. She tried to wipe away the tears as casually as possible and was grateful that Corvidae didn't say anything else. "I need to go. I'm starting to get cold, being soaked to the bone like this."

She stood quickly and Corvidae rose beside her. "Why don't you let me drive you home? Or call you a cab?"

That gave Ashley a badly needed laugh. "Thank you, but I'm okay to drive. I may smell like I'm wasted, but unless I get a buzz through osmosis, I'm fine."

Corvidae smiled. "Well, drive carefully and don't get pulled over. They'll get one whiff of you and lock you up without bothering with the breathalyzer."

Chapter 9
Ollie Comes Clean

Ollie tried to not check his phone every two minutes. He'd texted Ashley that he was free, and if she wanted to talk, he'd be happy to come over. If she wanted to see him, she'd contact him.

So, he wouldn't check it every two minutes. Instead, he waited until the clock over the TV showed it had been three minutes and picked it up.

He nearly dropped it when it buzzed with an incoming call. He answered so quickly he hadn't bothered to check the Caller ID.

"Hey." He winced at the desperate sound of his voice.

"Ollie," Drew said from the other side. "Is something wrong?"

Ollie sighed. "No. What's up?"

"I was just checking to see if Ashley came to see you. She tore out of here a couple of hours ago. I was hoping she'd be home by now."

Something twisted in Ollie's gut. "She's not here. What happened?" As Drew explained how Ashley had gotten angry with him, giving him what he deserved, Ollie grabbed his wallet, badge, gun, and car keys. "You need to talk to her Drew. She needs to know why you left. It might help her forgive you. Her being angry isn't good for either of you."

"No. Ollie, you promised me you wouldn't tell her."

Ollie had, but he was become more and more convinced that he wasn't doing either Ashley or Drew any favors in keeping that promise.

"I'm going to go look for her. No, let me do it," Ollie insisted. "She'll just get upset if you do. I know the places she'd go. In the mood she was in, I'd bet she went to Clancy's. I'll make sure she's…" Ollie trailed off as he glanced out the window. "Never mind. I'm watching her cross the street now. She's here. I'll make sure she's okay."

"All right," Drew said. It broke Ollie's heart to hear the relief in his voice. "Better not tell her I called to look for her, she'd just flip out on you."

Ollie ended the call just as Ashley came in the door.

He smelled her before he saw her, and he just thanked God she hadn't hurt herself or anyone else on the way over here. "Ashley, what's wrong? Are you okay?"

Ashley shook her head. "I don't know what I am. I wanted to tell you stuff. I was excited to tell you things, but then some jerk got in my face about Drew, and I nearly ripped his throat out. I might have if it weren't for Ian."

The unfamiliar name was like a punch in the gut. *"Ian?"*

Ashley just nodded. "Ian Corvidae. You met him. I ran into him while I was looking to get comic book stuff for Cole. That's part of what I wanted to tell you. I made Cole cookies without it being a five-alarm disaster, and he and Jay were thrilled with the things I got them. Cole was *happy*. I was so ecstatic, and proud. I thought that maybe I could do this. I could raise Cole."

"Of course, you can," Ollie insisted, pushing away his hurt feelings over hearing her speak of another man's name. It was nothing new. Instead, he took joy at the smile on her face. "I've told you that you're going to be a wonderful mother."

Ashley smiled through her tears. "When you say that, I can almost believe it. But then this asshole Caesar gets in my face about Drew."

Ollie frowned. "Jack Caesar?"

Ashley paced back and forth as she went over the details of her encounters, first with the internet tabloid reporter, followed by Darren Winters. "So here I go, ready to kill to defend Drew and next time I see my brother, I rip into him. What the hell is wrong with me?"

Ollie stepped in front of her, stopping her dead in her tracks. He touched her face. "Nothing. There's not a damn thing wrong with you."

Ashley placed her hands on his chest and gazed into his eyes. "You always say that."

"It's true." He wished she could understand just how much he believed what he said. "Ashley, you are the most amazing person I've ever known. You're fearless. So full of passion and love. You're fierce and tender at the same time." He poured his heart into his words, wishing for her to hear what he didn't have the courage to say through whatever alcoholic haze she was in.

Ashley smiled and traced his face with her finger. There was something in her eyes that he hadn't seen before. Her hand found the back of his head and she pulled him down into a kiss.

Ollie's heart leapt at the sweet taste of her, but he gently pulled away. It wasn't going to happen. Not like this.

Ashley stumbled back. "I should have known. I'm sorry." She reached for the door.

Ollie held it closed. "You're not driving like this."

She turned and shoved him. "Don't look at me like you care Oliver Miller. Do you think that was easy for me? I know how you see me. The poor Duncan girl with the stained jeans who hides in the fucking closet listening while her drunk asshole of a father tortures her brother." She swiped at the tears. "I'm nobody's victim anymore. I don't need your pity. And if you can't find it in you to love someone like me, then just stay the fuck away."

She grabbed for the door handle, but Ollie spun her around. Her back was against the door as Ollie got in her face.

"You think I can't love you?" Ollie said. "God dammit Ashley, are you fucking blind? I've been *in love* with you since we were twelve years old! I don't know how to do any *but* love you."

Ollie knew he was going somewhere he could never come back from. He'd probably beg her forgiveness in the morning, but tonight he was going to let it all out. He hated the way she flinched when he spoke, but he couldn't stop now. "I loved you when you beat up Brad Liverman for picking on me for my weight. You were a sight to behold in your pigtails, and pink puppy dog sweater, kicking him in the balls. I loved you when you pulled me onto the dance floor at eighth grade formal and danced as bad as I did so I wouldn't feel like an idiot. I picked out an outfit to match your blue dress in case you agreed to dance with me, even though I'd never get the courage up to ask. I loved you when you moved out of your father's house, when you said you'd die before you'd ever step foot in there again. I broke for you when your brother left, and I died inside when I had to tell you about Kelli. I've loved you for so long Ashley, I don't know how to do anything else."

Ashley shook her head. "It's not true. You've never said anything…" She heaved a breath. "You never let me know."

Ollie closed his eyes and feeling his knees go weak, he lowered himself to the couch. "I knew how you saw me. I'm the shoulder to cry on, the guy you turn to when your heart is broken. I pick up the pieces and smile for you when you conquer the world. I've always been there for you Ash, and I swear to God I always will. The idea of you not letting me scares the hell out of me." He buried his head in his hands. "And the only time you ever let me get close to really loving you the way I want to, to holding you and kissing you, it's because you're hurt and drunk. You can't see it when your sober, just when you've had one too many. I won't touch you when you're like that. I won't take that from you unless I know you want me to have it."

Ashley moved closer. "I never knew."

Ollie sighed. "How could you? I was too much of a coward to ever tell you. And God, I'm sorry for it. If you remember this tomorrow, I promise I'll do everything I can do to keep you in my life, but I can't pretend anymore."

Ashley knelt down, took his face in her hands and made him look at her. "I'll remember. Do you know how much I've had to drink tonight?"

Ollie shook his head. "From the smell of you, enough that I should arrest you for DWI."

She laughed. "You idiot. Darren Winters spilled my Guinness on me. Followed by his whiskey, then a tray full of beers." She sniffed her own clothes. "I haven't had a drop to drink tonight. I planned on getting good and drunk. It wasn't my first thought. I wanted to see you. I was so excited, and I wanted to share it with you. I was angry, and I wanted you in my corner. I was hurt and all I thought about was how you'd make me feel better. All I've wanted all day is you."

She smiled and took his hand. "So, Ollie Miller, are you going to send me away, or are you going to give me what I want."

Ollie felt as if the Earth were trembling, but realized it was him. Was she saying what he thought he was saying? Did she really mean it? "You're really not drunk? I mean you smell…"

She laughed. "You can either give me a breathalyzer, or you can get me out of these smelly clothes and show me how you really feel."

Ollie studied her. She hadn't stumbled once. Her words were not incoherent or slurred. And her eyes, her beautiful eyes that were the color of autumn leaves with a twinkling of the night sky in them, were clear and determined.

When she touched him, Ollie lost all traces of control. He crushed his mouth on hers, and for the first time in his life, he felt whole.

He tasted her like a man dying of thirst would lap

up water. She moaned, and that just made her more delicious.

"I know I smell horrible," she whispered in his ear.

He shook his head. "I don't care. I've wanted this for so long, I'm not going to survive if I have to wait for you to take a shower."

She grinned. "I was thinking maybe you'd like to take one with me." She took his hand and led him to his bedroom. "I got a glimpse of what you're packing. You've got no reason to be shy."

Ollie stopped, kissed her again, and then lifted her in the air.

In the bathroom, he put her gently on the floor. They each slipped out of their shoes. "I liked what I saw the other night, but I didn't get a very good look. Let me see what I'm getting."

Slowly, he gripped the sides of his white t-shirt and pulled it over his head. His face flushed as he dropped it to the floor.

Ashley gently placed her hand on his firm stomach and started to trace his abs. She grabbed his belt and tugged it lose. Her fingers found their way down the front of his pants, into his boxers.

When she gripped him around his manhood, his eyes closed and he rolled his head back with a moan. Within moments, he felt the rest of his clothes fall down to his ankles. He opened his eyes when Ashley let go.

He started to cover himself with his hands. "What's wrong?"

Ashley grinned. "Not a thing. I just wanted a good look." She stepped forward and ran her hands over him. "I can't believe that I've been missing out on this for so long."

He needed the wall to support him while she tasted his neck with her mouth.

"Keep your eyes closed," She whispered in his ear just before she backed away.

He heard the rustle of clothing being removed and kicked away. Ollie had fantasized about this moment since he was a randy teenager. He was about to see Ashley, all of her.

"Open your eyes," she commanded.

When he did, she was gone. "Ash?"

In answer, the shower started, and her hand appeared from behind the curtain. She beckoned him with a finger.

He stepped into the shower and found Ashley under the water. He auburn hair was wet, and water ran over her skin. "Do you like what you see?"

Ollie didn't respond. He just studied every inch of her as the water ran down between her perfect, small breasts, down her long beautiful long legs, and ran off near her tiny feet.

"Ollie?"

Her voice snapped him out of his trance. "I've dreamed about seeing you like this for so long. You're more beautiful than I ever managed."

He stepped forward, pressed his body to hers. His lips found hers has his hands roamed her body.

She reached out and found his body wash. "Wash me," She whispered.

Ollie took the bottle and squirted a small amount in hands. Slowly, he massaged into her long, luxurious hair.

She stepped under the water and rinsed the soapy

water out. Ollie felt himself throb at the sight of the suds running down her long, lithe body.

Taking more body wash, he started to slather it on, enjoying the feeling of her skin as he got to know every inch of her. His fingers touched the indentation of the small of her back. He kissed her neck as he felt her nipples.

The water ran hot, but Ollie's blood pumped ever hotter. One hand slowly made its way between her legs, where he found a different sort of wetness. She gasped in pleasure as he moved his finger.

Ollie kissed his way down her body, tasting the different textures of her skin as his mouth continued down, until he got on his knees in front of her.

"Oh God," Ashley moaned, and she braced herself against the wall. She knocked down the shampoo and body wash, which splashed on the shower floor. They were followed by a wash rag that fell on Ollie's head. Ashley managed a laugh between sighs.

Ollie stopped long enough to grin at her. He reached up, to feel her as she trembled from what he was doing. His hand found hers and he experienced a thrill he'd never known before as she threw her head back and groaned in pleasure.

He started to work his way up, but he had a hard time finding something to grab onto. His hand slipped on the slick tile wall and nearly fell, taking her with him. His face ended up in her stomach.

Blushing, he glanced up at her. "Sorry."

She smiled and offered a helping hand. "I'm not. That was amazing."

"I never thought I'd ever get to touch you like this," Ollie whispered as he ran his fingers through her hair. "I can't believe I'm naked in the shower with Ashley Duncan, the girl who could drive men wild with a glance."

Ashley smirked. "Funny."

"I'm serious," Ollie said. "Do you have any idea how incredibly beautiful you are?"

"You're only saying that because I'm wet and naked," Ashley replied.

"No." Ollie shook his head and pushed a strand of wet hair out of her face. "*God* no."

Ollie's eyes were intense as he stroked her hair. "Ashley, there is no one more beautiful than you. I've always told you that."

"You're nice," Ashley replied. "You've always been too nice. You deserve better than damaged goods."

"Stop that," Ollie commanded. "You're not damaged. You're strong. You're fierce. You're amazing."

She looked away and shook her head. "You're crazy."

Ollie gently used his finger to make her look at him. "I'm crazy over you. Always have been, always will be."

She traced his jawline with her finger. "You're the one who's strong. Maybe I wasn't ready for you before. Maybe I needed you to just be a friend before. I need more now."

He kissed her deeply. He felt the warm water wash away his doubts and hesitation. She seemed to melt into him, as if this was where she'd always belonged.

"I want you inside me," Ashley said as the sharp sound of water splashing off his broad chest echoed around them. She lifted her leg, and pulled him closer. "Show me what I've been missing."

His eyes widened. "Here? In the shower?"

She laughed and pulled him into a kiss. "You've never had shower sex before?"

Blushing, he shook his head. "I'm sorry."

"Hey, no reason to be sorry." She slid her hand down, and gripped him. "I think you're more than up for the challenge."

His breath heaved as he stood at the ready, hesitating.

Was this real? Was he dreaming?

Dream or not, he couldn't wait any longer.

She wanted him. All of him.

He gave himself to her.

With one motion, he was inside of her. He saw it in her eyes, that realization that no matter what, there was no going back for either of them.

He began to move with her, finding a rhythm and picking up speed. She grabbed him, pulling him closer.

They moaned in pleasure, then laughed at the sound of wet flesh smacking wet flesh. He slipped twice, kicking the bottle of body wash against the wall of the shower.

Never had he felt more alive. She began to cry out and he let out a low deep groan of ecstasy as he built in intensity until he finally emptied out, exploding within her.

She leaned against him as they fought to catch their breath. The water was starting to cool off. He rested his head against hers. "I love you."

Ashley shook her head. "Don't say that. You don't know what you're in for with me."

Ollie laughed. "Who in the world could know what they're in for better than me."

Ashley still didn't look convinced, but when Ollie held his hand out, she took it.

"Come on," Ollie said. "Let's get dried off. The water's getting cold."

As Ashley shut the water off, Ollie stepped back, right onto the shampoo bottle, which squirted out on the floor of the shower.

His foot slipped, and he stumbled. His arms started to pinwheel as he fell back. He got caught up in the shower curtain, and took it with him as he fell out of the shower.

"Ollie!"

His back slammed down on the bathroom floor with a thud.

Ashley scrambled to his side. "Oh God, are you okay?"

He took her hand. "Was it real? Did we just…"

Ashley nodded as she checked his head. "Yes, we did."

Ollie smiled and laid his head down. "Then I'm fine."

Ashley swatted at him. She glanced downward and snorted.

"What?

Ashley pointed. "Feel like going camping?"

Ollie propped himself up on his elbows and peered down at himself. The Star Wars shower curtain was lying across the lower half of his body, and was tented right where Harrison Ford's image was.

"Oh God." Mortified, Ollie closed his eyes and felt his face burn red.

Ashley chuckled. "I guess it's fair to say that Han shot first."

Ollie smiled and looked up at Ashley. "I love you."

Ashley grinned as she leaned over him, her wet hair falling down the side of her face. "I know."

Chapter 10
Broken

"Where's Aunt Ashley?"

With a small squeak of surprise, Lilly jumped at the sound of Cole's voice. She had been looking at the contents of a box, which she quickly shut and put back on the shelf, near a yellow stuffed lamb.

Cole saw her startled look and took a step back, his eyes going to his feet. "I'm sorry," he mumbled as he started to retreat.

"Cole wait," Lilly called. "Please come back."

Cole stood out in the hallway for a solid ten seconds while contemplating the idea of pretending not to have heard her, but he knew Lilly would just come find him. Slowly he peeked around the corner. "I'm sorry," he repeated.

Lilly smiled. "You have nothing to be sorry about. Come here." She patted the bed next to her.

Slowly and cautiously, Cole entered the room with downcast eyes. He didn't want to risk upsetting her. Not that Lilly had ever gotten mad at him. In fact, the only time she'd ever really seen Lilly get angry was on his behalf, although she was sure she'd heard her put both Aunt Ash and Uncle Drew in their places.

Lilly waited patiently, her smile remained fixed on her face, as Cole took his time coming in. He sat on the edge of the bed, several inches away from Lilly, and still avoiding eye contact.

Lilly inched a little closer. "You startled me. I was lost in thought."

"I'm sorry," Cole repeated for the third time.

Lilly turned to face the small boy. "Cole, you don't need to be sorry. You didn't do anything wrong. I'm not angry." She shrugged. "Maybe a little embarrassed. Did I squeak? I know I make a sound like a little mouse when I'm surprised."

Despite himself, the corner of Cole's mouth twitched. "A little."

Lilly shook her head and blushed. "Some people have told me it's cute, but I feel silly. I'm a grown woman." She sighed. "Okay, maybe I'm not *grown*. I imagine within a few years you're going to tower over me like your aunt and uncle do. Promise me you'll never pat my head, will you."

Cole giggled, finally relaxing. "I promise. They're bigger, but they listen to you. I think you scare them."

Lilly laughed as Cole glanced at the box on the counter, and the stuffed lamb. "You're wondering what's in that box, but you don't want to ask."

Cole's smile faded a little bit, but Lilly's didn't. She stood up and retrieved the box. "This just holds a few mementos. I've been thinking about someone recently, a boy I once knew. He and I were very close, and for a time, I thought we'd have a family together."

Cole looked at dark wooden box as she held it out to him. He traced the pattern of wild flowers that were burned into the top. It looked like some of the petals were blowing in the wind.

Lilly opened up the box, revealing a picture and notes. Cole reached in and pulled out the photo. The image of a teenage Lilly Danvers looked up at him. She was being held by a man who didn't look at the camera. His eyes were glued to Lilly.

He was tall, although not as tall as Uncle Drew. He had milk chocolate skin that reminded him of Jay. His arms were the size of Lilly's head, but he held her gently and tenderly.

"His name was Brooke," Lilly said. "Everyone thought we'd be the first couple to get married. I knew he had a dream of working in the FBI."

"Did he?" Cole asked.

Lilly sighed as she took the picture. "I'd like to think so. He and your uncle were best friends for a long time."

Cole's head popped up. "Is he the one that Uncle Drew punched? For hurting you?"

Lilly's eyes widened. "Drew punched Brooke?"

Cole wasn't sure what to say, so he kept quiet.

Lilly rose and went to the shelf, where she picked up the lamb.

While she did, Cole poked through the box. He didn't want to read the letters, but he was hoping there were more pictures. There weren't any. Just several notes, a man's ring from high school, and a plastic stick at the bottom which was white and purple with a small, faded plus sign in a window.

Cole glanced up as Lilly sat back down holding the lamb. "This was the last thing he gave me before we broke up. I know your uncle thought Brooke had ended things, but I did. It was the hardest thing I ever did, and probably the biggest mistake I ever made."

Cole took the lamb and frowned. "Why did you then?"

Lilly sighed. This time, she did put her arm around Cole, who didn't flinch much. "I was hurt. Devastated by something bad that had happened. And I thought he'd be better off without me."

Cole felt the soft fur on the lamb. "Why?"

Lilly didn't answer. "Because I was young, and stupid and just heartbroken."

Cole handed the lamb back to Lilly. "I don't understand."

Lilly hugged the small stuffed animal, holding it like a little baby. "Sometimes, neither do I."

She handed Cole the lamb again got up to put the box back into place. Just as she was positioning it just right, her phone buzzed. She pulled it out, read the text, and smiled.

"Who is that?" Cole asked.

Lilly reread the text, then sent back a quick reply. "It was your Aunt. She's hanging out with... a friend tonight. She'll be back late, so she'll see you in the morning. I think she and Drew got into a fight, so that's why he's probably avoiding the house, in case she comes home."

Aunt Ashley was always yelling at Uncle Drew. Sometimes, it was for fun, but other times she got mean. She always seemed to get angry, and when Uncle Drew apologized and walked away, she got sad.

"But she's okay? She's not missing? You're not lying?"

Lilly shook her head. "No sweetie, she's perfectly safe where she is." She sat back down and began to smooth the back of his hair. "Do you worry about that a lot? That something bad will happen to Aunt Ashley? Or Uncle Drew?"

Cole shrugged, his eyes on the lamb, his hand rubbing its fur. "And you. Bad things happen."

"I know," Lilly said. "You know the men who killed your mom are gone. They can't hurt you."

Without looking up, Cole nodded and pressed the stuffed lamb to his chin. He shifted away from Lilly so she wouldn't see his tears. "It's not them I'm worried about."

****

"What's with the goofy grin, Miller?"

Ashley had just reentered the room from the kitchen where she'd poured herself and Ollie a glass of wine. She hadn't bothered to get dressed, and was completely at ease with her own nudity in front of Ollie, who was enjoying the view.

"I finally got to kiss Ashley Duncan." Ollie had covered himself with a sheet, still bashful about her seeing him with nothing on.

She handed him his glass. "You got to do more than that, or don't you remember?"

Ollie grinned as he took a sip of wine. Shower sex with Ashley Duncan was not something he was likely to ever forget. Neither would he forget their more traditional, but at least in his mind, equally amazing repeat performance in his bed.

His bed.

Ashley Duncan was in his bed.

With him.

Wow.

"Your grin is getting goofier by the moment," Ashley said as she snuggled with him.

"I just can't believe that after all these years that I'm getting a shot at being with you."

Ashley kissed him. "You make it sound like you're the lucky one being stuck with me."

Ollie put his wine down, and turned to Ashley. "There is no place I'd rather be. Being here, with you? It's everything."

Ashley hid her face behind her wine glass. "Stop saying that."

"Why?" Ollie put his arm around her. "Ashley, it's true."

She stiffened at his touch. "Stop. I'm not the angel you seem to think I am. You're such a good man. You're decent, and kind, and patient and all the things I'm not."

She stood up, and grabbed his shirt to cover up. Frowning, she took her wine and stalked across the room to stare out the window. "You don't know the ugliness I came from. You say you know me, but you don't. Not really. I hid that from you for a long time. Every once in a while, I'd slip. Just a small detail, but I never wanted you to really see it."

Ollie slipped out of bed, pulled on a pair of boxers for modesty's sake and joined her. "Do you really think that I'd think less of you? Because of what that bastard of a father did to you?"

Ashley put her glass on a nearby shelf in front of a small replica of Dr. Who's Tardis, and turned to face him. "No. You would have been kind and decent, but you would know. And how could you ever look at me the same way again."

Ollie placed his hands on her cheeks. "I will always look at you as the strongest, bravest, fiercest person I know. The most beautiful girl. The woman who I want to spend the rest of my life with. Nothing could ever change that."

Shaking her head, she turned away. "You don't understand. You can't. You weren't there. You didn't live it. I wet myself." She stared back into his eyes which were filled with tears. "Drew would lock me and Kelli in the closet. We heard him scream for hours as Dad burned him with his cigarette. Drew could have ended it by just calling our names. I wanted to yell out where we were, but Kelli was shaking, terrified. So, I stayed quiet as my brother shrieked. And when Drew came to let us out, six hours later, I'd wet myself. I was a fithly, cowardly little girl who let her brother get tortured. It wasn't the first time that happened. It wouldn't be the last."

Ollie trembled with rage, but his voice stayed calm. "I'm so sorry. So sorry for what you all went through. But you survived, and I'm never going to let anyone hurt you like that again."

Ashley wiped away her tears. "So kind. So sweet. You watched me hook up with how many guys. None of them looked at me the same way you do. I know men don't look at me and see the woman they'd want to marry. The woman who they'd want to raise their children, but you at least looked at me as someone who could make a decent mother."

"Stop it," Ollie demanded. "You are exactly the woman I want to be my wife. The kind of woman I would want as a mother to my children. You know, old habits are hard to break. It's not easy for me to tell you this. I thought I'd work up to it, take you on a date or two first, but the hell with it. Every time I've ever imagined getting married, it was to you. Every time I've ever dreamed about raising a family, it's been with you. If I thought you'd say yes, I'd get down on my knees and beg you to marry me. Say the word, and we can fly to Vegas right now."

Ashley's mouth dropped open as she took a step back.

Ollie winced. "Too much too soon."

She covered her mouth and managed a nod. Once again, she turned away. "You don't get it yet. You just can't."

Ollie put his hands on her shoulders and turned her to him. She placed her head on his chest.

"I know I can't possibly understand what it is you've been through, but there is nothing you could say or do that could make me love you less."

Ashley found herself holding her breath as she stepped back and turned towards the wall. "You told me you were twelve when you fell in love with me. Is that true?"

"Every word." Ollie once again placed his arms around her. "I had some crazy idea of telling you. I wrote you a note, pouring my idiot heart out to you. I never had the courage to give it to you."

Ashley smiled. "I wish I could have read it."

Ollie kissed her head, then moved her glass of wine. He picked up the tiny blue British police box every Dr. Who fan knew as the Tardis and pulled off the top. With two fingers, he pulled out a small, yellowed piece of loose-leaf that was neatly folded into a tiny square.

"Better late than never." Ollie handed it to her.

With wide eyes and trembling hands, Ashley unfolded the decade old note and read.

Dear Ashley,

If I give you this note, you'll probably hate me, which is why I'll probably chicken out. What I really want to say is I ~~love~~ like you. I'm sorry if that bothers you. Please still be my friend.

Ollie

She read it three times before folding it up carefully. "I can't believe you kept this."

Ollie shrugged. "I think part of me wanted to believe someday I'd have the courage to give it to you."

She tried to hand it back to him, but he refused. "It's yours now. That's what it was meant to be."

Ashley held the note tightly in her fingers. "Can I tell you about something that happened to me when I was twelve?" She paused as she placed the note down.

"Drew was out hanging with friends. Kelli was hiding in our room, in case dad came home. I was hungry, so I decided to make something to eat. I tried scrambling eggs, but they burnt." She gave a half smile. "Dad came bursting in. Threw the pan in the sink and knocked me to the ground. I tried to get up, but he back handed me. I was flat on my back, when he leaned over me. Told me how it's a crime that I couldn't make eggs, because that meant he would be stuck with me since no man would take me. He figured Kelli would be a nice little punching bag for some asshole." She scowled. "Guess he was right there. Drew would leave, and he'd be stuck with me unless I could find a man to put up with me. And the only way I'd ever do that is if I learned to fuck."

She closed her eyes as she continued. "I can still smell the cheap beer on his breath, the smell of cigarettes on his clothes. He held me by the throat, and I couldn't breathe as his bloodshot eyes looked me up and down. I swear to God, I thought he was going to rape me. He probably would have if Drew hadn't come home. Drew kicked at him, and Dad broke his arm."

"Oh no," Ollie said. "Oh baby. I'm sorry. I never knew."

Ashley nodded in his chest. "Now you do. That wasn't the only horrible thing he did. He was always vulgar. Always saying things like that, but that was the one time I really thought he'd do *that*." She let him pull her into his arms. "I'm sorry, but this is what you're getting with me. I'm broken."

"No, you're not." Ollie kissed the top of her head.

"You need to see me for what I am."

"I do," Ollie said. "I know you're not perfect. I know you have a past. I love you. That's never going to change. And if you're broken, then I'll break myself to fit."

****

Jericho sat and watched the apartment all night. He'd already reported back that there was no chance to pin the bodies on Drew Duncan. That much was sure. They needed to give them a viable suspect. Someone that made at least a little bit of sense. Someone who people would believe was capable of something so 'monstrous'.

Jericho himself didn't find the murders monstrous as all. More amateurish than outrageous. Still, there was promise. He assumed that the real killer had come a long way in perfecting his hobby. Still, his early work showed talent.

Jericho was intrigued by the small amount of interactions he'd been able to observe between Cole and his new family. Clearly, they loved him, but did they *know* him?

Jericho hadn't learned much tonight. It was interesting, the way the Duncan girl interacted with that wimp Corvidae, before she came running to Miller and finally screwed his brains out. Interesting, but not relevant. He'd been tempted to call it a night when it was clear that the Duncan girl, having finally tired of crying and fucking, had gone to sleep, but he stayed. Professionally, there was little reason to justify that. There was nothing more to be learned, but he needed to understand these people that would raise Cole Duncan. It mattered, although Jericho didn't know why.

So, he waited all night.

As expected, the morning was more of a rush for the new lovers. There wasn't time for either to engage in a little morning nookie, which was disappointing. There was laughter, sounds of kissing, and an offer of breakfast by Miller, politely declined. She wanted to see Cole before school.

Jericho was taking a chance by staying to watch, but he was certain that a moment would occur that he needed to witness, and Jericho liked taking chances.

As he'd hoped, both Miller and the Duncan girl came out at the same time. Miller, ever the pussy, walked the Duncan girl to her car, getting in as many kisses as possible. He saw the grin she gave him before she pulled out from her spot and drove away, under the golden hue of the sun just breaking the surface of the sky.

Jericho watched Miller. He wore a stupid, love struck expression that remained glued to his face long after the Duncan girl was gone, confirming what Jericho already knew.

Miller was completely in love, something that Jericho couldn't comprehend. He could understand the satisfaction in finally nailing her. Ashley Duncan was a pain in the ass on good day, and a real bitch when she's pissed, but there was no denying she looked like a good lay.

Perhaps, one day, Jericho would take off the disguise and show her his true face and find out for himself. It would be an indulgence, but a hardworking man like himself deserved one now and again.

For now, however, Jericho needed to proceed with the mission. It was time to deliver someone else to the Ember Falls PD. Watching Oliver Miller come back out of his apartment and climbing into his car, Jericho knew just who that person should be. It would take some time to set in motion, but Jericho knew exactly what his next move would be.

Chapter 11
Scout's Honor

Ollie felt as if he'd floated into the station. There was a part of him that wanted to tell every person he saw that he and Ashley were together. They were… *something* at least. They certainly weren't just friends. Not after last night. Of course, they hadn't gone out on a date yet.

That was something he'd have to remedy. He wanted to take Ashley out on a real date. She deserved have him ask her out. He wanted to pick her up, bring her flowers. The trappings were important. She deserved them, and so much more.

"What are you grinning about, Miller?"

Ollie jumped at the sound of Polansky's voice. "Nothing." Gentlemen do not kiss and tell. "What's going on?"

Polansky scowled. At least Ollie was pretty sure it was a scowl. It was sometimes hard to tell with the cantankerous desk sergeant.

"The Chief has visitors," Polansky said. "Said to get you and Duncan. Where is he?"

"Right here." Drew came down the hallway. They each followed Polansky to the chief's office. As they walked, Drew leaned closer to Ollie. "Ashley didn't talk to me this morning, but she seemed calmer. Even happy. I don't know what you did, but thank you."

Ollie stopped, gulped and looked away. "Um... yeah. My um... pleasure?" He felt as if his face was on fire.

For a brief moment, Drew furrowed his brow in confusion, studying his partner's reddening face.

Ollie could see the moment understanding set in. He prepared himself to be punched, but was saved when Polansky knocked on the chief's door.

"Come."

Polansky swung the door open, and all color drained out of Drew's face.

* * * *

Sitting in a chair opposite the chief was a forlorn woman. Her wrinkled eyes were hidden behind glasses and her grim face bore the resemblance of someone who had lost all that was precious to them.

Behind her, stood a young man. He wore a sweatshirt from a nearby college, and he kept a protective hand on the woman's shoulder. His grim eyes watched Drew warily.

Drew did his best to ignore the sick sensation that threatened to overwhelm him. His chest ached from weight of guilt and the twisting in his gut. His heartbeat thundered in his chest as the door closed behind him, sounding in his mind like the slamming of a prison cage.

Also present was Ian Corvidae, who instantly offered his hand to Drew before he resumed his place near the college age boy.

Drew's eyes remained fixed on the woman and her son. "Mrs. Winters, I'm so sorry for everything your family has gone through. I'm sure you'd prefer I leave."

Before Drew could move, Chief Miller beckoned

him to stay. "Actually, Helen Winters and her son Sean came here to talk to you for a few reasons. First off, have either of you been in contact with Darren Winters since he left here?"

She indicated the chair in front of her desk, opposite Helen Winters.

Drew slowly sat, hyperaware of how close he was to Mrs. Winters. "I haven't seen him since yesterday."

Ollie stepped forward. "He assaulted Ashley Duncan at a bar last night. She doesn't want to file charges, but I think she should."

Drew's eyes snapped up. "What? Is she—?"

"She's fine," Ollie assured him

"You didn't know?" Ann asked. "About the altercation at Clancy's?"

Drew shook his head. "No ma'am. I was home, alone. I stopped over at the house while Ashley was out, to see Cole. I wasn't aware this happened."

"Helen," Corvidae said. "I'm sure Darren will show up. You told me yourself, this isn't the only time he disappeared."

Helen nodded. "Normally, I'd agree with you about my ex-husband, but this feels different. Darren was determined to finally get justice for Molly."

Ann leaned forward. "I assure you, we will do everything in our ability to do that."

Corvidae frowned. "I doubt Mr. Duncan had anything to do with Darren's disappearance."

Helen glanced towards Drew. "I remember you from when you dated my daughter. You were nicer to me than she was at times."

Drew's mouth was too dry to speak, so Helen continued.

"When I got to the hotel this morning, he was nowhere to be found. Detective Corvidae told me he took a cab back to the Hotel, but he wasn't there. His bed hadn't been slept in. I don't think he made it there. Even when we were married and the children were young, Darren always left his socks on the floor. There were no socks."

Ann turned to her son. "Detective Miller will look into it. We'll find him."

Helen fidgeted with a tissue that she held. "While I was there, at the hotel, I was approached by a man. A rather—" her lip curled, "rude and distasteful man. He called himself a reporter. His name was Jack Caesar."

Ollie hissed out a breath. "Ashley was accosted by him as well."

Corvidae nodded. "I was going to talk to you about that. He really upset her, and recorded her without her permission. I uh…" He glanced sheepishly towards the chief. "I took the liberty of relieving him of his recorder, saying it could be considered evidence."

Corvidae retrieved the small device from his shirt pocket, and placed it on the chief's desk.

"Caesar is a real piece of work," Polansky said as he snatched the device. "He works on stupid pieces. Aliens abduct baby, Bigfoot gets married. My favorite was how pigs were going to take over the world. Real Pulitzer Prize stuff. He stopped reporting some years ago, after he tried to do a hard news piece about a college kid getting raped. He did his version of an investigation and found someone who met the description. Printed his name and picture." Polansky shrugged. "Too bad the the kid he named was innocent and had a rock-solid alibi. The victim even insisted it wasn't him, but the damage was done. By the time they cleared it up, the kid got his ass kicked by someone for it, and was expelled from school. Broken bones, internal injuries. He was lucky to survive and is suing to get back into college. Caesar went dark after that, but I guess he's trying for a comeback."

Helen tore the tissue in half. "I'm well aware of Mr. Caesar's *credentials*. My son Sean was able to dig up quite a lot on his phone. Nevertheless, he said he's gotten wind of a name that he thinks is responsible for Molly's death. He said the man's name was Duncan."

Drew swallowed hard, and his eyes darted to Ann expecting to see her coming at him with her cuffs. "Mrs. Winters, please believe me I would never—"

Helen held up her hand. "Not you. Frank Duncan."

All color drained from Drew's face. He opened his mouth to respond, but nothing came out. He glanced toward Ollie, who also didn't know what to say.

Helen sat forward. "The Chief was telling us that she had complete confidence that you were innocent, and hoped to be able to conclusively prove that now."

Ann nodded. "We recovered DNA." She chose her words carefully, making sure to not say where they'd recovered it from. "I just got the report this morning."

Ann handed a file to Drew, which he opened to read. They had the identity of the last of the female victims. Cindy Wellington had disappeared a week before the dance where Molly had been taken. Moreover, she had been raped, and DNA had been left behind.

Corvidae stepped forward. "Are we positive? Could it be a mistake?"

Polansky bristled. "We may not be a big

department, but we know what we're doing. We have a pretty good idea it's from the killer."

Corvidae considered. "Have we found Frank Duncan?"

Chief Miller shook her head. "Until now, we were trying to look for him unofficially, more in connection with another matter, however this changes things."

"Mr. Duncan," Helen said, then she reached out to take his hand. "Drew. I know that you were treated unfairly, and it must seem like we're just out to get your family. I had a hard time believing you were guilty in Molly's case. I wish you would have agreed to meet me—"

"When did you ask to meet with me?" Drew asked.

Sean Winters stepped forward. "When you were in prison. Mom went to see you. You refused."

"I was never told." Drew was stunned. "I would have spoken with you. I would have wanted to tell you how sorry I was, but try to convince you I had nothing to do with it. I was desperate to tell that to anyone. I would have begged you to believe me." He wanted to beg her now.

Tears appeared in Helen's eyes as she squeezed his hand.

Sean knelt down by his mother's side, but addressed Drew. "The point is, you can help. If your father's DNA is on Molly, your DNA can verify it. We'll know if it was a partial match."

"Hold on," Corvidae said. "Mr. Duncan was already jailed for this crime with scant evidence. You're asking him to expose himself again. Without a court order—"

"I'll do it." Drew stood up and handed the file back

to Ann.

Sean blinked in surprise. "You're sure? I mean…" He glanced down at his mother who had put her hand over his. "I'm very grateful, but I understand what I'm asking. You could be implicating your own father."

Drew sighed. "I'm not going to lie. I'm not convinced my father is the person responsible for Molly's death. I can't say why without compromising another investigation, but none of those doubts have to do with any loyalty to him. If he's responsible, I will do everything I can to make him pay. I give you my word."

Sean offered his hand to Drew, who took it. "I remember when you came around a few times to pick Molly up. You were always cool to me. You let me sit in your car, even offered to show me how to drive."

Drew nodded. "I'm sorry I wasn't able to keep that promise."

Sean managed a small smile. "My mother taught me." His smile faded. "I hated you for a long time. Even today when you walked in, I had an urge to punch you in the face. It's hard to let go of that. I'm trying."

If it would help, Drew would let him.

"You're going to turn twenty-one soon, if I recall." Drew pulled a pair of cards out from his wallet and handed one to each of them. "That has my personal cell number on it. If either of you ever need anything, or just want to talk to me, please don't hesitate to call, night or day. Sean, I'd like the chance to take you out for your first beer if you're interested, after your birthday."

Helen stood up and placed the card in her purse. "You mean his first legal beer, of course." She smiled at her son who blushed. "I'm a mother. I know you're not an angel, but you're a good son, and a kind man."

She turned to Drew, and pulled him into a hug. "I'm very sorry for everything you've gone through. Thank you."

Drew returned the embrace, feeling lighter inside, if only by a little. If Molly's mother believed he was innocent, could others?

Ann pressed a button on her phone before offering her hand to both of the Winters. "My office will be in touch. And we'll do whatever we can to find Darren Winters."

The door opened and Sam came in.

"Office Rossi will show you out," Chief Miller said.

Sam offered Drew a nod of acknowledgement before she departed with the Winters.

Everyone waited a few moments until they were sure the Winters were out of earshot. Corvidae turned to the chief. "I'm confused. Not to put too fine of a point on it, but isn't it possible that Mr. Duncan's DNA might be in Molly Winters? They were dating, and I was under the impression that they had been intimate."

Drew ignored him, and instead addressed the chief. "You do realize that while this will help clear my name, it's probably not going to get us any closer to the real killer."

"Why not?" Corvidae asked. "Are you saying you don't believe your father is capable of doing these things, because from what little I've heard...? Well."

Drew held up his hand to stop Corvidae from talking. "Let me be clear, I have no problem whatsoever believing my father would be *capable* of raping and murdering an innocent girl, but there's more to this case than you realize."

Corvidae waited, hoping for more. "Such as?" Nobody answered. "Look, I get you want to keep this in house, and that I'm an outsider, but I'm here. I want to help."

Ann glanced around the room.

Polansky just shrugged. "It's your house."

Ollie stepped forward. "Ashley told me about how Detective Corvidae helped her out. Made it clear he didn't believe Drew was guilty."

Drew shrugged. "If Ashley thinks he's okay, I'm willing to trust him."

Ann sighed. "If we read you in, you have to give me your word that you don't report anything to the Governor's Office until I say so. We have our reasons, and it's not political."

Corvidae held his hand up, his three middle fingers up, while his thumb held down his pinky. "Scouts honor."

Polansky snorted. "Were you even a Boy Scout?"

Corvidae smiled brightly. "Absolutely. And I've got the merit badges to prove it. My favorite is the one I got when I was twelve in Ornithology. Did you know my name is a type of bird?"

Polansky rolled his eye. "The only bird I know about is the one on my middle finger."

Drew smiled, but when Ann gave him the nod, he became all business. "The murder of Molly Winters is connected to my sister Kelli's case. You're aware of the fact that two cops from this house were responsible, and that a third person, my sister's counselor, was arrested, but died at the court house."

Corvidae nodded. "Yes. I was under the impression that her death was under investigation. I guessed it might have been suicide. Not uncommon."

Drew shook his head and motioned for Corvidae to sit. "She was murdered. And we believe it was a hired hit."

With wide eyes, Corvidae took the offered seat and began to listen.

Chapter 12
Let's Chat

With magical memories of the spending the last three nights in Ollie's arms fueling her, Ashley raced through her day with a smile on her face and a sense of contentment that seemed foreign to her. It was unreal, like clothing that just didn't fit. What did feel natural was the realization that Ashley was running late as usual. She moved through the store at top speed, ever grateful for the fact that Marie's Deli had more than just cold cuts. Sam's Nana was coming over tonight to watch Cole while she and Lilly went to that self-defense class given by Ollie and Sam. She'd been waiting for this. The chance to beat up Drew.

Afterwards, she and Lilly planned to go out with Drew's fiancé Sam for a 'Girls Night' where they could drink, dance, and talk men. Ashley had plenty to talk about. These days, she went from deliriously happy girl ready to do cartwheels from being in Ollie's bed every night, to snarling bitch ready to gouge Drew's eyes out whenever she came close to forgiving him. And she was so proud of Cole who was loving going to school. Ashley was making Sybil look well adjusted.

Ashley carried her bags out to the small parking lot. She hadn't lied when she said it was nice having her brother back, but she knew she was pushing him to leave again. Could she ever forgive him?

Frank Duncan came out of the shadows, smoking a cigarette and reeking of whiskey.

Ashley was transported back to when she was an eight-year-old girl seeing her brother unconscious on the floor, and her father squeezing her throat and telling her about the vile things he should do to her.

"Go away Dad, or I'll scream."

Frank flicked away the cigarette, blew out smoke, and shook his head. "We need to have a conversation."

Ashley shook her head as she backed away. "No, you need to get the fuck away from me."

Her father was older now, but he was still fast as he closed the distance between them. Dropping the bags, Ashley was slammed against a nearby wall, her father's hand closing on her throat. "You're gonna listen, or I'm going to do what I shoulda done years ago."

With her heart pounding in her chest, Ashley lost her voice. Frank took that as her agreeing to listen.

"You need to tell your brother to get out of town, or he ain't gonna like what happens." His breath reeked, and his eyes were wide and desperate. "He and I had a deal. He needs to keep up his end of the bargain."

Ashley wanted to scream, but all she managed was a whisper. "What deal?"

Frank pointed a finger in her face. "You don't worry about that. He'll know. And he needs to believe I'll keep my end of the deal. He *knows* I will."

Ashley wanted to fight, but what could a little girl do against such a big man. He was huge, and she was just a sixteen-year-old girl on her way out to a party. A twelve-year-old, just home from a dance. A seven-year-old girl who had just lost her mother.

Ollie's voice echoed in her mind, like a ray of light in the dead of night. *I will always look at you as the strongest, bravest, fiercest person I know.*

Ashley found her voice, just as her knee found his groin. "Get *away*!"

Taken by surprise, Frank released her. Ashley smashed her fist into his throat and scrambled for her car, leaping over the bags from Marie's. She heard him coming for her as she used her key fob to unlock the doors and jump in the driver's seat. She hit lock just as her father reached her, smacking the window. She refused to make eye contact as she started the engine and quickly pulled away, screaming as she tore down the road.

****

Drew paced back and forth in the small office outside the police gym, nearly tripping as he did. He hated being in all of this padding, and was ready to rip it off. It wasn't the fact that it was uncomfortable, which it was, or that it didn't make him look an actor playing an alien in a really low budget B movie, which it did. It was because the self-defense class had just started and Ashley was nowhere to be found.

Ollie was worried too. They had both tried calling her, but she would only text Ollie back saying she'd be there. So, where was she?

As if he weren't upset enough over that, Sam was here to help Ollie. Drew wanted to get down on his knees and beg her to forgive him. He should talk to her. Tell her what she wanted to hear.

Drew winced as he pictured the look of revulsion in her eyes.

No, Sam wouldn't do that. Trust her.

As if she'd heard his thoughts, Sam entered the small room.

"Sam, can we please talk."

Dressed in her dark blue, Ember PD police issue sweatpants, Sam seemed taken aback. "Drew, now's not the time. We need you out there."

Drew scowled through the mask. "Has anyone heard from Ashley? I wanted to text her again, but I can't in this stupid outfit."

Sam gave him a small grin. "I think you look cute. And Ashley's here."

Relief surged through Drew. At least his sister was safe. "Sam…"

She put her hand on his arm, which he couldn't feel through the padding. "Not now. I promise, we'll talk. I'm going out with your sister and Lilly tonight. I'll call you tomorrow. Okay?"

It wasn't okay, but it clearly the best he could hope for, so he nodded and followed her into the gym.

Ollie was front and center, talking about how the best thing to do was avoid conflict, but in the end, it may come down to defending yourself. He directed everyone to the center of the mat, where Drew was made to attack Sam, only to have her repel the assault.

After knocking Drew to the ground half-a-dozen times, she jutted her chin towards him. "Don't try and take it easy on me, Duncan, I can handle anything you can throw at me."

Drew came at her from behind, getting her in a headlock. "I'm not," he whispered in her ear. "You're good, and Cole could probably kick my ass while I'm in this getup."

Sam jabbed her elbow into his gut, stepped back

and sent Drew flying over her shoulder. He hit the pad with a thump hard enough to earn a round of, 'oohs' from the class. Offering him a hand, she pulled him up. "That's not what I was talking about you moron."

Drew knew exactly what she was talking about, but it didn't matter. He should probably let her go. He was too damaged to be good for her.

After being battered about by Sam for several more minutes, the women in the class were asked to come up, one by one. Both Sam and Ollie guided each woman through the self-defense movement. Some of the students seemed hesitant, almost apologetic. Others thought it was fun, and laughed as they punched at Drew. Drew decided that he probably didn't need the padding to protect him from half of them, but he was grateful that his face was hidden. They probably would either hit harder if they knew who he was, or maybe just run from the room.

Lilly was the most surprising. She smiled sweetly at Drew, before using her small frame to flip Drew and flatten him. Out of all the students so far, she was the one who could handle herself the best.

Ashley was the last to come up.

She seemed reluctant to approach, which surprised Drew. He had assumed she was looking forward to clobbering him, but she was hesitant, almost distracted.

"Ash, is everything okay?"

Ashley didn't respond, she just listened as Ollie explained things one last time. She avoided eye contact with Drew and seemed exhausted. At Ollie's direction, Drew grabbed Ashley from behind. She struggled, wiggling about halfheartedly, until she heard her brother's voice. "C'mon Ash. I know you want to hit me."

Ashley slammed her fist full force into Drew's face. "You fucking bastard!" She kept relentlessly pounding at him, her face turning red, as she cursed. Her swings were wild and savage, her screams drowning into sobs as she attacked.

Drew made no attempt to stop Ashley as she continued to pummel him. The assault ended only when Ollie pulled her away.

"Ashley, calm down."

"Fuck that." Ashley pulled away from him. She jabbed a finger towards her brother as he pulled off the helmet and dropped it to the floor. "Fuck you."

Drew ignored the gasps and whispers as the class recognized him.

Turning on her heel, she stalked away.

"Ashley," Drew called.

He started to follow, but Ollie shook his head. "Let me. Something's wrong."

Drew watched him go after his sister, while Sam tried to dismiss the class. The students were buzzing about Ashley's explosion, pointing at Drew, and deciding they knew what happened.

Disgusted with everything, mostly himself, Drew went in the back office alone.

****

"Ashley, hold up."

Ashley paused as she approached her own car in the parking lot, but she didn't turn to face Ollie behind her. "I'm sorry I ruined your class, but I can't stand the fucking sight of him."

Ollie moved in front of her. "Why? What happened?"

Ashley scowled. "Why don't you ask Drew?"

"I'm asking you." Ollie placed his hands on her shoulders. "Talk to me."

Ashley closed her eyes, trying to calm down. Breathing heavily, she fought against the tidal wave of tears threatening to come. "He can't come back into my life and just expect me to forgive him. I can't…" Her breath hitched. "I *won't* forgive him."

Ollie gently pulled her into his arms. "I know you're twisted up, but you need to talk to him. He's torn up over leaving, but he thought he was doing the right thing, and—"

Ashley shoved Ollie away. The boiling rage did a good job of melting the grief that had threatened to overcome her moments ago. "You're taking his side? You fucking bastard!"

"Ashley," Ollie tried to step closer, but she backed away. "I'm always on your side."

"Bullshit." Ashley walked around him, heading to her car. "I should have known, now that you and Drew are buddies, you take his fucking side. Just like all men, you can't believe in them. Pieces of shit, each and every—"

Ollie put his hands on her arms. "You need to stop."

Ashley pulled free. "What the hell?"

"All men aren't pieces of shit," Ollie yelled.

"Don't tell me what I need to do," Ashley yelled as she fumbled with her keys. "You're just like all—"

"Just like what?" Ollie got in her face. "Just like all men? Like your brother? Like *Cole*? You're raising a little boy Ashley. You can't keep bashing men like that. We're not all your father."

Ashley gasped. "I can't believe you just said that."

Ollie tried to move closer. "You know how I feel about you."

Shaking her head, Ashley got into her car. "I know what you told me, but I never believed it. I should have known, I can't count on anyone, but myself."

Before Ollie could say another word, Ashley got in her car, slammed the door shut, and drove away.

****

Drew noticed the black car in front of the house as he pulled into the driveway and knew what it meant. Surprise inspection time.

As he approached the front door, he heard raised voices. One male, one female. This couldn't be good.

He opened the door to see two of his favorite people going at each other as if they were political talking heads. Sam's Nana, Rose Howard, was locked in verbal combat with General Paul McAlister, the man who gave him a home and a purpose after he left the marines. The General had been more of a father to him in the few years he'd known him than his biological father, who had been in Drew's entire life.

Rose threw her hands up in the air. "Don't give me that. We're lucky we got out of the eighties without all of us glowing in the dark."

The General sighed as he stood. "Hit me."

Rose's eyes widened. "Excuse me? Why would I do that? I'm not a violent person."

The General grinned. "Normally neither am I, although I can be, but that's beside the point. Go ahead, take a swing."

Rose stood as well, but made no move to attack. "What's that prove? You're bigger and stronger, does that make you right?"

"Yes," the General said. "People don't attack a target that will attack back. They attack where they see weakness. So best not to show any."

Rose hmphed. "Please. There's something to be said about being vulnerable."

"In a relationship, sure." The General shrugged. "Not for a country, or a military."

Just as it looked like they were going to continue, Drew cleared his throat. "All of this is fascinating, but should we really be having this *'discussion'* in front of an eight-year-old?"

Cole sat at the table, his head down and eyes closed.

Rose snickered. "He's out. He came down from his room to referee."

Drew shook his head. "When did you get in?"

The General glanced at his watch. "About nineteen hundred hours. I was told you were getting your ass kicked for jollies. How'd that go?"

Drew scowled. "Not well, but something tells me you already knew that."

Rose smiled. "Sam called. She was supposed to come back here, give me a lift home before she went for drinks with your sister and Lilly. My car wouldn't start, so she had to drive me here, but after whatever happened, Ashley asked for them to meet her at the bar right away."

Drew let out a breath. "Ash is okay?"

Rose nodded. "Upset, but otherwise fine. You want to talk about what happened?"

Drew collapsed in the seat next to Cole. The kid was out, but he looked so peaceful sleeping, Drew hated to move him. With a sigh, he shook his head. "Not really. Ash has a right to be angry with me."

The General scowled. "You're being a doormat. You need to talk to her."

Drew gently stroked Cole's hair. "I don't think I have anything to say that she wants to hear." He glanced to Rose. "Let me take Cole upstairs and put him in bed, then I can take you home."

The General held his hand up. "At ease marine. I can take her."

"You?" Rose raised an eyebrow. "Are you planning on listening to talk radio the whole way there?"

The General grabbed her jacket off the back of the couch. "I prefer Sinatra."

Rose pulled her arm back, and threw a roundhouse punch at the General, who gracefully stepped aside. When Rose lost her balance and started to fall, he caught her in his arms effortlessly. "Not a bad punch for a pacifist, but you advertised it by planting your foot and pulling your arm back." He raised her back to her feet, handed her jacket to her, and grinned.

"Next time, I'll hit you from behind."

The General opened the door for her. "I'll look forward it. We can revisit your thoughts on America policing the planet. Ever hear of this little dust up called World War Two?"

Rose's retort was cut off as the door closed.

Grinning, Drew got up and gently lifted Cole, using the same care he would if he were moving an IED. The kid was light. Too light. He'd filled out a little in the last few weeks now that he was in a home where there was always food, but he was still tiny for his age.

Slowly, he walked upstairs and down the hall to Cole's bedroom. Gently, he placed the boy down on his bed.

Cole's eyes shot open, and he screamed. "*No!*" His fist smashed into Drew's face as his legs kicked. His breathing became heavy and labored as he curled into a ball.

Drew stood with his hands up, wanting to hold Cole, but afraid to touch him. "Cole, it's okay. You're safe. Nobody's going to hurt you."

Shaking, Cole managed to look up. Drew waited until Cole controlled his breathing. He could see the panic replaced with mortification in the child's eyes as he continued to sob.

"Go away," Cole said with trembling lips.

Drew wasn't quite sure what to do, but he knew leaving was not an option. He grabbed a nearby chair to sit, so he wasn't towering over his nephew. He leaned down, attempting to make his body as small as possible. "I'm not leaving. It's okay Cole. You're safe."

Cole hid his face, but his eyes watched Drew. "I didn't do anything."

"Of course, you didn't," Drew assured him, keeping his voice soft and gentle. "I'm sorry I startled you. I was just putting you to bed, but you didn't do anything wrong. In fact," Drew rubbed his chin. "You've got one hell of a right hook."

Cole's eye's widened. "You're not mad?"

"Not at you buddy," Drew said. "I swear, I'm not angry with you. I'm very angry at your stepfather. He's the reason you're scared right now, isn't he?"

Cole's eyes darted around, as if he expected Edward Hunter to jump out of the closet.

"He can't hurt you," Drew said. "I promise, he can't get near you."

Cole shook his head. "You're going to leave. He'll wait until you're gone, and he'll come."

Drew moved off the chair and knelt by the bed. The motion made Cole jump and scamper away. "I'm not going anywhere. Cole, I'm never leaving you."

"Aunt Ash says you're going to leave." Cole wouldn't look at Drew. "Now that you messed things up with Sam, you're going to leave."

Drew gripped the edge of the sheet on Cole's bed. "I'm *not* leaving. I haven't given up on my relationship with Sam, but even if that's over, I'm not going anywhere. I'm never leaving you."

Finally, Cole looked at Drew. "You promise? You swear you won't leave them?"

Drew began to swear, when Cole's words registered. "Leave *them*?"

Cole swallowed. "Aunt Ash and Lilly. I don't want him to hurt them."

It took every ounce of self-restraint for Drew not to stand up and start tearing the room apart. "Is that what he said to you when he called? That he was going to hurt Aunt Ash and Lilly? Is that why you ran? To protect them?"

Tears came to Cole's eyes and his face turned red. He began to rock back and forth as he nodded. "I *can't* protect them. I *can't* fight him. I'm no good."

Unable to stop himself, Drew pulled Cole into his arms. "I won't let them get hurt Cole. I swear on my life, I won't let anything happen to any of you. I don't care if Aunt Ash curses at me every time she sees me. I will never leave her again. Please believe me."

Cole held on, nodding into Drew's chest.

Drew wasn't sure how long he stayed like that, holding his nephew as he wept, but it was the longest he'd ever been in physical contact with Cole. He held on until he felt Cole pull away.

"You're not going to tell them," Cole asked. "About me crying."

Drew grinned. "It'll be our secret, but Cole, there's no shame in crying."

Cole wiped his nose with his sleeve. "I'm not strong like you. I can't fight him."

Drew rubbed his chin again. "You're stronger than you think."

That earned a small snort from Cole. "Shit."

Drew messed his hair. A casual gesture, but the fact that Cole let Drew touch him was huge. "Cole, I'm not as strong as *you* think. Anyone can feel helpless. I don't think I ever felt as powerless as when Wilson and Harrington had you. Your mom, your aunt, and I, we grew up in a home where we never knew when the next hit was going to come, the next beating. I felt powerless to protect us back then, but the thing was, I *could* have ended it, if I had been smart enough and brave enough to find someone to tell. I never thought anyone would help. My dad was a cop. Not a good one, like Ollie and Sam. I knew the cops here wouldn't help, not then, but you have people you can talk to. People who you can trust. We're all here for you. And the more you tell, the better we can protect you."

Drew smoothed the hair on Cole's head. "Is there more you can tell me?"

Quickly, Cole shook his head. He looked out the window. "He just wants to make me scared. He won't come."

Drew frowned. Kid was lying, but it was more than they'd gotten out of him before. He didn't want to push. "Okay, but you know you can tell me anything. Or Aunt Ash or Lilly. Right."

Cole nodded.

"You ready for bed?" When Cole hesitated, Drew understood. "You want me to hang for a while? I'd offer to read you a story, but you probably read better than me."

Cole snorted. "I have my story." Cole reached over to his nightstand and grabbed a notebook. "Mrs. Hanley read a story that I started for Mrs. Collins. She offered me extra credit if I finished it. I worked on it last night, but it's probably no good."

Drew took the notebook. "I doubt that. Can I read it?"

Cole scowled. "You don't want to."

Drew spun around, put his feet up on the bed, and leaned back. "You better believe I do."

Cole nestled into the crook of Drew's arm. "Okay, but be honest."

"Always," Drew promised as he opened the notebook and began the story of Drake the astronaut. Within seconds, Drew was transported off the bed and into an alien world, complete with a monster who saw him as a pet. By the time he was finished, Cole had fallen asleep.

****

"Oh my God," Sam said. "You've got to let me use that. That story is priceless, especially for a cop!"

Ashley held up her beer in mock salute. "You got it. Ollie will hate me, but I think I accomplished that already."

Sam sighed as she reached for her beer. "Why would you say that?"

Ashley blew out a breath. "Because that's what I do. I fuck things up. I'm sure he's done with me for good."

Lilly took a sip of her club soda. "I doubt that. I don't think Ollie could ever stop loving you, even if he tried."

Ashley lifted her beer, but didn't drink. "Wait, you knew Ollie liked me too? Who else knew?"

Lilly and Sam exchanged glances.

Ashley put her beer down. "What?"

Lilly grinned. "It would be easier to tell you who didn't know. Which would be you, Dwight the handy man and *maybe* Cole?"

Sam shook her head. "No, Cole knows. He said something to Drew a while back."

Ashley scowled into her drink. "Well, shit."

They all laughed.

Finishing her beer, Ashley signaled for another round. "So, what about you. Why are you and my brother on the outs?"

Sam folded her arms. "Why do we have to talk about my issues with Drew, and not *your* issues with Drew?"

The server came, delivered two more beers and a club soda with lime. Ashley took a long pull on hers. "Because I'm buying this round. When you buy the next one, you can ask. I'll probably be too shit-faced to answer, but that's the chance you take."

Sam huffed. "I told you, there's something Drew isn't telling me. He's not lying. I know there's something about how he met Stephanie he doesn't want me to know."

Sam filled Lilly in on her own past, and what she did and didn't know about Stephanie and Drew. "I know I'm being silly. Drew loves me, and God I love him, but he admitted that there's something he doesn't want to tell me, and I just can't get past it."

Ashley leaned in, as if she was about to confess a big secret herself. "My brother loves you. I can see it in his eyes. I know it's killing him that you're on the outs, but I get why you're feeling that way. If I were you, I'd pin him down, and make him tell you."

Sam put her beer down and moved closer to Ashley. "I tried to talk to him, but he wouldn't budge."

Ashley gestured towards Sam with her beer. "If it's this important, you make him spill. You don't let my brother walk away again."

Lilly leaned into the circle. "Are you afraid that if Sam and Drew don't work it out, that he's going to leave town and you won't have your brother again?"

Ashley didn't answer, she just leaned back in her chair.

Sam picked her beer up. "You tell me that I should make him talk, but you won't try. Ashley, you need to talk to your brother about why he left."

Ashley shook her head, and pointed at both of them. "I said we're not talking about what happened tonight."

Lilly folded her arms. "Ash, I know how devastated you were when Drew left, and how scared you are that he's going to leave again, but you keep pushing at him, as if you're begging him to run."

Ashley didn't deny it. "Might as well get it over

with."

"He's not going," Sam said. "If I know anything at all, it's that Drew hates himself for leaving you. Even if you forgive him, he'll probably never forgive himself. He thought he was doing the right thing."

Ashley scoffed. "Bullshit. Why would he think that?"

Sam glanced away as she took a sip.

Ashley quickly leaned in again. "What has he told you?"

Sam shook her head. "No, you don't get off that easily. I gave my word that I wouldn't tell you, and you wouldn't believe it coming from me. You need to hear it from him."

Lilly smiled. "Seems to me, you both need a word or two with Drew. None of this is good for any of you, and it's certainly not good for Cole. He needs to know Drew is staying. If he's picking up on your fears, and you know how perceptive that little boy is, it's probably tearing him apart inside. If you won't talk to your brother for you, do it for Cole."

Ashley frowned, hearing Ollie's words in her head. She didn't want to hear how escaping from Ember Falls was more important to Drew than her, but maybe if he said it, she'd be able to forgive him. She downed the rest of her beer and stood up. "Fine then, let's go before my liquid courage wears off."

Sam rose up. "Really? Now? Are we too drunk?"

Ashley dug into her purse to settle the bill. "No, we're just drunk enough."

****

Drew saw the car lights, recognized the rumble from Lilly's car, and shut the TV. It didn't surprise him

237

that Lilly had ended up as the designated driver.

He'd just come down from Cole's room twenty minutes ago, having slipped out of the bed while the kid slept. Drew considered escaping through the back door, so he wouldn't have to face his sister, but she needed to be told that whatever problems they had, they needed to either work them out, or at least do a better job of keeping them from Cole.

Besides, maybe Sam would be with them, and even if she didn't want to talk, he just wanted to see her.

The door opened and Ashley was the first to enter, followed by Sam. Lilly came in and closed the door behind them. Drew expected his sister to tell him to leave, but instead, she folded her arms and sneered. "Okay big brother, time we had a little chat."

Great. It was an intervention.

Drew stood up. "While you're drunk?"

Ashley shook her head. "I'm not that drunk. Maybe too drunk to drive, but I know what I'm doing." She grabbed Sam's arm, pulled her forward. "She needs to know what secrets you're hiding."

Sam blinked. "Me? We were supposed to talk about you first."

Ashley waved a hand in Sam's face. "Shush."

Lilly stepped up. "Drew, both of them need to talk. They're buzzed, but not drunk."

Drew shook his head. "Great. Keep it down, I just got Cole to sleep, and—"

Ashley poked her finger into his chest. "Cole needs to know you're not going to leave him. He needs to know that this time you won't just disappear without a trace."

Drew felt his body tense. He tried to stay calm, to

keep his voice low so as not to scare Cole. "You're right, he's worried, because he hears you saying it over and over again. Dammit Ash, I swear I won't leave again. I'm sorry I left in the first place."

Ashley glared. "I don't believe you."

"I know that," Drew replied. "And I don't know how to convince you, but you *need* to believe me when I tell you I'm not going anywhere. If you can't believe it for yourself, believe it for Cole."

"Bullshit." Ashley stalked away.

"What do you want me to do?" Drew followed her. "Do you want me to swear on my life? Consider it done. Do you need me to get down on my hands and knees and beg you to forgive me for the worst mistake I've ever made?"

Ashley shoved Drew away. "I want to believe *in* you again! I want to know that the one person I always thought loved me isn't going to make another deal with Dad and then leave."

Drew felt as if the ground had fallen out beneath him. "What did you say?" He glanced at Sam and Lilly. Their puzzled expressions told him that this was something they didn't know about.

Ashley's face was red. "I saw Dad today. He had a message for you."

Drew's knees nearly buckled. "When? Where? Did he hurt you?"

Ashley didn't answer. "Don't change the subject by playing big brother."

"Dammit Ash, he's dangerous," Drew yelled, forgetting about the small boy upstairs. "I need to find him. What did he say?"

"He told me you and he struck some sort of deal."

Ashley accentuated each word with a jab of her finger. "*That's* why you left. All this time, I thought it was because you thought the whole town believed you killed Molly, but it was some sick, twisted agreement between you two. Now he says you better live up to your end of the deal, or else he—"

Drew grabbed her by the arms. "Did he hurt you? Did he put his hands on you?" His eyes found the small bruise on her neck. "Did Dad fucking do this to you?"

Ashley looked at him as if he were mad. "He's done far worse, and he's the one who limped away today."

"Oh God." Drew's voice was panicked, and he was beginning to tremble. "Where's Ollie?" Drew reached for his cell phone, nearly dropped it because his hands were shaking so badly.

Ashley rounded on him. "Leave Ollie out of it. What deal did you make?"

Drew wasn't listening, he kept trying to work his cell to call Ollie, until Ashley grabbed his phone away. "I need to get you protection. You can't go anywhere alone."

"Bullshit," Ashley said. "What are you playing at?"

Drew grabbed her again, desperation in his eyes. "I'm not playing. Dad is dangerous. You have to let me protect you."

Ashley tried to pull away. "Protect me? By leaving again? Is that what you're trying to tell me?"

"Goddammit Ashley." Drew back away, ran his hand over his head. He was like a caged animal. "Don't you get it? Don't you understand?"

Ashley held out her hands. "Understand what?"

Drew searched for a way out, a way to protect his

sister without going where he didn't want to go, but he was backed against the wall. He wouldn't lose another sister. "He told me if I came back home, if I had any contact with *anyone* in Ember Falls, I'd be sorry. He told me that he'd see to it that you and Kelli were found raped and murdered. He promised me as long as I stayed away, you'd be safe, but if I ever tried to clear my name, you'd both pay for it with your lives."

Ashley shook her head, and her eyes were glassy. "No, Dad was a monster, but he never… He had plenty of opportunities if he were going to do that…" She backed away from him. "We were out of the house. We were finally safe. Why the hell would you believe him?"

Seeing no other choice, Drew spoke about the thing he never wanted to remember. *"Because he had me raped in prison!"*

The house went silent as Drew's words reverberated through the room. Nobody breathed or moved.

Until Cole gasped from the stairs.

Chapter 13
Aftermath

Mortified beyond belief, Drew spun to see Cole sitting at the bottom of the stairs, his eyes wide, and his hand over his open mouth.

"Cole, I'm sorry. I…" Drew took a step towards his nephew, but stopped when Cole rose. He expected the boy to run to his bedroom and lock himself away from his uncle who was too weak to protect himself.

Cole launched himself towards Drew, wrapping his arms around him. Drew fell to his knees and held Cole.

"You're safe now. It's over," Cole whispered into Drew's ear, repeating the same words Drew had said to him earlier.

Crying, Ashley walked over, knelt by her brother. She started to reach out, but withdrew her hand. "Drew?"

Desperately wiping away his tears, Drew avoided looking at Sam. "They attacked me in the shower. I fought like hell, but there were three of them, and they were big. Hard core convicts. Told me my old man had a message. Take the plea. I thought they'd be satisfied with just beating me, but they weren't. A guard came by, but not until after—" He winced and looked away.

Ashley took his face in her hands. "Oh God Drew. I'm so sorry."

Cole used his thumbs to dry his uncle's tears.

Drew sat back against the couch, taking comfort in Cole's embrace. "I almost took the plea after that. I wanted to, but I couldn't when I realized that you and Kelli would think I was guilty. I couldn't live with that. I decided I'd fight even if it killed me. Then a few weeks later, I was being released. And Dad was there to pick me up." He shook his head as he recalled the moment. "I wanted to kill him on the spot, but I was shell shocked. I didn't even know I was being released until about fifteen minutes beforehand, and I desperately needed to get out of there."

Ashley tried to dry her tears, but they wouldn't stop coming. She moved closer to her brother, and Cole threw his arm around her as well.

"Dad drove me away from Ember Falls," Drew continued, not looking at anyone. He'd gone this far, he might as well finish it. "He pulled a gun on me. Not the first time, but this was different. You know how it was always him being angry that triggered the worst of it."

Ashley nodded. "I remember. He pulled his gun on all of us a few times."

"He wasn't angry." Drew shook his head. "He was giddy. Like he'd won the lottery. He was driving a new car. Wearing new clothes. He made me get out. I really thought he was going to kill me. Made me get on my knees. Put the gun in my mouth and told me that every single person in Ember Falls believed I'd killed Molly. She was thought of as a saint, murdered by me. You and Kelli wanted nothing to do with me anymore—"

"No," Ashley said, her voice cracking with grief. "Drew we never believed that. I tried to get in to see you at the hospital and the prison. We never stopped believing in you."

Drew closed his eyes. "At the time, after being in there for nearly a year, cut off, no letters, no contact, I thought maybe you did. Ash, I was all alone in there. Isolated. Terrified. And then he told me that if I ever came back, tried to clear my name, or even contacted either of you, he'd see to it that you and Kelli were raped and killed. God help me, he wasn't lying. He bragged about sending those bastards after me. I didn't know what else to do." He locked eyes with Ashely. "I'm so sorry for what I did. I'll never forgive myself, but you have to believe me, I never stopped loving you and Kelli."

Ashley shushed him, taking both her brother and nephew in her arms. "No Drew, you need to stop apologizing. I'm sorry. I should have known. I should have realized that you wouldn't just abandon me. I'm so sorry. Just promise me, you'll forgive me."

Drew held on to his sister, felt the last of the walls she'd put up since his return collapse, and together with Cole, they cried.

****

Sam stepped out onto the back porch, breathed in the cool, night air, and desperately tried to stop herself from sobbing. Drew needed time with Cole and Ashley, and she needed a moment to find the ground beneath her.

It all made such horrible sense. Frank Duncan had once threatened her grandmother when she'd reported her suspicions of child abuse in the Duncan home. He'd told Nana if she didn't stop pushing it, he'd have someone pay her granddaughter a visit. Someone who would enjoy doing unspeakable things to Sam while she was just a little girl.

Clearly, those were never empty threats. Sam shivered from a chill as she realized how close she'd probably come to becoming a victim herself.

"I thought you might have left." Drew came out onto the back porch, his eyes focused not on her, but on a fixed imaginary point in the distance.

Sam turned. "I wouldn't do that. I just thought you needed a little space with your sister and Cole. How is he?"

Drew shook his head. "He seems okay. Kept telling me it was all right. God…" Drew leaned against the back banister, keeping his distance from Sam. "That kid astounds me."

Sam smiled. "He has a lot of you in him. No matter how much pain he's in, he comforts and protects."

Drew took a deep breath and slowly exhaled. "When I started at McAlister, the General sent me to set up security at a shelter. It was run by a woman named Ellen. She'd been a victim as a kid, and had fought for survivors ever since. They had a Group Share meeting about to start, and I noticed a few men. I asked her if that was usual and if it really helped any to share like that. She must have read the signs in me. She invited me in, told me I could just listen."

Sam stepped closer, but Drew moved away. "That's all I could do was listen. I never shared myself, but that's where I met Stephanie. She'd been raped while visiting a witness in a hospital."

The image of the beautiful attorney, so scared at the hospital the other day, resurfaced in Sam's memory. Another piece falling into place.

"I never told anyone," Drew said. "Not even the General. I couldn't tell you."

"Did you think I couldn't handle it? Or that I'd see you as less of a man?" Sam took his face him her hands so he was looking at her, although his eyes still remained focused elsewhere. "Drew, you are the bravest, most caring man I've ever known. The fact that this horrible thing happened to you doesn't change that. Nothing does."

Drew looked at her for the first time since coming out on the porch. "I didn't want to tell you, but mostly, I just didn't want to say it. I've never said those words out loud."

Sam pulled him into an embrace. Her strong, brave Drew. His biggest secret, the one thing he refused to talk about. He'd laid it all out there because it was the only way he could see to protect his sister. "I love you Drew. Nothing will ever change that."

Drew kissed her. "I need you Sam."

Sam took his hand, pulled him to the stairs that led to the small apartment over the garage. They thundered up the stairs together. Drew opened the door and they entered. Neither bothered with the lights.

Their mouths tasted each other as their hands worked to pull off their clothing. This wasn't slow and gentle, but fast and driven by a frenzied want and desperate need. Feeling her skin against his, Drew lifted her up and carried her to the small bed, indulging in hot, hungry kisses, and feeling every inch of her body.

She found him ready, and herself aching to be whole with him. "I want you inside of me," Sam said, her voice desperate for him. "I need you to be a part of me."

Needing no further prompting, Drew thrust forward, and their bodies became one. He grinned at her moans of pleasure and watched as ripples of ecstasy overtook her. Gone was the control that he'd learned, replaced with reckless abandon.

Sam wrapped herself around Drew, lifting her body to meet his. Her hands roamed over his broad chest, her eyes remained locked on his.

She moaned as he drove her over the edge. Her chocolate eyes widened as she cried out, her body tensing from the tidal wave of ecstasy. She dug her fingers into his back as she held on while he pushed her into erotic rhapsody. He buried his face in her neck, and ravished her. The fervor of his movements climaxed as she whispered his name. "Fill me Drew. Make me whole."

Drew let out a primal noise from deep within as he emptied himself, losing himself in the rapture that was his love for her.

He collapsed over her, every inch of him exhausted. "I love you Samantha. Please tell me you're mine."

Sam took his hand, looked into eyes, and smile. "I'm yours forever."

Chapter 14
Superheroes and Villains

In a near panic, Ashley ran through the house. Lilly had left early to take care of business at the book store, and Drew and Sam hadn't yet emerged from the apartment over the garage. Cole sat at the kitchen eating the one breakfast that she knew how to make him without burning, a heaping bowl of Captain Crunch, while leafing through his favorite book.

She refused to tell him that she'd ruined his chance of going to the Dragon-Con. Somehow, she had to make this right, even if she had to steal someone else's tickets.

Jay was coming as well, and they only had twenty minutes before they were supposed to pick him up. Cole was dressed in a Halloween costume they'd ordered for the occasion, because he wanted to fit in. Every few minutes, he'd play with his emerald ring, and study the large plastic green lantern that his book was propped on. Jay was supposed to be dressed as the Dark Knight, whatever that meant.

Ashley had thrown on a Wonder Woman costume she'd worn years ago to a party. It was little more than a fancy one-piece bathing suit. When she bought the outfit, she'd gone for slutty, but now she needed to transform it into something that wouldn't get her arrested as she escorted two young boys through the convention. She found a pair of blue yoga pants that matched, and completed the ensemble with a red cape from an old costume from when Lilly had had gone as Little Red Riding Hood. On Lilly, the cloak went down below her knees, but on Ashley, it just reached her ass. Still, it gave her a little more cover.

The back door opened and Drew entered, holding hands with Sam. For a moment, her panic at not having tickets to the sold-out event were forgotten as she launched herself at her brother. "Are you okay?"

Drew returned the embrace, which was more than she deserved. "I'm good. I'm so sorry Ash…"

"Stop, please," Ashley said. "I should be begging for your forgiveness. God Drew, you never stopped protecting me, have you?"

Drew didn't answer. Her brother would never forgive himself for the impossible choice he was forced to make. That was Drew. Even now, she could feel him tense in their embrace. She looked at his face, saw him grimace. "Drew, don't ever apologize to me again for leaving."

He kissed her cheek, then stepped back and smirked. "Um, that's one hell of an outfit."

With those words, the panic was back. "Do I look like an idiot? I've got to get Jay and take him and Cole to this convention and try and score tickets on the fly."

Sam came over with two cups of coffee she'd just poured, and handed one to Drew. "I thought Ollie had gotten tickets a month ago."

Ashley scowled. "Yeah, but that was before last night. I laid into him real good. I was so angry after running into Dad, I let it spill over on both of you. I doubt he'll ever talk to me again."

Drew frowned. "This is Ollie."

Ashley took a breath and glanced at Cole. "Ollie is the most reliable friend, but I threw that away to try for something more. And then I ruined it, just like I ruin everything. I can't—"

The doorbell rang and Cole ran to get it. Opening it up, Cole was greeted by the Man of Steel. Cole grinned. "Wicked."

Ollie stepped in and did a twirl, his red cape floating in the air. Placing his hands on his hips, he struck the perfect Superman pose. "Up, up and away. You ready?"

Cole nodded. "Let me grab my lantern and book."

As he scampered in, Ashley realized she'd been holding her breath until Ollie looked at her. She expected disgust and anger. Instead, he wore the goofy grin she loved.

"Cole, why don't you go to the bathroom before we go," Ashley said.

With an eye roll, Cole took his lantern and thundered upstairs. Ashley quickly went to Ollie.

"I didn't think you'd be here today," Ashley said. "Not after what I'd said last night."

Ollie smiled. "I told you, I'll always be there. I know maybe you might be too angry to want to see me, but I wasn't breaking my word to Cole."

She grabbed him and pulled him into a kiss. "The only one I'm angry with is me. I'm sorry."

Ollie rested his forehead against hers. "I thought I was never going to get to kiss you again."

Ashley felt a surge of elation, not to mention a desire to use her magic lasso to tie Ollie up and have her way with him, but that part would have to wait. "I wish I could go with you, but I guess you only got three tickets."

Ollie grinned and pulled out four stubs. "I was kinda hoping you'd come. You look amazing." His eyes wandered up and down her body.

"I look like a dork." Ashley rolled her eyes. "Which means I'll fit in."

Ollie played with her cape. "I don't suppose I could convince you to wear this costume later tonight at my place?"

Ashley arched an eyebrow. "Perv. But I guess you deserve it for putting up with me."

Ollie pulled her close. "Being with you is worth it. I mean it."

Ashley felt herself blush at the intense way Ollie was looking at her, and it didn't help that Drew and Sam were discreetly watching from the kitchen, and grinning like idiots. "Give me a minute, will you. I need to talk with Drew."

Ollie glanced in his direction. "You really should go easy on him."

Ashley patted his chest. "We're good. He and I spoke last night, and…" Ashley closed her eyes, fought against the tears.

"What is it?" Ollie asked.

Ashley shook her head. "Not now, but I promise you, Drew and I are not in the same place we've been."

Ollie wore a concerned expression, but didn't argue as Cole was rampaging down the stairs. "Let's get in the car buddy. Your aunt will be out in a few minutes."

Cole ran to the door, hesitated and ran instead into the kitchen to his uncle, where he stared at Drew's sneakers. "I love you Uncle Drew," he said in a small voice. Before Drew could respond, Cole went running to the front door and outside with Ollie.

When Ashley approached, Sam excused herself. Ashley placed her hand over her brother's heart. "How much does Ollie know?"

Drew continued to stare at the door Ollie had just left through. "He knows about the threat to you and Kelli, not what happened to me. I don't think I'm ready to tell him. I know we're partners, but—"

Ashley shook her head. "You don't need to explain. I just want to make sure I'm on the same page. I do love you, you know. Even all this time, while I was furious at you, I kept flipping out whenever someone else said anything bad. You're my brother. You always protected me. I'm so sorry I wasn't there to do the same."

Drew's face went dark. "I've done a piss poor job of protecting you. I should have gotten you and Kelli away from Dad. I never should have—"

"Stop, please." Ashley fought the threatening tears. "You have to stop blaming yourself. None of this was your fault. There's one thing that I've told you since you've been back that's true, I don't need you to protect me like I did when we were kids. That doesn't mean I don't need you in my life. And…" She stopped to wipe away her own tears. "I can't do this now. I don't want Cole to see me crying and I'm right on the verge. Not to mention, how I look." She gripped the cape and gave it a small shake.

Drew snorted. "Ollie must love this."

Ashley bit her lower lip. "You think maybe you could ditch Sam tomorrow? You and I can spend some time alone together and talk. I haven't asked once about what you've done over the last few years, but I want to know."

Drew took her hand. "I'd like that."

She kissed his cheek again and gave him one last hug. "I'm glad I've got my brother back."

Then without looking at Drew, knowing if she did, the waterworks would start, Wonder Woman went out to join Superman and Green Lantern, and go pick up the Batman.

****

Sam held Drew's hand as he drove down the highway towards her place. It had been an intense night, but her bond with Drew felt stronger. She glanced out the window as they passed the entrance to the park where their relationship had started. She'd known Drew when they were children, had a schoolgirl crush on him. They'd met briefly at the station when Drew had brought Cole in to see his mother's body, but they hadn't really spoken. It was in that park where they first connected.

Sam glanced his way. "Have you given any thought to us getting married?"

He lifted her hand and brushed the engagement ring he'd given her with his thumb. "I thought this showed I did."

"No, I mean have you given any thought to *how* you want to do it? We haven't spoken about the actual wedding. Do you imagine a big wedding? A small one? Just running off to Vegas?"

He shrugged. "I want you to be happy. I know girls often dream of these things their entire lives."

"Some of us do," she said. "But as long as it's not

something that takes years to put together, or anything crazy expensive, I'll be happy. I do want this to be our wedding. Tell me what you'd like."

Drew grinned as he took a left onto Route Fifty. "Really?"

"Why not?" Sam asked. "It's your wedding too."

He hit the left blinker, expertly moved his truck around a Buick going ten miles below the speed limit, and then eased back into the center lane once it was clear. "Okay. Actually, I did imagine getting married when I was a kid. I always saw it outside."

She smiled. "An outdoor wedding? Oh, that could be fantastic."

He nodded. "Like right in the park where we met. I mean, that's where we started, right?"

Her heart melted. He saw it the same way she did. "There's a little gazebo not too far from where you and I ran into each other. I've seen people get married there. It would be perfect."

Drew reached over, brushed his fingers over her cheek. "Let's do it. Spring is just around the corner. I don't feel the need to wait. I don't have many people to invite. Ashley and Cole are the only blood I have in town that I'd want. Ollie and Lilly too. The General and a few other people from McAlister."

Sam's eyes watched the road. "Like Stephanie."

He frowned. "Yes, like Stephanie. I told you, there was never anything between us."

"I know," she said. "But I don't want you to invite her."

They remained silent as he turned off the highway, and came to a stop at a red light. Sam turned to Drew. "Let *me* invite her. I liked her, a lot. And I know she loves you Drew. Not in a romantic way, but in a way that I'd be crazy to not want her to love you. She's your family Drew, and that means she'll be my family too. She'll always be welcome in our home."

He took her hand, but avoided eye contact. "Thank you. Maybe I do have more family than I realized. Lilly and Ollie. Your Nana. Steph. The General…" Drew frowned. "Shit."

"What's the matter?"

Drew pressed on the gas, speeding down the road. "Have you heard from your grandmother since last night?"

She shook her head as she pulled out her phone. There were no messages. "I told her that you'd take her home last night. She didn't have her car with her."

The tires squealed as he took a corner too quickly. "The General came in last night. I found him and your Nana arguing about everything from nuclear disarmament to World War Two. He should have come back, but with everything that happened I completely forgot. Crap!"

"Easy," Sam said, although she was starting to get nervous herself. "I'm sure he's fine." She thought about calling, but as they were less than a block away, it made no sense.

"Hopefully your Nana knows where he went." He pulled into her driveway. "That's his car. It was in front of the house last night."

She undid her seatbelt. "Maybe they stayed up talking, and he slept on the couch?"

He shook his head. "They woke Cole up last night with their *discussion*. They were practically at each other's throats. The General is financing the investigation into what happened with Kelli. They sent an assassin who killed Diana while she was under police protection. If they wanted to take him out, last night would have been the perfect chance."

They both exited the car, quickly and quietly, while they each pulled out their clutch pieces. Using hand signals to communicate, they made it to the front steps and stood on opposite sides of the door. Sam used her key, and with their guns at the ready, they slipped inside.

They cleared the kitchen first, saw the empty coffee maker. Sam's heart started to pound in her chest. Normally, by this time of day, Nana would have started on her second cup.

The living room was empty, and the couch didn't appear to have been slept on. Swiftly, they made their way down the hall.

Muffled sounds were detectable from the main bedroom as they moved closer, followed by a sharp slap. The General's voice was the first they heard. "Just wait until I'm untied."

Drew reared back and kicked Nana's bedroom door open, burst in gun first, and screamed.

The General lay on his back, each hand strapped to a separate bed post. He was naked, covered only by Sam's equally nude Nana.

"Oh God." Sam turned and buried her face in Drew's chest.

The General smirked up at Rose Henry. "I told you I heard them. Maybe next time you'll believe me."

Rose glanced over her shoulder at her beet-red granddaughter, who was turning to flee along with Drew. "Maybe, I will."

Their laughter echoed down the hall.

****

Jericho sat, listened, and approved. Cole was having a good time at the convention. His interaction with the author he so admired couldn't have gone better and the kid seemed to be enjoying a moment of pure happiness. This pleased Jericho.

Jericho was also delighted that after such a rough night, the Duncan girl and Miller were acting as a unit. One little happy family. The mamma's boy cop had managed to tame the town slut. Good for him.

Maybe they were good with one another. The Duncan girl needed someone who could handle high maintenance. That much had been clear when she left that wimp Corvidae at the bar and ran to Miller. And Miller just needed to get laid.

Still, maybe together they were good for the boy.

Jericho didn't understand why that mattered to him, but more and more, it did.

He used his laptop to bring up a picture of Cole. They were so protective of him, yet they had no idea what sort of hell Cole Duncan escaped from. Jericho did. It was the same sort of hell that had shaped him.

His burner phone signaled an incoming text. A wicked grin spread across his face as he read the message. Time to play again.

Chapter 15
Going Out with a Bang

The sun had long ago retreated into the night, and only a sliver of the moon was visible, as if it were afraid to show its face in Ember Falls. Ollie sat on Ashley's front porch. The last of the winter chill was still hanging in the air, threatening to bite one last time, but Ollie didn't mind. Today had been perfect, holding Ashley's hand as they walked around the Dragon-Con with the kids, getting the rare treat of unhindered joy in Cole's eyes. Ollie hadn't kept his promise to protect his mother, but he wouldn't fail the child again.

Ashley came through the front door, took a seat next to him and snuggled into his arms. "Cole was out the moment his head hit the pillow, but he kept going on and on about what that author said to him. It's like he's bursting with all these emotions that he doesn't know what to do with."

Ollie kissed the top of her head, took her hand in his, and gave it a gentle squeeze. "He hasn't had a lot of experience with hope, pride, or just plain old joy, but you're changing that for him."

Ashley glanced up to him. "No, *we're* doing that for him. All of us. Drew has been amazing with him. Lilly is the rock that knows what to do, and you. Ollie, you came. You came because you said you would. Do you have any idea how much that means to me?"

Ollie smiled. "I'll always come. You should know that."

Ashley turned around and sat up. "I do. I should have known for years how much you loved me, but I was too much of an idiot." She placed her hand on his heart. "Not anymore."

She kissed him deeply and explored the inside of his mouth.

The chill of the air was gone, replaced by a sudden warmth that spread through Ollie's body. He felt his need for her as he tasted her lips, smelt the cherry blossoms from her perfume. Everything tingled.

"I want you in my bed Oliver Miller," Ashley said. "I don't want you to go home tonight."

He was ready to pick her up and carry her to her bed, when they heard someone clear their throats.

Ollie felt a different sort of heat in his face as he realized that Drew and Sam were there. The embarrassment quickly faded when he saw their eyes. "What's wrong?"

"We've been called in," Drew said, his eyes on his sister. "They spotted Dad. And he may have a hostage."

Ollie managed to untangle himself from Ashley and stood up. "Who?"

Drew shrugged. "Not sure, but we need to go. He's down in that abandoned supermarket across town."

Ashley held her arms across her chest as if suddenly cold. "You mean the one—"

"Where I was found half dead with God knows what up my veins?" Drew finished for her. "That would be the one."

Tires squealed as the General pulled up in front of the house. "You heard?" Everyone nodded. "Get in

Drew. Sam can ride with your partner."

Drew started for the truck when Ashley ran to him. "Be careful. I don't care what happens to Dad, but you come home tonight. Promise me."

Drew hugged her. "I'm not dying for him."

Ashley turned to Ollie. "You too. He's not worth your lives. Cole needs you both." She swallowed. "So do I."

Ollie kissed her again, then headed to Sam's side. "We'll be careful. I'm not about to die when I have everything to live for."

****

The General barely slowed down through red lights or stop signs. "You got your head on straight, Marine?"

Drew nodded, looking straight ahead. "Yes sir."

The General hit the turn signal, executed a right. "Your sister was right. You're needed. You're going to deal with this and go home. That's an order."

Drew kept his gaze on the street in front of them. "Yes sir."

The General accelerated, well past the speed limit. "You want to look at me when I talk to you?"

Drew shook his head. "No sir."

The General scowled. "I'm too old to feel embarrassed, and I don't think I owe you an explanation."

Drew didn't blink. "No sir, you don't. But you're like a father to me, and Rose is Sam's Nana, and nobody likes to see their parents having private time. So, if it's all the same to you, I'm going to pretend I didn't see what I saw. I don't think less of you, I just can't look at you or Nana right now."

The General made a left. He was forced to slow

down as they were in on a main street with more traffic, even at this late hour. "I see you and your sister seemed to have made some progress. You two talk about why you left?"

Drew nodded, relaxed a bit. "Yeah. She came home last night to have it out. Dad cornered her yesterday afternoon. I didn't have much of a choice. I told her what Dad said." He closed his eyes and swallowed. "I told her why I believed Dad. I never told you. Something happened in prison."

The General made one last turn, putting them on the street that would bring them to the abandoned supermarket where Drew had been found near death. "I'm proud of you. It's not easy for anyone to talk about sexual assault."

Drew's mouth fell open, and he turned to face the General. "You knew?"

The General sent him a weary sidelong glance. "Why do you think I sent you to help Ellen Hughes? I asked her to try and get you in that group."

Drew forced his mouth closed, looked away. All these years, the General gave no indication he'd known. He turned back to the General. "How?"

The General met Drew's gaze. "Does it matter? I've seen it before. In women *and* men. You needed to talk to someone, but you weren't ready to tell me. Until now. I appreciate how hard it was, but at least it got you looking at me again."

Drew turned away. Somehow, he managed to hide his grin.

****

Ollie pulled up in front of the old Wallman's Supermarket. The place had sold its last overripe banana days after Drew had been released from prison. Nobody really talked much about it anymore with the three new major chain stores in town. They'd be talking about it tomorrow.

Ollie spotted his mother at the front of the police line. He ran to the back of a nearby cruiser, pulled out a vest for himself, handed one to Sam. Drew was on his heels, doing the same for himself and the General.

Chief Miller was waiting for them. She handed them each a radio with a headset. "He's inside, with a gun to someone's head. I can't tell who it is, but they're in a chair. We think there's someone else in there, on the floor."

She handed a pair of binoculars to Ollie.

"Yeah, whoever is in the chair looks out, but I see the shape on the floor." Ollie handed the binoculars to Drew. "Might be dead."

Drew studied the scene. "This doesn't feel right."

Ann took another look. "He's desperate."

The General took the binoculars from Drew. "He's dumb as shit, but he's not that stupid. Do you have a sniper?"

Ann's eyebrows went up. "In Ember Falls?"

The General jabbed a thumb at Drew. "You've got two standing here, but I didn't bring the right equipment. We can have it here in about two hours."

Drew shook his head. "I don't think a sniper is the right way. I need to go in there."

Sam grabbed his arm. "Are you crazy? Drew, your father is a monster. You can't risk your life for him. Not after everything—" Her eyes scanned the faces around them. "*Everything* he did to your family."

Ollie saw something pass between them, something

that told him there was more he didn't know, but he didn't press. "I don't want to go home to Ashley and tell her you died trying to save that son of a bitch."

Drew shook his head. "I'm not risking my life for him. I *know* him. This is wrong."

Corvidae came running up to them. "What's happening?"

As Ann filled him in, Drew huddled with Ollie and Sam. "I'm telling you, we need to get in there. Dad has no impulse control. If he wanted to kill whoever it was in there, they'd be dead."

Ollie shrugged. "They might be. Nobody's moved."

Corvidae was studying the scene through the chief's binoculars. "Isn't that the problem?" He turned to face everyone. "Nobody is moving, *including* Frank Duncan."

Drew snapped his fingers and pointed. "Exactly. I've got to lay eyes on him."

Ann grimaced. "You need full body armor. No chances once you're inside. If he gives you a target, you drop him."

Drew nodded. "Deal."

Ollie stepped beside Drew. "Let's go. If something happens to you, it better happen to me. I'm not being to one to tell Ash that something went wrong in there."

A uniformed officer came up, started to hand out the body armor. Drew grabbed one set, handed another to Ollie.

Sam found one in her size. "I'm going too. We just started to plan out our wedding. You're not getting out of cake tasting that easily."

Corvidae started to get dressed as well. "I've got

tactical experience. And I love wedding cake."

****

Drew hugged the wall as he and Ollie entered from the right side of the store. They waited until he heard in his earwig that Sam and Corvidae had entered from the back.

He and Ollie would approach from the front, draw his father's attention, but Sam and Corvidae would be ready to take Drew's father out from the rear if needed. If it came to it, he wasn't sure if he preferred being the one to kill him or not. After everything his father had done Drew should want to take him out, yet he didn't yearn to be the one to pull the trigger.

Sam spoke in his earwig. "We're here. Drew, be careful. It's dark, but you're right. He's not moving an inch. Something's up."

With a nod, he and Ollie entered the room.

Frank Duncan stood nestled between two large refrigerator units. There was a body crumpled on the floor, and one in a chair. The person in the chair was starting to stir, but wasn't quite awake yet.

As they drew closer, the single light above head allowed them to see faces. Darren Winters, Molly's father, was lying dead at the feet of his son. His throat had been cut, but there was no blood. He wasn't killed here. His son Sean Winters was bound in the chair, and had a small trickle of blood from his left temple, but he seemed otherwise unharmed.

Frank Duncan was fully restrained and held in position to make him look like he had a gun to Sean's head, when in fact he was helpless. His face had taken a beating, and his nose was broken. Frank's eyes were wide with panic and pleading. He was trying to say something, glancing down towards Sean Winters.

Drew holstered his sidearm, signaled for Sam to come out. She was by his side, while Corvidae stayed behind where he could cover everyone just in case things went south.

"Mmmhrm!" Frank kept struggling.

Drew held up his hands. "Yeah, I see. Nobody touch anything." He used his earwig radio, which they had on an open channel. "Chief, you read? We've got a situation. My father's duct taped in position, his back is against a dolly, and his arm in secured to a board. Darren Winters is dead. Body was transported here, he's cold." Drew checked for a pulse, just to be sure. "Probably killed a few days ago. Sean Winters is taped to a chair. There's an IED wired underneath it."

Drew examined the wires. "It's a pressure trigger. If Sean moves, it goes boom. Not much of bomb, but it'll kill everyone near it, including Sean and my father."

At Drew's nod, Sam pulled the tape off of Frank's mouth. "Who did this?"

Frank spit out blood. "How the fuck should I know. Fucker got me from behind. I barely got a look at him. All I saw was a crumpled trench coat."

Ollie glared at Drew. "Jack Caesar."

Drew nodded, just as Sean groaned. "I've got to disarm this. Kid comes to, he's gonna panic. Blow us all to kingdom come."

Drew went back to studying the explosives, as he listened to the chief in his ear. "I don't think we can wait. The General can tell you, I've diffused these before, under far worse circumstances."

He got on his stomach, placed his head down low.

Saw the simple device. It was amateurish. A rudimentary set up, with a solid red light showing him the bomb was armed.

"But never with a member of your family attached to the bomb," Sam said.

Drew glanced at his father. "He's not family. He's just some asshole who got stuck with three kids he couldn't stand."

Frank spit at Drew. "You got no fucking clue. You ain't shit to me. You and your fucking sisters are nothing but a—Mmmph!"

His words were cut off as Sam replaced the duct tape over his mouth. She pointed a finger in his face to silence him. "You really are a stupid fuck. He needs to concentrate, or we're all going to get killed. And you need to stay still."

Drew reached into a pocket, pulled out a knife, and got to work. "This isn't complicated. The wires are exposed. I just need to—" He stopped when Sean's legs moved. "He's waking up."

Drew brought himself to his knees and held Sean in place as the young man's eyes opened. Groggy and unfocused at first, Sean's pupils started to move. His eye's widened in panic, and he looked ready to bolt.

Sam leaned down, gently touched his face. "Sean, you need to keep still, okay?" She kept her voice calm and quiet. "You're going to be okay, but you can't move until I tell you."

Sweat began to pour out of him, but he nodded.

"This won't take long," Drew said. "You're going to be fine, I promise you. When I say so, Officer Rossi will help you to the door."

Sam started to protest, but Drew shook his head.

"Once you have him safe, I'll make sure there's no secondary device on my father, then we'll cut him loose, and get out of here. Ollie should stay, he's had the body cam on me the whole time, not you. We've got to keep this clean."

Sam grimaced, but she didn't argue.

Drew laid back down, and got to work. He pulled out three wires, traced them back to the source. Placed the knife against the red one. "Here we go."

He cut the wire. The red light flicked off, replaced by a satisfactory green. Drew grinned and glanced at Sean. "Go."

Sam pulled him up. He was unsteady, but able to walk. They got a few feet, when she turned to face Drew. "You're coming?"

"Soon," Drew said. "I've got to help take out the trash."

Corvidae emerged from the shadows to take Sean's other arm. "Be careful Drew. Don't take any chances."

Drew nodded as they walked off into the darkness towards the door. He waited until he knew they were out before he turned back to his father. "Let me make sure there's no secondary device, then we can cut him loose. You ready to cuff him?"

Ollie nodded and moved closer to Frank. "You think there's something there?"

Drew took out a small flashlight. "The first one wasn't very well done. If there is a secondary device, I can't imagine that it's…" His eyes widened, and his mouth went dry.

"What is it?" Ollie asked.

There was a beep, followed by a flashing red light.

Drew looked up at the father that he hated, and the

man who was becoming his brother. And he knew what he had to do.

****

Sam handed Sean off to a set of paramedics, who started to give him a cursory exam, before they transported him. She headed back towards the store.

"Where are you going?" Ann asked.

"Back in there," Sam answered as she headed for the door. "I want to make sure they get out okay. I don't trust Frank Duncan."

The General pulled on a vest. "I'll go with you. If Drew found a secondary device, I can help. I was disarming bombs while you were—"

The store exploded. The windows blew out with fumes of fire, and the force of the blast knocked Sam to the ground, the door she was opening still in her hand.

"Drew!"

Chapter 16
Bombs, Bugs and Loofahs

Ashley burst into the ER, yelling out for Drew and Ollie. People watched her, but nobody seemed to know anything. She followed the line of cops, hoping they'd lead to where she needed to go.

There was a gaggle of five uniforms, each standing with Styrofoam cups of coffee. One of them, an older cop with grey hair and a few extra pounds was shaking his head. "Man, they're going to have to pick up pieces of Duncan with tweezers."

Ashley's heart froze and suddenly she couldn't breathe. She started to stumble backwards, and the room began to spin.

"Ashley!"

Someone took her arm, helped her into a chair. "Are you okay?"

She shook her head, tried to form words, but forgot how to speak. Glancing over, she saw familiar eyes. What was his name?

"Ashley can you hear me?" Corvidae said. "Do you need me to get a doctor?"

Ashley could barely see through her tears. She shook her head. "No. No, I don't…" She was shaking so badly, Corvidae's face was blurred. "I need my brother."

Corvidae smiled. "Okay, let me take you to see

him. He's just down the hall."

Ashley gripped the armrests of the chair. "What? Drew... he's not..."

Corvidae pointed down the hall, to the left. "He's right down there. He's fine, I can—"

Ashley bolted out of the chair, and raced down the hallway. She spotted another cluster of cops by a room at the end standing with the General.

Bursting past them, Ashley entered the room, and felt her insides melt. There on the bed, his face smudged black with soot, his mouth covered with an oxygen mask, was Drew.

She pushed past Sam and ran into his arms. "Oh God, I thought I lost you. I heard that there was an explosion, and someone was killed, and then..." Ashley gasped. "Ollie?"

Drew pointed to a curtain that divided the room just as Ollie pushed the drape open. Ollie tried to say something, but was cut off when Ashley crashed into him, and crushed her mouth to his. She didn't care that he tasted like charcoal, he was alive.

Ollie stroked her hair gently, and kissed the top of her head. "We're okay. Both of us. Just a little smoke inhalation."

Ashley nodded as she stroked his face. She glanced over at her brother. "I came in... there were cops... they said something about Duncan and I thought you were killed."

Drew's eyes closed for a moment. "It's Dad. He's dead."

Ashley blinked, unsure if she heard correctly. "Dad's dead?"

Drew swung his legs off the bed, stood with

assistance from Sam. "Yeah."

Ashley furrowed her brow. How was she supposed to feel about that? He father was dead. Most people would be devastated, but she wasn't. Should she feel a sense of relief? The monster they'd grown up with was gone. There was no more boogey man. Maybe joy? After all he'd done, death was the least he deserved.

The truth was, she didn't feel anything, and that was fine with her. What was important was here, in this room.

Ann rushed in and quickly went to her son. Ashley moved back to Drew. She took his hand and kissed his forehead. "You can't die on me. If anyone gets to kill you, it's me."

Drew began to laugh, but was overtaken with a fit of coughs.

Ann pulled away from her son and closed the door after the General stepped in. For several minutes, she'd been Ollie's mother and nothing but. Now, she was back into cop mode. "What happened?"

"I'd like to know that too," the General said. "You said the bomb was rudimentary. You've disarmed far worse than what you described to me."

Drew stood holding on to both Sam and Ashley. "The first one *was* simple. You could google how to make a better IED. The wires were exposed, there was no dead man trigger. I could have talked Cole through disarming it. The secondary device was a whole different story." He shook his head. "More powerful, and this one was remote activated. I saw it turn on. It had a timer. It gave me ten seconds. There wasn't enough time to get Dad out of there."

Ollie stepped forward. "I saw it in Drew's eyes, the

moment it activated. He leapt up from the floor, grabbed me and tossed me into a nearby freezer. The kind you get your meat from. I didn't know what the hell was going on until I heard the explosion. I felt the ceiling come crashing down. Drew was on top of me. If he hadn't reacted in that instant, I'd be dead."

Ann came over and her cop face slipped again. "Drew, I can't thank you enough. I know how awful your relationship with your father was, but it couldn't have been easy to choose my son over your own family."

Drew took her hand. "I did choose my family."

He and Ollie locked eyes. Something unspoken passed between them, something that made Ashley tear up yet again.

"Well, that's lovely." The General wore a scowl, and his eyes weren't misty at all. "Do you two need a few moments to seal your love, of could we discuss the ramifications of this?"

Corvidae held up his hands in a shrug. "I'm not sure I understand what the ramifications are, beyond the fact that Duncan and Miller are lucky to be alive. Maybe I'm still shell-shocked, but I'm lost."

The General eyed him coolly. "I guess they don't put much stock in critical thinking in the worst of circumstances in the State's DA, but at McAlister, I expect my people to be at the top of their game at *all* times." He turned to Drew. "You want to take a crack at it, or do you need a lollipop and some time to pet a puppy."

Drew straightened out. "We're being set up. Make us think that Dad killed Molly and the others, but we know he didn't have the means to hire a hit like what happened to Diana and Vic. That was professional. So was this. The killer wants us to look one way, so we don't look the other."

Ollie nodded. "It was ballsy too. Whoever is doing this, they're not just a hired gun. They think of themselves as an artist."

Corvidae snorted. "He's a lunatic, not Picasso."

Ollie shook his head. "He's a monster. Most likely a sociopath, but I bet if you asked him, he'd be the first to tell you how he considers what he does an art. Each killing, in his mind, is a masterpiece." Ollie frowned. "Well, maybe not Vic. That was probably just him… what do you call it? Mixing colors, laying out his tools and priming the canvas. Vic wasn't part of his work; his murder was just needed to create his masterpiece."

Corvidae frowned. "So, he didn't care about Officer Miranda's killing the same way he cared about Diana's? I don't get that."

"Imagine it this way." Ollie folded his arms, with one hand on his chin as he spoke. He looked like a professor patently explaining something to a student who was having a problem wrapping his head around the concept that had been presented. "Vic was a means to an end. That doesn't mean he didn't take pride in what he did, but he didn't put the time into making it art. He enjoyed it the same way a painter might enjoy doodling, but it lacked the depth of his other killings. Vic's death was a tool. I hate to talk about Vic like that, but—" Ollie shrugged, appearing almost embarrassed.

"But that's exactly how you have to look at things," the General said. "You have to be able to try and see it from the killer's eyes. And that meshes." He turned to Drew. "You were right about him. He's sharp." He turned back to Ollie who was turning red. "If you ever decide you want something besides being a detective in Ember Falls, let me know. Anyone who can profile Jericho as accurately as you, has a place in my organization."

Ann's proud smile faded into a scowl. "I'm sorry, but who?"

The General grinned. "I've got your killer for you. We should talk back at the station once these two are released."

"That can wait," Ashley said. "They were nearly killed. They need to get cleaned up, get some rest. Can't this wait until Monday?"

Ann shook her head. "I'm afraid I have to agree with General McAlister. This has to be a priority." She turned to her son and Drew. "Go home, get showered and changed. Then meet me at the station. Let's find out who we're dealing with."

****

Ashley and Ollie sent each other goofy grins as they hurriedly got dressed. Ollie, so distracted by the sight of Ashley pulling on her pants that he put his shirt on backwards.

Rolling her eyes, Ashley reached over and gave the t-shirt a tug to show him.

Ollie blushed. "Oops. I guess my head is still spinning. At least I didn't fall out of the shower this time."

Ashley leaned in and kissed him hard. "I'd offer to scrub your back again, but you've got to get going."

Ollie pulled on his shoes, making sure to put them on the right feet, and stood up. He glanced around the room. "Did I drop my shield and gun on the table on the way in here?"

Ashley rolled off the bed. "Yeah, I think it's right next to my purse. Why don't you let me take you through a drive through at least, grab coffee and donuts for everyone?"

Ollie opened the door for her. "Sounds like a plan."

Ashley started to head out, then snapped her fingers. "I took off my earrings before we climbed in the shower. Go get your stuff."

Ollie kissed her again before heading out. He glanced at the clock, saw they had fifteen minutes.

Ollie went to the kitchen, saw his stuff next to Ashley's purse on the tall bar counter. He grabbed his gun and shield and knocked over Ashley's purse. It fell to the floor, spilling out gum, keys, a small notepad, pens, some small thing he didn't recognize and women's hygiene products. "Crap."

"What?" Ashley asked as she came in.

"Nothing." Ollie knelt down to start picking things up and shovel them back into her purse. "I'm a klutz is all." He picked up the small, black item that was no larger than a paper clip. "Hey Ash, what's this…?"

Suddenly it clicked.

Ashley bent down to get a closer look. "I don't…"

Ollie quickly put his finger to his mouth, shushing her. He pointed to the device, then to his ears.

"Let's go," Ollie said as casually as possible. "They're going to be waiting on us."

****

"I give you Jericho." The General tossed a large file down on the chief's desk.

Ann pulled it forward, flipped it open, and began to read. There were detailed notes, affidavits, police reports, redacted documents from government agencies such as the FBI, CIA, and Homeland. There were lists of dozens of victims, crime scene photos, trial transcripts and more. "This seems extensive, but you know what I don't see?"

The General crossed his arms. "A picture of the bastard himself. He's very good. I aim to prove we're better."

As Ann continued to read, Polansky looked over her shoulder. "This guy sounds like a psychopathic punk."

"That he is," the General said. "But he's smart, efficient and downright deadly. He was hired to take out a witness under FBI scrutiny. He managed to do so right under their noses."

Polansky snorted. "Doesn't sound too hard."

The General cocked an eyebrow. "There were six agents active at the safe house. Two in the back, two in the front, and two in the house. One was in the bedroom while the witness took a shower, the door ajar. Jericho managed to cut his throat without anyone the wiser."

Polanski stopped reading over the chief's shoulder and sneered. "How'd he'd manage that?"

The General folded his arms. "Jericho had come in while the wit was out over the past week. He'd created a hidey hole from the roof to the ceiling above the bathroom. He also had a recording of the vic, singing."

Ollie furrowed his brow. "Singing?"

The General nearly smiled, a sign that as much as he hated Jericho, he had to admire his skill. "Victim was a lover of Opera. The agents on the case said he was always humming a tune, but he really belted it out in the shower."

"Don't we all?" Ollie shrugged. "I prefer old Barry Manilow, but everyone sings in the shower."

"Not like this guy." The General pointed at the file. "He was good, but so was the recording Jericho had made of his shower performance from a week earlier. He was in and out before anyone was the wiser. The agents found him only because the recording ended."

Polansky went back to reading. "What opera?"

"Don Giovanni," the General said.

Polansky pursed his lips and shrugged. "Good one. Pavarotti did an amazing version of it. That ain't an easy one."

Ann looked up and stared at Polanski, who turned red. "What? I sing in the shower too."

With the first smile she'd had all night, Ann went back to the file. "So, we're dealing with an elite hired gun."

The General nodded. "Elite, deadly and just a little bit insane."

"Insane?" Corvidae frowned. "How do you get that? It takes intelligence to pull off the sort of things you're talking about."

"No doubt," the General agreed. "Most likely he's got a genius IQ. He's methodical, he's efficient, and he's a chameleon. He blends in. He assumes identities. He's gone to the funerals of some of the people he's murdered. Spoken to the widows. We've got reports that he's an expert in prosthetics. He can appear to be old and young. Imitated nearly every race and nationality. He's shown up fat, skinny and everything in-between. He assumes a new identity every time he surfaces. Some fake ones, other times, he'll use a real person. I've checked. Nobody has heard from Jack

Caesar for two weeks, including his ex-wives, his buddies or his bookie. It was the bookie that started to worry first."

"Great." Drew stood with his arms folded, a scowl on his face. "So, we really have no idea who he is."

"We know one thing," the General said. "He's not done. He always sends someone connected with the case a letter when he's finished."

"What kind of letter?" Ann asked.

The General walked over to her desk, reached down and flipped to the back of the file. He picked up a laminated page. It was blank, except for a large letter J in a fancy font.

"Oh," Ollie said as he glanced down at it. "You mean an *actual* letter. I guess he's signing his masterpieces."

"It's ego," Drew said. "He wants people to know it's him. He wants to say, 'hey, look at me. I was able to do all this. Slip by your best and brightest.' Look at how he took out Diana. In the middle of a freaking courtroom, surrounded by cops and McAlister Security men."

The General nodded. "We don't know his real name, but every alias he's used has had a J in it. First or last name. James, John. Johansson." The general pointed to a picture on the board of Caesar. "Jack."

Chief Miller got up, went to the board. She studied the picture of Diana, an unflattering mug shot. Next to her, was a picture of Vic Miranda in uniform. "You said he comes to funerals?"

The General nodded. "At times. We're not sure how many, but he definitely likes to rub shoulders with people grieving for the ones he's killed."

Ann sighed. "We'll have to stake out Vic's wake. That's coming up in a few days."

Ollie grimaced as he stood by his mother. "Son of a bitch. You really think the bastard is going to show up there at Vic's place?"

"It would fit," the General said. "Of course, Officer Miranda was just killed so he could take his place. Diana was the real masterpiece. He might be more likely to show up at hers."

"When is that?" Corvidae asked.

Chief Miller went back to her desk. "At this point, I don't know. Nobody has claimed her body. She wasn't married. Had no siblings. Her mother died a decade ago. If she has any other relatives, they haven't claimed her."

Ollie frowned. "What about her father?"

Ann shrugged as she sat behind her desk again. "As far as we can tell, she doesn't have one. No mention of one anywhere. We talked to a few colleagues. She told a few that her mother was her only family. Never knew her father."

Ollie's frown deepened, but he didn't say anything else.

"We've got a professional serial killer," Drew said. "He doesn't just do this for money, but I'd guess he doesn't come cheap either."

The General shook his head and raised his eyebrows. "Not with the toys he's bringing to the party. That poison laced gum he used to kill Diana? You can't get that out of a vending machine. It was expensive, and dangerous. And this." The General held up the small device Ollie had brought in. "Top of the line. It's similar to ones we use. Deactivated now. With your permission, I can have someone from McAlister come and study it. We have experts. It would be better if we could take it to our headquarters, but I understand we need to maintain the chain of evidence."

Ann leaned back in the chair, sighing and rubbing her temple. "I hate to ask this, but how much is something like that going to cost? We may be handling a high stakes murder case, but we're still on a small-town budget. And after tonight, I may not be able to keep the State out, let alone the feds."

Corvidae walked forward. "I understand why you want to keep it in-house, but maybe it's time to let the State take over?"

The General folded his arms. "I've got no reason to believe that the State can do any better a job on this. As far as the cost, it's on the house, Chief. I don't take kindly when assholes try and blow my people to smithereens. I intend to see this to the end, whether you like it or not. I'd much rather work with you. You may be a small-town police department, but both you and your department handle yourselves as well as any department in the country, and I've worked with most of them. I trust you, I *don't* trust whoever the State might send in."

Corvidae cleared his throat. "You realize the State sent me in."

The General glanced casually at Corvidae. "I do. And you've got a decent enough record."

"You checked me out?" Corvidae seemed more shocked than angry.

"You bet your ass. Problem?"

Corvidae seemed to consider. "Depends. If I get tired of the gig with the state, could I apply to

McAlister?"

The General gave a bored shrug. "Anyone can apply. That doesn't mean you'll get in."

Corvidae pursed his lips, as if trying to decide if he were amused or insulted.

Ann stood up, clearly wanting to move the conversation back to the investigation. "Our next step is to search Frank Duncan's home. Ollie, I know you've been through a lot tonight, but I need you there. Body cam on."

"I'm too wound up to sleep." He turned to Drew. "You good?"

"Not Mr. Duncan," Ann interjected before Drew could respond. "Sorry, but this time I need you to be treated as a witness. We'll do the search without you. It's not a reflection on you personally, but it just needs to be this way."

Drew scowled. "I know that house better than you do. My sisters and I found every conceivable place to hide, trust me."

"I *do* trust you." Ann eyes slid to her son for a moment, before returning to Drew. "More than you could know, but this time, at least until we can go over the place ourselves and document it, you stay away. After that, I'll ask you *and* your sister to come and take a look."

Drew unfolded his arms, narrowed his eyes and felt a stab of panic. "Ashley doesn't need to…"

The General held his hand up, and gave Drew a glare that told him to shut his trap. "She spent just as much time there as you. And she's tougher than you think she is. She doesn't need you to shield her. She needs you to support her. Nobody is going to force her to go, but I expect you to put it out there. It's her choice if she wants to help, and it's not your place to take that choice away from her. Are we clear?"

Drew stiffened. "Yes sir."

Ann walked to Drew, put her hand on his arm. "It might help her heal. Your father can't hurt either of you again."

Drew was far from convinced that was true, but he held his tongue.

There was a knock on the door. A moment later, Sam popped her head in. She was in a fresh uniform, and her hair was back in its traditional pony tail. She jabbed her thumb in the general direction of the squad room. "Morning shift is about to go out. I've given them a heads up about what happened, but since Ollie was involved, I think they'd all like to see him for themselves. You know how much they like him."

Ollie grinned and turned a slight shade of pink. "Um… yeah, sure."

Drew studied Sam. She was avoiding eye contact. Was she embarrassed to be seen with him? He thought they'd worked everything out.

But as soon as Ollie passed her by, Sam grinned and motioned for everyone to follow them. Quickly, they walked down the hallway and into the squad room.

As they rounded the corner, they saw about twenty officers, all standing at attention by the front desk. Each trying their best to hide smirks.

Each member of the squad was in full uniform, their hands behind their backs in a traditional Parade-Rest stance. Each wore a large, white towel wrapped around their waists.

Polansky cleared his throat loudly. "Attention!"

The officers all saluted Ollie, allowing their towels to fall to the floor. A moment later they removed their hats and held them in front of their crotches.

The pink tinge in Ollie's cheeks was replaced by a burning shade of red as his mouth formed a perfect 'O'. He glanced around, at a complete loss for words. Ann hid a laugh behind her hand before heading back to her office. The General and Corvidae exchanged bemused expressions. Drew just shook his head. This had his sister's handiwork all over it. He wasn't sure what it all meant, and was quite sure he didn't want to know.

Giggling like a school girl, Sam handed Ollie a long loofah brush. One of the civilian workers was recording the entire thing on her cell phone.

Ollie put his head down, winced and laughed. He straightened up, saluted them with the loofah and pointed to the door. "Dismissed."

Chapter 17
Home Sweet Home

The moment Drew walked in the front door, Cole was on him in an instant, skidding to a stop at his feet. His eyes were scared as they examined him up and down, looking for missing body parts. "It's all over the news. Aunt Ash said you and Ollie were in the building that got blown up."

Ashley came over herself. "I told him you were okay. It takes more than a little bomb to stop you, but he wanted to see for yourself."

Drew grinned down at his nephew. "I'm fine, and so is Ollie. We breathed in some smoke, but nothing to worry about. Ollie will see you soon."

Cole nodded and backed up. "I wasn't worried or anything. I just wanted to know."

"Of course."

Cole studied his uncle, the fear draining from his face, being replaced by boyish excitement. "What happened? Did you see the bomb go boom?"

Drew laughed. "No, I had to take cover so I didn't go boom with it, but I heard it and it was loud."

Cole grinned. "Wicked. I can't wait to tell Jay. His dad deals with bombs too."

Lilly tapped her watch. "Cole, we need to go or you'll be late for school."

Cole ran to the kitchen, grabbed his bag and slung

it over his shoulder, and started to follow Lilly out to the car. He paused at the doorway and looked back at Drew. "The news said someone got blowed up. Who was it?"

Drew glanced over to Ashley. She hadn't told him. Cole knew enough about their father to not want anything to do with the man, but he didn't need to know his grandfather had been blown to bits right before school. Drew had promised he'd never lie to Cole, but now wasn't the time to explain it. "Nobody important. I'll tell you about it later."

Cole grinned and ran out to the car.

Drew stood by the window, watching him go. Ashley watched by his side. "He was beside himself. I told him because I didn't want him to hear it at school, but I promised I'd seen you both and that you and Ollie had already been discharged. Still, he needed to see you with his own eyes. I'm glad you were able to stop by. Do you have to go back to work, or can you get some rest?"

Drew sighed. It was against his better judgment, but maybe the General was right. He was right about pretty much everything else. "They're at Dad's house, doing a search. I've been told to stay away, at least until they have a thorough pass through. After that, they want me there." He swallowed hard. "Chief Miller asked if you'd come too. You don't have to do it."

The color drained from Ashley's face, but she nodded. "I can go. I want to. I'm not letting you face that alone." She took his hand. "We're in this together."

They stood together for a few moments in silence, before Ashley spoke. "Do you want to take a nap at least? You must be exhausted."

Drew stretched. "Not really. I don't think I could fall asleep. I'm hungry more than anything else."

Ashley smiled. "I can take care of that."

Drew sighed. "I've already had one close call today, I don't want to risk another."

She smacked his arm. "Funny. I was going to take you out to breakfast. Have you been to Kate's Corner? It's not too far, opened about a year ago. They make the best breakfasts. Let me take my brother out."

Drew smiled and followed her to the door. "You got it. Oh, Sam wanted me to make sure you got a video she sent you."

Ashley laughed. "Yeah I did. I should probably explain."

Drew opened the door for her. "No. You really, really shouldn't.

****

Drew had to admit, even if Ashley couldn't cook to save her life, she knew good food. He ordered Country Eggs Benedict; poached eggs over biscuits, together with a fried green tomato and a delicious homemade hollandaise sauce. He washed it down with plenty of strong coffee and simply enjoyed spending the morning with his sister.

Ashley leaned in. "What are you grinning about?"

Drew reached out to take her hand. "You. This." He shrugged. "*Us*. Ash, I've wanted this for so long. I know you don't believe me, but I thought of you every day. I missed you." He shook his head, sure he was screwing up what he wanted to say. "I've been back awhile now, but this feels like the first time I really have *you* back. I know I messed up, but…"

"Stop." Ashley squeezed his hand. "Stop doing that

thing where you blame everything on yourself. I deserve as much of the blame as you do. You wrote to me after you left. I refused to read them. I could have gotten you back in my life years ago, if I hadn't been so…" She closed her eyes. "We both made mistakes. We both blamed you, but it was *never* you. It was Dad. That son of a fucking bitch did this to us. He can't do that anymore."

Drew nodded. "It's weird, isn't it? Dad's dead. He was our father, but honestly, I can't think of one good memory with him. He never made any effort to hide the fact that he hated us."

Ashley took a sip of her own coffee. "I know. It was like we were responsible for some great sin, or injustice that befell him. I've wondered if he resented Mom for getting pregnant with three of us at the same time, but you know what? Why didn't he just leave? I mean, sure we would have been orphaned once mom died, and I'm not saying the foster system would have been great, but it had to be better than that nightmare of our childhood."

Drew grimaced. If he had been smarter, known who to talk to, he could have gotten his sisters out of that hell hole.

"You're doing it again, aren't you?" Ashley pointed at him. "I can see it in your eyes. You're blaming yourself."

Drew nearly lied. "Yeah, I guess old habits die hard."

Ashley took his hand again. "It's going to take time. We'll get there. This time, nothing is going to get between us. We can't do anything about our pasts, except forgive ourselves and each other and move on.

But we're going to make things different for Cole."

Drew nodded. "Damn right we will."

A waitress came by, took their plates and left a bill. Drew reached for it, but Ashley snatched it away. "My treat, remember?"

Drew didn't complain as she pulled out her credit card. As the waitress took it to the register, his phone buzzed. He pulled it out. "It's Ollie. They want to know when we can get there."

Ashley swallowed the last of her coffee. "We can be there in ten minutes."

Drew typed that into his phone, but didn't hit send. "Ash, I went to see Dad right before Kelli's funeral. It brings it all back. I was a little kid with a broken arm when I walked into that house. You don't have to do this. I can take you home, or to the bookstore."

Ashley took her credit card from the waitress, scribbled in a generous tip, and started to get up. "If you go, I go."

She headed out to her car, with Drew trailing behind her. "Ash, would you just think about it? I know that house as well as you do. I know everyplace he could use to hide something…"

Ashley turned on him. "No, you don't. You weren't the one that was usually hiding from him. That was me and Kelli, locked in a closet, listening to you scream. You think I don't know why he wanted you to call for us? Do you understand why he did that?"

Drew stared into the street. "He was an abusive asshole. He wanted to spread the pain around."

Ashley stepped into his line of sight. "He was, but that wasn't it. Dad understood that even as an eight-year-old boy, you were capable of so much more love, and decency than he was ever was. He wanted to break that. He needed to take that away from you. And for a short amount of time, he probably thought he did. He convinced you that leaving to protect us was the same as abandoning us. And Goddammit, he used me to hurt you. So, I'm going back into that house today. With or without you. I'd rather have you by my side."

Drew finally made eye contact. "It was hell, going in there with the General. Having him see that piece of me. It's going to be harder to go in there with you. To remind you of who we were. I don't know if I'm strong enough to handle it."

Ashley pulled her brother into a warm embrace. "This time, let me be strong enough for the both of us."

****

Ollie stood on the front porch of the Duncan home. Although they had been friends since they were kids, this was the first time he'd ever come into this house. Ollie could feel himself shake with rage whenever he tried to picture the terror that Ashley had been in, and him none the wiser. There had been times when she'd shown up at school, sometimes quieter than normal, other times quicker to anger at any perceived slight. He'd ask if she was okay, or if he could do anything, and she insisted everything was fine. It was all a lie. She was never okay.

How many nights did Ollie sit at home, fantasizing about asking Ashley for a real date, while she cowered in her closet listening to her brother being tortured while she held Kelli?

"You all right, son?"

Ollie sighed as he turned to find the General by his side. "I just..." Ollie paused, turned off the body cam.

"I hate that we're bringing them here. They're going to have to relive their childhood nightmares on record." He pointed to the small, black rectangular device that was clipped to his shirt pocket. "We've been through this place, but Mom insists we can't afford to miss anything."

The General nodded. "And she's right. She's already getting pressure to have the state or feds come in, and she's not going to be able avoid a federal takeover, not once it's official that Jericho is involved."

Ollie rubbed the bridge of his nose. "I know she wants to solve this in- house, and I get why. A lot of this stems from the corruption of the Ember Falls PD from before Mom took over. She's worked hard to erase that stain, but if this requires the State or Feds to take over, it'll look like Mom can't care for her own department. Besides, Vic was ours. It should be someone wearing an EFPD shield that brings him in."

"What's important is that someone brings him down," the General said. "And that we clear up this mess. Drew deserves to have his name fully exonerated, beyond any doubt. And Cole deserves to grow up not having to defend him. But there's something else. Something struck you back when we were in your mother's office."

Ollie glanced down the street, knowing Ashley and Drew would be arriving any moment now, and for the first time in his life, he wasn't eagerly awaiting her arrival.

"It's Diana's father," Ollie said.

Frowning, the General raised an eyebrow. "I thought your mother said there wasn't one in the picture."

Ollie exhaled sharply. "Yeah, I went over that with Mom on the way over here. No father on record. No pictures at her place that indicated there had ever been one in her life. She was raised by a single mom, now deceased. No siblings."

"It happens," the General shrugged. "Some men cut out the moment they hear they have a kid on the way. Some women never tell the guy because he's bad news. Neither way is really fair to the kid, growing up without a father."

Ollie spotted Ashley's car turn the corner and head down the block towards them. "The last thing I heard from Diana was her calling out for her father."

The General scowled. "You sure?"

Ollie nodded as Ashley pulled her Nissan into her father's driveway. Brother and sister seemed reluctant to get out of the car.

"Crystal. I'll never forget that moment," Ollie said as he scooted down the steps to greet Drew and Ashley. Ashley buried herself in his arms, and he could feel her tremble.

Ollie kissed the top of her head. "I realized, I never really said anything to either of you. Y'know…" He shrugged. "About your dad. I mean, he was your father, but…"

Drew shook his head. "He was no father to either of us. He as much said so last night. Thank you for your sympathy, but it's not needed." He glanced up at the doorway where Ann was waiting for them. "If we're going to do this, let's get it over with."

As they climbed the porch to their childhood home, a herd of cops came out through the back carrying kits and evidence bags.

"Thank you both for coming," Ann said. "We've been through the house. Your father wasn't one for record keeping, so we haven't found much of anything. I can tell you that we have noted that he has a lot of expensive items in his home. We were wondering if you had any idea how he paid for it all."

Drew shook his head. "When he picked me up at prison, he had what looked like a brand-new truck. All the amenities. I also noticed stuff when I came to speak with Dad before Kelli's funeral. The General was with me. He'd lined the house with expensive crap." He glared at the house. "It was still a shithole."

"We don't have any idea where Dad got his money," Ashley added. "He never gave us any. He hated to keep food in the house for us to eat."

As the last of the cars pulled away, Ann placed her hand on the doorknob, but didn't twist it open. "I've sent everyone back to the station. I didn't think you'd need an audience. Officer Rossi is inside waiting. We need to make sure both of you are covered by a body camera. I'm sorry, but if we find anything, I don't want it questioned. Detective Miller will stay with Ashley, and Officer Rossi with your brother. If you'd prefer that I and General McAlister stay outside, we'll understand."

Ashley stepped all the way onto the porch. "You're both family."

Ann reached out to take Ashley's hand, the veneer of police authority dropping as she gave a small squeeze of affection. A moment later, she was all business as she nodded to her son. "Camera on."

Ann opened the door and invited Ashley and Drew into their childhood home.

****

Drew fought a wave a nausea when he breathed in the air in his father's home, but the sight of Sam standing in of the living room, making notes in her police memo book made him feel more solid. She quickly shoved it into her back pocket and came over to Drew. Her camera was already on, but Drew didn't really care as he wrapped his arms around her.

"You got this," Sam whispered in his ear.

Chief Miller stood in front of them, motioned for them to look around. "I know it's been a few years, but just look around. Anything that stands out that might be important, or any place you think your father may have hidden anything at all, please let one of us know."

Ashley had her arms folded as if she were cold. She studied the living room. "It's the same ugly wallpaper, but new furniture. Dad never liked to do any work around the house, so I guess that makes sense." She turned to the big screen TV. "That's new, not that we ever watched TV in here. This was Dad's room."

There were ashtrays filled with the remnants of cigarettes and ashes, much of which had spilled out onto whatever surface they were on. Bottles of beer and Jack Daniels littered the room. Some on the floor, some on the couch and chair. The place was a mess, disgustingly so, but there was little that could help their case. "There's an air vent by the window," Drew said. "I think it could be popped out. Any chance there's something there?"

Ollie shook his head. "We've checked them. This one here," he pointed to the one near the window Drew was indicating. "It comes out, but we looked, there's nothing there."

"But that's the sort of thing we need to know," Ann said.

After a few moments longer, they moved into the kitchen. "Did you check the oven?" Ashley asked. "Dad didn't cook. He was worse at it than I was. By the time we were ten, Kelli and Drew made most of the meals."

Sam walked over, pulled out a flashlight, and opened the oven. She took a few seconds to inspect inside. "Nothing, but some grease stains from things that spilled over."

Ashley leaned on the counter near the stove. "I still remember the morning we all turned thirteen. Kelli wanted us to celebrate together. Dad had spent the night out, which wasn't uncommon, so Kelli had made this omelet, one big enough for all of us. Just as she was done, Dad came in and took it." She looked at Drew. "You got so angry."

Drew clenched his jaw. "Kelli was in tears. We didn't really have any money to get presents for each other. I used to mow laws in the summer, shovel driveways in the winter, but it wasn't much. That was Kelli's way of telling us she loved us, and Dad just ruined it. Thought it was funny as hell. I don't think he even realized it was our birthday."

Ashely wiped away a tear. "It was all *his* food, which he allowed us to eat out of the kindness of his heart."

Drew snorted and turned away. "His heart was a black, soulless pit."

Ashley didn't laugh. She held her hand two inches above the right-front burner. "He shoved your face this close, didn't he?"

Drew stormed over, pulled her hand away. "It

doesn't matter. It's over."

"Is it?" Ashley didn't budge. "You didn't fight when Kelli turned the stove on, you remember why?"

Sam's hand went to her face, and Ollie's eyes went wide. Both reactions deepened Drew's humiliation. "Let's move on." Drew tried to walk away, but Ashley yanked him back.

"He told you if you fought, he'd burn Kelli and me. You were going to let him burn your face."

Drew glared at the stove, resisted the urge to kick it. "He was lying. Dad wouldn't have been able to explain the burns on my face away. He was usually careful to leave the bruises where nobody could see them."

Ashley placed her hand over his heart. "You don't see it, do you? I'd let myself forget because it was too painful to remember, but you just refuse to see how much you endured to protect us."

Drew closed his eyes. He didn't want his sister looking at him like a savior, or see the pity in the eyes of his fiancée. He didn't want to hear about how he was her hero. He'd been useless. There was no escaping that reality. He pulled away, and left the room without making eye contact with anyone.

They continued to tour the house, stopping at a trio of class pictures, one of each of the Duncan triplets as kids. Ashley's hand trembled as she touched the one of her sister. "Kelli was always so pretty. I don't have any of these pictures from when we were little. Do you think we can take them?"

Ann smiled. "Not now, but eventually. I couldn't help but notice that these are the most recent ones."

Ashley kept her eyes on the picture of Kelli.

"These were first grade. Last ones we took and brought home before Mom died. She put them up. Dad wasn't interested. I don't think we ever got them again."

Drew tried to talk Ashley out of following him downstairs. The basement was always dark, cramped and one of her least favorite places, but she insisted. The cellar was stuffed with things their father had bought that he never used or had gotten tired of. Golf clubs, weights, gaming equipment, two barbeques, bikes, a canoe and old furniture were lying haphazardly around. Ann went through the inventory. "There were a few laptops, besides the newer one we found upstairs, but we've removed those. We'll see what's on them. I don't suppose either of you could guess his password."

Drew shrugged. "Not our birthday, that's for sure. I couldn't even guess right now."

They headed upstairs next. There were four bedrooms. Both Drew and Ashley admitted that if there was a place to hide anything in the master bedroom, they wouldn't know about it and the fact was it was such a filthy mess nobody wanted to touch it. They started in the second largest room. It was mostly empty, with a small dresser and a chair but no bed. Ashley stood in the empty spot where one would go. "This was Mom's room. Once she got sick, she slept here. Had a bed, no TV. Just magazines and a few books."

Drew opened the closet. It was empty. "Dad threw out everything that was Mom's." He gave a humorless laugh. "Except us."

They went into Drew's room next. He felt a little embarrassed to have Sam see the posters on his wall of different bikini models, but he had been a horny teenage boy who never had the chance to redecorate. If that was bad, he definitely didn't want her to look under the bed.

There wasn't anything there that didn't belong, so they moved on to the last bedroom, which Ashley had shared with Kelli.

The walls were still the same pale blue that Drew had helped them paint it while their father was on a weekend bender. Ashley had grabbed most of the things that were important to her, or anything she'd thought Kelli would want, so the room was barer than Drew's, who hadn't been in his since the night before his arrest.

Ashley headed for their closet. Drew launched himself across the room. "What are you doing?"

Ashely kept her eye on the door. "I want to look in there."

Drew put himself between his sister and her closet. "I can look, you don't need to go."

Ashley was starting to tremble, but she didn't move. "

Yes, I do. I need to go in there."

Drew put his hands on her shoulders. "Ash, let me. I know you wanted to be here for me, and that means more to me than you can know, but I can't let…"

"I need to go in there," Ashley yelled. "I need to know I can go inside that damn closet without hearing you scream."

Drew pulled her into a hug. "I'm okay. It wasn't that bad."

"Bullshit," Ashley said. "Don't you think I know why you got that damn tattoo?"

Drew kept shaking his head, arguing with her, tears falling from his eyes. He wouldn't budge.

"Marine, stand aside," the General ordered. He

stepped next to Drew, getting right in his face. "You can't keep what's in that closet from hurting her if you stand between her and her demons. This may be the hardest order you ever have to obey, but I expect you to obey it. Stand aside."

Drew froze, holding his sister, stroking her hair.

"Don't make me repeat myself," the General warned.

Slowly, painfully, Drew stepped aside.

Ashley gripped the doorknob to the closet, and opened it. She grabbed Ollie's hand as she entered. She glanced down, her eyes fixed on an old shoebox, before she retreated out and ran to the window that she opened, gulping down air. Drew was by her side in an instant.

"Are we done?" Drew's voice was laced with anger. "Can I get her out of here?"

Ann sighed, but nodded. "I'm sorry to put you through this for nothing, but we had to try."

Ashley turned and surprised everyone by grinning. "Somethings off in there. I had to see for myself. I wasn't sure if I'd remember right, but I did."

Sam glanced at the closet, then back to Ashley. "What is it we missed?"

"The pile of shoe boxes? The white one, on top of the green one, on the pink one?" Ashley pointed. "The white one is the smallest. It's on top, but I used to always stack them the opposite way, to smallest one on the bottom."

Sam pulled out her phone. She checked the pictures she'd taken of it earlier. It was exactly how it was now, the smallest on the top. "Why?"

Ashley folded her arms across her chest. "I wanted

to know if Dad ever got in there. There was a board under that box that came up. Hard to spot. Kelli and I found it one time while we were waiting for Drew to let us out. Kelli would store snacks and water in there. There were times we'd be in there for hours."

Drew nodded. "I remember sometimes you had a water bottle for me when I let you out. You'd put it against the latest burn. I just never really thought about it."

Ashley pointed once again. "I think I let something slip once, the first time I saw Dad after I'd left. We ran into each other at the grocery store. I told him how it was my food, and I didn't have to hide it in the fucking closet floor. He must have found it. Check it, Ollie."

Ollie entered the closet. Pulling on gloves, he waited until Sam had a flashlight on him to give plenty of light for the camera. He moved the boxes and felt around the floor. Finding a nick in the floorboard, he used a tweezer for evidence collection and opened it up. "Shine that light in here Sam."

Drew stood by his sister, his hands on her shoulders, and waited.

"Son of a bitch," Ollie said. He came out of the closet, and held up a long string with a small USB device attached to it. "Recognize this?"

Both Drew and Ashley shook their heads.

Ann took it and dropped it in an evidence bag. "Well, looks like this may not have been for nothing after all."

Ashley grinned as she pulled her cell phone out. The smile faded. "Shit, it's a message from the school. Mrs. Hanley wants to see us. Something's up with Cole."

Chapter 18
The Diabolical Galactor

Ashley approached the school with nearly as much trepidation as she had her father's home.

The school was empty. Jay's aunt had picked up the boys and taken them to Jay's home to work on their comic book. She and Drew marched down the halls, ready to do battle for Cole. For the last week, he'd been looking forward to coming to class, and while the majority of that had to do with his new friend Jay, a lot of the credit belonged to Mrs. Hanley. Cole liked her, and that was amazing in and of itself. They had been told that Cole wasn't in any trouble. Mrs. Hanley simply needed to see them.

"Feels weird being back here huh?" Drew said. "I keep expecting Mrs. Petoskey to come out yelling at us for being here without a pass."

Ashley managed a small laugh. "Or Mr. Fitzgerald telling us to get to class and not take the scenic route."

The both turned the corner and made their way down to Mrs. Hanley's class. Outside the hallway there were papers proudly displayed, essays about a variety of books. Ashely grinned as she pointed to Cole's. He'd gotten an A Plus on his treatment of 'A Call to Courage.'

Drew took a picture. "Did either of us ever get an A plus on anything?"

Ashley took a moment to skim the report, which she'd read before Cole had handed in, but concentrated on the remarks from Mrs. Hanley, who was glowing with praise. "We all did once, but I don't know that our blood tests count."

With a snicker, Drew knocked on Cole's class room door.

Mrs. Hanley was smiling and friendly, but right away, Ashley could sense she was upset. Still, her affection for Cole was plainly obvious as she spoke. "Cole is a sweetheart. He listens well, and he's adjusted to his new class better than I expected. He's still shy around the other kids, but thankfully Jay isn't, so I think that compensates for a lot." Mrs. Hanley motioned them to her desk. "I've had to focus his attention a couple of times. Nothing serious, but once in a while after lunch, he and Jay might still be chattering about something as I'm trying to get the class to pay attention. I've never had to reprimand them or anything. Usually just calling their names gets them to settle down."

Drew leaned against the teacher's desk. "I'm assuming that's not why we're here. Cole loves coming to school, and you can't possibly know how huge that is for him. I really don't want to do anything that'll change that."

Mrs. Hanley seemed to melt. "Neither do I. I know Cole has had a very rough past, plus what happened to his mother, and then being kidnapped." She shook her head and sighed. "God, I can't even begin to imagine what that little boy has been through, and the fact that he's adjusting as well as he is, well, that's a tribute to what you two and his other guardian has done. Lilly Danvers, right?"

Ashley nodded. "She wanted to be here, but she's at work and this was short notice. I thought it would be all right if just the two of us met with you."

Mrs. Hanley gave Ashley a reassuring smile. "I'm thrilled the pair of you came in so quickly. Sometimes I'm lucky if I can get either parent to respond."

"We take everything about Cole very seriously," Drew said. "He is our top priority. Can I ask why we are here? Is Cole in any trouble?"

Mrs. Hanley shook her head. "No. If this had been anyone *but* Cole, I would have probably not have even called, but well…" Mrs. Hanley reached into her drawer, pulled out a homemade comic book. "They had this in class today. I asked to see it."

Ashley groaned. "I'm sorry. Cole and Jay are working on their own comic. I guess they were so excited they had trouble putting it away for class. We'll talk to him."

Mrs. Hanley placed the comic on the table before them. "The presence of a comic book in class isn't anything new. Normally, I would have just told them to put it away, but I took a look in it. The content is probably not so over the top compared to what's out there these days, but it's a little inappropriate for a fourth-grade classroom. I talked to the boys, individually."

Ashley started to reach for the comic, but Mrs. Hanley kept her hand over it.

"I want you to understand that I was careful how I spoke to the boys. I started with Jay, told him the comic was well done and very exciting. He was enthusiastic and referred to Cole as his best buddy. When I asked Jay about the pictures in here, he told me that he just drew the story that Cole had created. I gave Jay no reason to think there was anything wrong. From Jay's perspective, he was just making sure I understood Cole's contribution."

Ashley and Drew exchanged confused looks. Finally, Mrs. Hanley handed Ashley the comic. She started to flip through it. At first, she didn't see anything wrong. Detailed pictures of their hero Captain Nova, his black, star studded uniform prominently featured in most panels.

As Ashley continued to flip through the pages, Mrs. Hanley continued. "When I spoke to Cole, he seemed very excited to talk about their creation. I thought I was doing well to hide my concerns, until I asked about the pictures towards the end. He closed down. I asked what inspired the idea. He told me nothing, but for the rest of the day, Cole seemed shaken. Even scared."

Ashley flipped to the end, where the comic went to the secret lair of the intergalactic menace, Galactor. The character was huge; larger than life, with smoke coming out of his mouth and nostrils as if he were breathing out while smoking a cigarette. Galactor wore armor, with a large belt that carried keys. His skin was pale, and scarred. His face was cruel and hungry. On the fifth panel, Galactor entered a dark room. In the sixth, he talked about having a rough day, and needing to relax. The next panel had him making a fist, with lighting emanating out, illuminating the room. Ashley turned the page, to find Galactor surveying a collection of prisoners. All women, wearing rags. Little lines near their skin indicated the women were trembling from the cold, and little dialogue bubbles made it clear they were starving.

Each woman was bound by chains that glowed with a sinister energy. Galactor laughed as he tried to decide who he wanted to use to entertain him. The last panel showed one of the women crying as Galactor held up a small key.

"I could be overreacting," Mrs. Hanley said. "I know that children often use art to express things that they can't put into words. And while Jay is the artist, it was, as they both admitted, Cole's ideas coming to life."

Confused, Ashley looked to Drew, ready to ask him what he thought. She froze at the look on his face. Pale white, eyes wide with fear. It was the same look Drew got whenever their father was on a rampage and Drew didn't think he could protect her or Kelli.

Mrs. Hanley rose, but stayed behind her desk. "I'm going to assume that this means something to you."

Drew winced as he nodded. "Who else has seen these?"

"Just myself," Mrs. Hanley said. "Both boys told me that they didn't want anyone else to see it until it's done."

Drew picked up the comic with hands that were shaking. "I can't explain this, but you have to keep this as quiet as possible. I don't want this getting out. I need…" Drew's voice cracked. "I need to take this. Please."

Mrs. Hanley nodded. "I'll tell them that I gave it to you, and that while the comic is well done, shouldn't be brought to class. I'm sorry, but I don't think other parents would want their kids seeing that. Having said that, you may not want to take this away from Cole. It might be the only outlet to share with you how he feels about his past. I don't know what this represents but—"

"I do," Drew grabbed the comic. "Thank you for everything. I can't even begin to tell you how much gratitude I have for how you handled this. I'll keep you informed as much as I can, but I might be very limited in what I can say."

Mrs. Hanley nodded. "I understand. His therapist will want to keep things confidential."

Drew scowled. "Cole isn't seeing a therapist, at least not yet. He refuses. But this," he held up the comic, "will be involving an open police case, so I have to advise you to keep it all to yourself."

Mrs. Hanley slowly lowered herself into her chair. This time, her own face was going white. She reiterated her promise to not tell anyone.

Ashley followed her brother. "Drew, what is it?"

Drew just shook his head. "Not here."

They exited the building, and quickly made it to Ashley's car. Drew got in, closed his eyes and gritted his teeth.

"You're scaring the shit out of me, Drew." Ashley started the car, but didn't put it in drive as she wasn't sure where to go. Her mind was spinning, and her heart was racing. "Talk to me."

Drew ignored her as he pulled out his cell phone. He put it on speaker and held it where Ashley could see that he'd called Ollie.

"Hey, Drew." Ollie's voice sounded tired. "We haven't tried to get into the thumb drive yet, but we will soon. I can't tell you when—"

"Forget about that for now Ollie," Drew interrupted. "I'm coming to the station. It's about the mass grave."

Ashley's eyes widened and she'd suddenly forgotten how to breathe.

"What about it?" Ollie asked, his voice sounded sharper now.

Drew reached for his sister's hand. "We may have discovered an eye witness who can shed some light on what happened."

Ashley was shaking her head, not wanting to believe what her brother was saying. Hoping he was wrong, praying he was completely off.

"Who?" Ollie asked.

Drew closed his eyes, and Ashley knew he was fighting against the need to say the words that he needed to say. Words that would make it real.

"It's Cole."

****

Drew burst into Chief Miller's office without knocking. He barely noticed Polansky standing behind her desk, or Ollie and Sam in nearby chairs, rising as he came in. The General stood at the front right corner, his hawk like face set in stone. Corvidae was opposite, waiting eagerly. Drew tossed Cole's comic book on the chief's desk, opened to the last few pages.

"Take a look at that. Tell me that I'm wrong." Drew closed his eyes and waited. "Please."

Ann took her time, studying the illustrations, reading the dialogue. She then used her laptop to pull up a picture of a keys. They were the keys that had been hidden in a box near the dump site where they'd found Kelli and the grave of four women and one man. All of the women's bodies had been constrained by chains and a lock that matched the keys.

The design was simple, a short stub of a key, with a single tooth, and a circle at the end. It matched the key in the drawing, perfectly.

"I don't understand." Ann shook her head as she continued to study the comic. "Cole couldn't have witnessed the murders. They all took place before he was born. The male victim was the last, and best estimates tell us he was buried six months after you were in prison. Cole couldn't have seen this, but…" She looked at the chains again. The way they were wrapped around Galactor's victims, a crisscross pattern that held their arms and legs in, was exactly the same. "Mr. Duncan, I have to ask, is there anyway Cole could have seen crime scene pictures? Gone through your phone? Your computer?"

Drew shook his head. "None. I don't have these pictures on my phone, and the laptop I use is very secure. McAlister issue secure. Even if he got on while I was logged in, the pictures are in an encrypted file. I've been very careful, not only because of the nature of the investigation, but because I wouldn't want to risk Cole seeing these. I've never even opened them at home. Wherever Cole saw this, it wasn't from me."

Drew went on to explain how Jay was the artist, but it was all coming from Cole's mind. "Chief, what do we know about the male vic?"

Ann retrieved the correct file. "Male, approximate age early twenties. Estimated height, just under six feet. Build was thin. Blonde hair. He was killed quickly. His hands and feet were burnt, teeth removed, which is what's making it so difficult to identify him. Why?"

Drew glanced towards the General, who listening intently. "How well does that match Rodger Ganty?"

Ollie came forward. "You mean Cole's biological father? I thought he skipped out before Cole was born. He was a loser. I tried to talk to Kelli about him before she met Edward. Rodger was already bitching about how Kelli should get an abortion, but Kelli refused. I remember thinking it was for the best when he took her money and left."

Ashley, who had been quiet, turned to Ollie. "You tried to look out for her then, but she was afraid of trying to raise a son on her own, so she hooked up with Edward Hunter within a week. She didn't put Rodger's name on Cole's birth certificate because he never wanted to be a father, but neither did Edward. He told her that he understood they were a package deal and took both of them out of Ember Falls up north to Cheyanne."

Ashley shivered. "I only met him twice. I never liked Edward, but at the time I didn't think much of any man. Kelli told me he was different. He'd been really patient with the fact that she wasn't able to have sex yet. That said something to her. She thought maybe he was one of the good ones, like Drew. I um…" She glanced towards her brother, and he could feel his heartbreak knowing what was coming next. "I wasn't in a mood to agree. I just didn't want to think any guy was a good guy. We had a fight and she left town. I tried to contact her, to ask about the baby, but she never responded. I thought she just had decided not to forgive me, but she told me that she'd never gotten my messages. Edward wouldn't let her have any contact with anyone from Ember Falls. He told her…" Her breath caught in her throat. "Kelli said that everyone in that town was nothing but a dead body buried in a shallow grave, and that if she wasn't careful, her and her little brat would end up the same way."

Ashley was crying, shaking her head as she started to plead. "I thought about it when Kelli was killed, but Ollie told me he was in jail, so I assumed it was just more of the same crap he'd used to control her. I swear I never thought…" She buried herself in Ollie's arms.

Drew put his hand on her shoulder. "It's not your fault. None of this is."

Polansky leaned over the chief, studied the homemade comic book. "Look." He pointed to the panel that showed one of the women chained up. "The lock is right over the heart, that's exactly where it was on each of our DB's. It's hard to argue coincidence."

"I don't believe in coincidences," the General said. "Not like this."

Corvidae crossed his arms. "I'm afraid I'm not following. The kid wasn't born by the time our vics were put in the ground. At best, he was one or under. He can't have knowledge about this unless it was leaked. He's never seen these bodies."

The General narrowed his eyes. "I don't think he has. Not *these* bodies. Marine, play it out."

Drew turned towards the General. "Whoever murdered Molly and the others is clearly a serial killer. Killers like that don't just stop unless they're stopped. If they die, or are arrested, even for something unrelated, but they never stop. They can't, it's a compulsion. Edward Hunter killed Molly Winters, and the others. He then left Ember Falls, taking Kelli and Cole with him. Somehow, Cole must have known what Hunter was doing. My guess is that if we check out Cheyanne, we'll find similar bodies."

Corvidae seemed to consider this. "So why didn't the kid say something? He's away from Hunter now. He's safe."

Ollie ran his fingers through his hair. "He doesn't feel safe. How can he with that monster out there? Remember when Cole ran away? Edward Hunter called the house, spoke to him. Cole won't talk about it, but my guess is that Hunter threatened him."

"Not him." Understanding washed over Drew like a tidal wave of scolding hot water. "The other night, after the self-defense class, Cole was asleep downstairs. I carried him to bed and he woke up swinging. He's been scared I'm going to leave because if I go, who will protect Ashley and Lilly. That fucking bastard told Cole if he talked, he'd be coming here. Not for him, but for Ashley and Lilly. He's keeping quiet to protect *us*."

"Cole has asked me how fast I could get to his house," Ollie said. "I always assumed he was scared of Hunter coming for him, but that was just part of it. If we take down Hunter, Cole will talk. If he's positive that talking would be the best way to protect his family, he'll do it."

Corvidae picked up the comic book himself, flipped through the pages. "If this is true, that puts Hunter well out of your jurisdiction. He's still in New York State, but not here in Ember Falls. I can call it in, have the State come review the evidence. Then we can go get him."

"Screw that," Drew said. "I'm not officially a part of the EMPD yet, so I don't have a jurisdiction. I'm going to find Edward Hunter and drag his ass here, kicking and screaming."

"You're not going alone," Ollie said.

Ann got up. "Ollie, I can't stop Drew, but you have an EMPD shield. You can't go."

"That's an easy solution." Ollie pulled his shield off his belt, placed on his mother's desk. "Consider that my resignation if you need to, Mom. I love Cole. I plan on being a part of the family that raises him. I'm helping to take the son of a bitch down."

"Hold on." Corvidae glanced at the comic. "He's still in New York State. One county can easily cooperate with another. I know the police chief in Cheyanne. His name is Stevens. He's a good man. It'll take you a couple of hours to get there. Let me reach out, they can make the official arrest, have him transported. But to do this right, we need to get Cole's statement."

Drew nodded. "Let's go now."

He held up his hands. "Hold on now, you can't play both sides here. You need to stay far away from any questioning of the minor child witness. Quite frankly, all of you should. I should handle that." He looked at Chief Miller. "Here, under your direct supervision, but let me be on point until we get Cole's statement."

Ann came around her desk. "It would make more sense. Corvidae and an officer from the EMPD. No, not you Rossi," she quickly said as Sam stepped forward. "You're engaged to Cole's uncle. Let's get Miranda's partner in here. Bryan O'Malley. He deserves a piece of this."

Corvidae pulled out his phone. "Give me a few minutes. I can make the arraignments in Cheyanne, then I'll go get the kid. I'll take Ashley with me. He's a minor, so he should have an adult present at all times. If you two head out now, you can get to the Cheyanne police station before dark. Stevens will be waiting. But let's keep this on the down low for as long as we can. Keep in mind, we still have Jericho to deal with, and for all we know, he might be listening as we speak."

"Not likely," the General said. "This entire station has been thoroughly swept for bugs by McAlister. And believe it or not, you each passed through a scanner on the way in. Unless you climbed in through a window."

Corvidae headed for the door. "I still say we don't take chances. We know Jericho is good. We shouldn't leave anything up to chance." Without waiting for a reply, Corvidae left the room, phone in hand.

Drew walked back to Ann. "I'm leaving now. The sooner we get the son of a bitch, the faster Cole will feel safe." He looked towards the General. "You want in?"

The General scowled as he considered. "I think I want to be present when Corvidae questions Cole. Make sure he doesn't fuck it up."

Drew turned to Ashley next. "You take care of Cole, and this nightmare will be over before long. All of it."

Ashley nodded, her eyes watery, but full of steely resolve.

Drew and Ollie headed for the door. "Detective Miller," Ann called.

Ollie turned around, his eyes set.

Ann tossed him his shield. "Take that with you. You still represent the EMPD. Behave yourself accordingly."

With a nod, Ollie replaced his shield and followed Drew to find Edward Hunter.

****

Just as Drew and Ollie were getting in their car, Corvidae came running out to them. "Okay so when you get into Cheyanne, go right to the police station on Barrett Street. You have GPS?"

Drew nodded, pointed to the dash. "The General also had the cars swept. They're clean."

"Perfect," Corvidae said. "I called Chief Stevens directly, but kept it brief, so you'll have to lay it out for him. He knows me and knows you're coming, but I asked him to not tell anyone until you get there. Keep it off the radar, at least until you're in Cheyanne. I'll take care of things here. And look, I can't imagine how angry you guys are. I know I'd be ready to rip heads off if it were my nephew, but try to play it by the book. Or at the very least, the Cliff Notes."

Drew nodded as Ollie started the engine. "You just better be gentle with Cole. He's been through a lot."

Corvidae held up his hand like a boy scout. "I promise. I've taken statements from kids before. I know what I'm doing."

Drew stared out the window, suddenly feeling unsure. "Maybe I should stay. Cole might want me there."

"Hey, you need to do this," Corvidae said. "I'll take care of Cole. I swear."

Drew thought it through. He desperately wanted to put his hands on Edward Hunter. He'd wanted that for a very long time. Finally, he nodded. "If you need me, call."

He gave the signal, and Ollie pulled out of the parking lot and headed towards Cheyanne.

****

Ashley had been crying at the station, but by the time she'd climbed into Corvidae's car, she'd become very angry. She sat with her fists clenched as she imagined her brother and Ollie ripping Edward Hunter limb from limb. She wanted a shot at the bastard.

What had Cole seen? How close did Hunter come to showing him what he did to women? The thought of that sweet boy being threatened by Hunter made Ashley want to scream.

"You've got two minutes to get that out of your system," Corvidae said.

"What?" Ashley spun around, trying to piece together the syllables that she'd heard into a sentence that made sense.

"You look ready to scream you head off," Corvidae said. "And I can't say as I blame you. So, if you want to scream, scream. But do it now. When we get there, Cole needs to see you calm and in control."

Ashley glanced out at the mailboxes as they passed. "I don't do calm and in control very well. Cole knows that."

Corvidae smiled. "I'm sure he does. And based on everything you've told me, everything I've heard, Cole will probably know something's up the moment he sees you. Kids like that, who grew up in homes like you did, they learn fast to pick up on things. But if you're afraid, he'll be more afraid than he has to be. You want to show him that it's under control. It might be the hardest thing you ever had to do, but you *can* do it."

Ashley nodded. She kept telling herself over and over again, it would be okay. Cole would be fine. This was the start of making everything better for him. They would arrest Edward Hunter, and throw him in jail where he'd rot for the rest of his miserable life.

"Dammit," Ashley said as she pulled down the vanity mirror. "I do better angry. I can't let him see me cry." She wiped away the tears and flipped the mirror up again as they pulled into the Jay's driveway. "Stay here, will you? Cole doesn't know you. You'll make him nervous."

Corvidae smiled. "Sure."

Ashley got out and ran to the front door. She'd texted, so hopefully Cole was ready. She hated the fact that she had to pull Cole away from Jay. Not only was he Cole's first friend, but this was the first time in his life that Cole had gone over to someone else's house.

Cole was sitting in the living room, eating homemade cookies that were distinctly not burned, and playing a video game with Jay. Jay's aunt came over. "I'm sorry that you have to take Cole so soon. We were hoping for him to stay for dinner."

Ashley forced a smile. "I'm sorry too. Jay is such a sweetheart. I'd love it if Cole could come back another day, but something came up and we need Cole."

Cole was studying Ashley, ignoring his game. His onscreen character was being devoured by zombies. "What's wrong?"

"Nothing sweetie." Inwardly, Ashley winced. She was putting too much happiness forward. Cole was seeing right through it. "But really, we have to go."

Hesitantly, Cole got up. He grabbed his bag, but didn't move towards the door. Instead he looked out the window, spotting Corvidae. "Where's Uncle Drew? Weren't you with him today?"

Ashley nodded. "We spent the day together, but he had to go to work. That's someone who he's been working with."

Cole kept looking out the window to Corvidae. "I don't know him."

Happy and calm weren't working. "Cole, we need to go. *Now*." She pointed to the front door. "Say thank you to Jay and his aunt, and let's head out now."

Sighing his understanding that he had no choice, Cole thanked Jay's aunt, did some strange fist bump, slap and point thing with Jay, and followed Ashley out to the car. Ashely opened the back door and then went around to get in the front passenger seat. As soon as they were buckled, Corvidae pulled out of the driveway and headed for the highway.

Cole held his bag tightly as he looked out the window. "This isn't the way home."

Ashley turned in her seat to face him. "No, it's not. Cole, I don't want you to get upset, but we need to go to the police station. We just need to talk with a few people. You trust me, right?"

Cole scowled. "I didn't do anything wrong."

"No, of course you didn't." Ashley smiled and took his hand. "Ian, tell Cole he's not in any trouble."

Ian Corvidae grinned, looked behind him and winked. "Sorry kid, but fact is, you have no idea how deep in it you are."

Corvidae pulled a strange looking gun out, pointed it at Ashley and fired. Ashley spasmed violently while the gun emitted an angry buzz. She heard Cole scream just as she lost consciousness.

Chapter 19
Ornithology

"Don't even think about it, buddy," the man driving the car said.

Cole was frozen in place, unsure what to do. He tried to swallow the ball of panic that was stuck in his throat, but he couldn't manage even that. His eyes drifted towards Aunt Ashley who was slumped over in her seat. Was she breathing?

"She's not dead," the man said. "That was a Taser." He pulled onto a back road. His eyes never left the mirror where he watched Cole for more than a few seconds. "A Taser is a stun gun, in case you don't know. It's hard to be sure what you're aware of. I think you're smarter than most kids your age, but you are still a child. I feel as if I know you. I've heard a lot about you. Hell, I've heard you. You're special." He smiled wickedly. "I wonder if you know just how special."

Cole didn't feel special. He felt useless and helpless. Weak. Somehow, he'd let his aunt, someone he loved, someone who he knew loved him, be hurt. He knew everyone would come. Drew, Ollie, and Sam would stop at nothing to save them both, but if they did, he should go away. He was bad for them.

Maybe he was just bad.

The car made another turn, this one onto a dirt road. Cole's heart began to slam against his chest, as if trying to escape. Alone meant dead. He was going to die. Maybe everyone would be better off. But he had to do something for his aunt.

Slowly, he tried to reach for his book bag.

The car stopped. "Don't." The man didn't turn around, and his smile, still friendly and deceptively kind, never faltered. "I know what that little phone of yours can do. If you try for it, I may have to do something I'm not prepared to do. In fact," He turned, this time holding a real gun, which he pointed at Aunt Ashley's still form. "Hand it to me. Now."

Cole hesitated for a brief moment.

"Now!"

Quickly, he pulled the phone out of his bag, and held it up. The man reached over and took it. "Thank you. I'm going to drive a little father, then I'll need to stop. If you try anything, I'll kill both of you. If you behave, I promise to not kill you. Understand?"

Cole nodded.

The man drove down the road, past old abandoned buildings, into a barn. As he was coming to a stop, Ashley began to stir, mumbling Cole's name. The man casually reached around, put the device he'd used earlier to her thigh and pressed the button. Ashley cried out, and ripples of pain shuddered through her again.

"Leave her alone!"

Corvidae stopped, and Ashley lay still once more.

"We can't have her waking up just yet. I'm going to get out of the car. If you try and run, I'll kill her slowly. If you don't, I'll check her to make sure she's all right. I won't lie. I never lie once I've revealed myself. Understand that. I haven't decided if I'm going to kill her or not. Everything you do will help me decide. Understand?"

Cole nodded as he reached out and took Ashley's hand.

Smiling brightly, the man got out and came around to Ashley's side of the car. He opened the door, and half of Ashley's body fell out. Showing no care, the man pulled her out and deposited her on the dirt floor of the barn. "Get out and come around. Bring your bag."

Cole did what he was told. The man pointed to a spot near Ashley, so Cole stood there. The man knelt down, and put his fingers under the left side of her neck. "Give me your fingers."

Slowly, Cold held his hands out. The man grabbed his fingers, pulled them to her neck. "Press. Feel that? That's her pulse. Nice and strong. She's fine. Want to keep her that way?"

Once again, Cole nodded.

"Do what I say, when I say. This is the end game. It's going to end big, one way or the other." He stood up. "You can't run with her, so here's the deal. If you run, I won't chase you. I'll take her. I will give her to Edward Hunter. If you stay, I won't. I can't promise not to kill her, but I promise to keep her away from your stepfather. Do we understand? No nodding. Speak."

Cole swallowed so hard, his throat hurt. "Yes."

"Good." He went around to the back of the car, used a key fob to open the trunk. "This is going to be fun."

He pulled out a black bag, brought it to the front, and tossed it on top of Ashley's still form. "Open up the zipper. You're going to find duct tape. Use it on her ankles, her wrists, and then her mouth. Be careful not to cover her nose so she can breathe. When you're done, we're going to put her in the car. Then guess what I'm going to do?"

Cole kept his fingers to Ashley's neck, feeling her pulse, deciding that as long as his aunt was alive, he'd do whatever it took to keep her that way. "I don't know. Hurt me?"

The man frowned. "No. I really don't want to do that. I hope you believe that. I will if I have to, without hesitation. But I've never hurt a child before, and I really don't want to start with you. I feel... Connected to you. So, we'll see how it plays out. But if you do a good job, I'll let you use your phone to text your uncle. You want to do that, right?"

Cole nodded, then gasped, afraid he'd just broken the rules. "Yes, please."

"Very good." The man leaned against the car. "I want us to talk. I want to have a long conversation. I'm very interested in you. In your thoughts. And although I'm not delusional to believe that you'll see it this way, I'd like to be your friend. Do you believe that's possible?"

Cole felt himself start to tremble. What answer did he want? What answer would give him the best chance of getting Aunt Ashley out of this alive. "No."

The man smiled. "Honesty. Oh, how I like you Cole. I really do want to be your friend. So, to that end, let me formally introduce myself. You can call me Jericho."

****

Ollie and Drew drove mostly in silence. No words seemed needed as their minds were in the same, dark place. Their anger buzzed through the air like a hornet trapped in the car.

Drew glanced over at his new partner. Ollie had worked hard to earn that badge. He wore it well. He was everything that a cop should be, and he'd been willing to throw it all away for Cole.

Ollie was as honest as he was decent. And he deserved better than to have a partner that kept secrets.

"We need to talk." Drew felt his palms sweat, and a surge of panic in his chest that he fought to ignore.

Ollie frowned. "Are you breaking up with me?"

Drew managed a small smile. "No, not unless you show me the door. Ollie, you've become more than a friend and a partner. I meant what I said to your mom. I chose to save my family. You *are* family."

Ollie shifted uncomfortably. "Thank you. I always wanted to be friends. I'm glad you feel like that. It's mutual. Although, I never thought of you as the heart to heart sort of guy. More of the brooding and silent type. It's a little unnerving."

Drew tried to control his breath, afraid he'd hyperventilate.

Do it. It's Ollie.

"This isn't my strong suit, but there is something you don't know. It's possible that you'll find out because of that damn bug, but you deserve for me to tell you. The only people who do know are family. It's not easy. I uh…"

Pursing his lips, and frowning, Ollie gave Drew a sidelong glance. "Dude, whatever it is, just spit it out. I can't be that—"

"I was raped in prison," Drew blurted out.

Ollie's eyes went wide. He turned into a nearby rest area, and brought the car to a screeching halt. Killing the engine, he sat in stunned silence.

Drew kept his eyes straight ahead, but was acutely aware of Ollie staring at him. He could see Ollie's eyes moving back and forth as if he were reading invisible print very quickly. He was a good detective, and the truth was written all over Drew's face.

Breathing heavily, Ollie swallowed. "Your father. He arraigned it. You told me… Fuck!" Ollie winced as he hit the steering wheel. "God Drew, I'm so sorry. That's what he threatened to do to your sisters. That's what kept you away."

Drew nodded and turned all the way around. "Yeah."

They sat in deafening silence for what seemed like an eternity. Drew knew Ollie was searching for the right words, but there were none.

"I swear to God, if he weren't dead, I'd want to murder him again." Ollie's knuckles were going white from the way he was gripping the steering wheel. "What kind of monster was he?"

Drew rubbed his hand over his face. "I can't answer that. I never wanted to tell you this. I never wanted to face it, but it's out now."

Ollie nodded absently. "Who knows?"

Drew felt the urge for a cigarette worse than he had in weeks. "The General, but apparently he somehow divined that truth years ago. Stephanie, the lawyer from McAlister. And everyone who was in the house that night when Ashley forced me to tell her about the deal I made with Dad. Sam. Lilly." Drew swallowed so hard it hurt. "Cole."

"Cole?" Ollie ran his hand over his head.

"He heard us. Kid hears everything. I didn't see him there until I heard him gasp. I thought I'd lost him, but Cole ran to me. Kept telling me I was safe now." Drew managed to smile. "God, I love that boy. And I'm sorry to lay this on you, but you deserved to know. You've never once failed to stand up for my family, including today. If we're going to be partners, you deserve to know what you're taking on."

Ollie turned in his seat. "Drew, look at me."

Drew took several deep breaths, then turned to face Ollie. He wasn't surprised to see his eyes full of compassion and understanding. He'd expect nothing less of the man his sister was in love with.

"I didn't stand up for your family today," Ollie said. "I stood up for mine. Ashley, Cole. *You*. You guys *are* my family. And since were having this moment of true confessions, you should know I want to make that official. I sorta, kinda asked Ashley to marry me. I don't think she believes I was serious, but I am. I'm not going to ask you for her hand or anything, but I hope I could get your blessing."

Drew felt the glacier of sickness and disgust with himself melt away. He returned Ollie's smile. "Ollie, I couldn't ask for a better man to be with her. I wish I had realized that when we were young. I'm sorry for—"

"Stop," Ollie insisted. "Drew, I get why you were the way you were. It's over. And you never have to apologize to me again. You went through a hell I couldn't even imagine. That's the past. Just like the horror that Cole went through. It's over, and we're going to make his future a happy one."

Drew began to breathe easier as his cell chirped. He pulled it out and glanced at the screen. "Cole's texting. He must be at the station. I feel like crap not being there." Drew held out the phone so Ollie could see.

Are you there, Uncle Drew?

Drew typed 'yes' in return.

Ollie restarted the engine. "Ashley is there with him. We'll deal with Hunter and get back."

Drew nodded, knowing that he'd wanted to go because he couldn't wait to get his hands on Cole's stepfather. Maybe he should have let the Cheyanne police handle it and stayed with Cole. Kid was probably pissed and with good reason, which is why it was taking him so long to respond.

I'm with Aunt Ashley and Detective Corvidae

Drew sighed, and responded.

I know, buddy. You're going to be fine. I love you.

Drew waited, feeling as if something was off. If Cole asked, he'd make Ollie turn the car around. He was cursing himself for leaving, with nothing but thoughts of ripping Edward Hunter to pieces. "We should have stayed. He needs us."

Ollie frowned. "You want to head back? They're expecting us in Cheyanne, but we can turn around."

Drew watched his phone, saw Cole was typing a reply. "Yeah. We both want in on taking Hunter down, but anyone can do that. Cole needs us."

Ollie nodded, put the car in drive and started to get into position to turn around.

You need to look up the name Corvidae. It's a type of bird. Goodbye. I love you... I'm sorry

"Hold on," Drew said.

Ollie pressed the brake. "What's up?"

He held the phone up, so Ollie could read. They exchanged puzzled expressions. Drew felt a sick feeling growing in the pit of his stomach. This was wrong. He brought up a search browser on his phone. "What the fuck is going on?" Drew typed Corvidae and waited for the results.

A picture of a black bird displayed as part of a wikki entry. He read the intro paragraph.

'Corvidae is a cosmopolitan family of oscine passerine birds that contains the crows, ravens, rooks, jackdaws, jays, magpies, treepies, choughs, and nutcrackers. In common English, they are known as the crow family, or, more technically, corvids. Over 120 species are described. The genus Corvus, including the jackdaws, crows, and ravens, makes up over a third of the entire family.'

Drew read it three times, trying to understand. Then he saw a word that was like an icepick through his heart. Jays.

The memory of Corvidae telling them that his name was a type of bird came flooding back.

J.

Jericho.

"Fuck, Corvidae is Jericho!" Drew screamed.

Ollie eyes widened. "He's got Cole and Ashley!" He gunned the engine, and aimed the car back to Ember Falls.

Chapter 20
Jericho's True Face

Cole had to endure a terrifying car ride sitting next to Jericho. When Aunt Ash had first woken in the back seat, she'd screamed a series of muffled threats and curses, none of which were clear, yet the meaning was easily understood. Jericho had grinned, finding Ashley's inaudible threats amusing, at least while they were in the middle of nowhere. Once they had returned to more populated streets, he had demanded she be quiet. Ashley had been unwilling to obey when the gun was levelled at her, but had complied immediately when Jericho had pointed the gun at Cole's gut.

Jericho had to want something. He had made Cole text Uncle Drew, telling him what to say. It hadn't made sense to Cole, but Jericho had promised that it would to his Uncle.

"He'll come for me," Cole said. "And when he finds us, he'll kill you."

Jericho had grinned. "It's hardly any fun if he's not looking. We'll see who's the better Picasso."

That had made even less sense, but Cole did what he was told. For now.

When they arrived in town, Jericho pulled into a garage of a house Cole didn't recognize. He killed the engine, and closed the door behind him. "Cole, I want you to go inside. Go into the living room and sit. Don't try and call anyone, the phone here doesn't work. The front door is unlocked, so if you decide to run, you can, but that will mean I'll have to leave with your aunt. She'll die a slow and painful death, but you'll be fine. I won't come for you. The choice is yours."

Ashley began to scream against the duct tape, her face going red and tears falling from her eyes. Cole couldn't understand the words she was saying, but the meaning was clear. She wanted Cole to run. Which is why he couldn't.

"You won't hurt her?"

Jericho frowned. "I can't promise that, but I don't intend to right now. I know that's not what you want to hear, but it'll have to do."

Cole turned to see Ashley, her eyes pleading with him to run as the air seemed to be sucked out of the car. "I'll be inside."

Jericho smiled. "Good boy. I won't be long."

It took Cole a good two minutes to remember how to make his limbs move. His legs felt like lead weights as he got out of the car. Once inside, he stood staring at the front door. He wanted to keep going. Couldn't he run to another house, bang on the door and beg for help? But what if nobody was home. Or worse, if they were and they came here and got themselves killed, and Jericho disappeared with Aunt Ash.

He felt that door calling to him. Inviting him to leave, to run screaming down the street outside.

Cole felt his upper lip tremble as he took another step towards the front door. He felt his hand twitch, wanting to reach out for the handle. He'd run. He'd try and get help. He'd call his Uncle Drew and Ollie.

And he'd have to tell them it was his fault Aunt

Ash was being killed.

Cole took a deep breath, as if it might be his last, and turned around.

Jericho came in pulling a struggling Ashley with him. She was thrashing her body in every direction, going limp, trying to body slam him, anything to get away, but Jericho's grip was too tight. He laughed as he dragged her towards the closet.

Cole rushed to stand in front of the door. "No, she's scared of small spaces. You can't put her in there!"

Jericho grinned. "Of course, I can. It's what's best for her, trust me."

Cole wouldn't budge. He kept screaming at Jericho to leave her alone. Ashley's eyes were wide with terror, as she wept.

"Move Cole," Jericho said blandly. "She goes in, or..." He pulled out a knife. "She gets the same treatment as your mother."

Weeping for his aunt, Cole stepped aside, and prayed that if they survived, Ashley would be able to forgive him. Jericho opened the door, kissed Ashley's head like a father might, and shoved her inside. She crashed into the back wall of the closet, her head hitting the bar that held a few wire hangers. With her hands and feet bound by duct tape, Ashley fell to the floor hard, the bar and coat hangers falling on top of her. Her wide eyes searched around, found Cole and she started to emit a muffled scream that faltered into a sob.

Cole closed his eyes, unable to stand seeing Aunt Ash, normally so fierce and strong, whimpering as Jericho slammed the door shut. Cole winced as the sounds of her high-pitched wailing mixed with the scraping sounds of a nearby dresser that Jericho pulled in front of the closet door.

Jericho grinned as he turned around. "Come Cole. I have some work to do, and then we'll chat."

Cole's eyes snapped open as he heard the muffled noises of Aunt Ash sobbing. She sounded broken and defeated.

Jericho glanced over his shoulder at the closet. "Do you know why she's terrified of closed spaces? It's really quite a moving story. I imagine she's in sheer hell right now. I can't help but wonder—"

Cole rammed his body into Jericho, taking him by surprise. He slammed his fists into the killer's legs and stomach, and didn't stop when Jericho pulled out a gun. At least until Jericho aimed it at the closet.

Jericho grinned. "Interesting."

Cole stared at the door as he wept. "Please, let her out. You don't understand."

"Oh, but I do."

****

Jericho spent an hour working on a small laptop. He had a police scanner nearby, where he listened to various Ember Falls Police channels. They had already started to look for him, heading to the barn. They wouldn't find Cole there, or anything that might help them find him. Just a vague clue that Cole was convinced that nobody would unravel.

Jericho let Cole sit near the closet where Ashley was trapped. Jericho had laughed at Cole's pitiful efforts to move the dresser, but it was just too heavy.

After several minutes, Cole had collapsed as close to the door as he could. He didn't know if Ashley could hear him. He knew that sometimes people who were terrified beyond all reason went into a sort of trance. How many times had Cole seen that catatonic look on someone's face? Sitting there, shivering in the freezing cold, unable to accept that they were in the last few hours of their lives. The lucky ones bored Edward so he'd kill them faster. Most weren't so fortunate.

Cole picked at the carpet as he wept. He wished he could at least hold his aunt's hand, to give her some comfort. "I'm sorry Aunt Ash. I know you probably can't hear me, but I love you and I'm sorry. I let this happen. He's here because of me. If Mom and I hadn't come to you..." Cole's lip trembled and he pawed at the tears. "Just hold on. Please. Uncle Drew and Ollie will come for you. And I'll go away. You won't be in danger anymore if I'm gone."

"I knew you were smart." Jericho snapped the laptop closed. "Your Aunt and Uncle talk about it all the time, but it's not just boasting. You do get it. If you hadn't come here, your family would be safe."

Jericho stood and walked over to Cole, who tried to scramble away. Jericho scowled. "Please, I thought we were past that. I have job to do, and I'm lucky enough to enjoy my work, but I won't hurt you if you don't make me. I've been handed the impossible task of protecting someone, and I have to fulfill that task, but how I do it is my business. Your Aunt's friend, Oliver Miller, he kept referring to me as a Picasso." Jericho smiled. "I liked that description. He got me, better than most of the law enforcement idiots that have come after me. How well?" He shrugged as he lowered himself to the floor. "I guess we'll see. I practically told him where we are."

Cole sneered. "No, you didn't. What did that thing

you made me write even mean?"

Jericho grinned. "Don't worry. I've got something else for you to consider." He paused, holding up a finger as he listened to the radio. They were about to find what they'd left behind at the barn. "I had it all planned out. I hadn't realized Hunter showed you—"

"I never told anyone," Cole whispered, still terrified Ashley would hear. He started to rock back and forth. He hadn't said anything, because he knew what telling would bring. Edward would know. He always knew. He'd know and he'd come and he'd do those things again.

"I don't think you even realize that you did," Jericho said. "But you let that horror feed your stories. You were getting ready to slay the unbeatable monster with your imagination, because I think he's got you convinced he can't be killed for real. Cole, he's a flesh and blood man. He *can* be killed."

Cole kept shaking his head, his fingers tearing into the carpet, and crying. He kept mumbling the words, "No, no, no, can't talk about it. He'll know. He always knows."

Cole was barely aware of Jericho as he knelt in front of him, frowning, until Jericho gently tried to touch Cole. Cole shrieked and crawled away on his hands and knees. He cowered under the dining room table.

Jericho watched him go. "Are you actually more terrified of your former stepfather who is nowhere near Ember Falls, than you are me?" Jericho sighed and sat down. "I understand terror. I really do. When I was your age, I watched my father do unspeakable things. I was named after him, you know. Except he always spelled our name with a G, while I preferred the J. I suppose that explains my attachment to that letter."

Jericho smoothed out the rug where Cole had pulled at the strands. "It's been a long time since I've felt fear. I would tell you that I simply cast it out, as if it were an act of sheer will. That's what I've often said on the few occasions that I've ever spoken about it." With a sad laugh, he shook his head. "I think you're the first person I've ever told that to who I wasn't ready to kill. You should be honored." He glanced at Cole who was lying on his side, sucking his thumb. "Ah well, perhaps when you're not so comatose. The fact is, I didn't find some inner strength. Something inside of me broke, and things like fear, and love, and compassion, were all gone."

He got up, grabbed a small blanket and tossed it on Cole. "Until today."

****

Drew was holding his breath as Ollie screeched to a halt near the abandoned barn. There were cops pouring in and out. Someone was already putting up crime scene tape, and every face looked grave. He was out of the car, before the brake was on. He ran full speed towards the barn when the General stepped out.

"They're not in there." He held his hand out to stop Drew in his tracks. "Just Cole's phone."

Drew closed his eyes. They were alive. They had to be alive. He wouldn't have taken them from here if he just planed on killing them.

"He tossed the phone here so we couldn't trace it." Ollie was rubbing his hand over his head. "He knew about it. We let him read the report from what happened when Harrington took him. Dammit."

"He didn't just toss the phone," the General said, motioning for them to follow him inside. "He left it for us to find. This is a game to him, and he's the only one who knows the rules."

Inside the barn, there were a few crime scene techs working under the watchful eye of the chief. Sam ran to Drew and hugged him. "We'll find them. They're going to be okay," she whispered in his ear.

Drew managed a small nod before he turned to Ann.

She held a note in one hand, Cole's phone in the other. "He's taunting us. He's telling us that he's smarter than us, and right about now, I don't know that I can disagree."

Drew took the note first.

If you confess your sins, your heart will be lighter.

Drew frowned, the words echoing in his head.

"Any idea what the hell he's talking about?" Ann held up the phone. "We're at a loss. The General thinks he left the phone behind on purpose, but the passwords have been changed."

"We're working on having it overridden at McAlister, but it's going to take time." The General took the phone. "He left this right out where we could find it. The question is why."

Drew held out his hand. "Give it to me."

Ann handed Drew the phone. Drew stared at the screen, back to the note, then back to the screen. With his thumb, he punched in a code.

The blank screen came to life.

"I'll be a son of a bitch," the General said. "What was the code?"

Drew scowled. "S-A-M."

"What?" Sam stepped closer to examine the phone herself. "Why would he choose my name? Does he even know that we're—?"

"Don't worry about that now," Drew said as he went app by app, looking for a sign. He was sure something was in here, something Jericho left for them. He opened up the notes app, saw Cole had used it to record ideas for stories and characters, but there was one note at the top that caught his eye, titled 'For Officer Miller'.

"He left a note," Drew said and held out the phone to Ollie. "For you."

Ollie blinked in surprise as he took it. After exchanging a puzzled look with his mother, Ollie opened the note.

I must confess, I didn't think much of you before I came to Ember Falls, but your insight is keen and your mind is sharp. You recognize that I am an artist, and you felt a chill in your blood where I first spilt blood because you sensed me close by. I thought you deserved to know that, for the game is not worth playing without a worthy opponent.

He read it out load, then handed the phone back to Drew.

"What the hell does that mean?" Ann asked.

The General took the phone from Drew, read the note himself. "I'll tell you what it means. Detective Miller did an outstanding job in profiling him, better than the rest of us, myself included. Jericho knows that. He's issuing a challenge." He looked Ollie in the eye. "Chess is no fun if you play by yourself."

Eyes wide in shock, Ollie nodded. "Okay, so he wants to play. He killed Diana, right under our noses. It was ballsy because he killed her in a room full of cops. We were there to protect her. We knew there was a threat, yet he managed to pull it off."

He paced as he thought. "He wants to do it again. He's telling us where he is, but it's couched in a riddle. If we're smart, we get to him first, but if not…" Ollie pressed the heel of his hand to his forehead. "Where he first spilled blood. He can't mean the first time he took a life. We can't possibly know where that was. The first kill we know about? He was there when the General went through that file."

Ollie clenched his fist, scowled and continued to pace, frustrating Drew. "Ollie, think. You get him. He's calling to you. What does your gut tell you?"

Ollie shook his head as his pacing increased. "If I'm wrong, if we go left when we should go right…" He sucked in a breath. "Jesus Drew, Ashley and Cole must be so terrified. I can't… I can't get this wrong."

Drew grabbed his shoulders, stopping him in his tracks. "Ollie, someone needs to make a call. *You* need to make it. I trust you. If you're wrong, it's not your fault, but you won't be."

Ollie stared into Drew's eyes, frozen to the spot. "He means… Here. In Ember Falls. First blood… Diana? I felt…" Ollie closed his eyes and winced. "Shit."

Ollie clenched his fists and gritted his teeth. Taking a deep breath, he opened his eyes. "Got it."

****

Jericho kept an eye on Cole who was still shaking and sucking his thumb, while he put into place the final details for his latest masterpiece. It was perfect. Jericho grinned, proud of himself. Considering this was something he had to come up with on the fly, it was pretty brilliant. As long as Oliver Miller eventually deciphered his clue. He assumed Miller was up to it, but didn't expect it any time soon.

The chatter on the nearby police radio escalated. He focused in as he stood. They'd already gone to the hotel that he rented, where they would find nothing of use, except the body of Jack Caesar who Jericho had been feeding leaks to suit his own agenda.

Where were they headed now?

"All units, Code Ten, repeat Code Ten until further notice. Converge on the court house. Be aware, this is a live hostage situation, and suspect is to be considered armed and extremely dangerous. Over."

"Code Eight. Keep the way clear for units. Suspect believed to be in Court Room Twelve. Adam One through Thirteen, respond. Over."

"All units. No Code Three. Repeat *no Code Three*. Keep those fucking sirens off. Do not announce your presence. Over."

"Adam Five to Station, we're almost Code Eleven, should we enter? Over."

Polansky's voice crackled through next. "Adam Five, negative, repeat negative. Wait for backup. Detective Miller en-route. Wait for his instructions. Do not exit your fucking vehicle."

"All units, this is D-Three." It was Ollie's voice. "En-route, ETA ten minutes. Keep the fuck back. Bastard is mine."

Jericho grinned, but couldn't help but feel a tinge of regret. "Oh, Detective Miller, or should I call you D-Three. I can't say I'm not a little disappointed. I expected better."

With a sigh, Jericho got up and unplugged the laptop he was working on, and carried it into the living room, near where Cole was. "I'm sorry, but this might scare you."

Jericho lifted the laptop up in the air and smashed it down on the mantel of the fireplace. He kept doing it, until the computer fell into pieces. He saw Cole gasp and jump, but didn't stop until the laptop was completely wrecked. He removed the grate of the fireplace, and tossed in most of the components, leaving a few scattered pieces on the floor.

He stood up and studied the scene carefully, making sure everything was in place. Satisfied, he flicked on the switch for the fireplace and watched as the flames came to life, and the corpse of the computer started to burn.

He went and knelt by Cole, who scampered away. He frowned. "I'm truly sorry that I frighten you. I wish I didn't. I hope you can believe that someday you'll thank me. We're going to be friends. I'm going to set you free. I understand your terror. I was there myself as a child, so I know it's no small feat to overcome, but we'll do it together. I promise you, as much as the very thought of Edward Hunter terrorizes you, you'll be stronger once you face him, and he's gone."

Standing, he headed towards the closet, where Cole's Aunt had been silent with not so much as a whimper, for some time. "I need to deal with your aunt, then we'll leave."

Jericho started to push at the dresser, which began to move, when he heard Cole shriek. "Get away from her!"

Cole slammed into Jericho and began to punch.

Jericho was shocked, and awestruck. The child was small, but he knew how to use his fists. "Cole, you need to let me complete my work." He tried to push the child away, but Cole kept punching, kicking and slamming his entire body. Jericho grabbed him by the shirt. "I'm impressed young man, I truly am, but I have to finish."

Cole never stopped. Not when Jericho shoved him to the floor, or when he pulled out a gun before pushing the dresser nearly away from the door. He rammed back into the killer, kicking, screaming and punching, until with one last sigh, Jericho hit back, sending Cole flying across the room.

Cole landed hard on his side, but he struggled to his feet as Jericho finished pushing the dresser away from the closet. "I admire that spirit, and I'm thrilled you have that fight still in you. That's how I know you'll feel better when we destroy Edward Hunter."

He grabbed the doorknob, and pulled the closet open.

Ashley burst out, screaming as she jabbed the tip of a wire coat hanger at Jericho, puncturing his left eye. As Jericho howled in pain, she knocked the gun out of his hand and clawed at his face. "Cole! Run!"

Chapter 21
The High Ground

Finding his legs, Cole ran. He slammed into the back of Jericho as Ashley continued to try to shove the hanger farther into his skull. For a moment, it seemed like Jericho would topple over.

Jericho kicked Cole away, and smacked Ashley hard. Jericho stumbled back, his hand over his wounded eye, and cried. "You fucking bitch."

As Jericho began to search for his gun, Ashley grabbed Cole's hand. "We've got to run."

Pulling Cole to his feet, she ran to the front door and pulled it open.

"Cole! Ashley!"

Drew and Ollie appeared, guns drawn. Relief flooded through Cole for one hot, bright moment.

Jericho grabbed Ashley by the hair and yanked her back inside.

Cole fell, caught by Drew. "You're all right. You're safe."

Cole began to fight against his uncle. "He's got her!"

"We'll get her," Drew said. "Stay with the General."

Cole was shoved into the waiting arms of General McAlister.

"Ease up son." The General held him firmly, but

gently. "Let your uncle take care of that prick."

****

Ashley tried to fight, but Jericho had her in a vice-like grip. She felt the cold tip from the muzzle of his gun on her as he pulled her inside the house, but she continued to buck and thrash. She stomped down hard on his foot, jabbed her elbow in his gut, and scratched at the arm that held her.

He responded by tightening his grip, cutting off her air supply as he pulled her towards the back. Her vision started to get blurry when she heard Sam's voice. "You've got nowhere to go."

Jericho shifted directions. He backed up into the stairwell, dragging her upstairs. Her feet hit each step as they went. It was a narrow staircase, and Jericho took no care to prevent her head hitting the walls. He got to the top step, right before the landing. Drew was the closest, with Ollie and Sam right behind him, but nobody had a decent shot. And they couldn't flank him as they tried to do downstairs. "Back off, or she's dead."

"All right!" Drew held his hands up, his gun pointed away. "All right, let her go."

Jericho shook his head, sending blood splattering onto his captive. "Not a fucking chance. Why would I do that?"

Drew took a breath, stepped forward. "Because you can have me." He fell to his knees, tossing his gun to the lower step and held up his hands. "Put the gun to my head. Use me to barter for whatever you want. Let Ashley go."

Ashley tried to yell at her brother, to tell him to just shoot the bastard even if the bullet went through her, but she couldn't form the words. Her brother was exposed, ready to die for her.

Jericho's eye exuded puss and blood. "Tell them to back off."

Drew turned around, made eye contact with Ollie. "Get back." He motioned to both Ollie and Sam. "Please."

Ollie shook his head. "I'm not leaving…"

"I've got this!" Drew pointed to the door. "Ollie, I need you to back off. Do what you do best and take the high road. Leave the low road to me."

Ollie scowled, but nodded. With a snarl towards Jericho, Ollie and Sam fell back, out of view.

Drew moved up a step, staying on his knees, and moving farther away from his gun. "It's just us. Let my sister go. Please."

Jericho grinned. "It's not going to be that easy for you. I've been listening you know. I know all your secrets. I know you. I have no doubt you'd die for your sister. Maybe you'd even like that. You can stop suffering. Stop hating yourself for your failures."

Drew moved closer. "I don't want to die, if that's what you think. I've got too much to live for, but yes. I'd die for Ashley."

Jericho loosened his grip on Ashley's throat, but just enough for her to breath. He leaned his frame on the wall for support. His eye was oozing, but he appeared calm. Nearly serine now that he was the only one with a gun. "I'm probably not getting out of here alive, and I'm all right with that. If it had to happen, I'm actually glad it's happening here. I feel connected to all of you. I know you think that's bullshit, but like yourself, I grew up with a monster for a father. Far worse than yours, in fact. I don't say that in a dismissive way. I don't want to diminish what you and your sisters went through, but as bad as it was, there are worse things."

Drew moved up one more step with his knees. He forced himself to talk in a calm and soothing voice. "I can believe that. I'm sorry."

Jericho frowned and tightened his grip on Ashley. "Don't do that. Don't try and relate to me, so I'll lower my guard and my gun. It won't happen. I lied to you in every encounter we've had, but not here. Not now. Not as you see my real face." He laughed and tilted his head. "Such as it is. I won't lie, so neither can you, or she dies. Understand."

Drew nodded, understanding. "I *am* sorry to hear of any child being hurt and terrified. And I can't help but wonder if that's what turned you into the type of monster that can kill so casually and enjoy it."

Jericho considered. Slowly, he released his grip so Ashley could breathe. She gasped for air, her chest heaved and her knees nearly gave out.

"Like I was saying, I know I'm most likely not getting out of here," Jericho said. "But before I die, I would like to have a conversation. I was clearly hired to stop you from looking any further into the disappearance of Molly Winters. You may want to think about having that investigation halted. My client is desperate to bury that secret. I must be loyal to my client to the end. I *am* a monster. That much is true, but I am not without honor."

Drew scowled, but stayed silent.

Jericho smiled. "You have a hard time with that, I see. I don't blame you, but it's true. You should realize something. I would not have killed Cole. I admire all of you for how you've dealt with the boy. He's beginning to trust you. I don't think you can fathom, at least not yet, how hard that is. You think your life growing up was rough?" Jericho's face grew hard, and his grip tightened once again. "You have no idea."

Ashley groaned, and Jericho loosened his grip, almost apologetically this time.

"What do you know about what Cole's been through?" Drew asked. "I know you had us bugged, but you can't know what he's been through more than we do. You learned what you know through listening to *us*."

Jericho shook his head. "So disappointing. It's too bad you decided to stay and not Oliver Miller. I thought you would be the challenge, and you are formidable, but it was Miller who intrigued me. How did you figure out I was here? Tell me."

Drew moved up one more step. "It was Ollie. He put it together. Where you first spilled blood. We thought Diana, but Ollie realized that she was your second kill in Ember Falls, not your first. You killed Vic across the street. And when we came out of Vic Miranda's house, Ollie felt like he was being watched."

Jericho grinned. "Yes, he did. I saw that moment. Miller's got good instincts."

Drew narrowed his eyes. "He's the best. He'd be here in my place if he could be."

Jericho frowned. "Did you tell him…?" He paused. "Does Miller know that you were raped in prison?"

Drew clenched his jaw.

Jericho started to squeeze Ashley's throat.

"All right," Drew said. "Please. Leave her alone.

Okay, I told Ollie about… that. He did what I expected him to do. He accepted. He supported. Is that what you want to hear? You want me to yell it out? We're on a fucking open frequency! I just announced it to the entire Ember Falls PD."

Drew moved up the last step, so he was as close as he can get to Jericho. "Please, I'm begging you."

Jericho sighed. "I have to kill one of you, I suppose. I can't let myself be taken without killing one last time. It would look bad. Even to the death, I am a professional. Still, I can't decide who will suffer more. You if I kill your sister, or Ashley if she sees me blow your brains out." He shrugged. "I suppose I could kill her, then you."

Drew looked up and snarled. "If you kill her, I will tear you limb from limb."

Jericho grinned. "You'll try, but you're not that fast. Who should it be? Who could Cole survive best without?"

Jericho repositioned the muzzle of his gun so it was behind Ashley's head. He could pull the trigger and aim it at Drew in a fraction of a second. "Should Cole lose his aunt, or his uncle?"

Drew tensed, ready to strike. "Kill me. Ashley will be a great mother. And Cole couldn't ask for a better man to be his father than Ollie."

Jericho smiled. "A valid argument. Ashley, would you care to add your two cents?" He loosened his grip on her throat enough to let her speak.

Ashley gasped for air. "Don't hurt my brother. Let me protect him for once in my life." She managed to turn to her brother, to see the pleading in his eyes. "Drew. Don't die for me."

Jericho shifted the gun, aiming it directly at Drew who bowed his head to accept his fate. "You should have seen Cole. I gave him the chance to run twice, but he wouldn't leave his aunt. He was nearly comatose in fear because I told him we were going to see Edward Hunter, but he broke out of his trance to fight for her. I hadn't thought I was capable of feeling pity or sympathy, but he managed to reawaken both in me. I don't know if I believe he wouldn't be fine living a life like mine, but for what it's worth, I think you've already saved him from embracing that darkness. Let that give you comfort in your final moments. Once they hear the shot, I expect them to come at me." He pressed the gun against Drew's skull. "I'll try my best as I defend myself not to take Ashely out, but I can't make any promises. My aim might be a little off today."

Ashley was crying, begging for Jericho not to shoot her brother, but it didn't matter. Jericho wasn't angry, or desperate. He was resigned.

"Any last thing you want to say to your sister? From what I've heard, you two still have a lot to talk about. We don't have time for a long heart to heart, but is there any one thing you want her to know? Or a message to give to someone?"

Slowly, Drew looked up. His eyes locked with Ashley's and he smiled. "I love you. And Ollie *is* the best." His eyes hardened as he glanced to the right. "Now!"

Ollie came around the corner at the top of the stairs, grabbing Jericho and yanking him away, just as Drew moved right, shoving the killer's gun hand to the left. A shot rang out, and a piece of the banister shattered.

Ollie had Jericho in a headlock and was pulling him up, trying to haul him away from Ashley. Jericho refused to let go.

Ashley found her footing. Twisting her body, she reached up, grabbed the coat hanger still protruding from Jericho's eye, and yanked it out.

Jericho screamed in agony as Ashley toppled down the stairs, taking Drew with her. They landed in a heap on the bottom of the landing.

Drew struggled to get up to go help Ollie who was thrashing back and forth at the top of the stairs. Jericho fought like a wounded beast, desperate to take down its prey before its own slaughter.

Jericho backed Ollie into the old-fashioned wall clock at the top of the stairs. He jabbed his elbow into Ollie's gut and managed to break free. Grinning once again, Jericho moved down a step and aimed his gun at Drew's heart.

"Drew!" Ashley threw herself over her brother, covering him with her body as a shot exploded.

Ollie pulled his weapon, and fired three shots into Jericho's back. The killer tumbled to the floor and landed near Ashley and Drew. His eyes wide and blank.

Ollie thundered down the stairs to check Jericho for signs of life. He kicked Jericho's gun away and pressed a finger to the killer's neck to check for a pulse.

"Ollie! Ashley's been hit!"

Ollie rushed over as Drew gently turned his sister around. Her shirt was stained in blood. Drew was pressing the wound while Ollie was yelling into the radio. "Suspect down, we need medical in here. Ashley's been shot, get that fucking bus here now!"

Drew used his free hand to hold his sister's.

"You're going to be okay Ash. You're not done giving me a hard time. You're going to be fine. It's just a scratch."

Ashley winced, but managed to smile. "You're not getting rid of me that easily." Her eyes found Ollie as he dropped to his knees and took her other hand. "Or you. We haven't even gone out on a proper date yet."

With eyes swimming in tears, he leaned down and kissed her forehead. "Wherever you want once you're better. I'll even take you shopping and hold your purse."

She grinned. "I do."

Drew and Ollie exchanged worried glances. Those words made no sense to either of them. "You do what?" Drew asked. "Protect me? You *did*. I wish to hell you hadn't, but you did."

She reached up and put her hand on her brother's face. "I did protect you. For once I was able to and I'm glad. I don't need my brother to stand in front of me anymore, but I do need you by my side. Always."

Drew began to cry. "I'll always be there. I promise."

"I know." Ashley wiped his tears away. "You always were, even when you went away. You were there." She turned back to Ollie. "But that 'I do' was for Ollie. You did ask me if I wanted to get married. I never answered. I do. I want to marry you, and be yours forever."

Ollie's eyes widened as the EMTs arrived. "I was thinking dinner and a movie for our first date, but why the hell not."

****

After a few moments, one of the EMTs looked up.

"It's not bad. Bled a lot, but she won't even need surgery. She's lucky."

As they worked, Sam and Ann came in and surveyed the scene. Finally, they lifted Ashley into a stretcher and were ready to transport her to the hospital. "Someone should go with her, but only one."

Ashley reached out for Ollie's hand. "I'd like my fiancé to come with me."

Grinning, Ollie kissed her.

"Fiancé?" Ann said. "When did this happen?"

"Just now," Ollie said. "We didn't have time yet for engagement announcements. I was thinking of ones with Han and Leia."

Ashley laughed. "Not a chance."

Drew grinned until Ann pulled him to the side. "Ollie got your clue, to go high. He was able to get in through a window. I'm familiar with the layout of this house. It's the same as one I had with Ollie's father. You can't see anything around that corner. You kept him focused on you. Good job."

"Thank you." Drew started to move to the door, wanting to go with his sister at least as far as the ambulance. And he was desperate to see Cole, make sure he was okay. Poor kid must be terrified.

He stopped when Ann placed her hand on his chest. "Drew, before you go out there, you have a right to know that we were listening in to everything on your open radio. We heard what you and Jericho talked about. I'm…" She paused and her eyes went moist. "I'm sorry."

Drew looked at the door, where the EMTs were ready to move Ashley outside. There was a big part of him that wanted to hide until everyone left, but he couldn't. His sister and nephew needed him. "I'll deal with it. If you want to reconsider your offer…"

"Drew," Ann said. "I'm so sorry for what happened to you. As a mother, my heart breaks for everything you've been through. As the Chief of Ember Falls, I can honestly say that we're proud to have you come on board. You may still be getting paid by McAlister Security for now, but you are one of us."

Stunned and touched, Drew put his hand over hers for a moment.

"Go," she ordered. "Cole's having a fit out there."

Drew nodded and followed his sister who had just been pushed outside. Sam was by his side, taking his hand. "I really thought I was about to lose you."

Drew scoffed. "You sure that wouldn't be a good thing?"

She pulled him to a halt. "Stop that. You are everything I ever wanted and so much more."

Before Drew could respond, a small voice called out. "Aunt Ash! What happened?"

The General let Cole go so he could run to his Aunt's stretcher. Drew crossed the distance. His heart broke as he heard Cole begging his aunt's forgiveness. Promising that if she could just be okay, he'd leave her so she'd never be in danger again.

"Kid really does take after you," Sam whispered in his ear. "He needs you to show him that it's okay to be loved. And to be protected. You need to show him how to forgive himself for things he couldn't control."

Drew pulled away and went to his nephew. Cole refused to make eye contact with Ashley as she insisted nothing was his fault. Cole kept shaking his head, crying, and refusing to listen. Drew knelt down in front of him. "Cole, look at me."

It took a long, painful minute for Cole to look up.

"Thank you," Drew said. "I know how terrified you must have been, but you protected your aunt. Kept her alive. You didn't leave her. You're the reason why Jericho didn't kill her. Thank you for being so incredibly brave."

Cole shook his head, weeping. "I wasn't brave. I was scared. The whole time, I was scared and I didn't know what to do. I'm not brave like you."

Drew put his hand on Cole's arm, felt him trembling, but not flinch or pull away. Progress. "You are braver than I ever was. I know how difficult it is to see that. I blame myself for what happened when I was a kid, and I have to stop. I think that's something you and I need to work on together, because I really don't think I'll make it without you. I know you blame yourself. I blame *myself*. What's say we start learning to blame the bastards that did this to the ones we love, okay?"

Cole nodded and let himself be pulled into a hug by his uncle.

They watched as the ambulance that Ashley and Ollie had been loaded onto was pulled away.

"I want to go with her," Cole said.

Ann approached them. "Your nephew should be seen as well. We can handle this. Officer Rossi," she turned towards Sam. "Take both of these brave men to the hospital. Go, and give my best to my soon to be daughter-in-law."

Drew smiled and started to steer Cole towards Sam's squad car. The smile melted into a grimace as he saw over a dozen cops, all staring at him. Polansky was there, looking out of place out in the field. All of them watched him with hard, cop eyes.

They knew. All it would have taken is for one cop to have listened to the open radio channel, and it would have spread like wildfire. Cops were the biggest gossips.

Cole stiffened and stopped, glancing up to Drew. "Uncle Drew, what's wrong?"

Before he could respond, Polansky stepped forward, and stood up straight. "Company. Atten*tion.*"

Each officer stood up straight, hands by their sides.

"Company," Polansky said. "Present arms."

As a unit, they saluted Drew.

Drew couldn't breathe as he searched their faces for the disgust or pity he expected to see, but saw nothing but respect.

"At ease," Polansky said. All hands went back to their sides. Just as Drew tried to find the words to express his gratitude, the officers started to applaud. Polanski stepped forward and held his hand out. "Good job. Now get the kid to the hospital."

The cops parted, and Drew and Cole went to the car.

Cole climbed in, and clicked his seatbelt into place. "What was that about?"

Sam started the engine. "That was them telling your Uncle Drew how much they respect him." She pulled away from the curb, and took Drew's hand. "He's one of us now."

Chapter 22
Making Plans

Three days later, Ashley sat snuggled on the couch with Ollie. The two of them looked as if they'd been a couple for over a thousand years. It wasn't so different from the way they'd always been, finishing each other's sentences, knowing what the other one was thinking. Whatever it was that kept these two apart, Drew couldn't be happier that they were together.

Ollie hadn't left her side since they'd gotten home that night from the hospital. It had only been a flesh wound, and cared for with a few stiches. Her neck was bruised, and her eye was black, but it was better today than it was yesterday. She winced when she had to walk, but she was able to move unassisted. She was healing.

They all were, Drew thought as he glanced at Cole who sat on the floor watching the end of the movie they'd chosen. Drew had worried that Cole would have regressed. He expected to find Cole curled up in a ball in the back of his closet, or ready to run again.

Instead, he seemed to have taken a small step forward. If he jumped when Drew entered the room, it didn't take Cole long to relax. Once he knew he was among family, he was fine.

He was still tightlipped about everything that happened with Edward Hunter. Bring it up, try and push, he'd get glassy eyed. He'd nearly had a panic attack at the mention of counseling. Jericho said at one point he was nearly catatonic. The mere mention of Hunter's name was still enough to make Cole tremble. Nobody was willing to push him that far, so for now, they would hold off.

Sam was not really paying attention to the movie, but staring at her ring. It was clear what was on her mind.

As the credits rolled, she caught Ashley's eye. "Are you really serious about you and Ollie getting married right away? You two haven't even been on an actual date yet."

Ashley responded by taking Ollie's hand. "Very serious. I've wasted enough time. You date to get to know each other. I don't think anyone knows me better than Ollie." She grinned. "Besides, I'm not taking any chance that he's going to realize what he's in for and run for the hills."

Ollie kissed her. "Never gonna happen. You want, we can pack up and get to Vegas now. I don't need any fancy wedding, I just need you."

Cole rolled over from the floor. "What's a wedding like? And why go to Vegas?"

"Cause it's Vegas, baby," Ollie responded. That earned a few chuckles.

It occurred to Drew that most kids saw weddings growing up, but Cole hadn't. "A wedding is in and of itself pretty simple. Two people stand together before witnesses. Someone officiates. That means they have the authority to actually make a marriage legal and valid. It can be a pastor, or priest. A justice of the peace like a judge, or even what they call an ordained minister."

"Which can be anyone these days," Ollie said. "You can sign up and register online. Everyone here could do it, except for Cole because he's too young."

Drew nodded. "In Vegas, there are tons of places where you can get married right away. It can be tacky, but it counts. So, people who want to get hitched right away can do that. Or just go down to the court house if they can't afford a big wedding."

"A big wedding?" Cole sat up, clearly interested.

Lilly pulled out her phone, moved from her chair to sit next to Cole on the floor. "Oh, a wedding is so beautiful. Most girls dream of wearing a white dress, being walked down the aisle by their father, who gives them away. There's a whole wedding party of a best man, maid of honor, bride's maids and groomsmen. There a so many different ways to do it." She showed her phone to Cole, who scrolled through pictures of weddings that Lilly had found. "They can be very expensive, not just for the wedding, but the reception afterwards, but it's so romantic."

"It doesn't have to break the bank," Sam added. "Drew and I were talking about doing it at the park. You can rent that spot with the gazebo for a couple of hundred. You get a caterer, set up some tents."

"Ooh, the park," Lilly cooed. "That was what? Wedding option number three?"

Ashley pursed her lips and looked off to a far corner of the room for a moment as she thought. "Yeah, more or less."

Seeing the confusion on everyone's face, Ashley laughed. "When we were kids, Lilly, Kelli and I would talk weddings. We had dozens of different plans, none of which…" She poked Ollie in the side. "Involved running down to Vegas and getting hitched at the Star Trek Experience by a Klingon."

Ollie made a show of being hurt. "But… *Vegas Baby?"*

Ashley brandished a fist, which Ollie kissed.

"One of the plans did include a triple wedding at the park," Lilly said as she stroked the back of Cole's hair. "The three of us up there, saying our vows together, but I doubt that would work now."

Cole handed the phone back to Lilly. "Why not?"

Ashley sighed. "Logistics. I want your uncle to give me away, but how can he do that if he was also getting married? I don't know…" She looked upset because she couldn't get it to work in her head.

"Hold on now," Sam said, sitting forward. "It *could* work. You could go down the aisle first with Drew, then I could have Nana walk me down. I'd just have to stay hidden until you were at the altar so Drew couldn't see me."

Cole frowned. "Why?"

"Its bad luck to see the bride before she walks down the aisle," Lilly explained. "One of those wedding traditions. Are you guys really thinking about a double wedding?"

Ashley and Drew exchanged glances. He could see the excitement in her eyes, and since Sam was already googling double weddings, he figured she was on board. Ollie made it crystal he'd do whatever Ashley wanted as long as it ended with him married to her. Drew also noticed that Ollie kept glancing at his watch.

"You order a pizza or something?" Drew asked as Ollie did it again.

Ollie blinked. "Huh? No, but Mom and the General are at the station, she said she'd stop by here. Said there was some stuff to talk about. I hate being out of the loop, being on administrative leave cause of what happened."

Drew frowned. The fact that neither he, Ollie, nor Sam were allowed on active duty while everything was being reviewed which was standard operating procedure. Ollie had killed Jericho, but it was a righteous shooting. Jericho was a known hitman, a deadly assassin who considered himself an artist in death. There was no way Drew could think of that this would blow back on Ollie.

So why did he seem nervous?

"I'd really like to have a double wedding," Ashley said. "It would be like we're living one of the childhood dreams for Kelli, and besides, I want to share that day with Drew. I just wish Lilly was getting married too."

For a moment, Lilly's face grew dark, but she smiled when Cole looked at her. "I don't think that's in my future, and even if it was, I'm not dating anyone. I'll be happy just being your maid of honor, if that's okay. I'll work with whoever Sam wants to pick."

Sam thought for a moment. "Ollie's my best friend around here. I've got Nana to give me away." She shrugged. "I don't suppose you'd consider double duty?"

Lilly lit up. "I would love to."

Ashley groaned. "Oh, you have no idea what you've just done. Lilly in wedding mode is scary. In double wedding mode is terrifying."

Everyone laughed as Lilly shook her fist at Ashley. "Now what about best men? Could Drew and Ollie be best men to each other while also being the grooms?"

Drew wanted to object. He had no problem with having Ollie be his best man. In fact, it would be an honor, but he still felt like he had no place filling that position for him. Although Ollie had forgiven him, he wasn't sure he deserved it.

And there it was again. He had to work on that, if for no other reason than for Cole. Ollie showed Cole how a good and decent man could forgive someone who had hurt them when they were truly sorry. It would be up to Drew to show Cole how to forgive yourself.

Suddenly an image formed in his mind. He caught Ollie's eye, and glanced down towards Cole. Seeing Ollie grin and nod his agreement, Drew smiled. "Hey Cole, would you be our best man?"

Cole blinked in surprise. "What does that mean? What do I have to do?"

Lilly placed her hand on his shoulder. "You'd be in charge of holding the rings on the day of the wedding. Making sure these two are at the church on time. I'm sure the General can help with some of that. He keeps Drew in line when no one else can."

Sam laughed. "And you'd be the one who has to throw them a bachelor party." She glanced at Drew and smiled. "He's nearly nine, I'm sure he can manage to throw together a nice, *safe* party for you."

Drew smiled. "I'm sure it'll be great. What do you say Cole? It'd would mean a lot to me."

"Me too," Ollie said. "I can't imagine it any other way."

Cole grinned. "Cool. Yeah, okay." He sealed the deal with a fist bump with each of the men.

"I need to use the bathroom," Ashley said. "When I

get back, let's find a wedding movie so Cole can see what to expect."

Immediately, Ollie, Drew and Cole were on their feet to help Ashley up. She let Ollie help her to her feet, but shooed them all away afterwards. "I can go pee on my own. Damn." Her phone rang. "Hello? Yeah hold on." She took her phone and walked to the kitchen.

As she left, Lilly started to search for wedding movies, came up with one of her favorites, all the while continuing to talk wedding plans. Ashley reappeared and pressed a hand over her stomach as she sat. "You in pain Ash?" Ollie asked. "You want some of those pills?"

Ashley frowned as if she hadn't heard Ollie. "No, I'm fine. Um…"

The doorbell rang and Ollie shot up. "That'll be Mom, I'll get it." He was to the door in an instant. A few moments later, the General and Ann came in. Lilly went directly into host mode, offering food and drink, all declined right away.

Something about the way the pair of them stood, side by side, bothered Drew. Too formal, too stiff. While they both asked if Ashley was okay, their eyes were mostly on him. Ann had the look of a mother about to tell her kids that Christmas just got cancelled. The General's face was not as passive as normal. It was hard to see, but Drew knew the man. Whatever bombshell they were about to drop, it had Paul McAlister shaken, and that wasn't easy to do.

"What's going on?" Drew asked, getting up. Whatever was coming, he'd take it on his feet.

"Mom?" Ollie asked.

The General stiffened. "Chief Miller needs to talk

to you Drew."

Ann sighed, turned to the General who just indicated that this was her show.

"Would you care to speak privately? You're not in trouble, and don't require a lawyer, but if you want one—"

"Out with it," Drew snapped. He wanted to regret his tone, but he needed to know what had the General concerned.

Cole scrambled to his feet and stood protectively in front of his uncle.

Ann shifted uncomfortably. "The General had one of his experts come in today. I'm sure you know Ari Patel."

Drew scowled, but nodded. "He's the best I know."

"Jericho was sloppy," the General said. "Smashed the computer and burned the pieces, but a component got tossed under the table. It's encrypted, but Ari is working his magic."

They were stalling. "If anyone can get that information, it's Ari, but you're not here to talk about that computer drive if Ari hasn't gotten through the encryption. What's going on?"

Ann frowned. "He started first on that USB we found at your father's. It was coded, but your man got through it like it was nothing. We found information regarding the original investigation of Molly Winters."

Instinctively, Drew took a step back. "I don't care what he had on there. I never hurt Molly. I'm not going back to prison."

The General stepped forward. "No son, you're not. I read the information myself. Included your missing medical records. You don't remember that night, do you?"

Drew shook his head, tried to force himself to relax, but it was hard when he felt the walls closing in on him. "No, I've told you before I just *know* I didn't hurt her."

"You couldn't have," Ann corrected. "You had an extremely large dose of Rohypnol in your system. Mixed with a smaller amount of ketamine. We think you were dosed at the pre-dance party with one, then the other *after* you left. There's no way you could have hurt Molly Winters. You would not have had the capability in the state you were in. There was some alcohol in your system, but not much. No other drugs."

Drew tried to picture it, but whenever he thought of that night, all he saw was darkness. "I don't understand? You're telling me Dad had this information? The information that could have cleared me? He fucking had it *all along*?"

The General sighed, his hawk like face grim. "I'm afraid it's worse than that. There were pictures, notes. A video taken from a nearby video camera from a time where Molly was still accounted for at the party. They didn't just try and pin it on you, you were set up. Right from the word go."

"Who set me the fuck up?" Drew screamed. "Who put me in that fucking place? I want a name. Was it…" He put his hand on Cole's shoulder. "Was it Edward Hunter?"

Cole started to tremble. The mere name of his stepfather terrified him, but he didn't move from his position in front of Drew.

The General narrowed his eyes. "It wasn't his idea to set you up. Drew, it was your father that volunteered to frame you. It was very clear in his notes. He couldn't believe they, whoever 'they' were, hadn't already thought of it. I'm sorry."

Drew staggered back a step. He knew his father had hated him. When he was younger, he believed it was just his drunkenness, but over time he'd come to accept that his father truly detested him and his sisters.

But not to this extent. Frank Duncan despised him, and if he weren't already dead, Drew would find him and rip him to pieces, bit by bit.

"It started with Hunter," the General continued. "It didn't end there. Based on Frank Duncan's notes, you were drugged on the scene, so Hunter could get to Molly. We don't know why he targeted her, but she *was* targeted. There was a meeting of some nature, where it was discussed how to get the blame away from Hunter. We don't know yet why they wanted to keep Hunter's name in the clear. I'm not sure that your father knew, but he suspected he had stuff on the old Chief and others. Refers to an underground sex club here in Ember Falls. I'm sure some of the big names were involved. He's got their names in code, but based on what he said, Molly might have been a part of it."

Drew pressing the heel of his hand to his head. "Molly was a part of some sort of sex club? Who else?"

Ann scowled. "We don't know. *Yet*. I intend to find out."

Drew thought back, pushed his brain to recall details that were buried under nearly a decade of fear and darkness. Memories he would have died rather than examine, he now fought to remember. "Molly used to say things sometimes… I just thought…" He swallowed hard. "I knew I wasn't her first, but every now and then she'd say things that made me think there'd been an older man."

Ann swallowed as she took a step closer. "One of the few details everyone could agree on was that argument the two of you had where she slapped you. Can you remember what she said to you?"

"I do. I told her…" He closed his eyes against the painful memory. "I told that I loved her." He looked towards Sam, his eyes pleading for forgiveness. "I was young and stupid, and she listened to me when I talked to her about…" He winced. "Fuck me. Of course, she was interested. She probably was using it to blackmail Dad."

Sam wrapped her arms around Drew. "It's okay. You didn't do anything wrong. And I was engaged once, remember?"

Drew felt trapped, but afraid to move. "She laughed at me. Told me she'd had been fucking other guys all along, and that they may be older, but they had the money to pay. I was just a pathetic wimp that didn't know how much of a bastard I was. I was shocked. It wasn't easy for me to say those words. I realized I was nothing to her. I guess I was always nothing."

Finally, he turned away. It was stupid. He once loved her, but had known for a long time that it was all based on a lie. Why did he feel as if he'd just been betrayed all over again?

"We still need to find Edward Hunter," Ann said. "He's not at his home in Cheyanne. In fact, there is no home. He was warned you were coming, and burnt it to the ground. No doubt thanks to Jericho. And because of Jericho's involvement, the FBI is coming in."

Lilly slowly lowered herself into a chair, looking

staggered. "The FBI?"

Ann nodded. "Yes, it was either that, or let State take over. The General made a few calls, and they seem willing to allow us to stay involved, based on certain conditions. I agreed. Edward Hunter is out there, probably getting as much distance between himself and Ember Falls as possible, but the answers to all of our questions are still here. Who wanted him protected? Clearly, someone who was a part of that sex club."

"If I had to guess," Drew said, turning back to them at last. "I'd say we should look at the state DA. Bob Reynolds."

"Why him?" Sam asked.

Drew scowled. "S-A-M. Jericho changed the code on Cole's phone from his mother's name to the name Sam. You thought it was because we're engaged, but that clue. *'If you confess your sins, your heart will be lighter.'* Reynolds used that line on me when I was in the hospital to try and get me to confess. Kept talking to me as if it were a forgone conclusion that I'd killed Molly and that everyone would see it. He was good. I couldn't remember what had happened, so I actually started to consider it. But the more he pushed, the more I pushed back. He has a son named Sam. I threw that in Reynolds face, asking if he was planning on questioning Molly's dealer, which was Sam. That earned me a good, hard slap. He'd have the political clout and probably the money to hire Jericho."

The General nodded. "It fits. We should have a conversation with Reynolds once the FBI has wheels on the ground. That would be Monday."

Ann stepped closer to Drew. "I am so sorry for everything Drew. I know we can't give you those

363

months of your life back, or the years you were in exile, but I want to make this as right as possible. With your permission, I'll speak to the editor of the Ember Falls Times, and any other news organization. This is going to be big news, and I will make it clear that you are completely exonerated. I know it's not much, but you should be able to walk around town without having people think such horrible things. I can do that."

Drew felt as if the Earth had shifted from under him. He'd always believed he was innocent. Knew for some time that the people in this room believed it too. He'd also accepted the fact that most people would believe him guilty. Could it really be that people wouldn't wonder? Was he finally free of the suspicion, and the weight of the guilt for something he didn't do? He'd sworn up and down that he didn't care what people thought, but now, in this moment where he knew every person in Ember Falls would know he wasn't a rapist and a murderer, he realized he had been lying to everyone, including himself.

He looked to Ann and tried to find the words to thank her. To everyone for believing him, but he couldn't speak. He could barely breathe.

It was Ashley who dried his tears and hugged him. "I have my brother back."

Slowly, everyone embraced him. Sam was last, and Drew held on to her the longest and the tightest. He buried his head in her neck. "I can marry you as an innocent man."

She kissed him. "You were always innocent. And now the whole world will know it."

****

Two hours later at the dining room table, Cole

listened as the adults continued speaking and tried to process what everything meant. It was very confusing, but he understood the basics. Everyone would now know Uncle Drew didn't do something horrible, but he couldn't understand why so many people assumed he did. Didn't they have to prove something before you could be punished?

Uncle Drew seemed dazed, like when someone hit you so hard you saw three of everything. If something like this had happened when he'd first met Uncle Drew, it would have caused Cole to hide, but not anymore. He was safe with Uncle Drew. With everyone here at home.

He understood that. He believed it.

Still, Cole couldn't help but wince whenever someone brought up his stepfather's name. When they did, they'd stroke his hair, or put a hand on his shoulder. They were trying to tell him that his stepfather couldn't hurt him.

He wanted them to stop talking about it. To stop saying his name. Cole was sure Edward could hear them every time they spoke it aloud.

"Hey," Drew said, while looking right at Cole. "I think we've covered this enough for today. And my head is spinning. Let's put it away. We were talking wedding plans before this. We've got the most important people in the wedding party around this table. We've got both sets of brides and grooms to be, we've got the mother of one of the grooms, and the father of the other." He smiled at the General. "We've got Lilly, our collective Maid of Honor, who I know is itching to get into planning. And Ollie and I have the best of all possible best men here." He offered a fist bump to Cole.

"Who needs to understand how he's supposed to tackle either of us if we panic and make a run for the door."

Cole giggled.

Ann smiled. "You're right, I've dumped too much on you tonight. I should leave and let you…"

"Nonsense." Ashley reached over and put her hand on Ann's. "You're family now Chief. You're stuck here with the rest of us."

Ann smiled. "I'm so happy you think that, but if we're going to be family then please, don't call me Chief. You can call me Ann or whatever else you like."

Ashley leaned over and gave Ann a hug. "How would Mom sound? I haven't had one since I was eight."

The tears in Ann's eyes told everyone that she'd love that.

Ollie was practically bursting at the seams when he stood. "Well, when Mom came over, I had no idea that she had so much to share. I asked her to get something for me." He moved his chair back, reached into his pocket. "This was something that belonged to my grandmother. You never got to meet her, but you remind me of her. Fierce and loyal and never afraid to speak her mind. My original proposal wasn't really romantic, so I hope this is a little better."

Ollie dropped down to one knee and held out a gold ring with a large square diamond on it. There were smaller stones surrounding the large one and more on the ring itself. "Ashley Duncan, will you marry me."

Ashley gasped, her eyes going watery. She had one hand over her mouth and the other on her stomach as she nodded. "Oh God, yes. We will."

Grinning from ear to ear, Ollie slipped the ring on

her finger and kissed her. Drew was on his feet in an instant to applaud. Everyone followed.

Cole kept waiting for the kiss to end. He felt funny watching, but at the same time, he was happy. Aunt Ash always smiled the most when Ollie was around.

Would Cole someday meet a girl that he wanted to kiss and ask to marry him? Maybe. Would she say yes? Probably not, but you never know. "Aunt Ash." He waited until she looked his way before he asked his question. "Why did you say *we* will?"

Ashley's grin widened even more. She sat between Ollie and Ann and put her hand on each of theirs. "What does it say that the kid picked that up and none of you did?" She took a deep breath, and looked into Ollie's eyes. "I said we because I meant *we*. That call I got earlier was from the hospital. They had results of my blood test. Seems that we'll have a very small window for this wedding. After the bruises fade, but before the baby bump starts to show. Ollie, I'm pregnant."

Ollie's eyes went wide, and slowly he leaned in to kiss Ashley yet again.

Cole decided that it wasn't so yucky to watch as everyone cheered. In the back of his head, he couldn't help but think that somewhere out there, Edward Hunter was planning to come here. Now Cole had someone else he needed to protect. He couldn't do that if he ran.

Now all he needed to know was, what a bachelor party was.

Epilogue
Professional Detachment

Special Agent Madison stepped off the elevator
and made his way to the office of the director of the
FBI Behavioral Unit. Betsy, the director's personal
assistant, smiled and tried to flirt. Betsy was very
attractive and most of the single agents as well as half
of the married ones would kill to have her look at them
like that, but Special Agent Madison barely noticed. He
knew why he was here, and he had no room in his mind
for anything else.

Betsy pressed a button on her phone. "Agent
Madison is here to see you sir."

The response came back, garbled in part because of
the system, but mostly because of the voice on the other
end. "Send him in."

Betsy motioned to the door. Madison gripped the
handle, took one deep breath to steady himself, and
entered.

Director Burkhart sat behind his desk staring at the
computer, not looking up or inviting Agent Madison to
sit. Madison didn't need to guess what he was reading.
Burkhart was studying his service record. He was trying
to intimidate Madison, to see if he could stand up to a
fraction of the pressure of what he was going to be
asked to do.

"You have an impressive record," Burkhart said.

"You correctly profiled the UNSUB from Scranton when the rest of the unit was off. Your work in the Norfolk case was exceptional. And you've earned high praise for what happened in Somerville. You certainly dealt with the victims well enough. Got them to trust you. That can't have been easy. It never is, not with children. How's your shoulder?"

Madison resisted the urge to roll it. "It's fine. Aches in the rainy weather, but nothing I can't handle."

Burkhart coughed, and took a sip of water, before standing up. "I'm concerned. You got personally invested in that case. As FBI, we have to maintain a certain professional detachment. You didn't. That's my personal and professional opinion. However, I'd like to hear your viewpoint."

Agent Madison was ready for this, but he still felt like slugging the man who he'd spent nights studying and years admiring. "You're correct. An agent is supposed to stay detached, and I got involved personally. It wasn't a weakness, it was a choice. Someone needed to step up, and I did."

Burkhart nodded and coughed again. He reached for his water. "There's talk about putting you on a case. A unit going on a manhunt across the nation."

"I'm aware," Agent Madison responded. "I know Special Agent Foster requested me. I'm grateful for the chance to be considered. If you decide I'm worthy, I'm sure I could be of use."

Burkhart seemed to consider this, but didn't respond. Instead, he reached into his drawer. "Sit down Madison."

As Madison did, Burkhart pulled out a stick of gum. "I don't know if you've ever smoked, but if you haven't picked up the habit, I'd suggest never starting."

Madison nearly grinned. "I used to. Quit years ago, because someone I loved asked me to."

Burkhart nodded. "Good. How is Abbie by the way?"

Madison knew this was part of the dance. And he knew what was coming. He was not going on the manhunt. "She's well."

"Excellent," Burkhart said. "And yourself? How are the nightmares?"

There wasn't a damn thing in his file about having nightmares, but that didn't mean squat. He was sitting in front of a man so good at profiling evil monsters from just scrapes of evidence, he could tell what they liked for breakfast. Burkhart could probably just read his mind, and this was one more test.

"I haven't had one in some time," Madison said. "I have no problem making use of the mental health services if they come back. It helped the first time. Abbie helped more."

Burkhart nodded, glancing at the picture of his family on his desk. "You're a smart man. The comfort from family is important. I want you to know I think you're a fine agent, and I've read your theory on the Ember Falls case. If it were me, I would want to go after Edward Hunter myself. He's smart, sinister and downright deadly. We need our best on this, and I'm tempted to honor Foster's wishes, but I've decided against it. I don't think we understand everything about Hunter. We need to. And at the center of this is a young boy named Cole Duncan. Kid still hasn't been put on record in this. I spoke with the Chief of Ember Falls. An Ann Miller. Any thoughts on her?"

Madison shook his head. "Not directly. I knew her son. Oliver Miller was a good guy at school. I didn't think much of the EMPD. They were corrupt and incompetent, but from what I've read they've been overhauled."

Burkhart gave him a single nod. "I'm sending you there. You'll coordinate with their PD. Interview all witnesses. Travel to Cheyanne and do the same. See if you can find any other of Hunter's dump sites. Get Cole Duncan to talk to you about what happened. Maybe all he saw was his mother being beaten, maybe he saw more. Find out. I know this has to be a disappointment to you. The Foster assignment could be career making, but after your close call on the last case, I'm not sure you're ready. Plus, you have a unique skill set that I need in Ember Falls. Your job is simple. Cole Duncan. Understood."

"Yes sir." Madison kept his voice passive, his eyes straight ahead. "Is there anything else?"

Burkhart studied him carefully for a long moment before shaking his head. "You have until Monday to be in Chief Miller's office. Dismissed."

Trying not to get up too quickly, Agent Madison stood, said thank you and left. He nodded towards Betsy and got on the elevator. He avoided eye contact with everyone as much as possible as he made his way to the parking lot and was in his car.

He sighed and pulled out his phone and finally allowed himself to smile. If the Director had assigned him to the manhunt, he would have thanked him and asked to be assigned to the unit going to Ember Falls. He was prepared to make the same arguments to Burkhart about why he should be assigned there that

Burkhart did to explain not putting him on the more prestigious unit. If Burkhart had refused to reconsider, he would have asked for leave. Failing that, he was prepared to resign with the FBI and go as a private citizen. No matter what, he was going home.

Agent Foster was a top agent, one of the best, and he'd love to work under her again, but not if it meant going on a fucking wild goose chase. They thought Edward Hunter was going to run. He would. For now.

But sooner or later he would return to Ember Falls. He'd want to punish Cole Duncan. There was something about the child that would make Hunter need to go back. But it wouldn't be a straight path to the kid. Hunter would make sure he hurt Cole as much as possible. And Madison hadn't just profiled Hunter, he also profiled Cole Duncan. The way to hurt Cole would be to take away everyone who loved him.

Madison didn't care if it cost him his entire career, or if she decided she didn't want to see his face. She could tell him she hated him, and call him the son of a whore that he was, but Special Agent Brooke Madison was not letting that monster get anywhere near Lilly.

Coming soon from Vincent Morrone:
Part 3, the final installment of the Torn Saga:
Torn to Pieces

Vincent Morrone

A word about the author…

Born and raised in Brooklyn NY, Vincent Morrone now resides in Upstate NY with his wife. (Although he can still speak fluent Brooklynese.) His twin daughters remain not only his biggest fans, but usually are the first to read all of his work. Their home is run and operated for the comfort and convenience of their dogs. Vincent has been writing fiction, poetry and song lyrics for as long as he can remember, most of which involve magical misfits, paranormal prodigies and even on occasion superheroes and their sidekicks.

As they say in Brooklyn: Yo, you got something to say? Vincent would love to hear from you at Vincent@vincentmorrone.com

~~~

Other Titles by Vincent Borrone

Torn Away
Book 1 of the Torn Series